THE SACRED ORDER

And The Mystical Legend Of Saint Francis Of Assisi

ROGER L. BROOKS

AR
PRESS

For Sabrina…

ACKNOWLEDGMENTS

First and foremost, to Saint Francis of Assisi, for whom the foundation of this novel came to be from my first trip to Assisi in 2004. The incredible life that you led and the example you set remains as strong today as it did eight hundred years ago.

To my good friend, Anthony Brunelli, for allowing me to create the story of *The Sacred Order* around your persona. Thank you for all the talks, hikes, rounds of golf, and podcast episodes we shared.

I am eternally grateful for the exceptional guidance, mentorship, and tutelage from James Bonnet, who spent countless Friday evenings teaching me his story model, *Stealing Fire from the Gods*. I will always cherish the video calls, retreats to France, and our trip to Italy, visiting many of the sites together.

There are many others who lent their names to this book who I'd like to thank—Ronald Brunelli, Richard Pescatore, Carol Brunelli (deceased), Louis Meisel, His Excellency the Most Reverend Marco Tasca O.F.M. Conv., Father Martin Breski O.F.M. Conv., Massimo Coppo, Father Amedeo Guida, Father James D. Tormey, Ms. Pirozzi, and Angelo Stillittano.

Sincere appreciation to the late Alan Watts whose philosophical teachings made their way to the pages of this book. Also, special thank you to his son, Mark Watts, and the entire team at AlanWatts.org for preserving the legacy of Alan Watts.

My gratitude also to the many people who generously assisted in the research of this book, providing both insights and access. I would like to acknowledge the Basilica of Saint Francis, Sacro Convento, Santa Maria degli Angeli, the Portiuncula, San Damiano, Hotel Giotto, Laurentian Library, Basilica of San Lorenzo, Basilica of Santa Croce, Casa Buonarroti, Antica Trattoria da Tito, the Vatican Museums, Basilica of the Twelve Holy Apostles, Basilica of San Pietro in Vincoli, and Santa Maria of Miracoli.

I cannot fully express my gratitude to the unmatched Debra Hartmann who has so eloquently provided the final edits to this work. She and the team at American Real Publishing, including Roger Harvey, London Koffler, Glendon Haddix, and Tara Monaco all hold a special place in my heart and I am thankful for all that you do. Thank you especially to Alisha Brunelli for the stunning cover design. Much appreciation to some of my early beta readers, editors, and advisors, including Elizabeth Cohen, Dr. Patricia Ross, Claire Gault, Mikael Short, Kristen Tru, and Joe Sweeney who sparked the idea for the subtitle.

And finally, to my family for putting up with me for nearly fourteen years. To my mother, Nancy Brooks, and my father, Roger Brooks, and my sister, Stephanie Pirozzi, and my brother-in-law, Steve Pirozzi—all of whom have been both supportive and helpful in reading the progression of this novel. To my sister-in-law, Romina Stanton for being an early beta reader and my brother-in-law, Ray Stanton for providing constant support of my endeavor. My daughter, Alexis Brooks and my son, Roger L. Brooks, II—everything I do is for you, including the creation of this story. And my beautiful wife, Sabrina—amazing front-line editor, confidant, Italian interpreter, soulmate, and without a doubt the most amazing woman on the face of the earth.

PRELUDE OF TRUTHS

The Franciscan Order, founded in 1209 by Saint Francis of Assisi after a divine vision, quickly rose to become one of Christianity's most influential—and enigmatic—movements. Its three branches include the First Order (friars), the Second Order (Poor Clares), and the Third Order (lay persons), whose members have included luminaries such as Dante Alighieri, Michelangelo Buonarroti, and Joan of Arc. These figures, while serving God, profoundly shaped human history and transformed our understanding of faith, art, and the pursuit of divine truth.

The virgin birth of Jesus Christ—His miraculous conception through the Holy Spirit while Mary remained a virgin—stands as one of Christianity's most profound and contested mysteries. Treasured as a cornerstone of faith, its true nature has been debated, studied, and safeguarded by theologians for over two millennia.

All depictions of Vatican architecture, Renaissance masterpieces, and historical locations in this novel are authentic and rendered with meticulous accuracy.

CHAPTER 1

Tor Bella Monaca, Rome, Italy
FEBRUARY 9, 2013, 11:44 PM

Ronald Brunelli's arms and legs stretched painfully away from his torso, bound by thick, fibrous ropes that cut into his skin like serrated wire. He had fought desperately only moments before, but now he lay defeated, trussed to a wooden cross that weighed down his battered body.

The sixty-eight-year-old man's breath came in sharp, ragged gasps as he again struggled against his restraints, but his efforts were futile. Pain seared through him, a relentless tide crashing against his will. He tried to form a coherent thought, but the agony clouded his mind, leaving him adrift.

Behind him, a voice broke the oppressive silence, chillingly close. "I'm losing patience. Your time is running out."

The words were followed by a rough yank on his blindfold, forcing Ronald's eyes to adjust to the dim, sterile light of the room and revealing his prison. As his vision focused, he realized where he was—an underground garage, the kind that would have once been filled with cars but now reeked of abandonment. The cold, metallic scent of a mechanic's workshop mingling with decay in the stale air amplified the hopelessness of his situation.

The figure looming over him was an enigma—an assassin dressed in expensive leather shoes, his suit mostly hidden beneath a pristine white lab coat. His face, sharp and cold, was framed by hair greased back into a tight ponytail, giving him an almost predatory appearance.

"What do you want from me?" Ronald rasped, his words dissolving into the air.

The man leered down at him, the sharp edges of his face twisted into a sneer. He stepped closer, his voice low but unmistakably menacing. "Why are you here, Ronald? Why are you in Rome?" His accent was hard to place, a strange blend that gave nothing away.

Ronald's heart raced as he strained to make out the details of his captor's face. The man was tall—strikingly so—with a lean, athletic build. But it was his eyes, cold and sterile, that sent a chill down his spine.

Panic clawed at Ronald's chest. He needed a lie, something convincing enough to keep him alive. "I'm here for a week, visiting my cousin. She's terminally ill," he said, hoping the story would suffice, though it was far from the truth.

Just hours earlier, Ronald had been enjoying the cool evening air during a walk from his hotel to a nearby café, where he'd ordered a simple prosciutto panini and an Italian soda. But on his return, two men had jumped him, blindfolded him, and thrown him into the back of a van. The vehicle had traveled for what felt like miles, heading eastward from the heart of the city. Ronald had counted the minutes in his head, his only frame of reference being a street sign he glimpsed through a tiny opening in the blindfold: Via di Tor Bella Monaca.

His captor's voice yanked him back to the present. "Your family holds the key to something that doesn't belong to you. I need answers, Ronald, or you will suffer."

Ronald's heart thudded in his chest as he squeezed his eyes shut, desperately trying to block out the growing panic. *Who told him? How does he know?*

When he opened his eyes again, he watched the assassin rummaging through a duffel bag, retrieving something from its depths. The man walked over to the van parked nearby, where a second captor stood watch. Ronald's thoughts scrambled as he desperately searched for any way out.

The assassin returned, towering above him with three iron spikes in one hand and, in the other, a heavy mallet.

Ronald tried a desperate bluff. "The carabinieri are likely on their way," he pleaded, his eyes squinting in the van's headlights.

The man only laughed darkly, then positioned a sharp iron spike at the center of Ronald's palm. In one swift motion, he drove it deep into his flesh with the mallet. The spike ripped through his hand and embedded itself into the wood beneath him as blood spattered across his attacker's coat.

Ronald's scream echoed off the cold walls, tearing from his throat, primal and raw, a sound he hadn't known he was capable of. His body arched against the wooden cross, every muscle rigid with shock as his mind struggled to process the horror.

"Your Franciscan brothers are not as loyal a bunch as you thought," the killer sneered, wiping Ronald's blood from his face with a casual flick of his sleeve. "Is this something you're willing to die for?"

Ronald's breath hitched. *They know.*

The truth that he had spent a lifetime guarding was known only to a select few. His ties to the Franciscan Order were as secret as the promise he had made to take the knowledge to his grave. But now, as searing pain coursed through his body, he knew his options had dwindled: speak or die.

The clanging sound of metal filled the air as the assassin held up the two remaining spikes, his eyes narrowing to slits. "You were warned never to set foot in this country again." His voice dropped to a dangerous whisper. "Now, where is it? If you don't reveal the truth, your son will be next."

At the mention of his son, Ronald's breath caught sharply. Anthony Brunelli—a renowned artist commissioned by the Vatican to paint a masterpiece for the Holy See—was his one source of hope. The reception for Anthony's artwork was set for the next morning, and now Ronald's panic surged. If they knew about Anthony, they knew *everything*.

"Wait! Please!" Ronald pleaded, his voice barely escaping his parched throat. "I will tell you what I know."

His attacker's lips curled into a cruel smile.

As the keeper of one of the most dangerous secrets in the modern world, Ronald recited the story he had sworn never to reveal unless his life depended on it, a story passed down from his father. The revelation of the Virgin Mary was a secret too dangerous to speak aloud, placed into the righteous hands of Saint Francis of Assisi. As he spoke, his throat was dry, the words barely forming.

The assassin simply shook his head, his smile broadening. "All of you make the same mistake," he said. "Tell a tale so outrageous it may just be believable."

Panic surged through Ronald. "Please, I've told you every-thing. I've told you the truth."

Without hesitation, the man struck another spike deep into Ronald's left palm, pinning it to the cross.

Ronald's wail filled the garage as his body convulsed once more, the agony unbearable.

Before the pain could fully register, the man positioned Ronald's feet one atop the other and hammered the final spike through them, securing him fully to the cross.

Ronald's voice broke into incoherent cries as the agony overwhelmed him. "Dear Lord God!" he moaned.

Ronald Brunelli had just been crucified.

Ｔ

As his vision began to blur, his life was slipping away, and he knew it. His hearing dulled, the world around him reduced to a muffled hum.

The assassin attached a large eye-hook clip to the base of the cross and began cranking a pulley, raising Ronald—feet first—slowly toward the high ceiling.

When the motion stopped, Ronald dangled upside down. Blood rushed to his head, and his vision darkened as he fought to remain conscious.

"Betrayal, Ronald, is the ultimate sin," the assassin whispered.

Through the haze, Ronald muttered, "I beg of you… please."

The killer's eyes narrowed, his tone deadly calm. "Saint Peter denied Christ. Now you will die as Peter did. My job here is done. *Buonanotte*, Ronald."

The garage door slammed shut behind him, leaving Ronald alone in the cold, empty stall.

"Lord, make me an instrument of your peace. Where there is hatred, let me sow love…" Ronald's whispered prayer wavered as his strength ebbed. His mind clouded, the crushing burden of impending death smothering down with unbearable finality.

But as the darkness closed in, a fragment of hope sparked within him. Eight hundred years of secrets, safeguards, and rituals had led to this moment. He knew there was only one person to whom he could turn. Barely conscious, he remembered the smartphone his son had insisted he carry, showing him how to use it just days before. A modern piece of technology Ronald had almost dismissed was now his only chance of salvation. It was tucked into the hidden pocket of his trousers, an inconspicuous place no one would have thought to search. His heart rate slowed as he clung to consciousness, praying his idea would work.

His body screamed in protest, his nerves frayed, but Ronald forced himself onward. Slowly, painstakingly, he cleared his throat. His crucified flesh sent fresh waves of agony through him, but he pushed past the pain. He had no other choice. *This is my last chance…*

In a final, desperate effort, Ronald wheezed out the universal command, praying the phone would respond to his request even though his voice was barely audible. "Hey, Siri…"

For a moment, nothing happened.

Then, to his immense relief, the digital assistant's familiar tone echoed faintly from the phone. "Uh huh?"

What Ronald attempted next would require every ounce of his remaining strength and nothing less than a miracle.

CHAPTER 2

Via Mariano Fortuny, Rome
7:00 AM

Arriving at Via Mariano Fortuny right on time, Dr. Vera Valentino found the location was far from what she had expected. Nestled on a dead-end street just five blocks northeast of the Piazza del Popolo and barely a mile from Vatican City, the unassuming building was tucked above a satellite office of the Confederation of Italian Agriculture. No grand façades or towering structures, just a quiet, inconspicuous building that seemed to shrink from attention.

For someone like Vera who had become accustomed to prestigious institutions and grand Renaissance halls, this setting seemed too modest, almost suspiciously discreet. But she wasn't easily surprised. Such unusual circumstances had become rather routine for her over the last few years.

At just thirty-six, Vera had achieved what few could dream of, having been named the director of the Laurentian Library in Florence. Not only was she the youngest ever to hold the esteemed position but she was also the first woman. It was a feat she took great pride in, albeit one she wore lightly. As the head of the Church's most important repository of knowledge, her role demanded respect and deference. She never sought the limelight, but her confident demeanor ensured it often found her.

Anyone watching her step gracefully out of her sleek Alfa Romeo Giulia and ascend the ivy-lined embankment toward the villa's gated entrance would have been momentarily spellbound. Vera was striking, not just because of her impeccable fashion sense—today, she wore a black jacket-and-skirt combination paired with knee-grazing leather riding boots—but because of her commanding presence. Her deep brown hair contrasted vividly with her piercing green eyes, exuding both elegance and determination. Above all, it was her quiet confidence that inspired awe.

Standing at the gate, awaiting her arrival, was Father Alessandro della Rovere. He shifted uncomfortably from foot to foot, his hands folded awkwardly across his ample midsection and his thin lips tightly pursed. His portly figure seemed out of place against the villa's serene backdrop. He was unshaven, his robe appeared rumpled, and the faint odor of stale sweat suggested he'd slept in today's clothes.

"I wasn't sure if I had the right address," Vera called out, flashing a disarming smile as she approached. "This place feels more like a safe house than an off-site Vatican office," she added, studying the priest's nervous demeanor.

Father Alessandro chuckled uneasily, dabbing beads of sweat from his forehead with a wrinkled handkerchief. He held the wrought-iron gate open for her, his discomfort apparent in every movement.

Vera leaned in, greeting him with the customary Italian kiss, one peck on each cheek. "And to what do I owe the pleasure of this meeting?" she asked, her grip tightening on her leather business bag.

"This won't take long, Dr. Valentino," he replied, his voice low and thick with an accent that never quite matched the formality of his position. "But what we discuss here must remain strictly between us. As far as anyone is concerned, this meeting never happened."

Though the four-story building appeared modest from the outside, Vera knew better. She had done enough covert work for the Vatican to recognize when appearances were meant to deceive. The villa, seemingly functioning as a retreat house for aging high-ranking priests and cardinals, boasted luxuries that the unassuming exterior deliberately concealed.

As they stepped inside, her trained eye immediately caught sight of strategically positioned security cameras. *What is this place?* she wondered, though she quickly refocused. Having been summoned by Father Alessandro della Rovere, the pope's most trusted personal secretary, speculation would have to wait.

Father Alessandro led her up a narrow flight of stairs, his breathing labored with each step, and then into a formal sitting room overlooking the foyer. The room exuded quiet wealth with its heavy silk drapes framing large windows, polished mahogany floors, and ornate furniture that spoke of old money and older secrets. He gestured for her to sit, then poured two steaming cups of espresso from an antique silver service. Vera sat, crossing her legs, while the priest remained standing, awkwardly clutching his cup.

"Vera," he began, his voice strained, "something urgent has come up. We need your expertise once more. His Holiness has personally directed this matter, which means I cannot divulge everything. But what I can say is that this investigation involves certain…important artifacts."

Curiosity piqued, she immediately retrieved a notepad from her bag. Her keen eyes caught the priest's gaze lingering too long on her legs, then quickly averting the moment he realized she had noticed his breach of decorum. She offered no reaction, though the uncomfortable memory of a previous incident surfaced briefly.

The priest continued, visibly unsettled by his own lapse. "This case requires absolute discretion. And though it comes from the Holy Father himself, we are operating outside official Vatican channels. That's why I requested to meet here."

She nodded. "Father Alessandro, I'm more than willing to assist. What exactly am I investigating?"

"It's not a what but a who," he said with a dry chuckle. "His name is Anthony Brunelli. He's an American artist."

Vera's brow creased at the unfamiliar name.

Before she could probe further, a sharp knock at the door interrupted them. Alessandro excused himself, leaving her alone with her thoughts. Instinctively, she pulled out her phone and began researching Brunelli. A series of images and articles filled her screen. *Anthony Brunelli,* she mused, studying his face. *Quite the accomplished man.* He was a renowned photo-realist painter, gallery owner, and even a documentary subject. His features, sharp and confident, were well-known among the artistic elite.

Alessandro returned, taking a seat on the sofa across from her.

"He's certainly distinguished," she commented, turning the phone to show him.

With a weary sigh the priest replied, "Yes, which is exactly why this is delicate. Brunelli holds information critical to the Church, but he can't know we're investigating him. He's been in Assisi for the past couple of months, and we've been keeping tabs. And what complicates matters even further is that he's been hired by the PCC, along with several other artists, to undertake an art commission. It's to be unveiled at a reception this morning in the Vatican Art Gallery."

Vera tapped her chin thoughtfully. "You're asking me to keep tabs on him without him suspecting?"

"Precisely." Alessandro nodded. "He's a man under constant scrutiny, so your approach will need to be subtle. I trust your discretion."

Vera shifted in her seat. "What exactly are we hoping to discover?"

The priest handed her a thick manila envelope, its contents detailing Brunelli's CV, press clippings, and other background material. "Everything you need is in here," he said. "But as for what we're after, I cannot disclose that yet. Let's just say it involves artifacts of historical significance, ones that could shake the very foundations of our faith."

She exhaled deeply. The PCC—Pontifical Council for Culture—was not an organization to be trifled with. It was one of the most respected branches of the Roman Curia, responsible for bridging the gap between the Catholic Church and modern culture.

She leaned forward, her voice soft but determined. "And you want me to infiltrate his life?"

He offered a sheepish smile. "In a manner of speaking, yes. But a warm introduction has already been arranged. He knows he needs help, and he knows you've been assigned to assist him. We need you to gain his trust, and through that trust, uncover what he may know. This isn't just about art, Vera—it's about the future of the Church."

"Could he be dangerous?" she asked, recalling other assignments that had turned volatile.

"No, not physically. But his actions—what he knows—could be detrimental. We need you inside his world, observing quietly while he believes you're there to assist him."

Vera's eyes narrowed slightly. She trusted Father Alessandro only because of his influence over her career, how her performance would reflect on him, and couldn't ignore the warning bells ringing in her mind. Still, she owed him a great deal. He had been instrumental in securing her position at the Laurentian Library as well as her more covert freelance assignments.

"As for tonight," he continued, "I've arranged for you to stay in a hotel here in Rome. No need to rush back to Florence." His beady eyes lingered on her for a moment too long.

Vera felt a familiar shiver of unease. A little over a year ago, when the two had traveled to Tuscany for an assignment, he had intentionally brushed her leg under the table during dinner. It had been slight but unmistakable. He had apologized, blaming immense pressure, vowing it would never happen again. She had believed him, reasoning that a priest's vow of celibacy must be difficult. *But if he were truly sorry, then why did his gaze still carry that hint of something darker?*

Her discomfort growing, she kept her expression neutral. "I hadn't planned to stay the night, Father. I should get back."

The priest's expression tightened but quickly recovered. "If that's what you prefer. But you'll need to attend the reception today, regardless. Brunelli will be there as one of the guests of honor. Be sure to stay out of his line of sight." He stood up, smoothing his wrinkled robe.

She followed, clutching her bag and offering a polite smile though her mind was already spinning with thoughts of the mission ahead. "Where exactly do the artifacts come into play?" she asked as the priest ushered her toward the door with unexpected haste.

His hesitation was brief but noticeable. "You'll know soon enough. The information Brunelli will come upon is not something even he will fully comprehend."

There was something in his tone that made Vera's instincts sharpen. She replayed his words as they descended the stairs in silence.

With the morning church bells tolling in the distance, their ancient bronze voices echoing across Rome, Alessandro ushered Vera out the door, leaving her with more questions than answers.

CHAPTER 3

The Vatican Art Gallery, Vatican City
11:22 AM

Anthony Brunelli shut his eyes tightly. Standing on the pristine marble floor of the artist's private lounge, he took refuge from the grandeur just outside. He leaned over the sink and splashed cold water on his face for a second time, hoping the shock would calm his nerves. Reaching for the hand towel, he noticed the intricate red insignia of the Vatican Art Gallery embroidered on the soft white fabric:

PINACOTECA VATICANA.

For a moment, he paused, towel in hand, reluctant to return to the reception. He wanted nothing more than a few minutes alone to take it all in, to bask in this moment of triumph. He looked straight into the mirror, and the man staring back was a confident, accomplished artist. His ice-blue eyes were sharp and focused, set deep beneath strong brows. A ginger stubble shadowed his face, blending into his thick auburn hair. For a man in his early forties, his reflection showed the physical build of someone ten years younger, no doubt the result of his love for hiking and his rigorous daily fitness routine.

More than any other day, Anthony needed to appear at his best today. He had woken at dawn determined to prepare meticulously for the occasion. He hadn't even checked his phone, opting to disconnect from the outside world, remain free of distractions. This day belonged to him, and everything—down to the clothes he wore—had been carefully chosen. His khaki linen suit and crisp, white-collared shirt, tailored a year ago for such prestigious events, felt perfect against his skin. The museum's electric shoe polisher hummed to a stop as he lifted his wingtips from the spinning brushes, inspecting their restored mirror-like finish. Running a hand through his hair, he took one last look in the mirror. The satisfaction on his face was undeniable.

As he stepped out of the lounge and into the gallery, he felt a familiar sense of awe sweep over him. He couldn't help but admire the masterpieces lining the walls. The Vatican Art Gallery, with its rich frescoes, timeless statues, and elaborate wood carvings, had been a place of reverence in his imagination for years. Growing up, he had immersed himself in the works of the Renaissance masters—men whose genius now surrounded him in every direction. To stand among their works was not only humbling but also profound. It was a moment of destiny that felt like the culmination of his life's journey.

Anthony's gift for art had manifested early in his childhood. His mother, an artist in her own right, had encouraged him to paint and allowed him to spend hours in her studio as a way to channel his boundless energy. By age ten, he had mastered drawing Snoopy, the beloved comic character, and soon after, his mind began to see the world around him as a canvas, alive with color and intricate detail. Every scene, every moment, was a potential painting waiting to be brought to life. That instinct to capture the world in hyperrealistic strokes had only deepened as he grew older. Now, as he stood in the hallowed halls of the Vatican Art Gallery surrounded by Renaissance masterpieces, he found himself visualizing the room as a painting and carefully noting the play of light and shadow across centuries-old frescoes and tapestries. It was second nature to him.

The gallery, virtually unchanged since its opening in 1932, housed 460 works of art—paintings, sculptures, and tapestries by some of the greatest Italian masters. Among them were the unfinished *St. Jerome in the Wilderness* by Leonardo da Vinci and Giotto's *Stefaneschi Altarpiece*. Usually packed with tourists, today the gallery entertained an exclusive group of nearly one hundred invitation-only guests. Waitstaff in crisp black uniforms weaved through the crowd, offering silver trays of prosciutto and melon, candied figs, and stuffed mushrooms while a violinist played a gentle, melodic tune in the corner.

A loud screech reverberated over the speaker system, suddenly cutting through the hum of conversation. It was followed by the sound of a hand tapping a microphone, drawing the crowd's attention to silence.

"Ladies and gentlemen, welcome." The president of the Pontifical Council for Culture stood at the podium, his voice commanding the room. His eyes scanned the gathering, and for a brief moment recognition lit up his face. Then with a small nod to the back of the room, he turned back to the assembled guests.

"It's a very special day for the PCC, for the artists before you, and for our Holy Father, Pope Benedict who made this day possible," he began, his voice rich with pride. "Two years ago, we set out on an ambitious task to find the most talented contemporary artists in the world, to create works that would stand the test of time. The selection process was arduous but rewarding. We reviewed more than five hundred submissions from artists across the globe. I'm proud to say that today we present twelve of the finest contemporary masters, each representing their unique art forms."

The room fell silent as cameras clicked and shutters snapped, the flashes from photographers creating a strobe-like effect as the artists seated atop the platform came into view.

Anthony, along with eleven other artists, sat beneath Raphael's *Transfiguration*, a work he had admired countless times. He recalled the words of Giorgio Vasari who once described the painting as "the most famous, the most beautiful, and the most divine." For him, this moment felt almost surreal. He was in the presence of greatness—not just the artists of history but also the extraordinary group gathered alongside him.

"And now," the president continued, "we will unveil the commissioned pieces."

Staff members took their places beside the draped works of art. A spotlight illuminated the velvet covering concealing the first piece. With delicate precision, two staff members removed the fabric, revealing the masterpiece.

"Our first unveiling is by Anthony Brunelli from the United States of America," the president announced to the hushed room. "This painting is titled *Assisi at Dusk*. It is an exterior panoramic landscape of the Basilica of Saint Francis in Assisi. The style is photorealism, and the size is fifty-four by sixty inches, oil on canvas. The work will enter the private collection at the Sacro Convento in Assisi."

The applause was immediate and resounding.

Anthony stood, giving a modest wave to the crowd as flashes lit up the room. His grin was wide, and he couldn't suppress the pride swelling within him. He had worked tirelessly on this piece, and now here it was, one of his crowning achievements displayed in the Vatican.

While the remaining artists were being introduced, Anthony felt a vibration in his suit-coat pocket and briefly glanced at his phone. It was a text message from his friend, Richard Pescatore. A mild-mannered man in his early sixties, with a slight build, he stood in the center of the room looking concerned. Anthony made eye contact with him, read the text, and quickly replied.

[Richard] *Did you talk to your father today? He's not here.*

[Anthony] *No, I haven't. This makes no sense. Call the hotel.*

[Richard] *I already did. They said he went out last night and never returned. I'm worried.*

Anthony pushed aside the flutter of concern, allowing himself to revel in the excitement of the moment.

In the back of the room, Dr. Vera Valentino took careful notes in her leather-bound journal, her handwriting elegant and precise. *Brunelli's talent lives up to his reputation. He seems well-loved by the art community and should be easy to work with,* she scribbled in neat Italian cursive.

CHAPTER 4

Exactly one and a half miles away from the Vatican Art Gallery, Father Alessandro della Rovere sat waiting behind the ornate wooden lattice of the confessional, nervously plucking at the edges of his robe. He gazed up at the beams of light streaming through the skylight in the dome above. The sunlight, cascading over his weathered face, deepened the cracks in his skin, making him appear like a figure sculpted from ancient, hardened clay. His mind drifted, unsettled, and his habitual nervous tic—tightening his thin lips—surfaced as it always did when he was lost in dark thoughts.

The sound of approaching footsteps echoed faintly across the marble floors. A figure knelt on the other side of the confessional, his imposing presence filling the small space.

Alessandro peered through the delicate lattice screen. The silhouette was unmistakable—a long, gaunt face framed by a greasy ponytail that grazed the back of a thick neck. His sharp beard caught the light, casting angular shadows.

"Enzo?" Alessandro asked softly, his voice laden with tension.

"Yes, it is I," the man replied. He crossed himself, bowing his head slightly. "Bless me, Father, for I have sinned."

Father Alessandro mirrored the sign of the cross, though the gesture felt hollow. He felt more fearful than faithful in the presence of Enzo. Leaning closer to the screen, he studied his manservant's scarred face with a mixture of dread and expectation. Alessandro's bushy eyebrows twitched nervously as his thick mustache quivered.

"Have you obeyed your command?" Alessandro's words held an edge, sharp and expectant.

"Yes, Father," the assassin responded without hesitation. "My work is done. The cross has been returned to storage, and the chamber has been bleached clean. Your urn…it's here on the floor. Still warm. I placed it behind the curtain."

Alessandro gave a knowing nod, his lips curling slightly. "The trophy. I recognize the smell." He inhaled deeply, savoring the familiar scent of incense mingled with burned flesh. "And what of the obligation, the secret that's been protected for eight centuries?" His voice was soft, but the question hung between them like the tolling of a distant bell.

Enzo shifted his weight, straightening his posture as if to underscore the importance of his report. "He confirmed everything. The full account of the Virgin Mary and the lore of the reliquary."

The legend, ancient and veiled in secrecy, spoke of a sacred reliquary protected by the Franciscan Order and a treasure buried deep within, something holy entrusted to Saint Francis of Assisi himself. Since Saint Francis's death, Franciscan friars had taken on the dual role of protecting the Church and the image of the Virgin Mary while ensuring the reliquary's existence remained hidden from the world.

Alessandro's breath quickened. "And where, pray tell, is it?" His voice trembled slightly, a reflection of the anticipation that now filled the small space between them.

Enzo's lips twitched in amusement. "Under pressure, he revealed that Benedict is involved."

The name hung in the air like a curse.

"Benedict? Then it must be inside the Papal Palace…or better yet, the pope's private vault," Alessandro whispered, his eyes wide with disbelief. "And you believe him?"

A slow, dangerous smile appeared as Enzo replied, "Threatening a man's son is a strong motive for truth."

Alessandro's relief was short-lived, quickly replaced by suspicion. "I had worried Ronald Brunelli might have taken the secret to his grave. Tell me, what else did he say?"

Enzo hesitated, carefully choosing his words. "He said his son, Anthony, knows very little…if anything."

A sharp exhale escaped Alessandro, frustration permeating the confessional. His fingers drummed against the wooden partition. "Then you didn't torture him enough. This can't be so easy, Enzo. I walk above Benedict's vault every day. There must be more."

Silence followed, broken only by the nervous tapping of Enzo's foot.

"Call Jean Lucca. Tell him to meet me at our regular spot near Saint Peter's." Alessandro's voice was firm now, commanding. "Your next assignment is the son. He's the artist." His tone dripped with finality. "The money and everything you need is in the bag hidden under your seat. Follow the instructions, then wait for my next order."

T

Enzo's breath caught for a moment. He hadn't been tasked with two assassinations in over three years—not since the last bodies he had disposed of in the shadow of Rome's great monuments. But the money. The lavish life he led in his penthouse in the heart of Rome depended on this work. He needed the reward.

"And the forty thousand euros we agreed to?" he asked cautiously, his foot tapping the bag beneath his seat with quiet urgency.

Alessandro's voice was curt. "It's all there." He gave Enzo one final glance through the screen. "Go outside, make the call, wait a few minutes, then leave. Oh, and"—he waved his hand dismissively—"you're absolved."

Enzo's pulse quickened, adrenaline coursing through his veins as he made his way out of the church. He dialed Jean Lucca without hesitation, knowing yet another forty thousand was now in reach.

The bright February sun cast its soft morning light over Piazza del Popolo. The vast square with its towering obelisk at the center was sparsely populated at this time of year. The ancient Egyptian monument, originally erected at the Circus Maximus and brought to Rome by Augustus in 10 BC, stood tall, its shadow stretching across the plaza. At each corner of the obelisk, lion statues spouted water into the fountain below.

Enzo strolled toward the lions, his steps measured and his eyes scanning the surroundings. He positioned himself behind one of the statues, finding solace in the anonymity the piazza provided. From his cloth bag, he pulled out the instructions and read them carefully, twice. With a flick of his lighter, the document ignited, curling into ashes as the wind carried its remains into the crystalline Roman sky. His gaze returned to the bag. Inside were the tools for his next role—an impeccably folded brown Franciscan habit, clergy credentials, and an envelope thick with crisp one-hundred-euro notes.

The noon sun now hung directly overhead, casting shade across the twin churches of Santa Maria that flanked Via del Corso. The assassin narrowed his eyes against the glare, momentarily drawn to the lion's mouth as water poured rhythmically into the fountain below. There was something eerily poetic about this setting. It seemed a fitting place to contemplate what lay ahead. As the lion's water continued its eternal pour, Enzo slipped on the Franciscan habit and straightened his collar.

After all, Anthony Brunelli would surely trust a man of God.

CHAPTER 5

The Vatican Art Gallery, Vatican City
12:40 PM

As much as Anthony tried, he couldn't shake the gnawing worry lingering in his mind. His father wouldn't miss what was undoubtedly his son's greatest professional achievement. *Where is he?*

The art reception was in full swing, filled with dignitaries and luminaries from around the world. But even among the applause and congratulations, Anthony's thoughts were elsewhere, a shadow of concern cast over his sense of triumph. He fidgeted in his seat as the final artist was being introduced. Scanning the crowd for the hundredth time, he hoped against hope that his father would appear, but the seat meant for him in the section reserved for the artist's immediate family remained empty.

Then, a soft tap on his shoulder interrupted his thoughts. He turned to see a cleric with a receding hairline leaning in. The man's demeanor was calm, though his presence carried an unmistakable air of authority.

"Anthony," Monsignor Amedeo Guida, the senior Vatican marshal, whispered, his voice barely audible above the low hum of the gathering. "His Holiness Pope Benedict wishes to see you."

Anthony blinked, momentarily flustered. He had been told all of the artists would meet the pope at some point that day, but to be singled out now—pulled from the reception—was unexpected. For a brief moment, he felt disoriented, caught between the mounting excitement of a papal audience and the deepening concern for his father. Then he rose slowly, glancing around as he tried to regain his composure.

The cleric motioned for him to follow.

Before leaving, Anthony turned and made brief eye contact with Rick. Pointing to the ornate mosaic tile floor, he mouthed the words, "I'll meet you back here."

Rick gave a small, knowing nod in response.

Outside the gallery, a Vatican vehicle—a modest four-door sedan—waited at the entrance, its engine quietly idling. The monsignor opened the back door and gestured for Anthony to enter. As the vehicle pulled away from the gallery, the artist tried to steady his nerves against the magnitude of the moment sinking in.

The car's destination was clear: the Apostolic Palace, the official residence of the pope. Anthony watched the Vatican's grand architecture they were passing, the majestic structures steeped in eras of history and power. Yet despite the imposing scenery, he couldn't shake a growing sense of unease.

☩

Standing at the periphery of the reception, Vera observed the subtle interaction between Brunelli and Pescatore. Her keen instincts, honed by years of covert work for the Vatican, had caught every nuance of the exchange between the two men.

She had taken careful note of the moment, her mind quietly filing it away for later analysis. She had been tasked with watching Brunelli, but her instincts told her that Pescatore might be far more significant than anyone suspected. Whatever lay beneath the surface of their relationship would need to be uncovered—and soon.

For now, she remained a quiet observer, blending seamlessly into the crowd as the ceremony continued. But her mind was already working, piecing together the threads of a mystery that was only beginning to unravel.

T

Back at the Pinacoteca Art Gallery, Richard Pescatore slipped quietly out of the rear entrance. The soft click of the door closing behind him seemed thunderous in the hushed atmosphere of the Vatican gardens. His departure went largely unnoticed, just as he had planned. He had arranged a very private meeting of his own, one that demanded absolute discretion.

He moved with purpose, his footsteps quick and silent as he navigated through the shaded pathways that crisscrossed the meticulously kept gardens. The afternoon sunlight filtered through ancient cypress trees, casting dappled patterns on the worn cobblestones beneath his feet. This meeting had been set in motion days before, and the timing now, with Anthony occupied and the eyes of the gallery fixed on the reception, was perfect.

CHAPTER 6

St. Peter's Basilica, Vatican City
12:44 PM

Directly beneath the majestic Apostolic Palace, hidden in the obscure depths of Vatican City, Father Alessandro crawled on his hands and knees, struggling to move quickly through the narrow, secret tunnel. His large frame scraped against the ancient stone walls, but he pushed forward, determined to reach his destination. The tunnel—an unmarked passage built by the della Rovere family generations earlier—did not exist on any Vatican map and only a handful of men alive knew of its existence.

The pectoral cross hanging from his neck dragged along the dusty floor in blatant disregard for the Son of God. There was no reverence in Alessandro's heart. His faith had long since been corrupted and his true devotion lay elsewhere.

At the end of the tunnel, he reached a cleverly concealed trapdoor, its entrance hidden within the intricate mosaic tiles on the floor of Pope Benedict's private vault. Built separately from the Vatican's secret archives, this vault held the most intimate and guarded possessions of the papal line—treasures and artifacts too powerful and dangerous to leave unprotected. The heavy smell of dry earth and ancient stone seeped through the trapdoor.

He opened the door, then whispered into the tiny microphone attached to his wireless headset, "I'm in."

Two henchmen followed him into the vault, their movements deliberate and cautious as their flashlights pierced the blackness. Another remained behind, standing guard at the tunnel's entrance.

Alessandro glanced at his watch, his impatience growing. "Move quickly! We've got less than ten minutes."

Father Jean Lucca Baloga, one of Alessandro's most trusted assistants, was scanning the shelves, his black-framed glasses reflecting the dancing beams of his flashlight. His fingers hovered over two large, red-bound binders on the bookshelf. "Is that what we're after?" he asked, his voice uncertain.

Alessandro shook his head impatiently and pointed toward the far side of the room, where a large stainless-steel safe stood upright. The insignia on the door—a red shield shaped like a chalice and adorned with a gold scallop shell in the center, a moor's head on the left, and a walking brown bear on the right—was unmistakable. Pope Benedict's coat of arms.

Jean Lucca wasted no time. Dropping to one knee, he pulled out his stethoscope, positioning the diaphragm against the safe's lock. Like a doctor listening to a heartbeat, he carefully began manipulating the lock with steady fingers despite the mounting tension.

Alessandro hovered impatiently above him. "Eight minutes until Benedict's meeting," he hissed. "Hurry!"

The seconds ticked by, but in less than a minute, the lock gave way with a soft click. The three-inch-thick door swung open, and Alessandro exhaled in relief. Inside, resting in front of a Kevlar backpack, was their target: an ancient limestone cylinder just under a foot in length. The cylinder was worn and smooth, its surface giving little away about the secrets it held within.

Jean Lucca carefully lifted the cylinder, his eyes wide with anticipation. "It's sealed shut," he muttered in frustration, examining the wax that kept the cylinder closed. He ran his fingers through his wavy dark hair, then rubbed his temples.

The third henchman, Fargazo, snapped pictures of the cylinder from every angle, ensuring they had a record of its appearance. Then, from his utility bag, he handed Jean Lucca a box cutter.

With surgical precision, Jean Lucca slipped the blade beneath the wax seal and gently pried it open. He handed the open cylinder to Alessandro, who immediately removed and unfurled an ancient scroll from within. But as he unrolled the fragile parchment, his expression darkened. He found only a single Latin word inscribed on its surface.

"*Incipe*," Alessandro read aloud, his frustration evident. "To begin? What the hell is that supposed to mean?" His voice was strained, his mind reeling. He had expected more—much more.

Scrutinizing the parchment carefully, he searched for any additional markings or clues. But aside from the Roman numerals LX and an odd symbol etched into the top-right corner, there was nothing of note.

"Damn it!" he cursed, his anger boiling over. He had spent a lifetime believing in the existence of something far more significant than this.

Desperation driving him, Alessandro held the limestone cylinder up to his eye, shining his flashlight deep into its hollow interior. As the beam penetrated the darkness, something caught his eye—a faint glimmer of another object hidden within.

A slow, malevolent smile crept across Alessandro's face.

Jean Lucca handed him a pair of long, rubber-tipped tweezers.

Alessandro extracted a second, smaller piece of parchment. This one was different, covered in ancient Italian script. His eyes widened as he read what he could of parts of the text, his hands trembling slightly. He paused, wiping the sweat from his brow. Whatever this document was, it held far greater significance than the first. He carefully placed it into a large zippered bag and stuffed it into the pocket of his cassock.

Meanwhile, Jean Lucca took photographs of both sides of the original scroll. Once finished, Alessandro returned the parchment to the cylinder and resealed it.

Jean Lucca worked quickly, using a small lighter torch to melt a candlewax stick. He squeezed the hot wax tightly to the cylinder, recreating the markings on the original seal using the photographs as reference. It was a flawless forgery—an act of art—but there was no time to admire the craftsmanship.

With the cylinder back in its place inside the safe, the three men made their escape. The stolen parchment lay secure in Alessandro's inner pocket as they crawled through the tunnel. His pulse quickened at the thought of what he carried—secrets powerful enough to shatter not just the foundations of the Church but everything the faithful held sacred about the Virgin Mary herself.

The trio raced through the secret passage toward the Vatican Necropolis, the ancient burial grounds beneath St. Peter's Basilica—an underground mortuary of the dead.

CHAPTER 7

The Apostolic Palace, Vatican City
12:52 PM

Through the corridors of the Apostolic Palace, a realm reserved for the Church's highest authorities, Monsignor Guida led Anthony through the layers of Vatican security. They cleared a discreet checkpoint before approaching the elevator. Each step brought them closer to their destination—the pope's private study, an inner sanctum few were ever privileged to see.

Arriving on the fourth floor, the monsignor guided Anthony down a long, marble corridor, its arched ceiling adorned with frescoes of heavenly scenes. The air was thick with history, each footfall reverberating through the centuries-old palace. As they approached a massive wooden door, two Swiss Guards—formidable in their ceremonial uniforms of blue, red, and gold—stood vigilant, their halberds gleaming in the filtered light. A brief nod from Guida and the door was opened, revealing the grandeur of Pope Benedict XVI's private study.

The room was an intimate reflection of both power and simplicity. An antique walnut desk stood at the center, flanked by towering shelves filled with untold years of leather-bound books. Leather chairs aged to a rich patina surrounded a beautifully carved coffee table in the middle of the room, inviting quiet conversation. The scent of frankincense hung lightly in the air, adding a sense of mystique to the space.

Anthony had only just begun to take in the room's quiet elegance when the rear door creaked open. Pope Benedict XVI entered, his white cassock and gold pectoral cross gleaming in the soft light. His ruby-red shoes, a mark of papal tradition, clicked softly on the floor as he approached, his demeanor one of calm authority.

"Anthony," the pope greeted him warmly, a gentle smile on his face. "At last, we meet."

He felt the magnitude of the moment, the significance of standing before the leader of the Roman Catholic Church. He bowed slightly, instinctively taking the pope's hand and kissing the Fisherman's Ring as was customary. The ring, a symbol of the pope's role as the successor to Saint Peter and a tangible connection to the Church's ancient history, gleamed in the light.

"It is an honor, Your Holiness," Anthony replied, his voice steady despite his heart racing. He had expected this meeting to be ceremonial, connected to the art commission. Yet something in the pope's demeanor told him there was more to it.

As Monsignor Guida excused himself and the heavy door closed with a soft thud, the pope gestured for Anthony to sit. They took their places around the coffee table, where two cups of black tea steamed in the silence.

"I have been looking forward to our meeting," Benedict began, his German-accented English gentle but firm. His eyes were piercing, yet there was warmth in his gaze. The Pope's presence commanded attention, though it was not overbearing—more a quiet strength.

Anthony nodded, trying to relax, though his mind buzzed with questions. "I must admit, it's quite a surprise to meet with you like this. I assumed the commission was the main reason for my visit."

The Pope took a slow sip of tea, his gaze never leaving Anthony. "The commission, yes. Your work is quite remarkable. I'm pleased that it will become part of the Church's legacy. But, Anthony"—his tone grew more serious—"there is something more."

Anthony's brow furrowed slightly. "More?"

Benedict leaned in, his eyes searching Anthony's. "You are aware of your family's connection to Saint Francis of Assisi, are you not? Your father has, no doubt, told you of this."

"Yes, of course," Anthony replied, his smile tinged with fondness. "My father has always spoken proudly of our family's ties to Saint Francis, but he's kept much of it between us. He taught me everything he could about Saint Francis and the Franciscan Order."

The Pope nodded, seemingly pleased. "Good, that is important. You see, your family's connection to Saint Francis is not just a matter of history, it's a matter of destiny."

Anthony blinked, caught off guard. "Destiny?"

"Anthony," the pope began again, his voice low, almost conspiratorial, "what I am about to tell you must remain between us. You came to Rome for the reception, yes, but perhaps there was another reason you were brought here." His words hung in the air, heavy with implication.

Anthony felt a chill creep up his spine. "I don't understand," he said cautiously. "What other reason could there be?"

Benedict set his tea down, his hands gently twisting the Fisherman's Ring. "There is a secret, Anthony. A sacred duty that has been passed down through the generations. Since the day I assumed the papacy, I have been the guardian of that secret. It is a secret of Saint Francis that has been protected for centuries by the popes, the Franciscans themselves, and by your family."

The room seemed to grow smaller, the walls closing in as Anthony listened intently. His pulse quickened, the magnitude of the moment overwhelming him.

"The first day I became Pope, I received a letter that instructed me to guard this secret with every fiber of my being. Every pope before me has done the same. And now, Anthony, I am passing this responsibility on to you." The pope's eyes were unwavering, his voice steady.

Anthony swallowed hard, struggling to keep his composure. "A secret? What kind of secret?"

Benedict's expression softened, but there was a hint of sadness in his eyes. "There is a sealed limestone cylinder, Anthony, that has been kept in the private vault. None of us have opened it. We were commanded not to. But now, I have made my decision. The time has come, and I am entrusting it to you."

Anthony's mind raced. His family's cryptic passion for Saint Francis suddenly took on a whole new meaning. *But why me? Why now?*

"To know that there's a personal connection to Saint Francis through my family is humbling," he said, trying to steady his thoughts. "But to be entrusted with such a precious artifact…I don't even know what to say or what to do."

The pope smiled, though there was a hint of solemnity in his eyes. "It is not just an artifact, Anthony. It is a responsibility. You see, it is known and written that the age would come when this holy office would pass the responsibility to a chosen son. You, Anthony, are the chosen son."

"The chosen son for what?" Anthony asked, his voice barely above a whisper.

Benedict's gaze was unwavering. "To see this obligation through. It is your duty now."

Anthony felt a crushing sensation settle on his chest. He had spent his life immersed in art, in the solitude of his studio. The notion of being thrust into an ancient obligation was overwhelming, something he wasn't remotely prepared for. His father had tried to prepare him for this possibility, as he had been prepared a generation before, but he never expected it to come in such a way.

"What exactly am I supposed to do?" he asked, his voice edged with uncertainty.

The pope's voice was gentle but firm. "That, Anthony, is a question only you can answer. It is between you and Saint Francis now." He picked up his teacup, then added, "Let us finish our tea, and I will take you to the vault."

Anthony's skin prickled with dread as he lifted the cup to his lips.

CHAPTER 8

Halfway around the dome of Saint Peter's Basilica in the imposing Vatican Government Palace, Richard Pescatore sat alone in the grand lobby, his body heavy with exhaustion from the day's events. He rubbed his tired eyes, and even in his weary state, he couldn't help but appreciate the splendor around him. Every detail of the luxurious vestibule—rich drapery, intricately carved furniture, and crystal-studded chandeliers—spoke of an opulence that was almost breathtaking.

But as he took in the grandeur, Richard's mind drifted to darker thoughts. He was all too aware that these beautiful surroundings had been built on generations of power, greed, and duplicity—everything that had driven a wedge between the Church and its people. The contradictions weighed heavily on him, stirring a mixture of admiration and disdain.

Glancing at his watch, Richard frowned. The minutes dragged on, and his impatience was growing.

"Signore Pescatore?" A young priest's voice broke the silence. "Father Alessandro will see you now."

Richard stood eagerly, his joints stiff from sitting too long. The priest gestured for him to follow, leading him to the elevator. They ascended to the second floor, and once the doors opened, the priest directed Richard into a small, dimly lit conference room.

"Signore, please wait here. Father Alessandro will join you shortly."

The room was modest compared to the opulent lobby below, yet there was a quiet elegance to it. The polished wooden table in the center gleamed under the soft light, and a few ornate paintings adorned the walls. Richard settled into a leather chair, tapping his fingers lightly on the table as he waited.

Moments later, the door swung open, and a slightly out of breath Father Alessandro entered. His cassock was askew, and beads of perspiration glistened on his brow. He wiped his forehead with the sleeve of his robe before extending his hand.

"*Buongiorno*, Signore Pescatore. I'm Father Alessandro, and I'll be your main point of contact here at the Vatican." His voice was formal, though there was an undercurrent of haste in his tone.

Richard shook his hand, studying the priest's face with a sense of familiarity. There was something about Alessandro— his eyes, his manner—that struck him as someone he had encountered before, though he couldn't quite place it.

As Father Alessandro set a file folder on the table, Richard's curiosity deepened. He kept his eyes on the priest, trying to piece together the vague sense of recognition gnawing at him.

"Signore, I'll need to make a copy of your passport," Alessandro said, breaking Richard's train of thought.

Richard unzipped the inside pocket of his jacket and handed over his passport. As Alessandro left the room, Richard's gaze fell to the label on the file folder in front of him: Richard Pescatore, 1968. His neatly typed name stared back at him, pulling him deeper into contemplation.

When Father Alessandro returned, he carried not only Richard's passport but also several legal-sized envelopes, their edges crisp and clean.

"Signore Pescatore, the pontiff signed off on your documents yesterday," Alessandro began, placing the envelopes on the table. "Everything has been prepared for the release of your funds. This process will be quick."

Richard nodded, though his mind was still on the strange sense of recognition. He picked up a pen as Alessandro slid the documents across the table, directing him where to sign. As he scrawled his signature, his eyes flicked briefly to the payment ledger. The Vatican City Bank was preparing to release the payment owed for his decades of service—an untraceable sum paid in bearer bonds. The figure caught his eye: $1,287,209.90. He frowned slightly, the number a stark reminder of the transactional nature of his work and the Church's inner dealings.

"Your funds have been held in a high-yield account, accumulating interest over the years," Alessandro explained, his voice even. "The final payout will be slightly more than the amount listed here."

With a quick, practiced motion, Richard signed the final document, officially authorizing the release of the bonds. His work for the Church—more than four decades of protecting Anthony Brunelli—was now complete. The bonds were unregistered, untraceable, ensuring that his dealings would remain hidden from any prying eyes.

Father Alessandro watched as Richard finished signing, then continued, "Signore Pescatore, your duties have ended. You are no longer authorized to provide assistance to Anthony Brunelli. Is that clear?"

Richard nodded, his lips pressed into a thin line. "Clear," he muttered.

Alessandro handed Richard a carbon copy of the paperwork stapled to his business card. "You've done extraordinary service for the Church. On behalf of His Holiness and the entire Holy See, we thank you."

Richard remained silent, tucking the documents and his passport into his jacket pocket.

Alessandro continued, "Now, take this receipt to the Vatican Bank just before St. Anne's Gate. Ask for Father Tormey. He'll be expecting you."

As Richard stood to leave something nagged at him. The feeling of familiarity refused to let go. "I'm sorry," he said, turning to Father Alessandro, "but I can't shake the feeling that we've met before. You look very familiar to me."

Alessandro's eyes met his, and for a moment, something unreadable flickered across his face. But then, with a dismissive smile, he tilted his head slightly. "I don't believe we have, Signore."

The words felt practiced, rehearsed, as if Alessandro had said them many times before. He guided Richard toward the elevator, his demeanor calm though something about his presence remained unsettling.

"Press zero to reach the lobby," Alessandro instructed, his voice carrying the faintest hint of impatience. "And if you need anything further, don't hesitate to contact me."

They shook hands, and as Richard stepped into the elevator, he noticed Father Alessandro's gaze linger on him for a second too long. The doors closed with a soft click, and Richard found himself alone once more.

As the elevator descended, Richard reached into his pocket, pulled out his handkerchief, and wiped his hands clean.

CHAPTER 9

Emerging from the elevator, Anthony followed Pope Benedict into his private vault, his breath still catching up from the extraordinary news he had received. The small room they entered was packed from floor to ceiling with ages of artifacts, precious books, and cherished gifts passed down from Pope to Pope. The space, no more than twenty feet by twenty feet, felt intimate, yet its historical impact was overwhelming.

The Persian-style carpet in the center of the room caught Anthony's eye, though it was slightly askew. Beneath it, a portion of an intricate tile mosaic pattern peeked out. Oddly, Benedict bent to adjust the rug with a quick sweep of his ruby-red shoe. The gesture seemed uncharacteristic of the meticulous pontiff, and Anthony couldn't help but wonder why it had been left out of place to begin with. However, his curiosity was soon diverted as he took in the leather chair in the far corner—a place of solitude and reflection, complete with a kneeler, an end table, and a lamp. Clearly, this was where the pope came for moments of private prayer and contemplation.

"Over here, Anthony," Benedict said softly, drawing his attention to the west wall where a stainless-steel safe bore the chalice of the pope's coat of arms.

As Benedict knelt to unlock the safe, Anthony's gaze wandered across the room, landing on two large, red-bound binders resting on a chest-high shelf. But his thoughts about what might be in them were interrupted as the pope removed a limestone cylinder and a Kevlar backpack from the safe and handed them over with great care.

"Anthony," Benedict began with severity in his voice, "here we are. The moment has come. This cylinder has been passed down through the popes for generations."

Anthony held the cylinder before him, marveling at its essence and craftsmanship.

"As you can see, it's airtight and sealed. Inside the backpack, you will find tools and gloves to help you open it. Be careful when you open the cylinder, especially with any artifacts you find inside."

Anthony examined the cylinder more closely, turning it over in his hands, feeling the cool, smooth surface. There was an air of mystery around the object, as if it held something far more significant than its modest size suggested.

"And when you do open it," Benedict continued, "do so in a private, secure place. It likely contains information that will require careful consideration—what to share with the Church, and what should remain undisclosed. This journey you are about to embark on is not just a search for something tangible. It is also a spiritual pilgrimage. Humility will be your guide, and through faith, you will find understanding."

As the pope's words sank in, the hefty toll of responsibility grew heavier on his shoulders. This was no ordinary task. He was being entrusted with something far greater than himself.

Benedict retrieved another item from the safe—a fragile parchment, yellowed with age and protected by a laminate sleeve. It was a document commemorating the more than two hundred popes who had kept this secret safe through the centuries.

Anthony carefully read some of the names aloud, each written in elegant Latin script. "Honorius the Third, 1224; Julius the Second, 1503; Leo the Fourth, 1605; Clemens the Eleventh, 1700; John Paul the Second, 1978." Then quietly, his voice filled with awe, Anthony said, "It's remarkable."

"The Lord works in mysterious ways," Benedict responded. "Despite the turmoil the Church has faced, the admiration for Saint Francis and this secret has never wavered. Even the antipopes respected the cylinder, leaving it untouched."

Anthony's gaze returned to the cylinder in his hands. It seemed almost impossible that something so small could carry so much history, so much power. "Your Holiness," he inquired, his voice calm and assured, "what's the purpose of the backpack?"

The Pope smiled gently. "I had it custom-made for you, Anthony. It is the safest way to transport these artifacts, similar to what we gift to new Swiss Guard recruits."

Anthony nodded, understanding the significance. Benedict was referring to the Pontifical Swiss Guard, the world's oldest standing army, known for their colorful striped Renaissance-era uniforms. Together with the Gendarmerie Corps, they hold responsibility as the military police for Vatican City, Holy See, and its extraterritorial properties. The army was established in 1506 by Pope Julius II and charged with serving and protecting the pope and the Apostolic Palace. The backpack, like the Guard's armor, was a safeguard against any ambiguity that lay ahead.

As his heart raced, the magnitude of the situation became even more apparent. His family's connection to Saint Francis was something he had never fully grasped until now. And yet, here he was, in possession of a letter believed to have been written by Saint Francis's close confidant, Brother Leo, on the saint's behalf.

Benedict's tone grew more serious. "Do be cautious, Anthony. There are those who do not wish for you to succeed no matter what you're called to do. Guard the backpack and its contents with your life." Reaching into his pocket, he handed Anthony a small gold card.

It was unlike anything Anthony had seen before—metallic, cold to the touch, with a microchip embedded inside. The words *Accesso Completo* were etched into its surface.

"This pass," Benedict explained, "will grant you and a guest unaccompanied access to anywhere within Vatican City and beyond. You will be able to enter any art collection, catacomb, or secret area within our domain. It is your key to the truth."

Anthony nodded and slid the card into his wallet, aware that he now possessed one of the most powerful items in the Vatican.

"In addition to the access card," the pope continued, "there is someone I have arranged for to help you, a resource to provide you with oversight, to sort through and interpret any ancient documents. I know of this woman personally, a doctor in archaeology and art history. She's the best in the world. And do not trust anyone else in handling, interpreting, or authenticating all that I've given you, or anything additional that may come your way. You may confide in her, and of course, you may continue to confide in your guardian, Signore Pescatore. I am grateful for the role he has played in guiding you all these years."

Anthony nodded again and smiled. "That makes me feel much better. I had already considered that I might need assistance from both."

Benedict's final words carried an unmistakable resonance. "Do begin by immersing yourself in the teachings of Saint

Francis. His life was a testament to the virtues of peace and harmony for all creation, and a profound commitment to the poor and marginalized. In his example, you may find inspiration and guidance for your own journey. Also seek the counsel of those wise in history and faith. There are lessons from the past, and those well-versed in it may help illuminate your path. As an artist, you have been blessed with the ability to see the world through a unique lens. Use your creativity and intuition as tools to uncover what's been concealed. Remember, what you are seeking may not always be in the form of physical objects or locations but could be found in the connections you make with others and the insights you gain along the way. Be open to the unexpected, for it is often in the unforeseen that the divine chooses to reveal itself."

Anthony's expression remained resolute. "Your Holiness, I'm honored you're trusting me with this. I know it's a big deal, but I'm ready to take it on. Whatever comes my way, I'll handle it. This is a privilege, and I'm fully committed to seeing it through."

"Bless you, Anthony. You are approaching this with sober intentions, and I can't ask for anything more than that. There is, however, one last item and one last request I'd like to ask of you," Benedict said. "There are many things I have done in my life that I regret, but I want you to know that I have been completely faithful to this obligation. I have not discussed this with anyone, not even my closest advisors. Anthony, my son, you have a very special tie to Saint Francis. Stay focused on your task and don't let anyone dissuade you. You have been bound to uphold this order since your birth. It is sacred, but should you find that this cylinder contains information that challenges anything, including the views of the Catholic Church, you will need to decide what is best for the greater body of Christ. Once you leave here, go forward with God's grace, and may you find the knowledge and wisdom needed to complete what's been willed. My request is this. Please keep me in your prayers and intentions."

Anthony felt a sudden surge of devotion. "You have my commitment, and I am profoundly honored, Your Holiness," he acknowledged. "I'm going to approach this with the same intricacy of my work, along with a deep understanding of its significance."

Benedict looked at the Kevlar backpack and then up at Anthony. "It is settled then. You must do what has been willed without fail. Follow your instincts. You will understand soon enough."

Exiting the vault, Benedict reached for the two red-bound binders on the shelf. Anthony happily carried one of them to assist.

"Any final questions, my son?" Benedict asked as the elevator doors slid open.

Although self-doubt set in, Anthony did not want to disappoint the most recognizable religious figure on earth. "I admit, I'm feeling far outside my element with this directive, but at the same time, I'm very competitive so I want to see this through," he said with a wide smile.

With the backpack slung over his shoulders, Anthony stepped into the elevator.

As they returned to the fourth-floor study, Father Alessandro appeared, his face eager. "Holy Father, the senior advisory staff has gathered as requested."

Benedict checked his wristwatch, acknowledging Alessandro with a nod, and turned toward Anthony. He motioned the sign of the cross over the artist's head while reciting a prayer in his native German. "Farewell, Anthony. Father Alessandro will give you the information to contact the art historian and see you out from here."

As Alessandro escorted Anthony out of the study and down to the lobby, he said, "Mr. Brunelli, I'm sure His Holiness explained that he has arranged to provide you with some professional assistance to support your cause. Dr. Vera Valentino is a notable art historian and the Vatican's leading restoration expert. Her specialty is in ancient artifacts. She's based in Florence and is expecting your call." He handed Anthony Dr. Valentino's business card along with his own.

"Thank you," Anthony returned. "I'll be sure to reach her if I run into any challenges." He tucked both business cards into the inside pocket of his jacket.

"Very well, Anthony. And in the meantime, if there's anything you need, do not hesitate to contact me."

As Anthony left the Apostolic Palace, he thought about how what had begun as a friendly introduction to the supreme pontiff had transformed into a far greater calling. The crushing burden of history, of faith, and of his family's obligation now rested in his hands.

CHAPTER 10

St. Peter's Square, Vatican City
2:28 PM

Walking swiftly through the vast, open square of St. Peter's, Anthony turned to his friend and protector, his face clouded with concern. "Have you been able to reach my father, Rick?"

Rick's expression mirrored Anthony's worry. "I spoke with the hotel clerk earlier. They said he never returned last night."

Anthony's heart sank further. He had barely finished debriefing Rick on his conversation with Pope Benedict before they were hailing a taxi to return to their hotel. The restless streets of Rome bustled outside as they rode in tense silence. Rick kept a watchful hand on the briefcase between his feet, while Anthony's hand rested protectively on the Kevlar backpack wedged between them.

Feeling the heavy mantle of the day settling in, Anthony pulled out his phone for the first time since the meeting and scrolled through his unread messages. There were the usual texts from art collectors, clients, and well-wishers, but one stood out—the most important one, from his father. It was time-stamped 12:11 a.m., hours after he had disappeared.

He read the message, his eyes scanning the cryptic words. "Tony, I hope you receive this. Please listen, I have little time.

Your birthright is intact. What I have taught you is now under-way. I love you, dear son."

Anthony's closest friends and family called him Tony, a name that carried warmth and familiarity. But his father's choice of words sent a chill to his bones. He quickly showed the message to Rick.

"You understand this?" Rick asked, his brow furrowed.

Anthony's voice was tight. "Yes. It's a message I hoped I'd never receive. He's in serious trouble."

Rick's confused expression deepened, an unmistakable sense of urgency now present.

Scrolling down, Anthony found a second message with a pin of his father's last known location——Viale Santa Rita da Cascia 101. Just days earlier, he had shown his father how to share his location via text, hoping it could be useful in an emergency. Now, that lesson proved vital as Anthony clicked the link and the map app loaded the coordinates.

"He's twelve miles outside of Rome!" His panic rose. He immediately dialed his father's number, but the call went straight to voicemail.

As the taxi crawled to a stop in front of their hotel, Rick's eyes reflected Anthony's own growing fear. "We need to call the authorities."

Just three blocks from Piazza del Popolo, the Residenza di Ripetta hotel was discreet, its presence marked only by a small gold nameplate on the stone façade. It was a far cry from an American-style hotel.

Anthony rushed through the entrance and up the grand staircase to the front desk. His desperation was apparent as he spoke to the clerk. "My father is staying here, and he's been missing since last night. It's not like him to disappear without any word. I'm very concerned about his safety. Can you please give me access to his room? I need to see if there's any sign of where he might have gone."

Rick stood by his side, offering silent support.

The clerk frowned sympathetically. "I understand your concern, Signore. I received a phone call earlier inquiring about your father."

"Yes, that was from me," Rick chimed in, giving a slight nod.

"Unfortunately, we have strict privacy policies in place, and I can't grant direct access to another guest's room without permission. However," the clerk continued, his eyes squinting as he scanned the computer screen, "I see the reservation was made under your name, Signore Brunelli. Is that correct?"

"Yes, yes, it was," Anthony reacted. "And I'm paying for the rooms."

"Very well," the clerk said. "We can accompany you to the room and open it for you, but we'll need to remain while you check for any information about your father's whereabouts. Should we also contact the local authorities, or perhaps the American Embassy?"

"Yes," Anthony answered immediately. "Please, let's contact them right away."

After a brief consultation with the hotel manager, the clerk returned with Ms. Pirozzi, a woman whose calm, authoritative presence reassured them both. She walked with them toward the elevators, speaking in measured tones.

"Signore Brunelli, I understand how concerning this must be," Ms. Pirozzi said in a calm, reassuring tone. "Our priority is your father's safety, and we will assist you in every way we can. My assistant is calling the American Embassy as we speak, and I'll accompany you to your father's room so you can look for any clues. Let's take this step by step."

As they neared the door to Ronald Brunelli's room, the air grew thick with anticipation. Ms. Pirozzi slid the key card into the door. With a click, the lock disengaged and the door swung open, revealing a room that appeared undisturbed.

Anthony immediately moved toward his father's suitcase, which lay open on the bed. His heart raced as he unzipped a small interior pocket, precisely where his father had told him to look if anything went wrong. Inside, he found a legal-sized envelope filled with neatly stacked papers. On top, a folded piece of lined notebook paper bore the words: For My Son, Tony.

"He left me a note," he whispered, his throat tight with emotion.

Out of respect for the private moment, Ms. Pirozzi stepped outside the room to call her assistant. Her voice faded into the background, professional but concerned.

Anthony stared at the note in his hands, feeling the enormity of the situation settle in his chest. His father had prepared him for this moment, warned him that their family secret held dangerous consequences. Just days before his departure for Assisi to begin his commission, his father had told him, "Tony, there are those who would rather we not honor our obligation. If anything happens to me, promise me you'll see it through. I'll leave everything you need to know."

Taking a deep breath, Anthony unfolded the note. Rick stepped closer, reading over his shoulder. The words were stark, final. He folded the note back up, placed it into the envelope, and tucked it securely into the Kevlar backpack. It was not something meant for others to see.

"The polizia are on their way," Ms. Pirozzi informed them as she reentered the room. "They will be here shortly."

The room fell into an tension-filled silence as they waited. Not long after, a sudden knock at the door shattered the quiet.

Ms. Pirozzi opened it to reveal a man in plain clothes holding a coffee cup in one hand.

"I'm Captain Daniello Rossi," he said, flashing his badge.

Ms. Pirozzi shook his hand. "Thank you for coming so quickly." She stepped aside to let him in. "I'll leave you to speak with Mr. Brunelli and Mr. Pescatore. If you need anything, I'll be outside the door."

As she exited, the captain turned to Anthony and Rick, his demeanor focused. "Tell me what's happened," he said, his voice calm but serious.

Anthony and Rick exchanged a glance, sensing the heightened threat of the situation.

"The American Embassy has emphasized the urgency of this matter," Captain Rossi added.

"My father, Ronald Brunelli, went missing late last night," Anthony began. "I received a message from him, but I didn't see it until earlier today. He also sent me his location."

Anthony handed his phone to the captain, showing him the pin drop.

Rossi's eyes flickered with recognition, though he kept his face neutral.

"We're very concerned," Rick added. "It's not like him to vanish without a trace."

Captain Rossi nodded, taking a photo of the text message. He then asked Anthony for his father's cellphone number, which he quickly wrote down in his pocket notebook. "We'll track his phone activity and follow up on any leads. Do you have a recent photograph of your father?"

Anthony pulled up the most recent image on his phone, a picture of his father wearing his favorite jacket. "He's about six feet tall," he said, showing the image to Rossi.

"That's helpful. Please send it to me." Rossi gave him his number, and within moments, the photo arrived on the captain's phone. He glanced at the screen, then locked eyes with Anthony. "We'll distribute this to our team immediately."

Anthony took a deep breath, his voice steady but urgent. "Captain, I've tried calling his phone several times, but it goes straight to voicemail."

Rossi nodded. "We'll look into all of his activity. And in the meantime, we'll investigate the location he sent to you. But just so you know, the law requires that we wait twenty-four hours before launching a formal search for a missing person. Given the circumstances, however, we'll get a head start." The captain winked.

Anthony hesitated, lowered his gaze to the floor. "I have a bad feeling, Captain," he said before glancing back up. "Something doesn't feel right."

Rossi raised an eyebrow. "We'll handle this thoroughly, Mr. Brunelli. Let's hope he turns up soon, but if there's any foul play involved, we'll be ready." As he departed, he shook their hands firmly and gave each of them a business card. "We'll be in touch with updates. Rest assured, we'll do everything we can. And if there's anything you learn in the meantime, please contact me right away."

Left in the quiet aftermath, Anthony and Rick exchanged a look—a blend of hope and fear.

With the folder of information in hand, Anthony again felt the unyielding grip of his father's note bearing heavily on him. He knew what it meant. His father had passed the torch, and there was no turning back. "Where do we start?" he asked, his voice low. "Do we go to the location he sent?"

"No," Rick placed a reassuring hand on Anthony's shoulder. "Let the police focus on finding your father. Every hour counts, and I'll be checking with them daily—multiple times if needed." He squeezed Anthony's shoulder. "But right now, your father gave you instructions in his letter. You need to focus on that. He told you specifically to contact the minister general, Friar Tasca. That's what you need to do. Trust me to handle things here. I'll call the moment—the very moment—there's any news about your father."

T

As Richard walked to his room, he pulled out his phone and dialed a number in Rome.

After several rings, an elderly voice answered, "*Pronto.*"

"*Pronto*, Friar. It's Richard Pescatore. I've got a very serious problem on my hands."

CHAPTER **11**

The Villa at Mariano Fortuny, Rome
4:15 PM

Alessandro was late. He hurried up the dead-end street to the unimposing villa, his heavy gait thumping the cobblestones. Just the day before, he had tasked the brilliant Dr. Valentino with a critical mission that he hoped would move his plan, untold years in the making, closer to fruition.

His uncle, Cardinal Pietro della Rovere, waited on the villa's terrace. Spotting Alessandro below, he barked down, "Alessandro, what's taken you so long!?" His voice, sharp with displeasure, cut through the cool air in clipped Italian.

Pietro was one of two elder cardinals stationed at the villa. Both held powerful positions within the Congregation for the Doctrine of the Faith, or CDF, the oldest and most controversial arm of the Roman Curia, originally established to defend the Church against heresy. Its modern role was to safeguard Catholic doctrine, a task many believed was no longer being fully upheld. Cardinal Pietro della Rovere had helped his nephew Alessandro into the coveted position of secretary to the pope.

Alessandro's primary duty was simple yet profound—to keep close watch on Pietro's greatest political victory, ensuring the stability of Pope Benedict XVI. Pietro had always taken full credit for orchestrating Joseph Ratzinger's election to the papacy, a feat he mentioned often. Few had expected Ratzinger to be chosen, given the long-standing pattern that front-runners rarely became Pope. The surprise election contradicted the Christian ethos of elevating the overlooked, a fact Pietro reveled in.

As Alessandro entered the villa's foyer, he came face-to-face with his uncle. "My apologies for being late," he panted. "Benedict just concluded a two-hour meeting with three of his most trusted advisors, including the minister general. None of them said a single word as they departed, which concerns me."

Pietro's eyes narrowed. "Right now, I'm far more interested in what you mentioned on the phone. The leadership is gathered, waiting to hear your findings firsthand. Now, what have you discovered?"

With a flicker of pride, Alessandro reached into his jacket and produced a plastic bag containing the parchment he had retrieved from the pope's vault earlier that day.

His uncle looked down at the artifact with suspicion. "What is this?"

"I removed it from Benedict's private vault," he replied, his eyes gleaming with satisfaction. "This could make all the difference for our cause."

"And I will pretend I didn't see this priceless artifact mishandled in transit," Pietro replied, his voice heavy with reprimand. Alessandro began to speak, but his uncle cut him off with a hard stare and a raised hand. "Let's make sure we know exactly what we're dealing with before we brief the leadership. Now, what does this document contain?"

Alessandro's beady eyes glittered as he replied, "It's the evidence we've been searching for." He took the next few minutes to brief his uncle on his findings, reading the highlights from the parchment and asking that he trust him to present the full discovery.

Pietro remained impassive. "For your sake, I certainly hope you're right." He carefully placed the parchment in a leather binder and motioned for Alessandro to follow him inside, where a dozen cardinals awaited the briefing. Before entering, he leaned in and whispered to his nephew, "And if you are right"—he then pulled away and bobbed his head in approval—"you will be rightfully rewarded."

Not even the Roman Curia was aware of the villa at Via Mariano Fortuny, other than Pietro and Cardinal Stefano Ferraro, head of the leadership and the highest-ranking cardinal in the CDF. The underground group housed there was called the *Ramorosso*, meaning "Branch of Red," founded in 1556 by the corrupt Cardinal Giovanni Pietro Carafa who would later become Pope Paul IV. For five centuries, the Ramorosso had thrived by manipulating authority, infiltrating the Catholic Church, and extending their influence into the government and modern media. Their primary goal was to control the Roman Curia, and through it, the cardinals. For whoever controlled the cardinals, controlled the pope. And that was the ultimate power.

Father Alessandro followed his uncle into the Ramorosso's secret meeting room. He had only been allowed entry on two previous occasions, when he was made secretary to the pope and when he had been chastised for failing to persuade Benedict to revoke John Paul II's reforms.

Cardinal Stefano Ferraro, the head of the Ramorosso, had led the clandestine group for the past decade. In his mid-eighties, he was tall and gaunt, with thinning, slicked-back hair, glossy black eyes, and skin so pale it seemed to glow in the dim light. Born into a powerful lineage, Ferraro's rise within the Church was a product of both his formidable intellect and ruthless ambition. Thirty years prior, he had been granted the associate priesthood at the Archdiocese of Reggio Calabria-Bova in Southern Italy, not because he sought to run a parish but because that was the expected path for cardinals. It mattered little that the priest looked nothing like his swarthy counterparts. Reggio Calabria-Bova was Ferraro's birthplace, a region known for its pervasive corruption, making it the perfect front from which he could run his secretive empire.

The only difference between Ferraro and the then notorious Cardinal Carafa was that Carafa had decided he must become pope himself, forcing his election in 1555. Even then, Carafa's opposition had nearly won out, with him barely securing the majority vote needed. Ferraro, on the other hand, had known the papacy was far too public and vulnerable a position. Instead, he opted to rule from the shadows, manipulating the cardinals and the Roman Curia to maintain control.

"We need to bring this meeting to order," Ferraro commanded, his voice cutting through the murmurs of the cardinals seated around the table, deep in their own private conversations. He tapped the underside of the table with his ornate wooden rod, drawing their attention.

The group turned their focus toward their arriving guest, Pietro's nephew, and the room fell silent.

Ferraro surveyed the room with piercing eyes. "As you are all aware, the Ramorosso has wielded control over the papacy since the Renaissance. We now find ourselves at a critical juncture where our future and our very survival hang in the balance. Let us now turn our attention to Cardinal della Rovere, who will provide the necessary updates."

"Thank you, Cardinal Ferraro." Pietro stepped forward. "Brothers, I ask you to prepare yourselves for what I and my nephew, Alessandro, are about to disclose. For ages, we have believed that Francis of Assisi, the great peacemaker, held the key to a secret that, if revealed, could shatter the very foundations upon which our Church stands. The revelation I am about to share strikes at the heart of our faith. I speak, of course, of the Blessed Virgin Mary and the doctrine of the virgin birth. At least, this is the narrative passed down through the ages."

He paused, allowing the substance of his words to settle before continuing. "The Ramorosso exists solely to shield the Church from truths of this magnitude. To preserve this secret, we have maintained an unyielding grip on the papacy. Popes throughout history have taken oaths of protection, often without fully understanding the significance of what they guarded. They were told only one thing, that the cylinder in question must never be opened, its contents never revealed, until a divine message from Almighty God made such a time known."

Pietro's gaze swept the room, then his voice grew more deliberate as he said, "Today, we believe that moment has come. Alessandro is here to offer critical insight into this revelation and to share what this Brunelli artist has uncovered since my last update." His eyes darted to Alessandro, granting him silent permission to speak.

Alessandro stepped forward and looked directly at Ferraro. "Cardinal Ferraro, we're tracking the artist, Anthony Brunelli. He met with Benedict, but the pope hasn't shared his plans even with me. However, Benedict has been very discreet and spent a fortune on the art commissions, far higher than he should have, and we believe that was meant to distract from this other Brunelli business."

"Did you speak with the artist's father as instructed?" Ferraro asked, his dark eyes narrowing.

"Yes, he's been intercepted." Alessandro couldn't help but sneer. "Unfortunately, he was…uncooperative. And for that he was eliminated."

"He's dead?" Ferraro questioned, his snakelike nostrils flaring.

"Yes. But before his death, we managed to extract the necessary information. We are now trailing his son, Anthony, and his guardian, Richard Pescatore."

"You better hope there's not a trace," Ferraro said sharply. "And if there is, it's on you."

"I want both of their cell phones tapped immediately," Pietro directed to his second-in-command. "Do it now."

"And Pescatore? Has he attempted to collect the funds we discussed previously?" Ferraro asked.

"Benedict already approved, and the transaction has commenced. Pescatore has the bonds, which we intend to intercept. We purposely gave him bearer bonds because they're unregistered and untraceable. No records are kept of the owner or the transactions involving ownership—"

"It was my understanding that the Vatican Bank discontinued the circulation of bearer bonds, no? For financial transparency?" a Cardinal's voice interrupted.

"They've stopped circulation of the bonds for the most part, but we do keep some on hand for situations such as this," Alessandro explained. "So, we must recover them before they're exchanged."

"You don't have to convince this group of the urgency," Ferraro said, bracing the conference table with his bony hands as he slowly rose to his feet. "That's our money, Alessandro. Get your hands on it quickly. It will fund our cause for the next two years at least."

"Now, Alessandro, tell us your findings," Pietro prompted.

Alessandro leaned forward, clearly pleased with himself. "We have long known that Ronald Brunelli's family is connected to the secrets held by Saint Francis. We were determined to uncover what that secret is. When Ronald returned to Rome—despite our threats to never do so again—we knew something significant was about to happen."

"Cardinal Ferraro, as we all know, information has been passed from father to son through the Brunelli lineage for centuries," Pietro interjected. "We are only now discovering exactly what that entails. We must assume the son knows everything and that he's now in charge."

Ferraro smiled, but it didn't reach his stone-cold eyes.

Alessandro waited for his uncle's approving nod before continuing. "Benedict took the artist into his private vault, and when Brunelli left the Apostolic Palace, he was carrying a Kevlar backpack. I recognized it instantly. It's the same one from the vault. It holds the ancient cylinder. Because of our history with the Brunelli family, we anticipated this moment. Using the secret tunnel our forefathers so cleverly provided, we intercepted the cylinder yesterday by breaching the vault." He paused for effect, his small audience hanging on his every word.

Several of the cardinals gasped audibly.

Alessandro didn't miss a beat. "Inside the cylinder, we found an ancient parchment. Unfortunately, it wasn't what we expected. It bore just one word, *Incipe*."

"*Incipe*?" a voice with a thick German accent echoed. "In the beginning?"

"Yes, the Latin word has a number of possible meanings, *in the beginning, begin, begins with*—something like that," Alessandro confirmed. Admittedly, Latin wasn't his strong suit in school. "That one word does not tell us much of anything."

"This is true," Pietro acknowledged.

The men around the table grumbled and whispered to each other.

Ferraro cleared his throat. "Enough," he commanded earnestly, and the conversation died at once.

"We left that parchment inside the cylinder. It was obviously a worthless scroll. I was at first disheartened, but that is not all we found." He let his words hang in the air and savored the audience resting in the palm of his hand. "When I looked deeper into the cylinder, I found another ancient parchment. And now I have reason to believe that Francis was hiding proof of the ultimate lie, the ultimate betrayal and secret that we need to finally take full control of the Church."

The cardinals leaned in almost simultaneously, and Alessandro knew his moment had arrived. The scornful expression he wore vanished, replaced by one of pure satisfaction.

Pietro reached into his leather binder and retrieved a plastic bag, holding it aloft for all to see before sliding it across the table to Alessandro, accompanied by a pair of protective black cotton gloves. "My nephew has uncovered undeniable proof," he declared. "Proof that Jesus was not the product of the Annunciation. Evidence that Mary, the Virgin Mother of Jesus, was not exactly a virgin as the Bible claims."

The room erupted in chaos. Elderly men shifted uneasily in their chairs, some crossing themselves, others recoiling in visible disgust. "This is blasphemy!" one of the elders cried, his voice quivering with outrage.

Alessandro ignored the outbursts, his gaze steady on the parchment before him. "This ancient document recounts a different story, one where Jesus was conceived not through divine intervention but through an act of violence. We have known of this rumor for over five hundred years, but this is the first historical document we can point to that actually speaks to it."

The cacophony of moments before dissolved into an eerie silence that seemed to linger like smoke in the air.

Alessandro seized the moment to continue. "Three years following the crucifixion of Our Lord Jesus Christ, Pontius Pilate, who presided over His sentencing," he read, "was cast from his station by the decree of the Emperor Tiberius. Summoned to Rome to account for his deeds, Pilate carried with him writings that he claimed as evidence, disputing the divine nature of Christ's birth. It was said Pilate sought to quell the spread of the Christian faith and shield himself from the judgment of the emperor. In these writings, he asserted that the Blessed Virgin Mary had suffered a grievous assault by an unknown wanderer and that Joseph, her betrothed, assumed the semblance of a father to the child to shield her honor as they journeyed unto Bethlehem for the census."

"This claim is profane!" one of the elders shouted, rising to his feet. "We all know Jesus was the product of a sanctified birth and divine conception."

"And what about the angel Gabriel?" a second elder added. "Shall we dismiss the divine messenger as well? Who are we to deconstruct the sacred word of God Himself?"

The elder's fiery declaration referred to the biblical account of the Annunciation, in which God sent the angel Gabriel to a young virgin named Mary. Gabriel greeted her with a proclamation that she would conceive and bear a son, Jesus, who would be called the Son of God. Though a virgin, Mary was told the Holy Spirit would descend upon her, making the miraculous conception possible. In an act of faith and obedience, Mary had responded, "May your word to me be fulfilled."

Ferraro turned sharply toward the two disruptive elders, his expression unyielding. "You both are excused. Leave this meeting at once!" he commanded, his voice cutting through the tension.

The elders hesitated for a moment but begrudgingly departed, leaving a heavy stillness in their wake.

"And for the rest of you, if you think the lightning that struck Saint Peter's dome this morning wasn't a sign for us to electrify this church before disaster unfolds, you have another thing coming. Now let's focus, shall we?"

Ferraro asked Alessandro for the pair of protective gloves, then motioned impatiently for the letter to be handed over too. Growing haste was intense among the cardinals waiting in anticipation for their leader's approval of Alessandro's discovery. They had been promised untold riches, derived from indefinite extortion, should an event like this ever transpire, and all they needed was for Ferraro to confirm the validity of what Alessandro had found.

Ferraro placed the parchment on the wooden table in front of him. Clutching a large magnifying glass in his viselike grip, he did not utter a word while taking in each letter written on the ancient scroll. The only sound that could be heard was the slight crinkle of the paper.

"This is the most significant find of our existence, Father Alessandro," he said thoughtfully after reading it through.

Alessandro felt pleased. Receiving praise from Ferraro was a rare happening.

"But," he said, changing his tone, "as I look closely, the remainder of this parchment has been deliberately ripped away. I can see there are letters that were torn beneath!" He held the ancient scroll aloft so everyone around the table could see its jagged edges. It was obvious there had previously been more writing beneath the tear. "At first glance, this appears to confirm what we have long heard about the virgin birth. I will have to study it some more, but at least now this gives us a hint as to what Saint Francis was up to. We must silence Anthony Brunelli."

"I'm already on it. As far as we can tell, he's only focused on his work and is far more distracted than his father," Alessandro offered. "It's doubtful that he knows anything about this secret of Mary, especially now that we have the parchment, but he still poses a threat. He has the original cylinder, and now, under direction of Benedict, he's also been given access to our very own Dr. Vera Valentino. He's aware that his father is missing and called the American Embassy to start a search. That will keep him distracted. And we do have one thing in our favor He is a little too impressed with himself and his success."

"That will certainly make it easier for us," one of the cardinals said with a sneer.

"Let's make him a business proposition…an offer he can't refuse," another cardinal proposed, and laughter multiplied in the room.

With alarming anger, Ferraro slammed his fist on the conference table, and once again the room went still. "This is anything but humorous," he snapped. "I want—"

Just then, one of the property's armed guards hastily entered the room and approached Ferraro with a soft-toned brief. After conferring out of earshot for only a few moments, Ferraro's face turned ghostlike as he turned to Alessandro.

"You may not have acted fast enough," Ferraro said, scowling. "Our sources have already intercepted a phone call. It seems Ronald Brunelli was able to somehow instruct his son. I wonder, Alessandro. Did this happen posthumously?"

The cardinal's repulsion cut through Alessandro's soul.

"The Brunelli son has contacted Minister General Tasca, and they're meeting tomorrow morning at Santi Apostoli at ten a.m. sharp. The minister general told Brunelli it's urgent they meet."

"It could be the second half to this parchment," Pietro said, his gaze distant. When his eyes flicked back to Alessandro, he cowered slightly at his expression. "If it's true, then we must be there to intercept this exchange."

"I will send in the Vatican police," Alessandro offered, though hesitant to suggest anything to his superiors, especially with Ferraro in such a fervent and unpredictable state.

His face still ghostly pale, Ferraro said, "If it's the second half of this parchment, we must intercept that meeting." He turned to Alessandro, his expression one of repulsion. "Brief our contact and have the Vatican police stop Brunelli before he arrives there tomorrow morning. We need to uncover what the Franciscans are protecting once and for all." The high priest's thin mouth tightened. "And you need to have a come-to-Jesus meeting with Benedict, Alessandro. Make it clear he must co-operate or we'll leak this Virgin Mary story to the media. And don't come back until you have the second half of the letter or whatever it is the minister general holds!"

Growing unbearably hot, Alessandro started to sweat, knowing absolutely everything was at stake.

CHAPTER 12

Santi Apostoli, Rome
4:45 PM

Shifting his bare feet on the rough clay tiles of the porch, Massimo Coppo anxiously pressed the buzzer at the Franciscan Brotherhood Headquarters at Santi Apostoli. Clad in a simple sackcloth habit, a rope cincture tied around his waist, Massimo looked every bit the part of a humble monk. His walking stick rested by his side, and his feet, calloused, swollen, and tinged purple, bore the marks of a life of extreme poverty and sacrifice. A large, tan bandage covered his right heel, where dried blood crusted at the edges. His thick, salt-and-pepper hair formed an uneven mushroom-style cut.

Despite the discomfort his body endured, Massimo's eyes, bright aqua blue and sharp, revealed a man at peace with his chosen path. A self-proclaimed monk seeking to emulate Saint Francis of Assisi with every fiber of his being, he took joy in his extreme poverty and slept each night on a wooden bench under the portico at the Basilica of Saint Francis in Assisi.

The door opened, and a friar with a warm smile greeted, "Come," and then gestured for Massimo to follow.

As they made their way through the modest offices, Massimo's discerning gaze roved the humble surroundings. The simplicity of the headquarters reassured him because the lack of opulence reflected the values Saint Francis had lived by—chastity, poverty, and obedience. It reinforced Massimo's trust in the modern-day Franciscans, who, unlike much of the world, seemed to stay true to the spirit of their founder.

Massimo knew the minister general had summoned him for a reason. The call for this meeting had come the previous evening, and although it was not their first encounter, today's gathering felt different. Something was shifting.

The friar led him to a door at the end of a long corridor. "Signore," he called softly, gesturing for Massimo to enter.

Inside, Friar Tasca greeted him with a warm embrace. "Massimo, my friend, I'm glad you came. Tell me, how is everything in Assisi?"

"Yes, Friar, Assisi remains pure and my mission endures." Then, with his customary humility, Massimo relayed a recent incident. He had been arrested for creating a public spectacle—stripping himself of his sackcloth and preaching in his undergarments.

Tasca gave a knowing smile. "I admire your conviction. Your actions, as always, speak of your devotion to the spirit of Francis, but do be careful not to stir unwanted attention." The minister general's expression grew somber. "Massimo, what we have prayed for, what we have prepared for all these years, is now set in motion. The time is upon us, and your role—your sacred duty as a Time Watcher—is more critical than ever. Forces of evil have been unleashed, and the Church stands on the brink."

Massimo leaned in, his worn hands tightening around the handle of his walking stick. "I'm not sure I quite understand. What has precipitated this?"

Tasca sighed, his eyes clouded with concern. "Our dear friend Ronald Brunelli is missing. We believe he's been captured, though we pray for his safety. His son, Anthony, whom you know now, takes on the mantle of responsibility. He will return to Assisi soon, and when he does, you must help guide him and protect him. The task ahead of him will be monumental. Nothing must prevent him from fulfilling his calling."

Massimo absorbed the significance of Tasca's words, his heart heavy with the oppressive force of what was to come. "How can I be of service?"

The minister general's gaze softened as he chose his words carefully. "Anthony will need your guidance, your wisdom. Enlighten him, help him see the path he must walk. His task will seem overwhelming, but with your counsel, he will be prepared." He placed his palm on Massimo's forehead, offering a solemn blessing. "May God keep you, our beloved land of Assisi, and all that we hold sacred, safe and pure as it has always been and as it must remain."

Massimo raised his head slowly, his sharp blue eyes glowing with reverence and his weathered face serene yet resolute. His voice, though soft, carried the conviction of centuries of faith. "My commitment is unwavering," he whispered, the profound depth of his vow echoing in the room.

Filled with admiration, Tasca's eyes sparkled with quiet pride. "*Pax et bonum*," Tasca intoned in Latin, his voice rich with soberness.

"*Pace e Bene*," Massimo responded in Italian, his words laced with both sincerity and finality. He offered Tasca a humble nod as he rose to his feet, his hand gripping his walking stick as though preparing for a journey far longer than the steps it would take to leave the room.

T

As the hermit departed, the minister general sat in quiet reflection, his mind turning over the striking similarities between Massimo's humble devotion and the spirit of Saint Francis. He had seen many devout men in his lifetime, but none had mirrored the spirit of Saint Francis so closely.

No one else alive knew Massimo's true role. When the Ordinary General Chapter elected him to a six-year term as Minister General in 2007, he became the 119th successor to St. Francis. One of his first acts had been to secretly appoint Massimo as the official Time Watcher—a position specifically intended to coincide with his term, which the pious monk fulfilled with honor. When he'd been re-elected in January, Massimo had also accepted a second appointment to continue his stealth service.

One thing was certain—the days ahead would not be easy, but Massimo's steadfast spirit might be the key to not only helping Brunelli but perhaps saving the spirit of the entire Church.

CHAPTER 13

Residenza di Ripetta, Rome
5:25 PM

In the dimly lit sanctum of his hotel room, Anthony stood before an ancient mystery now embodied in the form of a thick, aged envelope laying on the desk. The soft light from the nearby lamp bathed it in a gentle glow, casting long shadows that seemed to deepen the significance of the moment. His father's words still echoed in his mind—cryptic references to their family's sacred duty, an unspoken bond tied to Saint Francis of Assisi. This was no ordinary envelope—it was a passageway to the unknown, a key to unlocking a lineage steeped in faith and secrecy.

The air was heavy, as if the very atmosphere held its breath alongside him. Anthony felt the looming shadow of the ages engulfing him, as if his ancestors were standing silently by, watching, waiting. His father's voice reverberated in his memory, urging him forward, reminding him this was more than a personal journey. It was a pilgrimage through time, one that bound him to a legacy far greater than himself.

With steady, almost reverent hands, Anthony carefully removed the letter from the envelope. A sense of foreboding mingled with sorrow as he unfolded the pages. This was his second time reading his father's message, and the emotion was no less potent.

"To my dearest Anthony," the letter began, "the legacy of our family and its sacred duty now falls to you."

The words were simple yet profound, laced with an urgency that he hadn't fully appreciated until now. His father had written of a covenant with Saint Francis, a bond that stretched across generations, linked by objects of immense spiritual power. These ancient artifacts, guarded by the Brunelli family since days of old, held within them secrets that could change everything.

He finished reading, his father's instructions burning into his mind:

Your grandfather was adamant that I understood how incredibly revered these documents are to our family and that I express the importance of them to you. They can only be opened when we know it is time. This is the time. By now, the pope should have given you something of importance. If you are in possession of that gift, please open it only after reading the entirety of the documents in this envelope and any others the pope supplied. You will also need to be in contact with Minister General Tasca. He too holds critical information you'll need.

The force of his father's directive was unmistakable as Anthony gently withdrew the remaining contents from the envelope. A cascade of ancient documents spilled out onto the desk—parchment yellowed with age, sealed letters, and cryptic manuscripts from his lineage. It was as though he had unlocked a vault of secrets, the sheer mass of his family's guardianship laid out before him.

The afternoon light faded to dusk as he poured over every detail of the documents. This was more than just a collection of family papers. These artifacts from a forgotten era were laden with meaning and mystery. Some contained detailed accounts of secret pilgrimages to Assisi, others cryptic references to a grave that seemed to shift with time, and then there were symbols he didn't yet understand. His thoughts turned inward, wrestling with the significance of what lay before him.

The hotel room around him slowly transformed into something more, no longer just a simple, modern space but a sanctified chamber. The documents, no longer mere paper, seemed to pulse with life, whispering to him, weaving a narrative that tethered him to a history older than he could have imagined.

As night fell, he reached into the backpack and retrieved more documents written in ancient Italian. He put on the protective gloves Pope Benedict had provided before carefully handling the letter—a one-page script signed by his ancestor, Antonio Brunelli, many centuries ago.

With the help of his laptop, he began transcribing the document into English, laboring over the ancient Italian dialect. Each word seemed loaded with meaning, demanding careful consideration. When he finished, he read the words aloud, his voice trembling under the staggering impact of what they conveyed:

Our kin hath been greatly blessed with a bond to Francis of Assisi, who hath been called unto the Lord. Though but four and forty years of age, he was wise far beyond his years. It is said he shall soon be welcomed into sainthood. Ere Francis was struck with grievous illness, he did entrust unto me a solemn and tall charge, a task that demandeth mine own steadfast will as well as the will of those who shall follow in mine stead. This charge, though seemingly simple, must be kept with utmost devotion until such time as His Holiness decreeth its hour hath come.

Anthony paused, letting the words settle in the stillness of the room. The continuation of the letter spoke of a sacred charge bestowed upon the Brunelli family, to safeguard a scroll of immense significance, hidden with Antonio at his burial site, a location known only to the family. As Anthony read on, a dark history unfolded before him—his ancestor's flight from the Inquisition, the looming specter of the Church's wrath, and the ultimate sacrifice Antonio was prepared to make.

The words lingered in the air as he leaned back in his chair, the magnitude of his inheritance descending on him. The clock on his nightstand showed 11:45 p.m., yet sleep felt distant.

He steadied his breathing and opened the folder from his father, his attention drawn to a particular parchment his father had marked as essential. His eyes narrowed as he studied the text—an intricate maze of medieval Italian script interwoven with Roman numerals. His eyes burned with fatigue, but he cracked his knuckles and set to work, carefully working to translate the cryptic message:

N. MCLXIX • Lo luogo de la mia nascita • Uno homo de povertade riposa • Entro una chiesa sontuosa • Non piangere per lo 'Colle dello Inferno' • Ma gridare, 'Colle dello Paradiso' • Perciocché 'Dio ha audito' • Lo terreno sacro è confirmato qui • Ove lo mio scriba celato dimora • M. MCCXXXI

Anthony creased his brow, the ancient words swimming before his tired eyes. The meaning eluded him, and though he made some progress, the full picture remained just out of reach. The clock struck midnight.

Cutting through the quiet with a sharp trill, his cellphone rang. He glanced at the screen—Rick Pescatore.

"I hope you have some good news," Anthony answered, exhaustion evident in his voice.

"The priest who assisted you earlier, what was his name?" Rick's tone carried an urgency that cut through Anthony's fatigue. "Do you have his business card?"

Anthony's mind briefly wandered back to the Vatican. "Yes, give me a second," he said, retrieving the two business cards from his jacket. "Let's see, his name is Father Alessandro della Rovere."

"Yes, that's who I thought." Rick's voice tightened. "I have a suspicion that there's some connection here with the disappearance of your father, but I need more time to verify. Watch yourself, Anthony. I'll be in touch as soon as I can."

The warning in Rick's voice left a chill in the air.

Anthony placed both business cards on the desk, Dr. Valentino's name catching his eye. She would be the key to deciphering what he couldn't, yet fatigue overtook him. Glancing at the clock—12:20 a.m.—he decided that after eight hundred years, this could wait another night.

T

Anthony's phone jolted him awake at five a.m. The name Louis Meisel glowed on the screen. It was his longtime art dealer, the man solely responsible for launching his career. Swallowing a wave of fatigue, he answered.

"Tony, did you get my email?" Louis's voice was sharp, urgent.

"I haven't checked my inbox in a couple of days," he replied, rubbing sleep from his eyes. "What's going on?"

"There's a commission offer on the table—three-quarters of a million dollars," Louis said in a breathless rush. "We need an answer now."

That number sliced through Anthony's lingering drowsiness like a blade. He sat up against the headboard, heart suddenly awake. "Who's the client?"

"A sophisticated collector in Bavaria. He's been following your recent Vatican commission and wants you for a new project. This could be huge, Tony. Career-defining huge."

Anthony inhaled slowly, the enormity of the offer colliding with the task that already weighed heavily on his conscience. "Louis, I'm not sure I can take this on right now."

"Are you out of your mind?" Louis's voice rose, laced with frustrated disbelief. "This is a once-in-a-lifetime opportunity. I've got Clive waiting in the wings if you say no, but the client wants you—specifically you. You're the first choice."

Anthony's mind drifted for a moment, envisioning Louis in his Prince Street office in SoHo, the very cradle of the photorealist movement. Louis, who had coined that term in 1969, had shepherded the genre from obscurity to international acclaim, championing the work of Richard Estes, Chuck Close, Charles Bell, Tom Blackwell, and countless others. His guidance had carved out a space for Anthony's own talents. Yet, as his gaze drifted toward the stack of ancient documents spread across his hotel desk, he could almost feel their silent pressure. They weren't just old papers—they were the legacy of his family and likely something even more sacred. The kind of heritage that, once touched, could never be put aside.

He exhaled, steadying his voice. "What's the size of the piece, and where's the subject located?"

"I negotiated a five-by-seven-foot painting of his palace in Bavaria," Louis answered, his tone easing, hopeful again. "Architecture and light. Exactly what you're known for."

Anthony stood on a precipice. On one side was the monumental promise of a commission that could further anchor his career. On the other lay the beckoning shadows of his ancestry and the fragile sheaf of centuries-old documents, each page a whispered plea from the past. Until now, his path had always seemed clear. But this morning, clarity eluded him like a thin glaze of oil paint that refused to set, its contours blurring somewhere between the vivid highlights of ambition and the timeworn shadows of legacy.

The $750,000 commission was the pinnacle of everything Anthony had imagined, an artist's ultimate validation. For years he had strived to capture not just what the eye could see but the elusive spirit beneath—the intangible shimmer of emotion, the subtle pulse of life's hidden truths. Until now, his brush and canvas had belonged solely to him, an extension of his will and vision. But this moment felt different. It reached beyond his studio's familiar walls, beckoning him into a realm where history's currents ran deep and dark, where art and faith intertwined in ways he could scarcely comprehend.

"If he needs an answer so soon, Louis, I'm sorry," Anthony said at last, his voice steady yet edged with regret. "I must decline. I'm involved with this family-secret thing that I really can't get into right now. If he truly wants me, he'll have to wait."

A stunned silence crackled across the line before Louis's voice erupted, incredulous and furious. "This is everything you've ever wanted! I promised I'd bring you to this point, and here it is, laid out at your feet! You'd turn it down for what? A secret you can't even explain?"

Anthony's chest tightened. The artist in him howled to accept, to forever secure his name among the master photorealists. Yet something older and infinitely more potent tugged at him. An ancestral whisper threading through generations of blood and sacrifice spoke of duties not bound by contracts or fame. It reminded him that some legacies were forged not by ambition but by the fierce preservation of truth no matter how deeply it might be buried.

"I'm sorry, Louis," Anthony said, his voice softening. "But I have no choice." He hesitated, then found himself sharing the story of his father's disappearance.

Louis's art dealer persona vanished, replaced by genuine concern. "My God, Tony, why didn't you tell me sooner? I can be on the first flight out tomorrow." The news seemed to land like a physical blow—Louis had known his father for over twenty years.

"Thank you, but no. Rick's handling things here." Anthony rubbed his temple. "But there is something. Could you check on my mother? She's…" He trailed off, unable to fully articulate her distress.

"Say no more. I'll call her right now." Louis paused. "And, Tony? Whatever you need, whenever you need it—I'm here."

The call ended, leaving the silence of the room to press in like an unseen hand. He set the phone down as though it were something dangerous. Outside, the world carried on, but inside, he knew there would be no returning to the man he'd been only moments before.

For now, his painter's instinct would remain still. There were older stories to unearth, darker corridors demanding his attention. The brush could wait—truth would not.

CHAPTER 14

Before beginning his packed day, Anthony Brunelli made one final adjustment: moving the Snoopy luggage tag from his suitcase to his Kevlar backpack. It was a simple precaution, ensuring he could be reached if the bag went missing, and a lucky charm that had accompanied him on every journey for twenty-five years.

The city stirred with the energy of a typical Roman morning, yet something felt distinctly off. Anthony couldn't put his finger on it, but as he stepped through the hotel's lobby at the Residenza di Ripetta, it was almost as though the world had slowed down. The usual hum of life was absent and the staff seemed to move mechanically, their smiles thin and distracted. The lobby's usual charm, always bustling with travelers, felt hollow.

He exited into the street, expecting to be swept up in the rush of locals and tourists, but the atmosphere was eerily subdued. Normally a vibrant artery of the city, Via del Corso was filled with pockets of people standing still, engrossed in hushed conversation. There was an obvious tension, like the moments before a storm.

A cluster of pedestrians huddled near a café, their eyes fixed on the large TV screen broadcasting inside. Anthony pushed through the crowd, the soft murmur of voices in Italian barely registering until the words flashed across the screen, translated into English:

"Benedict XVI gives up the pontificate."

The impossible had happened. Pope Benedict had resigned. The shockwave of such an event—something that hadn't occurred in nearly 600 years—reverberated through his mind. He hadn't expected the unraveling of history to be so personal, so present.

His phone vibrated sharply in his pocket, pulling him out of his stupor.

"Hello?"

"Anthony? This is Friar Marco Tasca, we spoke yesterday. Are you on your way?" The urgency in the friar's voice was evident.

"Yes, I got distracted, but I'm just ten minutes away. What's going on?"

"Please, hurry. Meet me at the side entrance. I'll explain everything when you arri—"

The call cut off, leaving Anthony's questions unspoken.

The Church of the Twelve Holy Apostles, or Santi Apostoli, had always felt like a sanctuary hidden in plain sight. With its origins dating back to the sixth century, it was built on ancient foundations and originally dedicated to the apostles Philip and James. Amazingly, an ancient crypt was found with its relics still intact when the church had undergone repairs in 1873. The foundations had since been excavated.

Friar Tasca, Minister General of the Franciscan Order, met Anthony just outside the gate. His face, usually calm and composed, was tight with concern. Without a word, he led Anthony through the courtyard toward the sacristy, his pace hurried, his expression strained.

"You've heard about Benedict?" Tasca asked, glancing at Anthony as they passed through the stone passageway.

"I have," Anthony replied, his voice echoing slightly in the narrow corridor. "Why would he resign?"

"There's no time to get into the details right now," Tasca said, his voice dropping as they neared the sacristy. He stopped, unlocking a heavy wooden door. "But I'll tell you this, things are far worse than they seem."

Anthony paused at the angst in the friar's tone. "What do you mean?"

Friar Tasca opened the door, ushering them inside the sacristy. The dim light cast long shadows on the old stone walls, adding to the growing sense of uneasiness.

"Earlier today, there was…unexpected activity here at Santi Apostoli," Tasca began, his voice now a near whisper. "Someone was clearly listening to us, Anthony, when we spoke yesterday evening. They're trying to intercept what you're here to retrieve."

Anthony's pulse quickened. "What are you saying?"

"The Vatican police," Tasca continued, his eyes scanning the small, enclosed space. "They were here, searching for something. They left to get a search warrant. They'll be back soon."

Anthony's mind raced. "That doesn't make sense. Benedict himself told me to contact you. But wait…is this somehow tied to his resignation?"

Tasca shrugged. As the pair continued breezing through the sacristy, the minister general spoke over his shoulder to Anthony, who was tracking close behind. "There's more to this than we understand. Someone powerful is influencing the Vatican police."

"I'm sorry, Friar Tasca, but I'm lost."

"Look, Benedict found himself in the middle of a huge scandal," Tasca confided, lowering his voice. "Leaked documents of corruption, bribery, and the misappropriation of Benedict's own finances. He had no choice but to appoint an independent commission to investigate."

He paused, seeming to gather his thoughts before continuing. "They uncovered corruption of all sorts, from suspect contract work to the misappropriation of funds throughout Vatican City, but it's unknown where it originates. Not to mention, there was the slew of blackmail and mounting sexual scandals that took place on his watch."

Tasca's words shattered in Anthony's ears, and he suddenly felt ill-prepared. He told himself to relax. "Are you saying his resignation was a plea bargain?"

"No, Benedict did this on his own terms," the minister general said, prodding Anthony to walk even faster. Stopping in front of the main doors of Santi Apostoli, Tasca took out a large key ring from his pocket. He engaged the lock, bolting the doors shut to prevent any visitors from entering. "Here's what I do know. An independent three-member Cardinal commission was set up, and over the past eighteen months, they produced a three-hundred-page, two-volume report outlining all kinds of incriminating evidence." Tasca wiped his brow as his glasses slipped down.

Anthony's mind stuttered, recalling carrying one of the two large red volumes from inside Benedict's vault, up to his study.

The minister general stopped and solemnly addressed Anthony. "I met with Benedict yesterday, along with a small number of his senior staff. It was right after you left. He told me you were there and that you'd be reaching out to me. He didn't tell us he was resigning, but I knew that was one of the possibilities. What he did say is that he was making a monumental decision, without any pressure from the Curia. He said his intentions and motives are pure." Tasca looked at Anthony thoughtfully, then continued, "The Holy Father resigned not out of weakness but profound humility, recognizing that the burdens of the papacy required a strength he could no longer summon both in body and mind. It was revealed today that the report I referenced is now under a seventy-five-year moratorium to be held in the Vatican Secret Archives. That means eighty percent of the world's population will have passed before the report is released."

Anthony winced. "Okay," he chuckled. "So, I guess the answer is we'll never truly know. At the same time, I don't believe the timing of all this is coincidental. The pontiff knew what he was doing and wanted to make sure I was committed to take on my obligation. And the fact that you were meeting with him right after me confirms his positioning for what was about to unfold."

Tasca nodded in agreement. "So let me quickly bring you up to speed, because it's important you know this information. Earlier this morning, my assistant ran into my office in a panic. The guard's desk had called, saying Vatican authorities were in the sanctuary demanding to see me immediately and that there was an emergency. I rushed down and was met by two Swiss Guards, Vatican gendarme, and other plain-clothed men who stood in front of the stairs leading to the crypt. One of the men dressed in a business suit demanded I bring him the scroll, which I denied having any knowledge of. After giving them permission to search the church, the sacristy, and our administrative offices for nearly two hours, they came up empty-handed. Then, as they were about to leave, one of the men located the vault. They demanded that I open it, but I refused. Despite my refusal, they said they would return with an official search warrant."

Now clearly understanding the urgency, Anthony felt alarmed. As they hustled down the center aisle toward the vault, he couldn't help but be drawn to the ceiling. There, he noticed a pair of ceramic angels sitting atop the triumphal arch of the sanctuary. It was the glorified shield of the Franciscan Order displaying two crossed arms with blood-filled, nail-spiked holes visible in each palm. One represented Jesus of Nazareth, and the other, Francis of Assisi. Despite their rush, the symbolic sight of the shield made an impact on Anthony. He wished that he had listened more carefully all those years to what his father had told him about why Saint Francis was paired so closely with Jesus.

Tasca continued toward the altar ahead of Anthony, then down an open stairwell that descended into the ossuary. Anthony shivered as he passed displayed relics, wondering how many bones of the dead had found their final resting place there.

"This is where the Vatican police searched," Tasca said, his eyes wandering the closed quarters.

"How would they know to come here?" Anthony asked.

Tasca turned to meet his gaze. "Someone is obviously trying to use Benedict's resignation to gain access to what I'm about to give you."

"Why?"

"For the same reason they've always feared Saint Francis."

"Fear Saint Francis? I'm officially confused. What reason is that?"

"There's no time to explain." Tasca once again promptly removed the key ring from his pocket. He unlocked an iron door that opened into the dimly lit, barrel-vaulted niche of the crypt. He walked to the far corner where earlier the Vatican police had removed a large stone from the wall, exposing an iron safe.

Working the combination, he opened the safe and pulled out two objects.

Anthony's eyes widened. The first was an exact replica of the limestone cylinder Benedict had given him the day before.

Tasca held the cylinder reverently for a moment before handing it over. "Anthony, this cylinder has been passed down through the minister generals for generations, and now it belongs to you," he said.

Anthony paused, noting that the minister general's words nearly mimicked what the pope had told him the day before. He quickly opened his Kevlar backpack and placed the second cylinder safely inside.

Tasca then handed Anthony a leather satchel. "This contains a few documents, all in protective sleeves. One is a letter thought to be written by Brother Leo on behalf of Saint Francis to Pope Honorius. It has been handed down through the ages, to be read only by the reigning pope and the *chosen son*. As mentioned, Anthony, that son is you."

After turning to close the safe, he hustled up the stairs and back through the sacristy, talking to Anthony in between breaths. "You need to leave quickly. Is there anything else you need from me?" Tasca asked.

"Well, I'm off to Assisi. Do you have a reliable contact there in case I run into any difficulty?"

Without hesitation, Tasca scribbled a name and number onto a scrap of paper. "Friar Martin Breski. He's an American, stationed at the Sacro Convento in Assisi. I'll call to alert him."

Anthony slipped the note into his pocket, nodding his thanks, then dashed into the streets of Rome.

Within seconds of his departure, the Vatican police arrived and raced into the Church of the Twelve Holy Apostles.

T

The winding road to Assisi was both familiar and foreign to Anthony. The hills of Umbria stretched out before him, their skeletal trees standing like sentinels against the pale sky. As he approached the ancient hill town, the pressure of the past pressed down on him, a reminder that the answers he sought next lay in the very ground beneath his feet.

Anthony glanced at the now English-translated text he'd been able to decipher early that morning. The instructions his father had passed on echoed in his mind as he drove. "After you visit the minister general, immediately head to Assisi. Translate this text to locate a third artifact." Cryptic, yet filled with purpose. It had a rhythm and a sequence, and based on prior conversations with his father and what the writings provided, he had an immediate intuition as to where the final artifact might be.

N. 1169 • The place of my birth • A man of poverty rests • Within a sumptuous church • Do not weep for the "Hill of Hell" • But cry out, "Hill of Paradise" • Because "God has heard" • The sacred ground is confirmed here • Where my hidden scribe dwells • M. 1231

With winter's grip beginning to loosen on the Umbrian landscape, Anthony guided his rental car through the rolling hills toward Assisi. The ancient town loomed ahead, its storied stones cloaked in the soft, cool light of February. The journey from Rome had been a solitary one, the stark landscape mirroring the artist's own road of uncertainty. Now, as the medieval silhouette of Assisi perched on its hilltop emerged from the swirling winds, a complex tapestry of anticipation and memories gripped him.

Turning off the main road, Anthony navigated the narrow, winding streets. The town was quieter in the embrace of winter, its cobblestone pathways and ancient buildings holding the chill in their foundations. Here, life moved at a contemplative pace, the air filled with the muted sounds of the season—the distant call of a bird, the soft tolling of church bells cutting through the crisp air, and the low murmur of locals moving about their day.

The remaining quarter mile of ascent never failed to move him. Each time he made the final climb, it felt like the first. The overwhelming presence of Assisi provided a sense of calm and confidence. He entered the small lot adjacent to the hotel structure and found his usual parking spot open, then let the engine's hum fade into silence.

It had only been a week since he departed, yet it felt like months had passed. Exiting the car, he was greeted by the cold, a stark contrast to the warmth of the car's interior. The air was sharp, laced with the scent of burning wood from nearby hearths mingling with the earthy aroma of the surrounding countryside's breeze. He drew in a deep breath, letting the essence of Assisi fill his lungs, a cool yet comforting welcome from the town that held pieces of his family's past.

Before him, Hotel Giotto stood as a timeless guardian, its façade a testament to the enduring heart of Assisi. Approaching the entrance, he paused, the burden of history and personal journey merging in the shadow of the hotel's main doorway. The threshold marked more than a physical crossing—it was a gateway to the mysteries that awaited him and an unfinished reconciliation he needed to mend.

The hotel's lobby welcomed Anthony with its familiar embrace, the air inside carrying subtle hints of aged wood and history. Here, as winter's tale wove its final threads, he stood on the cusp of a reunion that would unfold beneath the watchful gaze of Assisi, a town suspended between the past and the present, between the chill of winter and the promise of spring.

Standing at the front desk, the proprietor's daughter, Lara Figli, lowered her head, her long dark brown hair pulled into a tight ponytail, perfectly accentuating her face.

As Anthony approached, he was met by a cold silence, punctuated only by the distant echo of footsteps on terracotta tile. "Lara," he said, his voice hesitant. "How are you? I hope you're not still upset."

Lara's expression hardened, her usually warm gaze distant and guarded.

The source of her anger lay in recent events that had up-ended their professional relationship. During Anthony's last visit, a local journalist who frequented the hotel had overheard a conversation between him and Lara's father. What began as a discussion about Anthony's commissioned painting had quickly evolved into a mild confrontation about the artist's perceived flirtations with Lara.

The proprietor, though admiring Anthony's work, had been clear in his warning. "Do not lead my daughter on" had been a directive born not of disdain but of paternal protection.

Days later and desperate for a story, the journalist had published an article that changed everything. The piece highlighted the Vatican commission and Anthony's stay at the hotel, but more damagingly, it insinuated a budding romantic connection between him and Lara. The article painted her in an unprofessional light and suggested her involvement was influencing the hotel's prestigious connections. Humiliated and dismayed, Lara had initially come to believe Anthony might have intentionally revealed details of their relationship to gain publicity for his work.

The sun had barely crested the Umbrian hills that morning when Lara, her usual serene self, was shattered by the sight of the morning's paper. Though days had passed since the article's publication, seeing Anthony again had likely made her think about the thinly veiled insinuations, the scandalous implications of the article and brought a fresh wave of humiliation. The words had cut like a dagger, betraying her trust. The journalist had suggested her involvement with Anthony was not just a breach of professionalism but a calculated move to elevate the hotel's status through his Vatican commission, casting a shadow over her family's hotel, their reputation, their legacy in Assisi. Despite being laced with inaccuracies and assumptions, it had also held a mirror up to Lara's most guarded secret—her unspoken feelings for Anthony.

"Lara, you have to believe me. I had no part in this," Anthony had said the morning she confronted him with the article in hand, his words hanging heavy in the air between them.

But in Lara's eyes, the damage had been done. For two days, she had remained silent and then he had departed for Rome. Her once excitement at attending the reception at the Vatican Art Gallery had abated.

Now that he'd returned, Anthony wrestled with the substance of his heritage—a secret bound tightly to his heart, its full truth a burden he could not fully share even with Lara. The afternoon light filtered through the windows, casting patterns on the floor that seemed to dance with the hesitancy he felt within.

He stood across the check-in counter from Lara, his expression a mixture of hope and apprehension. "Lara," he said softly, reaching across the space that divided them, "I want to once again apologize."

Lara raised her hand, signaling him to pause. Her deep brown eyes, usually a reservoir of strength, now shimmered with the pain of betrayal—not from Anthony but from the unforeseen consequences of their intertwined fates. "I saw the security footage, Tony," she said, her voice steady despite the storm of emotions. "I saw the journalist…a regular here. He was eavesdropping on your conversation with my father."

A silence engulfed the room, heavy with the wholeness of her admission. Anthony's heart sank in the realization of how deeply the situation had wounded her. He struggled to think that someone had been in fact snooping on his intimate discussion with Lara's father, which not only ended amicably but carried an open invitation to return at any point in time.

"I know you didn't speak to that journalist, that you weren't responsible for the article," Lara continued, her words deliberate. "And I'm sorry I didn't call sooner to let you know."

Anthony leaned in, the distance between them now charged with a deep intensity. "Lara, I wish I could undo the hurt, the damage caused by that article. If there were any way to take back the pain it brought you, I would find it no matter the cost. And if there's anything I can do to make it up to you, I will."

Lara met his gaze. Their respective apologies, raw and honest, swayed between them in a delicate thread of sincerity.

"There's a reason I've rushed back to Assisi, Lara. And I must be honest, it's a purpose that goes beyond what's happened between us or any article," Anthony said, his voice carrying the encumbrance of his unspoken truths. "It's a matter deeply personal and…it's complicated, but I could really use your help."

Her curiosity sharpened by the seriousness of Anthony's tone, she nodded her head, a silent gesture of her willingness to listen, her support unwavering despite any hint of uncertainty.

"There's something I haven't yet told you. It's about my family, about a legacy that's been passed down through generations. I've been charged with a task, one that connects us to Assisi, to its spiritual history." He chose his next words carefully to conceal the full depth of his secret. "There's an object I've been instructed to find here, something very important that's been hidden for a long time."

The mention of a legacy and a lost artifact sparked a flicker of intrigue in Lara's eyes, but it was the evident struggle in

Anthony's admission that drew her closer. She must have sensed the boundaries he was navigating, the delicate balance between revealing enough to enlist her help and preserving the sanctity of his family's secret.

"What is it, Tony? How can I help?" Lara asked, her voice a blend of concern and determination. "What is it that you need to find?"

He was fully aware that she was part of Assisi's in-crowd and had inside access wherever she went. Should anyone need a favor, Lara knew someone who knew someone else who could get anything done. She knew where all the bodies were buried in Assisi, both literally and figuratively.

"It's going to sound strange, but I have to dig something up…from a very old grave." He hoped his expression and tone conveyed this wasn't the sometimes devious humor he'd shared with her in the past.

"Okay, I can see you're serious," she said, offering a tentative smile.

"There's a relic, an artifact of significant historical and spiritual value, believed to be hidden within an ancient grave of one of my ancestors here in Assisi."

Absorbing the density of his words, she paused before venturing, "And you need my help to find this grave, to uncover this artifact?" Her voice held a blend of curiosity and caution.

"That's right," Anthony admitted. "But it's not just about finding it. It's about recovering it discreetly, later tonight, and I admit, I can't do this alone."

Lara sat back, seeming to consider the implications of his request. This was no small ask but a venture into the unknown, threading a delicate balance between discovery and disturbance. And it was only fair that she should measure the presence of her family's reputation, given that it had recently taken a significant blow.

"Tony, you realize what you're asking could disturb endless years of rest, of history?" she posed. "There are very strict rules here in Assisi when it comes to the disturbance of its soil."

"I understand, and believe me, I don't take this lightly. But I assure you, the significance of this artifact is directly related to the essence of Assisi's sacred past…and it's so important that I must take the risk. I promise, we'll take every precaution, respect every rite and tradition, but I must see this through," he replied, his sincerity undeniable.

"Okay, I'll help you. But we proceed with the utmost respect for the site and whatever we may find. We'll need to be cautious, discreet, and prepared for whatever comes our way."

Anthony turned toward her, knowing his next request posed an even greater risk. He hesitated, shifting uneasily. "Lara, were going to need more help than just the two of us. This isn't just about being careful and quiet—the stone slab isn't going to move itself."

Lara nodded, her eyes signaling he needn't say more. "My cousins—you've never met them," she said, carefully weighing each word. "They're loyal, strong, and each has a deep connection to Assisi and its history. They'll do anything for me…and for you, they'll hold your complete trust."

The air seemed to thicken with the implication and potential liability of widening their circle. Yet in that moment, an unspoken agreement sealed their pact and a new chapter in their quest was set to begin. The involvement of Lara's cousins would bring not only the physical strength they desperately needed but also a deeper bond of unity and trust between them.

CHAPTER 15

Under the cover of darkness, the cool night air settled over the cemetery of Assisi. The faint scent of damp earth mingled with the night fog created an eerie calm. The silence was broken only by the crunch of boots on gravel as Lara and her four cousins approached Gate #3. Each carried an iron crowbar slung over a shoulder. Their breath clouded in the crisp air, illuminated by the steady beam of Lara's flashlight. Dressed in all black, Lara led the group. Her slender coat hugged her figure, and a baseball cap shadowed her sharp, determined features.

Upon reaching Anthony at the gate, Lara introduced the men to each other. "Anthony, I'd like you to meet my very faithful cousins, Fabrizio, Federico, and Valerio and Giuseppe."

Anthony gave each man a nod they returned, and then he said, "Thank you for coming."

"This feels like a scene from a heist movie," Fabrizio, her eldest cousin, remarked with a raspy chuckle. Behind him, Federico and the twins, Valerio and Giuseppe, shifted nervously. "But just so we're clear, we're not stealing any corpses tonight, right?"

Anthony flashed a half-smile, though his eyes remained vigilant, scanning the shadows. "No corpses," he assured them.

"We're only here for something far more valuable and far less disturbing."

The group's laughter eased the tension, but Anthony's focus never wavered. His mind churned through the steps ahead, his resolve unshaken despite the daunting task. He led them to an impressive family plot nestled against the cemetery's perimeter wall, between Gate #3 and #4. The marble tombstones gleamed faintly in the dim starlight, each etched with the name *Famiglia Brunelli*.

His hands trembling slightly in the cold, Anthony crouched to inspect the nearest tombstone. The beam of his flashlight revealed the engraved name, *Aristide Brunelli*. He traced the letters with gloved fingers, a lump forming in his throat as he felt the connection to his great-great-grandfather across the decades. While the sight reassured him he had found the correct family plot, something gnawed at his consciousness. Something wasn't right.

"This cemetery only dates back to the mid-1800s." He exhaled deeply as he ran a hand through his hair. His voice carried a tinge of frustration, and his shoulders sagged with disappointment. "I'm looking for something much older—medieval, 1200s to be exact." He rose to his full height and turned toward Lara. "Do you know of any cemeteries that predate this one?"

Lara tilted her head, her brow raised in thought. "Let me think," she murmured, brushing back her ponytail. As someone who knew Assisi's every hidden corner, her encyclopedic knowledge was her greatest strength. She'd once told him that in her younger years, she had been the most sought-after guide in the town, captivating visitors with tales of its sacred history. She continued, "There are other gravesites scattered throughout Assisi, but most of them are heavily restricted. What exactly are you looking for?"

Anthony hesitated, the significance of his family's secret forcing him to consider if he could trust her fully. Her dedication to preserving the sanctity of Assisi and her respect for Saint Francis's legacy left little room for doubt, so he decided it was a risk worth taking.

He stepped away from Lara's cousins, creating a private space for their conversation. "Lara," he began, his eyes darting between her face and the surrounding darkness. "I need to show you something. This might help you understand." He removed the Kevlar backpack from his shoulders and knelt to unzip it, the sound seemingly amplified in the quiet cemetery. From within, he retrieved a delicate bundle wrapped in protective fabric. Peeling back the layers with care, his hands shaking slightly, he revealed one of the documents, its parchment aged to a soft, golden hue and its edges frayed by time.

Lara's breath hitched as her flashlight beam danced over the fragile artifact. The marvel in her expression was unmistakable. Her free hand instinctively moved to cover her mouth, stifling a gasp. "Is this…original?" she whispered.

"It's real," Anthony confirmed. "It's been passed down through my family for generations. My father entrusted it to me."

With trembling hands, she held her flashlight over the document as she carefully scanned the ornate Latin script. The aged ink was faint but legible, and the cryptic message stood out in careful, medieval hand.

> N. MCLXIX • Lo luogo de la mia nascita • Uno homo de povertade riposa • Entro una chiesa sontuosa • Non piangere per lo "Colle dello Inferno" • Ma gridare, "Colle dello Paradiso" • Perciocché "Dio ha audito" • Lo terreno sacro è confirmato qui • Ove lo mio scriba celato dimora • M. MCCXXXI

Anthony then read the English translation to her, his voice barely above a whisper.

N. 1169 • The place of my birth • A man of poverty rests • Within a sumptuous church • Do not weep for the "Hill of Hell" • But cry out, "Hill of Paradise" • Because "God has heard" • The sacred ground is confirmed here • Where my hidden scribe dwells • M. 1231

"What do you make of it?" he asked, watching her closely while keeping one ear tuned to their surroundings.

Lara read the words aloud, her voice hushed but deliberate as if invoking a spell. After a moment, she glanced at him, her expression thoughtful. "This phrase here—*Dio ha audito*—God has heard. That's key," she said, pointing to the passage with a leather-gloved finger. "There's something you couldn't have known. There was a man, Simone di Pucciarello, a prominent merchant in Assisi who lived during the time this was written. He donated the land where the Basilica of Saint Francis now stands. His name is significant. Simone comes from the Hebrew name *Shimon*, meaning 'he who hears' or, more literally, 'God has heard.' This can't be coincidence."

Impressed with her knowledge, Anthony's eyes widened. "You think the grave I'm looking for is on the Basilica's land?"

"I'd bet on it," Lara replied confidently. "Simone's land is the only place this message could point to." Her expression darkened as she glanced at her cousins standing nearby, crowbars slung over their shoulders, their breath visible in the cold night air. "But there's a slight problem. That land is part of the Basilica complex, and it's under tight restrictions. I have no immediate way to get us inside, at least not tonight."

Anthony nodded, his mind racing. "I might have a solution." He patted the front pocket of his jeans, then took off his glove and withdrew a small, folded piece of paper. On it was a seven-digit number scrawled in Friar Tasca's distinctive handwriting. "I think this might help us gain access."

Lara's expression shifted to one of cautious optimism. She gestured for her cousins to follow. "*Dai, andiamo!*" she said in urgent Italian. "If this note is right, I know exactly where we need to be."

The group moved swiftly under the soft glow of the stars, their destination now clear. For the first time that evening, Anthony felt a flicker of hope surge through his chest. The grave of his ancestor, hidden for centuries, might finally reveal itself and with it, the secrets that had bound the Brunelli family to Saint Francis's legacy.

Just past midnight, Friar Martin Breski awaited Anthony and his companions at the guard post situated between Sacro Convento and the Lower Church of the Basilica. The friar, a tall, prominent man with a calm demeanor, greeted the group warmly despite the late hour. His light brown eyes reflected both curiosity and purpose. Anthony realized that he had likely been briefed earlier by Minister General Tasca, assuring him unrestricted assistance.

Anthony and Lara stepped forward, pulling Friar Martin aside for a private word. The cool night breeze carried the scent of ancient stone and incense from the Basilica. "Friar, I appreciate you meeting us at this hour. I'm searching for an ancient tomb, 1231 to be exact. We have reason to believe it's within the grounds of the Basilica."

Friar Martin raised an eyebrow, seeming intrigued but unalarmed. "A tomb, you say? We have plenty of those. You've come to the right place." He smiled, the corners of his eyes crinkling with warmth. With a curt nod, he motioned for the group to follow.

Their footsteps echoed softly on the cobblestones as the friar led them through the quiet Basilica grounds, toward the interior courtyard cemetery. Within minutes, they passed through an ornate iron gate and found themselves standing in the private cemetery, enclosed within the massive Basilica complex. The air hung cool and still, carrying a faint floral scent from the dried bouquets that adorned the statues and graves. Starlight filtered through the gnarled branches of centuries-old olive trees, casting ethereal shadows across the ancient tombstones. Anthony walked side by side with Friar Martin as the group moved deeper into the grounds. Behind them, Lara's cousins followed silently, their crowbars concealed beneath their coats.

"Friar Martin," Anthony said quietly, "I believe one of these graves belongs to my ancestor."

"If your ancestor is from Assisi, it's certainly possible. The land for the Basilica was donated to the papacy countless years ago, to comply with the Franciscans' strict vow of poverty. They couldn't own land themselves. At the time of construction, anyone who contributed significantly to the building of the Lower Church was granted a burial plot here on these grounds. These benefactors also received a forty-day indulgence—a reduction in penance—from Pope Gregory IX."

"A forty-day indulgence?" Anthony murmured, his voice tinged with fascination. "So the Church granted them less time in purgatory in exchange for their contributions?" He chuckled.

"Indeed," Friar Martin replied. "The Church taught that these indulgences would shorten the soul's time in purgatory after death." He gestured broadly with a sweep of his arm, the wide sleeve of his black robe trailing in the faint light. "And as you can see, the main cemetery is quite small, no more than thirty tombstones and a few were damaged by the earthquake in 1997."

The group moved slowly, their flashlight beams dancing across weathered names and dates etched into the stone markers. None bore the Brunelli name. Friar Martin then led them toward a shaded portico encircling the cemetery, where rows of additional tombs were embedded along the stone walkway. Six raised tombs sculpted in the shape of human bodies protruded from the ground, their inscriptions worn with age.

Anthony's breath caught as his flashlight illuminated one particular tomb. Unlike the others, this one bore no name, only a pair of dates engraved in Roman numerals. His hands trembling slightly, he crouched to inspect the carving, his heart racing as he recognized the significance of the numbers: N – MCLXIX. M – MCCXXXI.

"Here it is!" he exclaimed, his voice breaking the stillness. He pointed at the tomb with trembling fingers. "These dates match the ancient letter exactly."

The others gathered around, their expressions a mix of awe and anticipation. Momentarily stunned, Friar Martin broke into a knowing smile.

Anthony wasted no time, directing Lara's cousins to proceed with care. Federico and Giuseppe positioned their crowbars along the edges of the tomb's marble slab while Valerio and Fabrizio stood ready to assist. Working in practiced synchronization, they carefully pried it loose. The stone groaned under its mass as they lifted it just enough to rest it at a slant, exposing the dark cavity within.

Anthony leaned forward as Lara shone her flashlight into the opening. His breath hitched as he spotted what he had been seeking—a limestone cylinder identical to the other two in his possession. He reached into the tomb and retrieved the object, cradling it as reverently as a priest would handle a sacred chalice.

The others looked on in hushed awe, their shared sense of discovery profound in the night air.

Lara broke the silence. "I take it you've found what you were looking for?"

Anthony nodded, holding the cylinder up to the faint light of the waxing crescent moon. Its seal remained intact, its intricate carvings mirroring the designs on the other two. "Yes," he whispered, his voice thick with emotion. "I have."

Under Anthony's direction, Lara's cousins gently returned the marble slab to its original position, ensuring the tomb appeared undisturbed. As he secured the cylinder inside his backpack, a sudden movement caught his eye. The shadow of a human figure wearing a habit loomed briefly on the upper level overlooking the courtyard. The silhouette was unmistakable against the starlit sky.

"Somebody's watching," he said through clenched teeth, his voice tight with unease. He nudged Friar Martin and gestured toward the spot, but by the time the friar turned, the figure had melted into the darkness.

Despite the lingering tension, he tightened the straps on his backpack, a sense of accomplishment grounding his resolve. The fullness of his family's legacy rested heavily on his shoulders, but tonight had changed everything. For the first time, all three cylinders—the keys to a mystery spanning generations—were in his possession. At last, he could unlock their secrets.

CHAPTER 16

Hotel Giotto, Assisi
12:55 AM

The faint hum of the caravan's engine dissolved into the night as Lara's cousins drove away, their task in the cemetery complete. Anthony watched them disappear into the darkness, each having tucked away a six-pack of Peroni, their simple reward for the evening's work.

Anthony caught her eye and stepped closer, his fingers brushing against her hand. "I can't thank you enough for this, Lara," he said, warmth in his voice tempered by the night's discoveries.

Lara hesitated, then softened. "You're welcome, Anthony." She gripped his hand briefly before releasing it. "Is there anything else you need?"

"Actually, yes," he said, massaging his temple. He let out a weary sigh. "I hate to ask for another favor after everything you've done, but I need a secure, well-lit space to examine the materials. These documents…they're invaluable, and I can really use the space to lay everything out in front of me."

Lara's lips curved into a faint smile as she moved behind the front desk, her fingers dancing across the computer's reservation system. "You're in luck. There's an old wine cellar in the basement that's been converted into a small conference room. Private, secluded, and yours for as long as you need."

She retrieved the key and led him down three flights of stairs into the hotel's hushed basement. The dim corridor opened onto the wine cellar, its brick walls and vaulted ceilings exuding an air of both history and security. She unlocked the heavy door, revealing a modestly furnished room with a long wooden table and a row of leather chairs.

"This should do," she said, pressing the key into his palm before stepping aside. "I'll leave you to your work," she added, lingering at the threshold.

He placed his Kevlar backpack on the table, then turned to her, exhaustion giving way to genuine warmth. "This room is perfect, and I couldn't have done this without you, Lara. Thank you."

As the door clicked shut behind her, Anthony engaged the deadbolt and released a deep breath. He sank into one of the leather chairs, the day's events kaleidoscoping through his mind like fragments of an ancient puzzle. His muscles protested, but his thoughts remained sharp and focused. This moment—what his family's legacy had been building toward—was the culmination of centuries of secrets and sacrifices.

Drawing himself up, Anthony pulled on his white cotton gloves—a habit now ingrained—and carefully extracted the three limestone cylinders from his backpack. He arranged them in a precise row on the table, then retrieved Benedict's toolkit. Inside lay an array of specialized implements—a box cutter for removing wax seals, felt-tipped tweezers, paperweights, preservation bags, markers, and labels. From a side pocket, he produced a magnifying glass, tape measure, and spare gloves.

He began by labeling each cylinder to preserve their origin. The box cutter sliced cleanly through the wax seals, and he carefully preserved each fragment in labeled bags. He extracted the first scroll using the tweezers, unrolling it with measured movements. The parchment stretched larger than expected—

over a foot when fully extended—but bore only a single Latin word boldly centered: *INCIPE*.

A frown deepened across Anthony's face as he turned the parchment over. The reverse side revealed two Roman numerals, LX, and a mysterious symbol tucked into the upper-right corner. Perplexed by the lack of writing, he carefully set it aside and moved to the second cylinder.

The process yielded another scroll, similarly sparse with only *IN PUNCTO* centered on its face. The reverse mirrored the first with another symbol—a small cross—and the Roman numerals, XX. As his flashlight swept the cylinder's interior, it caught an unexpected glint. He retrieved a second, smaller parchment covered in ancient Italian script.

With growing anticipation, Anthony turned to the final cylinder. Inside lay a scroll matching its siblings, bearing the solitary word *ALTRIX*. Its reverse displayed a new symbol and different numerals, XXX. Like its predecessor, this cylinder concealed an additional parchment, though this one bore ragged, torn edges.

He arranged everything before him in meticulous rows, each item labeled and cataloged. A final sweep with his flashlight confirmed the first cylinder's emptiness, while the second and third had yielded hidden treasures. The table now displayed a constellation of ancient mysteries—three scrolls with their cryptic Latin words, two weathered Italian parchments, and the growing certainty that he was unraveling something far vaster than he'd imagined.

Exhaustion crept at the edges of his consciousness, but he pushed it aside. Opening his laptop, he translated the Latin words:

Scroll #1: Incipe – Begin

Scroll #2: In Puncto – Point

Scroll #3: Altrix – The Wolf

The translations only deepened the mystery.

Anthony slumped back, kneading his temples in frustration. The words hung disconnected, their meaning tantalizingly out of reach. The ancient Italian documents had proven even more confounding since their full context remained elusive.

By 3:00 a.m., exhaustion finally overcame determination. Anthony secured the room and retreated to his suite, though sleep remained a distant prospect. His mind churned with unanswered questions and fragmentary clues. Four hours later found him back in the wine cellar, the intensity of the mystery bearing down harder with each passing moment. Despite fresh eyes and renewed focus, the puzzle remained maddeningly opaque, its secrets just beyond his grasp.

At last, he admitted defeat. This lay beyond his expertise. Reaching into his bag, he withdrew a business card. The embossed name felt like a lifeline—Dr. Vera Valentino.

He dialed the number.

Two rings, then a crisp female voice answered. "Pronto?"

"Hello, um, hi…Dr. Valentino?" Anthony stumbled.

"Yes, this is she," came the reply in English.

"My name is Anthony Brunelli. Father Alessandro gave me your contact information. He said you might be able to help."

"Yes, Anthony, hello, I've been expecting your call," she cut in, her tone warming with reassurance.

"Wonderful. I have several documents here and have so many questions," Anthony explained. "Some are in Latin, others in an ancient form of Italian. I've tried translating them, but…it's beyond me. Is this something you can help with?"

"With pleasure," Dr. Valentino answered. "Where are you now?"

"I'm in Assisi, at the Hotel Giotto," he said, relief seeping into his voice. "I know this is last minute, but—"

"Not to worry," she interjected, her confidence unwavering. "Hold tight. I'll be there by noon."

CHAPTER 17

Santi Apostoli Rectory, Rome
10:15 AM

The morning light filtered through the lace curtains of the third-floor rectory at Santi Apostoli, casting soft patterns across the worn oak table where Richard Pescatore sat opposite Friar Basilio Heiser. The retired minister general, now eighty-three years old, commanded the same presence that had marked his years of leadership and his dark eyes were sharp despite the wear of time. Dressed casually in black slacks, a collared shirt, and a gray cardigan, Heiser projected quiet authority, though his slightly undone clerical collar hinted at the man behind the role.

Richard shifted in his chair, his hands loosely clasped in front of him. It had been years since they had last spoken, and Heiser's warm greeting lingered in the air like a faint incense of memory.

"Richard," the friar began, his voice gravelly but steady, "how wonderful it is to see you after all these years. I feared I might not have the chance again."

Richard offered a soft smile, though his mind churned with the looming shadow of why he had come. "You haven't changed a bit, Friar. It's good to see you as well." His tone carried respect and determination. "I wish I could say this was just a social visit."

Heiser leaned forward slightly, curiosity sparking in his eyes. "To what do I owe the pleasure then?"

Richard hesitated briefly, collecting his thoughts. "As you may know, I came to Rome for Anthony Brunelli's art reception at the Vatican Art Gallery. But things have taken a turn. Anthony's father, Ronald, has gone missing, and Anthony has been plunged into fulfilling a family obligation he barely understands. I'm doing what I can to help him, but there's something else…something I can't shake." He slid a business card across the table. It bore the embossed name Father Alessandro della Rovere. "I recently met a priest," he continued. "He seemed familiar, but I can't place him. I thought if anyone might know who he is, it would be you."

Heiser picked up the card, his expression unreadable as he studied it. A flicker of recognition passed across his face, and he set the card down with deliberate care. "Ah, yes, Alessandro della Rovere." His gaze lifted to meet Richard's. "You know him, Richard. Though not by that name."

Richard's face tightened with bewilderment. "I do? How?"

Heiser leaned back, folding his hands in his lap. "Because Alessandro della Rovere is the man you knew as Alex Minos. He was enrolled in the seminary with you at Rye Beach."

The blood drained from Richard's face as memories crashed over him like a wave. His fingers gripped the edge of the table, knuckles whitening. "Alex Minos?" The name emerged as barely more than a whisper. The face that had been nagging at his consciousness suddenly snapped into focus—younger, clean-shaven, but unmistakably the same man. "I knew there was something about him, something I couldn't quite—" He drew a sharp breath. "But how? Why the change of name?"

Heiser nodded, watching Richard's reaction carefully. "His family, the della Rovere, had fallen into disgrace, and his father adopted the name Minos to protect him. Alessandro later reclaimed his birth name when he returned from seminary, shortly after your own departure, Richard."

The words "your own departure" hung heavy in the air, stirring memories he had long tried to suppress. That night in 1968 when his life's trajectory had been altered forever still visited him in dreams. He'd been kneeling in the seminary chapel, lost in evening prayer, when Minister General Heiser had appeared beside him. The conversation that followed had stripped him of his intended vocation and set him on an entirely different path—guardian to a newborn Anthony Brunelli whose family's connection to the Franciscans remained shrouded in mystery even now.

"A directive, not a request," Richard murmured almost to himself, remembering Heiser's exact words from that night. He looked up at his former superior. "You told me I had qualities essential to the task. That I would understand in time." His voice carried the abundance of decades of unspoken questions.

Heiser rose and moved to the modest kitchen, the soft clatter of an espresso pot breaking the tension. "Let me make you something special while we talk," he said, measuring coffee grounds. "Did you know the cappuccino owes its name to the Capuchin friars? Named for the color of our Franciscan habits. Like all things in God's plan, Richard, it represents perfect balance—each element transformed by its connection to the others."

Richard watched him work, recognition dawning in his eyes. "You're talking about more than a cappuccino, aren't you?"

"When you were asked to leave the seminary," Heiser continued, carefully pouring steamed milk over the rich espresso, "you were answering a different kind of calling. Your role with Anthony was no less sacred than the priesthood, perhaps more so." He placed a cup before Richard, a delicate angel swirled into the froth. "You served us well. You are indeed an angel, Richard."

He cupped his hands around the warm vessel, letting its heat ground him in the present. "Thank you, Friar. I appreciate that."

Heiser disappeared briefly, returning with a stack of file folders. "There's more you need to see." He selected one and slid it across the table. "This belonged to Father Reginald. When he passed two years ago, he arranged for his personal files to be sent to me. Among them was this."

Richard opened the folder, his eyes widening as he scanned the pages. They contained detailed notes on a young Alessandro della Rovere—his movements, his connections, and most disturbingly, a letter written in the familiar scrawl of a young seminarian he had once known as Alex Minos.

Heiser's voice softened. "When you left the seminary, Alessandro overheard our conversation. He took notes and sent a letter to his uncle, Pietro della Rovere. His notes are revealing."

As Richard read through the documents, his cappuccino grew cold. The letter detailed Alessandro's bitter resentment at being overlooked and his determination to uncover the Franciscans' secrets. A muscle worked in Richard's cheek as pieces of a decades-old puzzle fell into place. He looked up from the papers, his expression grave. "Tell me about Alex's—I mean, Alessandro's uncle. Is he still alive?"

"Not only is he alive, Richard, but he's also a Cardinal," he revealed, his words causing Richard to still. "Though the della Rovere family has lost much of the immense influence they once wielded, they're desperately clinging to the remnants of their power. And, Richard"—Heiser leaned forward, his voice dropping to barely above a whisper—"I must ask, what exactly are you trying to uncover?"

"I need to understand what Alessandro is planning," Richard said, his voice steady but charged with determination. "I remember the della Rovere family well from my Renaissance studies. It's eerie to think he's part of that lineage. Now that I know his connection, I can't help but wonder if he's been waiting all these years for something to resurface."

Heiser nodded gravely. "The della Rovere family has always been ambitious, Richard. Alessandro's current position near the pope is no coincidence. They're part of a clandestine group with deep roots and no hesitation to eliminate obstacles."

Richard clenched his teeth. "This…this is chilling."

A heavy silence filled the room, punctuated only by the faint hum of activity elsewhere in the rectory.

Heiser appeared to be weighing his next words carefully until he finally broke the stillness. "Do you still have the emergency number I gave you all those years ago?"

Richard retrieved a worn Post-it Note from his wallet. "I do."

"Call it when you leave here," Heiser instructed, and for the first time that day, his usually steady demeanor faltered, a hint of weariness clouding his expression. "Tell them who you are. They'll know what to do."

"What about the files?" Richard asked, his gaze shifting to the stack of documents.

"Take them, but handle them with extreme care." Heiser's voice hardened as he continued, "The della Roveres operate like the Inquisition itself—ruthless, methodical, and willing to silence anyone who threatens their interests. They'll protect their legacy at any cost." His words lingered in the air, heavy with forewarning.

Richard absorbed the significance of the situation, but his resolve remained unshaken. He had spent too much of his life looking after Anthony for a purpose he hadn't fully understood to turn his back now.

The morning sun had intensified by the time Richard reached his rental car with the stack of folders secured beneath his arm. He settled into the driver's seat, the scope of the documents looming over him like the secrets they contained. He extracted Alessandro's notes from one of the folders. The yellowed paper crackled beneath his fingers as he unfolded it, revealing a familiar, angular handwriting that transported him back decades.

Uncle, there's a plot unfolding within the Franciscans. The minister general came from Rome to meet with one of the seminarians. He's an American named Richard Pescatore. I didn't catch everything, but fortunately, I overheard most of their conversation.

Alessandro had recalled and documented their exchange with chilling precision.

Heiser: What I have to ask of you is exceptionally important to the Church, and out of all the young men enrolled here, you are best positioned to undertake this responsibility.

Pescatore: I'm not sure what I have to offer. My family is not wealthy. I have no real ties or connections.

Heiser: That is precisely why I've chosen you. You possess exactly what I'm looking for—a pure heart. You are one of the most trustworthy young men among your peers. Your role will be vital, part of an obligation that dates back generations and has the potential to affect millions of lives.

The notes continued, Alessandro's bitterness seeping through every word.

> As you can imagine, Uncle, hearing that conversation enraged me. Our family made the Franciscans who they are today. We've done more for them than any other family in history. If they knew my true identity, they would have chosen me over that sycophant, Pescatore. It's time we reclaim our rightful place. We must uncover whatever secrets they're hiding and use them to dismantle their hold. God would not condone their secrecy.

A cold certainty gripped Richard as the scope of the threat crystallized. The della Roveres weren't merely seeking revenge. They were orchestrating the systematic dismantling of centuries of tradition and trust.

He turned to a memo written in Father Reginald's precise hand.

> It was obvious from these scribbled notes that Alex wrote a more formal letter to his uncle, Pietro della Rovere. Richard Pescatore departed the seminary with the minister general around midnight. The next morning, I announced that Richard was no longer with us and reinforced the policy that no one was to contact him. A few days later, Alex disappeared in the middle of the night. I haven't heard from him since.
>
> -Father Reginald

Richard exhaled slowly, his fingers finding the worn Post-it Note in his wallet. The emergency number, faded but still legible, seemed to pulse with newfound urgency. He dialed with steady hands. As the phone began to ring, he braced himself.

The line clicked. "Identify yourself."

Richard inhaled deeply. "My name is Richard Pescatore. I need your help."

Hotel Giotto, Assisi
11:50 AM

Dr. Vera Valentino arrived at Hotel Giotto before noon, her presence commanding the room before she even spoke. Her heels clicked against the tile as she crossed the lobby, a subtle yet confident rhythm that hinted at the sharp intellect beneath her polished exterior. Lara had been anticipating her arrival ever since Anthony mentioned she was coming, explaining that the Vatican had arranged for professional assistance.

Vera Valentino was a name Lara had long admired, a figure gracing prestigious academic journals and European lifestyle magazines. In person, she was even more striking. She exuded a blend of sophistication, intelligence, and elegance that few could rival.

"Dr. Valentino, welcome to Hotel Giotto," Lara greeted, her voice steady. "Mr. Brunelli is expecting you."

"Thank you," Vera replied with measured grace, her emerald-green eyes scanning the space.

Lara maintained her professional composure as she escorted the Vatican representative to the hotel's conference room. As she guided her to the elevator, Lara observed Vera's natural authority, the kind that required no announcement or validation. Arriving at the conference room, Lara opened the door and introduced Anthony before excusing herself with discretion.

"Dr. Valentino," Anthony began, extending his hand, "thank you for coming so quickly."

"It's my pleasure, Anthony. And please, call me Vera," she replied, her handshake firm but not overpowering.

Dressed in a perfectly tailored navy suit over a cream blouse, Vera was elegance personified. Her dark brown hair, smooth and slightly curled at the ends, framed high cheekbones and penetrating eyes that missed nothing. Anthony had met his fair share of impressive women, but there was something about her—an aura of confidence and brilliance—that left him momentarily speechless.

Vera rolled in a sleek hard-shell case and placed it against the wall before turning her attention to the table of documents and artifacts carefully displayed. Her gaze flicked between them with curiosity and discernment. "Before we begin, Anthony," she said, "do tell me about yourself."

Anthony cleared his throat. "Well, I'm from the US, a professional artist by trade, and actually, I just finished up a commission for the Vatican. Maybe you're familiar with it?"

Vera smiled. "Please, enlighten me."

"Three months ago, Pope Benedict handpicked me, along with eleven other artists worldwide, to create various works of art. Mine was a painting of the Basilica of Saint Francis." He glanced toward the ceiling with a knowing gesture. "It brought me to Assisi," he added with a self-deprecating smile, "though my focus has certainly shifted since then."

"Understandably so. And these artifacts? May I?" she asked, gesturing toward the documents.

"Of course."

Vera slipped on a pair of gloves she pulled from her case and then approached the table. Lifting one of the parchments, she examined it under a magnifying glass, tilting it to catch the light. The fibers of the parchment and its faint ink seemed to whisper their secrets as she scrutinized them. After several moments, she turned to him.

"Anthony," she said, her voice quiet but firm, "if these are authentic—and at first glance, they seem to be—you may be holding a cache of documents more valuable than gold."

Anthony's lips quirked upward, amusement dancing in his eyes. "Well, I haven't exactly had time to even consider their value."

"Few surviving artifacts are linked to Saint Francis, let alone manuscripts he might have *touched*." Her expression sharpened. "And how exactly did you come into possession of these?"

"That's a story in itself," Anthony admitted. "The first cylinder came directly from Pope Benedict. The second was given to me by Minister General Marco Tasca, the head of the Franciscan Order. The third"—he pointed—"I retrieved from a grave that had been sealed for eight centuries."

Vera stared at him, wide-eyed. "My God, Anthony. Who are you? One of the Borgias?"

Anthony laughed. "Thankfully, no. Just a Brunelli. Although," he added with a playful glint in his eye, "there might be some Medici blood somewhere in there."

Vera smiled but couldn't hide her wonder. "Did you meet with the pope directly?"

"Yes," Anthony replied, his voice softening with respect. "It was the day before he resigned."

"Fascinating," she said, her tone tinged with awe. "And did he give you any direction for these documents?"

"Not much, only to follow my instincts. He literally told me it was between me and Saint Francis. I'm still trying to fully comprehend what he meant by that."

Vera stepped back, processing his words. "Well," she said after a moment, "you're in excellent hands. My job is to authenticate and translate these documents, and perhaps uncover their deeper purpose."

Anthony nodded, his trust in her growing but not yet absolute. "I need to ask, how can I be sure you weren't sent to intercept these documents for other reasons?"

Vera's demeanor shifted to one of quiet authority. "Anthony, I understand your concerns. Let me assure you, I am not here to undermine you. I am the director of the Laurentian Library in Florence, a position that demands both expertise and integrity. The Vatican entrusted me with this task because there are few others qualified for it. The documents will be treated with the utmost care, and your secrets are safe with me."

Anthony studied her for a moment, then nodded. "I appreciate your transparency, Vera. Pope Benedict assured me I could trust you completely"—he smiled warmly—"and I can see why. These last few days have been overwhelming, but having you here gives me confidence that I can actually see this through." He clapped and rubbed his hands together. "Let's get started."

Vera laughed. "I wish it was that easy. First, I need to understand all the details. Tell me more about you and your family's involvement. How did this all come together?"

Over the next hour, Anthony shared the complete story beginning with his family's long-held secrets, the mysterious disappearance of his father, and finally recounting the extraordinary events that had led him to this moment. Vera listened intently, her expression shifting between concern and determination. When he finished, she began studying the limestone cylinders with particular interest.

"These cylinders," she murmured, running a gloved finger along the carvings, "are remarkable. They've survived nearly eight centuries in pristine condition. That alone is extraordinary." Her fascination deepened as she considered the implications. "Three cylinders, three separate locations, eight centuries…and all perfectly preserved." She met Anthony's gaze. "That suggests bold intent, doesn't it?"

"I'd say so," Anthony remarked, watching her methodical examination. He opened his laptop and indicated his translated version of the Latin text found on each scroll.

Scroll #1: Incipe – Begin

Scroll #2: In Puncto – Point

Scroll #3: Altrix – The Wolf

Vera raised an eyebrow. "You did well, but your translation of Altrix isn't quite accurate. While it can mean 'wolf,' its primary meaning is 'nourisher' or 'caretaker.' It suggests something—or someone—that fosters growth, possibly spiritual."

"No argument from me," Anthony admitted. "I only used a basic translation tool."

"And Pope Benedict confirmed your family's connection to Saint Francis?" Vera asked, her tone probing but respectful.

"He did. He was the one who brought it up, in fact. It's been verified not just through my family's lineage but also by the minister general of the Franciscan Order. Everything ties back to the stories my father shared with me growing up, though I admit, I didn't appreciate their profound truth until now."

Vera studied him thoughtfully before turning her focus back to the documents. After several minutes of careful examination, she set down her magnifying glass and made notes in her pad. "Anthony, here's where we stand. These documents appear authentic on the surface. However, I'll need time to confirm that with absolute certainty. If they are genuine, the next challenge is decoding and transcribing the texts. That will require meticulous work to uncover the deeper meaning behind what you've found."

"I'm ready for whatever it takes," Anthony replied. "Just tell me how I can help."

Vera offered a small, reassuring smile. "For starters, I need your patience. Authenticating and interpreting documents of this significance is no small task. I'll need uninterrupted time to do it properly."

"Consider it done," Anthony said. "And where will you do all this? Here in Assisi?"

Vera shook her head. "No, no. I'll need to take everything back with me to Florence. The resources at the Laurentian Library and at the university will be invaluable for this work."

"That's fine," Anthony said quickly, his enthusiasm building. "I'll go with you."

Vera held up a hand. "That brings me to my second request," she said, her tone turning serious. "While I'm authenticating the documents, I need you to take this time to truly immerse yourself in Saint Francis, not just as a historical figure but as a man who embodied a spiritual philosophy that could hold the key to all of this. There's no better place to do that than right here in Assisi."

Anthony hesitated, considering her words. "You know," he said slowly, "the pope told me the same thing, to immerse myself in Saint Francis. Between what he said and what you're saying now, I'm starting to realize how important this is. Everything has been thrown at me so fast, but you're helping me see the bigger picture." He gave a sheepish laugh. "Honestly, I'm so far out of my element with the documents that diving into Saint Francis sounds like a welcome change. My only hesitation is the pope's warning not to let the documents out of my sight."

Vera leaned forward, her expression firm but reassuring. "I believe I'm the one exception to that instruction," she said, her voice carrying a quiet conviction. Her smile reflected their growing trust. "Before we wrap up, Anthony, was there anything else Pope Benedict requested of you that we haven't already discussed?"

He leaned back, replaying his conversation with the pontiff. "Let's see… He assured me that no one had ever seen or tampered with the documents under his watch. He mentioned there were things in his life he regretted, but he said he remained completely faithful to this obligation. He also told me that in the end I might have to make some tough decisions but to do what is best for the greater body of Christ. I'm pretty sure those were his exact words."

She nodded thoughtfully, making notes. "And my final question for now, did the pope tell you what you're supposed to do with the documents or give you any specific instructions?"

Anthony shook his head. "No, he didn't. All he said was to do what's been willed."

Vera's gaze moved across the artifacts displayed on the table, a quiet intensity in her expression. Finally, she turned back to Anthony. "Brava! Let's make a promise to each other right here and now. If anything significant or unexpected happens—anything that could change the course of what we're doing—we come to each other first. Deal?"

Anthony extended his hand with a faint smile. "Deal. But with one small exception—can you give me a ballpark idea of how long this will take? I like to have some sense of a timeline."

"It could be as soon as a couple of days, but realistically, don't be surprised if it takes a week or more. Once I begin sorting and analyzing everything, I'll have a clearer picture," Vera replied, brushing dust from her gloves.

Together, they carefully collected the artifacts and returned them to their respective limestone cylinders before sliding them into Anthony's Kevlar backpack. Vera paused, her fingers tracing the worn edges of the luggage tag.

"Snoopy?" she asked, her smile sincere. "You don't strike me as the Peanuts type."

"My first art lesson," Anthony said, a warmth crossing his face. "I learned to draw by copying Snoopy in grade school. Became known as the kid who could draw a perfect beagle. This tag's been with me on every trip since high school."

"So, the famous Anthony Brunelli owes his career to Charlie Brown's dog?" Vera teased, carefully securing his backpack in her equipment case.

"Don't tell the art critics," he whispered with a conspiratorial wink. Then, he glanced at Vera's case, a hint of lingering doubt in his eyes. "Just reassure me one last time that these will be stored somewhere absolutely secure."

"Anthony," she said, lowering her head slightly and peering over her reading glasses, "these will be in the Laurentian Library, an institution from which nothing has been stolen in over five hundred years. I promise you, they will be safer there than anywhere else."

His tension eased, and a genuine smile spread across his face. "Alright," he said with a resolute nod. "Let's do this."

Anthony carried Vera's equipment case as they walked to her car. "I'll be in close contact as I gather information," she said, watching as he carefully placed the case in the backseat of her Giulia.

"Thank you, Vera. Safe travels," he said, stepping back.

Vera slid into the driver's seat, gave a quick wave, and pulled onto Via Fontebella, her car accelerating smoothly up the narrow, winding street.

Leaning against the ornate iron fence at the southern edge of the parking lot, Anthony listened as her car faded into the distance, its faint hum swallowed by the quiet hills. The Umbrian countryside stretched before him in serene splendor, medieval Perugia standing powerfully in the distance, its tranquil beauty a stark contrast to the complexities of his unfolding journey.

Somewhere in those documents, locked within ages-old secrets Vera now carried, lay the answers he sought. Standing there, anticipation coiled tightly within him, not just for what Vera would uncover but for the deeper connection he would forge with Saint Francis, a figure who now felt more pivotal to his journey than ever before.

CHAPTER 19

The Basilica of Saint Francis, Assisi
3:15 PM

Anthony stood inside the magnificent Basilica of Saint Francis absorbing the hushed sanctity of the space. The Basilica had always been a marvel to him, but today it seemed more than a historical masterpiece. It felt alive, pulsing with purpose and meaning he had never before grasped. Built just two years after Saint Francis's burial in 1228, this structure had served as a beacon of faith during the Middle Ages and remained one of Christianity's most revered pilgrimage sites in the world.

The Basilica's architectural duality drew him in anew. The Upper Church, with its soaring Gothic arches and vibrant frescoes, seemed to touch the heavens themselves. In contrast, the somber intimacy of the Lower Church echoed the humility and simplicity that defined Saint Francis's life. Beneath it all lay the crypt where the saint himself rested, a quiet, sacred space where history and eternity intertwined.

Months earlier while working on his Vatican commission, Anthony had spent countless hours in the Upper Church, captivated by its exquisite Gothic art. His focus then had been purely technical—the brushstrokes, the layering of color, the intricate interplay of light and shadow. He had marveled at the genius of artists like Giotto, Cimabue, and Pietro Cavallini. Yet, for all his admiration, he had viewed their work through the detached lens of an artist, studying form over function, technique over theology. Now, standing in that same sacred space, something had shifted. The frescoes were no longer just breathtaking masterpieces—they were stories, parables painted with divine purpose. Understanding Saint Francis, he realized, would require more than studying his legacy. It demanded a connection with the heart of the man, his life, and his mission.

He turned to Giotto's *Legend of Saint Francis*, the series of twenty-eight frescoes adorning the walls of the Upper Church. These paintings, inspired by Saint Bonaventure's writings, chronicled the saint's life through narrative scenes rich with symbolism. Anthony's father had spoken of them often, recounting their significance with admiration. He remembered his first visit to Assisi as a teenager, standing in this very church while his father pointed out details in the frescoes. His father had mentioned that Saint Bonaventure's writings served as the blueprint for these works, a detail that had stuck with Anthony because he was considering attending St. Bonaventure University at the time.

Settling into a pew beneath the frescoes, Anthony allowed their beauty and message to wash over him. The narrative style unfolded like a visual scripture, each group of three scenes revealing pivotal moments in Saint Francis's journey. His gaze drifted to the north wall, drawn to one specific fresco, *St Francis Giving his Mantle to a Poor Man*. The scene showed the saint offering a richly adorned cloak to a man in rags. Anthony found himself transfixed by the golden material that gleamed with an almost otherworldly vibrance. This was no ordinary garment, but perhaps the saint's most precious possession. The image prompted Anthony to question his own generosity. While he often donated prints of his work to charity, the thought of giving away something truly valuable—a possession he cherished—felt far more challenging.

As he crossed the nave, other frescoes captured his attention, each one illuminating another facet of Saint Francis's life:

Sermon to the Birds—testament to his profound connection with nature

Saint Francis Preaching before Honorius III—the moment of divine endorsement

Stigmatization of St Francis—the miracle marking him as Christlike

Death and Ascension of Saint Francis—his solemn farewell after a life of unwavering faith

St Francis Mourned by St Clare—the enduring bond between kindred souls

Though he knew most scenes by name, he now realized how little he had engaged with their deeper meaning. These weren't merely historical events but acts of transformation, sacrifices that had shaped not just a man but an entire movement.

His gaze lingered on *Stigmatization of St Francis*. The scene of Francis bearing Christ's wounds—the ultimate sign of devotion and sacrifice—seemed to hold a message for him, though its meaning remained tantalizingly out of reach.

Afternoon light streamed through the stained-glass windows, casting shards of red, blue, and gold across the stone floor. Anthony paused before each of Giotto's frescoes, enthralled by the vivid depictions of Saint Francis's life. Though centuries old, the artwork seemed to breathe with a gentle pulse that drew him closer to the essence of the saint he sought to understand.

Yet, the more he lingered among these painted stories, the more his questions multiplied. *What could drive a man to surrender everything for a life of absolute poverty?* he wondered. *How could such profound humility spark a movement that echoed through centuries?* These were no longer academic curiosities. They were turning into personal reflections, challenging him to look deeper into the heart of Francis's mission.

Anthony exhaled, letting the last sunbeams catch flecks of color on his cheeks. He realized that while Giotto's frescoes provided a glimpse into Francis's life, another clue to the saint's enduring power might lie below, where his remains were laid to rest. If these images showed Francis's journey, perhaps the crypt would reveal the scale of his final resting place—a direct encounter with the sacrifice and mystery that still shaped countless lives.

With that thought, he turned away from the fresco's vibrant hues and allowed his gaze to settle on a modest stairway leading down. The soft echoes of the Basilica seemed to beckon him, urging him to follow the path of pilgrims and seekers before him. Clutching his notes, he set his sights on the crypt with a quiet determination rising in his chest. It was time to meet Saint Francis at the very heart of his legacy, entombed in stone yet living in spirit.

In the Lower Church, Anthony paused halfway down the nave, his gaze drifting to a narrow stairway leading into the crypt below. The air felt different here, heavier as though generations of devotion pressed gently on each breath. Following the worn steps downward, he reached the landing. His gaze fell upon an urn near the crypt's entrance, labeled with the name Jacopa dei Settesoli. Brother Jacoba as Francis had named her, Jacqueline Marle de Settesoli, the noble Roman woman who had stood by Francis's side at his death. Anthony felt a swell of emotion while imagining the saint's final hours and this steadfast benefactress ensuring he did not die alone. The crypt carried her presence too, bridging the ages with quiet grace.

At the foot of the stairs, an arched entrance was framed by simple stone. Anthony inhaled the cool subterranean air. Torch-like sconces cast flickering patterns across the walls, guiding him into the hush of history. In the half-light, precious marble mingled with bare stone, a mix of the neoclassical design once ordered by Pope Pius VII and the neo-Romanesque remodel in the early twentieth century. The blend of styles seemed symbolic, layers of time converging in a single sacred space.

In the distance, he noticed an ancient stone coffin secured with iron ties, enshrined in an open recess above the altar. This was where Saint Francis's remains had been hidden by Brother Elias, discovered only in 1818 after endless years of secrecy. The knowledge that Francis's relics had lain concealed so long sent a ripple of awe through Anthony. It was as if he had stepped into a secret woven by time itself.

Quietly, he approached the space around the altar. Four discreet tombs rested at the corners—Brother Rufino, Brother Angelo, Brother Masseo, and Brother Leo—the saint's most faithful companions now entombed around him, a testament to their devotion. Each name etched into the stone reminded Anthony of Francis's small circle united in humility.

He closed his eyes, letting the stillness seep into his bones. Soft candlelight danced on the walls, and each flame felt like an echo of past prayers. He thought of Francis's entire journey, the hidden remains discovered at Pope Pius VII's order, the subsequent designs, the final touches that had shaped this crypt into a shrine. And yet, despite the architectural shifts, the essence of Francis's life remained as tangible here as the rough stone at Anthony's fingertips.

A hush fell around him, deeper than silence, as if Francis's spirit lingered in the quiet corners. No matter how many layers of marble or stone had been stripped or added, the saint's humility and devotion still permeated the air. Anthony found his own trials momentarily dwarfed by the greatness of a man who had embraced poverty and compassion so entirely that it still resonated eight centuries later.

He knelt before the ancient coffin's stone. In that moment, he felt the potent intersection of faith and history, time collapsing into the present. A profound reverence welled within him, a hush of understanding that whatever mysteries he and Vera were chasing, this was the source—a love so immense it transcended centuries of secrecy, overcame grand designs and earthly ambitions, and forever changed the Church.

Anthony exhaled, sensing that he was but a pilgrim in the presence of something far greater than himself. He bowed his head in silent prayer, expressing gratitude for the saint whose body now lay just feet away and for the intangible legacy of unity and sacrifice that had guided millions to this crypt over the ages.

When he finally stepped back, the hush followed him like a secret entrusted to his heart. Each step felt like surfacing from a deep, holy well, leaving behind Francis's hidden tomb but carrying forward the saint's enduring call to humility, compassion, and a faith that dared to transform the world.

He sank into a pew, letting the sacred silence of Saint Francis's final resting place wash over him as he gathered his thoughts. His lingering questions turned to the guidance he would need. Someone who could offer more than intellectual clarity, a person who could challenge him to look beyond facts and artifacts, deep into himself. In his mind's eye, he glimpsed that figure—steady, insightful, grounded in Franciscan spirituality.

Massimo Coppo, the Assisi hermit who had urged him to explore Franciscan values. Just a month ago, Massimo had given him a book on Saint Bonaventure and encouraged him to read it. The volume remained unopened, a silent reproach to Anthony's reluctance to engage with his spiritual heritage. Now, with the richness of his family's legacy seeping through him, he felt a renewed sense of purpose. The thought of Massimo, with his profound connection to Franciscan life, whispered at the edges of his consciousness like a gentle nudge toward the path he knew he must take.

Rising from the pew, Anthony felt a strange yet comforting anticipation building within him. The way forward remained unclear, but for the first time in days it felt less daunting. There were answers to be found, both in history and within himself.

Understanding Saint Francis was no longer an abstract task. It had become personal, urgent, and now inexorably intertwined with his own destiny.

CHAPTER 20

The Basilica of Saint Francis, Assisi
4:44 PM

Anthony left the upper level of the Basilica and descended the brilliant stone steps toward the lower plaza. His mind churned, a restless whirlpool of emotions and unanswered questions.

His secret mission sanctioned by the highest echelons of the Church and intertwined with his father's abduction pressed heavily on his shoulders. Yet, despite everything, the introspective task given to him by the pope and reinforced by Vera to truly understand Saint Francis remained his focus.

His gaze swept across the expansive lower plaza illuminated in the soft, golden glow of the setting sun. It was then that he spotted the familiar figure of Massimo Coppo seated serenely beneath the portico. The barefoot monk's presence seemed to momentarily ease the storm within Anthony. For months, he had been captivated by Massimo, an enigmatic figure whose life seemed woven into the fabric of Assisi itself and whose devotion to Saint Francis ran deep, even beyond the hidden chambers of the Franciscan Order.

"Hey, Massimo!" Anthony called out.

The monk's face lit up with a grin as he recognized Anthony approaching. "Why, hello, Antonio! I didn't know you were in town. What brings you back to the glorious land of Assisi? How was the art reception?"

For a brief moment, Anthony was tempted to unburden himself, to share everything that had transpired since his last visit. But he held back, instead choosing to focus on the purpose that had drawn him to remain in Assisi once more. "The reception went well…very well, actually," he replied, offering a polite smile as he joined Massimo beneath the portico. Still, his true intentions simmered beneath the surface, waiting for the right moment to emerge.

Massimo reached for his worn walking stick. "Shall we?" he asked, gesturing toward the plaza.

Anthony nodded, falling into step beside him as they strolled along the cobblestone expanse.

Their conversations often began this way, meandering, lighthearted exchanges that seemed to mirror the rhythm of Assisi's streets. As they walked, Anthony's thoughts drifted to the first day he had met the hermit monk. He remembered how he had immediately noticed the monk's neatly trimmed beard, well-manicured fingernails, and an air of cleanliness that seemed at odds with his chosen life of poverty and exposure. It had puzzled him then, and still did now. How could someone so intelligent, so deliberate, willingly spend his days exposed to the harshness of the elements, living out the simplicity of Saint Francis's teachings with such unwavering purpose?

"Massimo, I'm back in Assisi because I need understanding—understanding of Saint Francis. But not the stories everyone knows. I want to know the man before he became a saint. What drove him, what gave him such determination?"

Massimo slowed his pace, his deep-set eyes meeting Anthony's with penetrating intensity. "Ah, Antonio, the spirit of San Francesco calls to many, but his path was not an easy one. His life was a poem written in the language of humility, compassion, and a unity with creation that few can grasp. But tell me, what is it you truly seek to understand?"

Anthony hesitated, cautiously choosing his words. He couldn't reveal everything, not the true purpose of his mission nor the secrets buried in the artifacts. Yet he yearned for the wisdom Massimo could offer. "I want to understand how he found such profound harmony through a life of poverty," he said. "How did he dedicate himself so completely to simplicity and still achieve a sense of peace?"

The monk nodded knowingly, as if anticipating the question. "San Francesco understood something fundamental about existence, Antonio. He saw divinity not as something separate or above but as intimately connected to all things. His harmony came from this radical understanding of love—love without boundaries, without expectation. To him, life itself was sacred and every creature, every breath was an expression of that sacredness."

Anthony listened intently, the monk's words stirring something deep within him. "And if someone were to try to emulate such a path, how would they even begin?"

Massimo's expression softened with gentle wisdom. "It begins with seeing," he said. "Not just with your eyes but with your heart. To truly follow in Francesco's footsteps, you must look beyond the surface, beyond the separations we so often impose. You must see the world not as fragments but as a whole, a divine tapestry where every thread matters. That is where harmony begins."

He turned to face Anthony fully. "You know, Antonio, this is something we've touched on before. Perhaps you weren't ready to hear it then, but now you seem more open. We've been taught to see ourselves as isolated, separate from the world around us. But Francis knew better. He understood that we are not strangers here, not something set apart. We are waves in the ocean of creation—unique, yet inseparable from the whole."

Anthony felt a profound shift within himself as if Massimo's words were unlocking doors he hadn't known were there.

"And so," Massimo continued, his voice taking on a meditative quality, "to walk this path is to awaken to the truth of your existence, not as something confined within the boundaries of your skin but as something expansive, interconnected. To see life and death, joy and sorrow as parts of a greater whole. That is what San Francesco understood so deeply. And that, Antonio, is the essence of existence."

The monk's words settled over Anthony like a warm blanket, comforting yet challenging. He felt as though he had glimpsed a deeper truth, one that would take time—and courage—to fully embrace.

He scratched his head, attempting to absorb the depth of Massimo's insights. They felt less like answers and more like a map that guided not his physical steps but the spiritual and moral odyssey awaiting him. Though Massimo's wisdom carried profound substance, Anthony sensed an underlying purpose behind the monk's measured words, as if they were breadcrumbs leading him forward.

As they walked, the plaza began to surrender to the cool embrace of evening, the air becoming crisp with the promise of night. The soft glow of spotlights illuminated the contours of the Basilica while the surrounding hills blurred into deepening shadows. Anthony felt a growing bond with Massimo, one not forged through shared secrets but through the wisdom imparted in their conversations. Under the watchful gaze of Saint Francis's resting place, an unspoken understanding passed between them.

"Massimo, it's clear that Saint Francis lived at a higher level of consciousness. But I can't help wondering, what was it really like for him during those times? What kind of world did he navigate? I feel like it's something my father tried to teach me, but the details have faded."

Massimo raised both eyebrows, his expression a mix of curiosity and gentle reproach. "Did you ever read the book of San Bonaventure I gave you a few weeks back?"

Anthony hesitated, slightly embarrassed. "No…I haven't yet. But I'm ready now. I want to understand."

"Antonio, you must read it," Massimo said, his tone firm yet encouraging. Reaching into the leather bag slung across his chest, he retrieved another book. "San Bonaventure had a profound connection to Francis. When he was a child, gravely ill with a rare disorder, Francesco prayed over him and his life was miraculously saved. But I'd also like you to read this." He handed Anthony a worn copy of *Saint Francis of Assisi* by G. K. Chesterton. "These two books will help you understand not only Francesco's life but also the world he lived in, its darkness and its light."

Anthony accepted the book, flipping through its pages as they continued to a nearby wooden bench. Massimo rested his walking stick against the portico's stone wall before settling beside him. Anthony remained engrossed in the book's yellowed pages, the faint scent of old paper mingling with the cool evening air.

"The times of Francesco were grim," Massimo began, his voice laden with historical significance. "It was a period of tension and futility. The Church forbade new ideas, demanding unquestioned authority as the sole intermediary to God. Laypeople were denied access to the Bible and couldn't even question the teachings forced upon them. Art and music were flourishing, yes, but so too was economic disparity. Cities like Perugia and Assisi were often at war while the papacy and the imperial throne clashed endlessly for power."

He gestured toward the hill overlooking the Basilica. "And here, on this very spot—once called the Hill of Hell—innocent souls were hanged or decapitated in mass executions. Their bodies were thrown into the abyss below, casualties of the Church's Inquisition. It was a time of unimaginable cruelty justified in the name of divine will."

Anthony shuddered, his gaze following the monk's outstretched hand. "This hill, where the Basilica now stands? It was an execution ground?"

Massimo nodded gravely. "Yes. The gallows stood here, a stark contrast to the message of love and compassion Francesco preached. The Inquisition, under the guise of protecting orthodoxy, was little more than a mechanism of fear and control. Its horrors were systemic and deliberate, yet the Church hierarchy turned a blind eye, rationalizing it as the will of God."

Anthony frowned, memories stirring. "I remember my father telling me about the Cathars, a Christian reform group annihilated in a twenty-year campaign. Tens of thousands slaughtered. It haunted me so much that I wrote an essay on it in college."

Massimo's expression darkened. "The Cathars, the Crusades, the Spanish Inquisition, the witch trials—it's the same story repeated again and again. Fear used as a tool of control. Francesco understood this and worked to dismantle it through love, humility, and service. His growing movement challenged the established guard, threatening those in power. But allowing him to form the Franciscan Order was a calculated decision. It kept him within the Church's jurisdiction while allowing his followers to serve the poor and the sick, tasks the Church itself had no interest in doing."

Anthony's mind raced, trying to reconcile the horrors of history with the profound harmony Saint Francis embodied.

"I'm surprised Francis wasn't considered a greater threat. His message…it must have rattled them."

The monk chuckled softly. "Oh, he was a threat, make no mistake. But Francesco's brilliance lay in his humility. He didn't seek to overthrow. He sought to transform. And by aligning himself with the Church—at least outwardly—he avoided the fate of so many reformers. His legacy endures because he understood how to navigate a system steeped in power and corruption while remaining true to his mission. He navigated the Church much like he navigated his own father, defiant yet resolute about his own purpose."

"So, how did he get his order approved?" Anthony asked.

Massimo gave a thoughtful nod, folding his hands calmly over his lap. "It's a wonder in itself, no? Francesco was no aristocrat, no Church official—just a man in tattered robes, preaching a life of radical humility. Yet he had a purity of purpose that even the highest churchmen couldn't ignore. When he first approached Pope Innocent III with his rough, hand-scrawled rule, many dismissed him as a fool or a dreamer. But the Holy Father, upon meeting him, discerned something extraordinary. Francesco's sincerity radiated beyond formalities and lit a spark of genuine renewal.

"So, in a time when the Church was entrenched in wealth and intrigue, Francesco's absolute poverty was both striking and convicting. According to tradition, Pope Innocent III had a remarkable dream in which he saw San Francesco physically bracing the crumbling walls of the Lateran Basilica—a symbolic vision of Francesco safeguarding the Church itself. Moved by this sign, Innocent realized Francesco was not merely a critic but a reformer whose love for the Church ran deeper than any institution. Of course, he first demanded Francesco demonstrate the fruits of his labor, and Francesco did so day by day, with every leper he embraced, every sermon he preached in the streets, and every hidden act of care for the forgotten. Eventually, the pope granted him a verbal approval that allowed Francesco to continue his mission, and it was formally sealed not long after, giving birth to what we now call the Franciscan Order."

Massimo paused, watching Anthony absorb his words. "The Franciscan Order—what Francesco called the Order of Lesser Brothers—was born out of a profound devotion to poverty, humility, and love. Francesco realized that genuine faith demanded not just worship but the willingness to live as Christ did, relinquishing possessions and embracing the marginalized. By embracing absolute poverty, they stripped away every layer of worldly vanity. In practical terms, Francesco and his earliest companions vowed never to own property, to rely on daily charity for food, and to pour out compassion wherever they went."

Anthony nodded slowly, his expression a mix of curiosity and awe. "So, they lived without the safety nets most of us cling to—no security, no backup plan…"

The monk gave a small, approving smile. "Precisely. Those vows of poverty, chastity, and obedience became the cornerstones of their new brotherhood. Poverty wasn't merely about giving up material goods. It was about recognizing the divine spark in each person and placing faith in God to provide. Chastity wasn't rigid denial—it was a commitment to love others freely, without binding them to personal desire. And obedience guided them to yield their own wills to God's grace and the Church's authority, shaping their personal ambitions for the collective good."

Anthony let out a measured breath, running a hand through his hair as he tried to imagine such a life. "I…I can't fathom how they kept so dedicated. If they didn't know where their next meal was coming from, how did they sustain themselves, or keep from losing faith?"

Massimo's gaze flickered with empathy. "They sustained themselves by grace, yes, but also by building community. When you share an unshakable commitment to each other and to serving the poorest, you find you're not alone. People saw them living with no ulterior motive, just to serve and love. And that selfless transparency stirred generosity and trust. It becomes easier to rely on frugality when your whole existence is anchored in humility and shared purpose.

"That's how Francesco challenged the Church's complacency, and why he lit a path for all humanity. This vow of simplicity was his shield, protecting the brothers from corruption, and his compassionate service to the poor was his sword, cutting through greed and fear. Their radical commitment stood as both a direct confrontation of worldly power and a living gift of hope for anyone, in any era searching for a purer way to follow Christ."

Anthony pressed a hand to his forehead, letting the depth of Massimo's explanation settle in. "I'd always assumed the Franciscan vow was just about giving up wealth, but you're telling me it's much deeper. It's really a spiritual framework for seeing the world with clarity, for living in pure honesty."

Massimo inclined his head. "Indeed. Francesco believed we're not separate from creation, nor are we meant to live at odds with one another. By choosing to let go of personal comforts, the brothers discovered a unity with all of life, one bound by service, love, and devotion."

Anthony exhaled softly, feeling a gentle stirring in his chest—an echo of the humility and conviction that had shaped Francis's path. "I hadn't realized how bold his message was… or how powerful it remains. It's no wonder people are still drawn to Francis after all these years."

For the first time in days, Anthony felt a flicker of clarity amidst the chaos of his thoughts. The monk's words were like light piercing the fog, illuminating the path he was meant to walk.

"Massimo, your insight couldn't have come at a better time," he said, rising from the bench with a firm hold on the Chesterton book. "Thank you."

The hermit monk smiled warmly, a touch of sadness in his eyes.

✝

Massimo watched as Anthony walked away, the measure of his journey evident in his stride. He knew the challenges ahead would test Anthony in ways he couldn't yet fathom. But he also knew that this man was exactly where he needed to be, on the cusp of revelations that would shape not only his mission but his very soul.

As Anthony's figure disappeared into the twilight, Massimo turned toward the Basilica. In the stillness of the plaza, the legacy and wisdom of Saint Francis whispered through the stones of Assisi, a beacon for those brave enough to seek its light.

CHAPTER 21

Hotel Giotto, Assisi
5:20 PM

Standing on the outdoor patio of Hotel Giotto, Anthony traced the contours of Assisi's landscape. The ancient town sprawled gracefully over the hillside, its terracotta rooftops radiating warmth under the soft evening glow. Beige and orange hues weathered by an age beyond measure stood in sharp contrast to the pale limestone walls of the medieval structures that breathed history into the crisp evening air. The rhythmic chime of distant church bells punctuated the tranquility, and carried on a gentle breeze, the faint scent of burning wood from hearths mingled with the aroma of wild herbs. The town was alive with the interplay of shadow and light, the setting sun casting intricate patterns through narrow alleyways and across quiet piazzas. In this sacred place, even the shadows held meaning. From this elevated perch, Assisi revealed itself as more than a mere place—it was a sanctuary suspended between Heaven and Earth. Its quietude brimmed with unspoken stories and whispered prayers.

Anthony absorbed it all, yet the picturesque view did little to calm his inner turbulence.

Venturing into the cobbled streets, he followed the incline toward the town square. His footsteps echoed against stones that had borne countless pilgrims before him. The intensity of his purpose pressed heavily, a quest entangled with his family's legacy, the pope's urgent directives, and the haunting mystery of his father's disappearance. Each step felt symbolic, as if the ground itself urged him to tread carefully, respectfully.

He couldn't ignore the pull of history, not as a spectator but as an inheritor. His connection to this place, woven through lineage and faith, was instinctual. He sought more than relics or secrets, *needed* to reconcile his identity with the legacy of Saint Francis, whose spirit lingered in every stone and shadow of this town.

The evening air brushed cool against his face, reminding him how swiftly time passed. Yet Assisi's ancient walls provided strange comfort, as if assuring him that while human lives were fleeting, some things—faith, legacy, truth—endured beyond mortal spans.

Drawn by an inexplicable urge to wander, Anthony descended into the maze of medieval streets. Stone archways curved overhead like protective embraces, their weathered surfaces holding innumerable years of prayers within their pores. The fading light painted the limestone walls in shades of honey and amber, while potted geraniums added splashes of crimson to wooden windowsills. Here and there, small shrines to the Virgin Mary nestled in wall niches, their candles flickering like earthbound stars.

A small shop caught his attention, its window display filled with framed portraits of Saint Francis and wooden tau crosses. The elderly shopkeeper was arranging his closing display when Anthony stepped inside, drawn to the simple wooden crosses hanging from brown cords.

"Ah, the tau," the shopkeeper smiled, lifting one from the display. "Made from Umbrian olive wood just like in Saint Francis's time. Each one carries the grain of these ancient trees." He turned the cross, letting the lamplight catch its natural patterns. "See these knots?" His weathered fingers rolled each one. "Three knots for the sacred vows—poverty, chastity, and obedience. Two knots on one side represent poverty and chastity, the single knot symbolizes obedience to God's will."

Anthony held the cross, feeling the smooth wood beneath his fingers.

"Just three euros," the shopkeeper added softly.

As he paid for the necklace, Anthony lifted it over his head and adjusted it around his neck. The wood felt warm against his skin and somehow right, as if it had been waiting for him. He thanked the shopkeeper and left.

While he passed the Chiesa Nuova built over Francis's childhood home, Anthony paused to study the worn steps. *How many times did the young Francis cross this threshold?*

Ancient melodies of Gregorian chants from one of Assisi's many churches wove through the streets like invisible threads connecting past and present. A group of brown-robed Franciscan friars passed silently by, their sandaled feet whispering against the stones, and for a moment, Anthony could almost imagine himself in Francis's time.

The narrow Via San Francesco led him past small shops closing for the day, their owners quietly exchanging *"buona sera"* as they locked their doors. He took in the scent of fresh bread still lingering from a nearby bakery and noticed the incense from the evening's vespers. An elderly woman draped in black lace emerged from a chapel, her wrinkled face serene as she clutched worn rosary beads. She nodded to Anthony as she passed, her eyes holding the same peaceful light he'd seen in Massimo's. In that simple exchange, he felt closer to understanding Francis's vision of universal kinship. It was all beginning to make sense.

Near the Piazza del Comune, he found himself before a simple stone fountain. Water trickled musically over its basin.

Local families had gathered in the square, their children's laughter echoing off ageless stones as they chased one another across the worn cobbles. A group of elderly men sat at their usual table outside the café, sharing tales over small cups of amaro, their faces animated in the warm glow of the piazza's lanterns.

Francis would have loved this scene, Anthony thought. *This simple communion of souls enjoying life's ordinary pleasures.* In their easy fellowship, their unconscious celebration of community, he glimpsed something of what Francis must have seen—the divine spark present in all creation, waiting only for eyes willing to perceive it.

Returning to the outdoor deck, he paused again to survey the expanse of rooftops and distant hills. Somewhere in that landscape, answers waited—not just about his family's history but about himself. He turned and entered the hotel, where familiar sounds greeted him: hushed conversations, aged wooden floors creaking beneath his feet, the subtle clink of glasses from the bar. Ascending the staircase to his suite, he felt the solitude of his task settle deeper within him. His room welcomed him with understated elegance—antique furnishings, soft lighting, and a quietude that invited reflection.

As evening settled in, Anthony lifted the leather-bound book Massimo had pressed into his hands after their conversation in the Basilica, *Saint Francis of Assisi*. The title alone stirred something in him as he opened to the first chapter, then lost himself in Chesterton's words.

The author painted Francis with such vivid strokes that Anthony felt he was discovering the saint anew, not as an icon in stained glass but as a flesh-and-blood man who had walked these very streets. Francis emerged from the pages as the son of Pietro di Bernardone, draped in fine silks, celebrating life with the careless joy of privileged youth. Anthony shifted uncomfortably in his chair, recognizing shadows of himself in the young Francis's love of luxury and pleasure.

He turned the pages slowly, absorbing Chesterton's account of Saint Clare, a girl of just seventeen from one of the noble families of Assisi, possessed of an "enthusiasm for the conventual life" that baffled so many onlookers. Her upbringing had promised the comforts of wealth and a well-arranged marriage, yet she defied her parents' will and slipped away in the dark of night to embrace Francis's radical call. Chesterton described it as a near "romantic elopement," except the object of Clare's devotion was not a suitor but the life of a Franciscan nun. She escaped her home through a hole in the wall, fled into the woods, and at midnight, Francis and the brothers welcomed her and lamp-lit torches guided her toward the convent she would found.

Chesterton lingered on the tension between such a "heavenly love" and the earthly alliances that society ordinarily celebrates. Clare's boldness and Francis's unwavering support made the story resonate like a passage from folklore, with all the thrills of a clandestine escapade. Yet behind the drama, Anthony saw something more—the seed of the Poor Clares. This was no flighty rebellion, but a determined act of faith by a young woman who believed that surrendering her privileged future would open a door to a higher calling. In an era when girls her age often married under parental dictates, Clare's choice to "elope into the cloister" was a radical and deeply spiritual defiance—a living testament to the transformative power of Francis's ideals. Reading of Clare's daring devotion reminded Anthony that Francis's radical empathy wasn't limited to guiding young nobles into cloisters.

Turning the page, he encountered another pivotal scene, one that laid bare Francis's compassion for all. His breath caught at the account of Francis's encounter with a beggar, the scene unfolding with stark clarity. Francis, moved by an impulse he couldn't explain, emptied his pockets while his companions laughed and his father seethed. Anthony closed his eyes, remembering his own carefully calculated charitable gestures. How many times had he donated old clothes, keeping the finest safely in his closet. Francis's spontaneous generosity stood in sharp relief against his own measured philanthropy.

The light outside his window had faded to deep blue when he read about Francis's brief stint in military conflict, a short-lived campaign in which he fought for Assisi against Perugia around 1202. According to Chesterton, those dark days, which culminated in Francis's capture and imprisonment, had acted as a forge that tempered his soul. Even after Francis's eventual release, when he momentarily tried to slip back into his old life of privilege, something within him had irrevocably changed. As Anthony took in these details, he recognized a familiar tension—the same pull between his comfortable life as a successful artist and a deeper calling that drew him back to Assisi.

Setting the book in his lap, he looked out his window to watch stars emerge in the darkening sky. Each point of light seemed to mirror the gradual awakening he felt within himself. This wasn't just research anymore…something deeper was taking root. Anthony continued reading.

Francis's world expanded before him. Here was a man who preached to birds and tamed wolves, who saw divine presence not just in church sanctuaries but in every leaf and stone. The words of the *Canticle of the Sun* took on new meaning—Brother Sun, Sister Moon, no longer mere poetic devices but expressions of a revolutionary understanding of creation's unity. Anthony found himself drawn to this vision of universal kinship, so different from his own carefully maintained boundaries.

Then, the account of the stigmata at La Verna struck him with particular force. Chesterton's words seemed to leap from the page. "To represent La Verna as the mere collapse of Francis is exactly like representing Mount Calvary as the mere collapse of Christ. Those mountains are mountains, whatever else they are…" Anthony felt the truth of it in his bones—suffering transformed into triumph, weakness into strength. He thought of his own struggles, his father's disappearance, the substance of his mission, then decided he would visit La Verna when he had the chance.

And finally, the concept of Lady Poverty captured his imagination—Francis's radical embrace of simplicity reimagined as a romance, a love story that defied the materialism of his age. "It was a road upon which even angels might fear to tread," Chesterton wrote, and Anthony felt those words resonate deeply.

He glanced around his comfortable hotel room, at his well-tailored clothes, the trappings of his carefully curated life. *What would it mean to love poverty as Francis had? Not just to accept it, but to court it, to choose it freely?* he supposed.

The more he read, the more Francis emerged not as a distant saint but as a mirror reflecting uncomfortable truths about Anthony's own life choices. Yet there was hope in that reflection too, the possibility of conversion, of finding a deeper purpose beyond the comfortable boundaries he'd drawn for himself.

Anthony closed the book and leaned back, thoughts swirling. Francis's transformation from privileged merchant's son to devoted servant of God seemed almost mythical, yet it rested on choices available to anyone—living with purpose, loving deeply, finding joy in simplicity.

Though unwilling to renounce his own comforts, Anthony could no longer ignore their role in his life. He posed a personal challenge rather than a philosophical one. Could an artist who had chased recognition and success for years find the courage to walk a humbler path?

The question lingered in the room's growing shadows, demanding answers he wasn't yet prepared to give.

Chesterton's portrayal of Francis as love's troubadour, preaching not from dogma but from mystical connection to the divine, offered both inspiration and challenge. His message of unconditional love and service without expectation resonated across countless lifetimes with an urgency Anthony could no longer dismiss.

As darkness deepened, his thoughts returned to Massimo. The barefoot monk's dedication now seemed less eccentric and more profound, a living embodiment of Francis's teachings. His words merged with Chesterton's. "Each one of us is a living reflection of the universe at work." The concept both puzzled and drew him.

The crossed arms of Christ and Saint Francis on the Franciscan shield surfaced in his memory, their symbolism of shared sacrifice and divine unity carrying fresh meaning. Beyond the saintly image, Anthony glimpsed the man who chose love and simplicity amid conflict and greed.

Closing his eyes, he let silence fill the room. What began as a search for answers had become a pilgrimage of the soul. Though daunted by Francis's legacy, Anthony felt a spark of courage here in Assisi's heart. The saint's radical love and humility offered direction for his mission and guidance for his own transformation. For the first time, he felt ready to take that first step.

T

Anthony's phone buzzed against the marble counter, Rick Pescatore's name lighting up the screen. His hands trembled slightly as he answered, but Rick's heavy tone told him every-thing before the words registered in his mind.

"Nothing concrete yet," Rick said quietly, the weight of failure evident in his voice. "But Captain Rossi's team found traces of blood in an abandoned garage off Via di Tor Bella Monaca. They rushed the DNA analysis. It's a match to your father's blood type and a swab they took from his hotel bath-room." There was a pause, then, "Tomorrow they're expanding the search radius to include the industrial district. Tony, I prom-ise you we're not giving up."

Anthony closed his eyes, his grip tightening on the phone as he processed the implications of blood in an abandoned garage. He wanted to drop everything, to join the search himself, but he knew that wasn't what his father would want. Not with what was at stake.

CHAPTER 22

The address scrawled on the slip of paper had brought Richard back to the familiar yet unassuming exterior of Santi Apostoli, the Church of the Twelve Holy Apostles. As he pushed open the massive wooden doors, centuries-old hinges groaned softly, releasing a gust of warm air thick with history. It was a welcome contrast to the brisk streets of Rome, which were just beginning to surrender to evening's embrace.

Inside, the Basilica's baroque splendor illuminated before him. Massive marble columns, their capitals adorned with intricate carvings worn smooth by time, soared upward to support the vaulted ceiling where gilt-edged frescoes depicted heavenly scenes in vibrant detail. Crystal chandeliers hung like suspended constellations, their warm light swaying across the golden grooves that traced paths along the nave's pillars.

Moving down the nave, his fingers trailed along the smooth edge of the pews, seeking comfort in their solid presence. Above, a familiar symbol caught his eye—the Franciscan Coat of Arms, the symbol of sacrifice and unwavering devotion. Richard paused, memories of his conflicted history with the order rising to the surface.

He approached the right-hand side, second pew from the rear, just as the instructions had specified. As he sat, uncertainty settled over him at this step into the unknown. The events leading to this moment crowded his thoughts, particularly the desperate call he'd made hours earlier to a number Minister General Tasca had entrusted to him years ago. That number had lain dormant until today. Ronald Brunelli's disappearance and Anthony's inherited family obligation had forced his hand. Father Alessandro della Rovere had made it clear his duties were finished, his authority to assist the Brunellis revoked. Yet still, he pressed on.

The faint scuff of approaching footsteps drew his attention. From the far corner of the sanctuary, a figure emerged, his pace deliberate yet unhurried. Dressed in the simple habit of a Franciscan monk, the man moved like a silhouette, his face obscured beneath the cowl of his hood. He paused briefly at the rear of the church as if attuning himself to the sanctity of the space before advancing toward Richard.

The voice that broke the stillness was low and raspy. "Richard Pescatore." The words, barely louder than a whisper, carried authority and mystery. With the monk kneeling so close behind him, Richard caught the austere scent of rough-worn wool and plain soap drifting up from behind him, the humble aromatics of a life devoted to simplicity and prayer.

Richard turned slightly but remained seated, his hands gripping the edge of the pew. The anonymity of the meeting felt deliberate, an unspoken testament to the significance of the moment.

The monk extended a small sackcloth drawstring bag, something solid shifting within. His hands were rough, the calluses and weathered skin speaking of years of labor and prayer. "Take this," he instructed. "But remember this warning. The risk you're about to take won't just threaten your life, it will test your very soul."

The warning hung in the air like incense, seeping into Richard's thoughts. He reached out and accepted the bag, its coarse fabric rough against his fingertips. The monk's presence seemed to dissolve as quickly as it had appeared, leaving him alone in the pew with the burden of what he held heavy in his hands.

He waited for several minutes, his focus now on the distant altar. The quiet grandeur of the church surrounded him, but his mind was consumed by what the bag might contain. With trembling fingers, he opened the sack. His breath caught at the sight of two ancient skeleton keys, their metal worn but sturdy, alongside a small, folded piece of paper. Unfolding it, Richard read the handwritten instructions. The neat script offered little comfort. These were not ordinary keys—they were relics, tools to unlock not just doors but secrets buried within the darkest corners of faith and the Church's forbidden past.

When he finally rose from the pew, his legs felt heavy with hours of waiting. He crossed himself and whispered a silent prayer, seeking strength for the journey he had chosen to undertake and knowing well its costs.

As Richard exited Santi Apostoli, the cool night air greeted him, sharp and invigorating. The bustling sounds of the city seemed distant, muted by the enormity of his mission. He tightened his grip on the sack as he stepped into the street, his resolve hardening with every step. Whatever lay ahead in the shadows of Rome's ancient secrets, he would face it for Anthony Brunelli, for the truth, and for the faith that had led them both to this moment in time.

The streets of Rome received him into their embrace as Richard walked away from Santi Apostoli carrying keys that would either illuminate truth or seal his fate.

CHAPTER 23

The Laurentian Library, Florence
9:10 PM

The city of Florence glittered under a deep indigo sky as Vera strode into the Laurentian Library, her heels clicking softly against the stone floor. It was past nine, and the library was silent save the hum of the air filtration system and the distant creak of settling wood. The staggering impact of Anthony's sacred duty pressed on her as she entered the lab, breathing in the familiar scent of old books.

She wasted no time, setting up her workbench with meticulous care. The limestone cylinders, parchments, and remnants of wax seals sat before her like relics from another world, their secrets waiting to be unlocked. She slipped on her gloves and began her analysis, each step deliberate and methodical.

The cylinders came first. Under the microscope, she examined the faint tool marks on the limestone, her trained eyes identifying patterns consistent with thirteenth-century carving techniques. Using X-ray fluorescence (XRF) and Raman spectroscopy, she confirmed the elemental composition of the stone matched quarries in Umbria used during Saint Francis's time. The results were promising, but they were only the beginning.

With a delicate hand, she unrolled the fragile parchments, their edges curling slightly in protest against the modern light and air. The Latin Gothic script, though faint, was unmistakable—a style prevalent in the early 1200s.

She leaned closer, examining the precise strokes of each letter. A small sample from the edge underwent radiocarbon dating, confirming its origin in the early thirteenth century. The ink passed her scrutiny as well, revealing the telltale composition of medieval iron gall ink.

But it was the wax seals that drew her sharpest focus. Two of the seals, intricately designed and weathered by time, aligned perfectly with the techniques and materials of the thirteenth century. The other seal, however, felt wrong. The wax was too smooth, its composition slightly off.

Frowning, Vera ran a series of tests, her instincts sharpening with each result. The chemical analysis confirmed her suspicions. The seal on the cylinder from the pope to Anthony was no anomaly but a likely sophisticated forgery crafted with disturbing precision.

Her stomach tightened as she contemplated the implications. *Someone altered this, but why? And who?*

As these questions swirled in her mind, her phone lit up with a series of missed calls from Father Alessandro, accompanied by a terse text message. "Vera, I need an update. This is urgent."

She set the phone down, fighting the urge to switch it off entirely. Alessandro's persistence had grown increasingly unnerving, his tone carrying an edge of desperation that now seemed suspicious. The timing of his message, coming just as she'd discovered the potential forgery, couldn't be coincidental.

The need for more sophisticated analysis drove her to carefully transfer the artifacts into Anthony's Kevlar backpack. Her destination, the Art Forensics Lab at the Florence Province Art Commission (ACF), a state-of-the-art facility funded by Italian Parliament and the University of Florence. Where the

Laurentian Library's tools had hinted at discrepancies, the ACF's sophisticated equipment would provide irrefutable proof. Vera had spent her early career years there, honing her skills in art restoration and analysis. If anywhere could unveil the complete truth, it was the ACF.

When she arrived, the facility stood nearly empty, its stark corridors illuminated by rows of LED lights that cast a clinical glow over the polished floors. The quiet suited her. Solitude had always sharpened her focus.

In the main lab, she breathed in the familiar scent of solvents and cleaning agents. The sophisticated equipment hummed around her as she calibrated the spectrometer, programming it to detect any trace of modern contaminants or chemical tampering in the wax seals.

As the machine worked, Vera's thoughts drifted to the parchments that lay before her, specifically to the letter she'd examined earlier that day from the third cylinder. She took it out to read its cryptic message again. "All will become clear to you when you uncover what I have hidden." The words seemed to pulse with significance, especially now.

The spectrometer's sharp beep pulled her attention back. The data scrolling across the screen confirmed her earlier findings that the seal from the limestone cylinder given to Anthony from Pope Benedict was a modern creation, its materials carefully chosen to mimic thirteenth-century wax but betraying themselves under closer scrutiny. The level of expertise required for such a forgery was remarkable…and troubling.

Vera pressed her temples, processing the implications. This wasn't just a clue. It was a warning. Someone with considerable resources and knowledge had tampered with this cylinder, and Father Alessandro's increasingly urgent messages suggested his involvement. His impatience, his pressing questions—everything pointed to a deeper conspiracy.

The overhead lights cast stark shadows across her workspace as she considered her next moves. Priority one, inform Anthony first thing in the morning about the forgery, but carefully. His trust in her was precious and fragile, and she needed this irrefutable evidence before leveling any accusation. Then she would have to confront Alessandro, though the prospect filled her with dread. If he was indeed involved, she was stepping into a dangerous game where the stakes exceeded anything she could imagine.

A sudden draft whispered through the lab, stirring the edges of the ancient parchments. Vera studied their delicate script, feeling the depth of eras upon eras sinking in on her. Whatever secrets these documents held, someone was willing to go to extraordinary lengths to control their narrative. And now she stood at the center of it all, knowing her next discovery could make her a target of those who wanted history's mysteries to remain buried.

The security lights outside cycled on, their harsh beams cutting through the window blinds in steady pulses. The night was deepening, and with it Vera's window of opportunity narrowed. But first, she needed to understand the totality of what she was dealing with…and who she could trust.

CHAPTER 24

Hotel Giotto, Assisi
5:52 AM

Anthony awoke to the muted light of morning spilling through the curtains of his room at Hotel Giotto. The echoes of his late-night reading lingered in his mind, Chesterton's words on Saint Francis weaving a rich tapestry of thought and imagery that had seeped into his dreams. The book lay open beside him, its pages a portal to a time when simplicity and grandeur coexisted in a way that felt both alien and intimately familiar.

A faint sense of purpose stirred within him, not yet fully formed but unmistakable. Dressing quickly, he stepped out into the cool air of Assisi. The urge to see La Verna—where Francis's legacy stood tangible—seized him with sudden intensity. Unable to ignore it, he climbed into his rental car, determined to make the ninety-minute drive.

When he arrived, he stepped onto the rocky path that wound up the forested slope toward La Verna, a place of secrets and devotions dating back to the thirteenth century. Although his breath came quickly in the crisp mountain air, each step seemed to slow time. Ahead, tall pines rustled in a gentle breeze as if ushering him forward to something profound. He clutched his notes and a small journal, heart pounding with anticipation.

He had read the history, how in 1213, Saint Francis of Assisi met the Count Orlando of Chiusi della Verna and his admiration for Francis's preaching led him to gift La Verna to Francis and his followers. How it became a site of countless spiritual retreats, culminating in the momentous day when Francis received the stigmata in 1224. Now Anthony meant to stand where that miracle had taken place, longing to sense for himself the echo of that centuries-old faith.

A friar in a simple brown habit greeted Anthony at the entrance. The monk's soft smile was a study in quiet warmth, one that made him think of Saint Francis's legendary gentleness. He bowed slightly, then led Anthony through the main gate, explaining that since Pope Alexander IV took the site under papal protection, La Verna's spiritual legacy had only grown. Within these walls, Franciscan friars still preserved the memory of Francis's last days on the mountain.

As they passed the Basilica di Santa Maria degli Angeli, built in 1218 by Saint Francis himself, Anthony felt as though he had stepped back in time. The stone walls rose austerely, speaking not of grandeur but of simplicity and devotion.

The friar paused for a moment, resting his fingertips against the venerable doorway. "This was one of the earliest chapels," he said quietly. "Francis prayed here before he climbed higher, seeking solitude."

They continued deeper into the complex, coming upon a corridor that led to the Chapel of the Stigmata built by Count Simon of Battifolle close to the place of the miracle. Every footstep on the ancient flagstones echoed with endless years of prayer.

"Twice a day," the friar explained, "the friars here make a solemn procession from the main church to this chapel, remembering Francis's suffering and revelation."

Anthony stopped as soon as the chapel came into sight. Soft light streamed through narrow stained-glass windows, illuminating the worn pews and casting ghostlike patterns on the cold floor. This was where Saint Francis had retreated in August of 1224, preparing in a 40-day fast for the Feast of Saint Michael. It was here, in the hush of prayer, that he received the stigmata, the five wounds of Christ, forever altering his life and the Franciscan Order.

His guide gave a final nod, allowing Anthony to enter alone. The hush inside felt almost electric, like a living silence that breathed with the faith of thousands who had stood there before him. The air smelled faintly of incense and candlewax. Though outwardly unassuming, the chapel's significance pulsed beneath Anthony's feet.

He approached the altar where a single taper burned in a rough-hewn sconce. A small wooden cross stood on the marble, and behind it hung a modest painting depicting the saint's stigmata. The painting's colors had faded over the centuries, yet the story it told remained vivid. Anthony closed his eyes, remembering how according to legend, Saint Francis had seen a seraph bearing the marks of the crucifixion and felt nails of light pierce his hands, feet, and side. He tried to envision the pain—the raw physical agony of Christ's wounds—melded with the transcendent love that compelled Francis to embrace it.

What must it have been like, he wondered, *to bear those marks as both burden and testament to faith?*

A sense of profound humility washed over him. The breadth of all he had uncovered in his quest—the truth behind countless years of guarded secrets—now converged in this single space. This was the heart of Francis's sacrifice and the beating pulse of the Franciscan way—a love so great it imitated Christ's own suffering.

Quietly, he sank to his knees, placing one hand on the cool stone floor. It was as though he could feel Francis's presence, not a distant relic of the past but an urgent call to live with the same total surrender and compassion.

"What strength it must have taken," he murmured under his breath.

He bowed his head, letting the magnitude of that moment sink in. The humility, the devotion, the sheer willingness of Francis to share in Christ's torment. All of it made Anthony's own struggles seem both smaller and yet more urgent. If such transformation was possible for a simple friar from Assisi, perhaps the world too could be changed by a greater calling.

After several minutes of silent reflection, Anthony rose with a renewed resolve, one shaped not by the worldly thrill of unearthing a sensational mystery but by the deeper realization that Saint Francis's stigmata was not about glory or spectacle. It was about an unbreakable bond with the suffering Christ, about bridging the gap between divinity and humanity through limitless compassion.

As he stepped back into the corridor, he found the friar waiting, hands clasped in front of his habit.

The monk offered a knowing smile, as if he understood the shift Anthony had just experienced. "You see now," he said softly, "how the wounds Francis bore were from his ultra-deep relationship with God, not for the life of the Church."

Anthony simply nodded. Words seemed inadequate. He looked once more at the chapel's humble façade before following the friar back along the ancient hallway. In his heart, he now carried a profound understanding and appreciation for what Saint Francis had endured. It wasn't just pain, it was an offering—one that resonated through the centuries, guiding hearts toward love, humility, and a faith far deeper than any suffering could eclipse.

The drive down the mountain passed in a reflective haze. The crisp alpine breeze followed Anthony as he navigated the winding roads back to Assisi, each turn reminding him of the fragile line between tribulation and grace. By the time he glimpsed the familiar skyline, his mind brimmed with questions and a quiet certainty that he had crossed a threshold in his own journey.

Upon returning, he made his way to the portico where he found his barefoot friend, Massimo, observing a group of tourists admiring the Basilica. With his sackcloth robe draped loosely around him, Massimo exuded an aura of serenity that stood in stark contrast to the restless thoughts still churning in Anthony's mind.

"Ready yet to become a monk and take a vow of silence?" Massimo teased, his warm smile breaking the quiet.

Anthony chuckled, though his laughter was edged with a solemnity that hadn't been there before. "You never know," he replied. "I finished the Chesterton book last night, and I made a trip to La Verna early this morning. It's making me rethink everything."

Massimo's expression softened, curiosity lighting his eyes. "Ah, Francesco's influence has a way of doing that. I'm happy you visited La Verna. Please, tell me about your experience there."

Anthony took a measured breath, recalling the hush of the site now marked by a chapel erected after the event and the presence of history embedded in every stone. "It's…difficult to explain. The place is so unassuming—almost austere, really— but you can feel generations of devotion spreading through you. I stood in that chapel, built to honor the very place where Francis received the stigmata outdoors, and it felt as though I was stepping into the moment his entire worldview shifted. I realized it wasn't just about pain but about love so profound he was willing to take on Christ's wounds."

Massimo's brows rose, and a gentle solemnity replaced his teasing grin. "Such a realization can shake a person to the core.

La Verna holds that power. Francesco's surrender, his unity with the divine, is woven into the very mountain."

Anthony nodded, his voice hushed as he replied, "It changed the way I see suffering. I always thought of it as something to avoid, but suffering can be purposeful, and for Francis it was a bridge to Christ, to the people he served. I sensed in those walls a call to live more deeply, to accept that true compassion sometimes involves sharing another's burden both physical and spiritual."

Massimo exhaled slowly. "Francesco's radical humility does that, reminds us that pain can be sanctified by love. And you…do you think it will alter your path?"

Anthony's gaze flicked to the Basilica, lingering for a moment. "It already has. I can tell you that for sure."

A warm pride shone in Massimo's eyes. "Then you've grasped the heart of his message. Sometimes a single day at La Verna can transform what reason alone never could."

Anthony offered a half-smile, a sense of quiet resolution settling over him. "I see that now. And I think…I think it's time to bring that understanding forward, to share it, just as Francis shared every blessing he received."

Massimo nodded, placing a supportive hand on Anthony's shoulder. "One step at a time, my friend. One step, and one prayer, at a time." They both nodded in unison. "And you say you finished Chesterton's book?"

Anthony paused, gathering his thoughts. "Massimo, you have no idea. Chesterton's words are helping me see the world as Francis did. He understood something fundamental, that we're not separate from the universe but continuous with it. He saw life as a harmonious pattern, a dance of energy. He knew that our physical and spiritual existence were one and the same. Once he let go of his ego and embraced this oneness, everything became clear to him. He stopped seeing life as a struggle and started living it as a symphony."

Massimo nodded, his smile deepening. "That's the best observation I've heard in a very long time. You've grasped the essence of Franciscan awareness. Francesco was a poet of the divine, someone who saw the extraordinary in the ordinary. To him, the world was not a set of separate pieces but a single, miraculous whole. He lived as if everything was part of a greater, beautiful rhythm."

The monks words resonated with Anthony, stirring something deeper within him. "I'm still calculating what drove him spiritually. What gave him such clarity?" His voice trembled with yearning as his gaze drifted toward the Basilica rising against the mid-morning sky.

Massimo motioned for Anthony to follow him to a quieter corner of the portico where the morning sun cast delicate shadows through the ancient arches. "One of the fundamental insights that Francesco left behind, which Chesterton especially tuned into, is that the attitude of Heaven is not serious and this should teach us about the attitude of this earthly life." Once again, he reached into the leather bag slung across his chest, taking out another book. He shuffled to a page folded at the edge. "There's a famous passage in this Chesterton book, *Orthodoxy.* Let me read it to you," he said. " 'Things like stones are subject to gravity. They are heavy, they are grave, they are serious. But in all things spiritual there is lightness, and therefore a kind of silliness. The angels fly because they take themselves lightly. And if that must be true of the angels, how much truer of the Lord of the Angels?' Our trouble today, Antonio, is that many times we take things too seriously, expect everything to make perfect sense, and then we get disappointed."

"Life becomes a constant anticipation," Anthony said, thinking of his own journey. "We're always waiting for that moment when everything will finally click into place."

"That's right," Massimo said. "True spirituality isn't about gravity. It's about lightness, joy, and participation in the play of life."

Anthony's eyes narrowed thoughtfully as he considered the radical simplicity of Francis's path. "So, Francis saw life not as something to figure out but as something to experience and embraced each moment like he embraced the lepers, without hesitation or fear. Or said differently, treating both poverty and plenty as welcome guests at the same feast."

"Marvelous, you've got it," Massimo said. "Francesco saw life as music. The goal of music is certainly not in the future but in the melody of the music itself. The goal of a symphony is not to reach the end of the symphony. If it were, the best orchestra would be the one that played the fastest." He chuckled. "And you don't dance in order to arrive at a particular place on the floor. You dance to enjoy the dance. Francesco believed existence is a kind of dance, a jazz performance where each moment is complete in itself. He taught us that the universe doesn't need to make sense to be beautiful—it's beautiful because it doesn't make sense. Francesco knew that God was playful, and he joined the dance."

Just then, Massimo's eyes sparkled with mischief as he began to sway while humming an ancient Umbrian melody that seemed to rise from the stones themselves. "Listen to the music of creation," he said. "Even the trees, the flowers, the mountains—they're all dancing and singing...*ca-jud-adoo, ca-jud-adoo, ca-jud-adoo, ca-jud-adoo, ca-jud-adoo,*" his voice broke, carrying the inflection of song. "But human beings think they're so special and are so serious and think they have to make sense of it all. There doesn't have to be sense to it.

Just join in, come on! *Ca-jud-adoo, ca-jud-adoo, ca-jud-adoo, ca-jud-adoo, ca-jud-adoo,*" he sang again.

Anthony bobbed his head while following Massimo's lead. "I love it!" he said.

"San Francesco knew that if we live life nonsensical and with humor, we'd find ourselves singing *Hallelujah* by the end."

Anthony snickered, but the fullness of Massimo's words settled deep within him. He felt his perspective shifting, the lines between the spiritual and the tangible blurring. For the first time, he began to see his journey not just as a search for answers but as an invitation to join a cosmic dance, one that Saint Francis had mastered on the very soil beneath him.

Massimo leaned closer. "And, Antonio, if you want to truly understand Francesco, go back and read the Canticle of the Sun. He wrote it when he was blind, near the end of his life, lying in a dark hut near San Damiano. Despite his suffering, he composed this hymn of joy, praising not just Brother Sun and Sister Moon but Brother Wind and Sister Water, Brother Fire and Sister Mother Earth. Even Sister Death received his loving embrace." Massimo's eyes brightened with reverence. "In his darkest hours, he saw what most of us miss—that all creation forms one divine family. He understood that we don't 'come into' this world. Rather, we come *out* of it just as a flower comes from the soil or a wave from the ocean. Each element, each creature plays its part in God's grand design. The wind that cleanses, the fire that illuminates, the earth that sustains— all are our siblings in creation. This was Francescos greatest gift to us, the understanding that we are part of the whole, bound together in one magnificent tapestry of life."

The morning bells of the Basilica began their melodic call to prayer, their bronze expressions floating across the ancient city. In that moment, Anthony's phone buzzed in his pocket, the modern world reasserting itself again.

Vera's voice was urgent. "Anthony, can you get to Florence sometime today? I've got some of the test results, and they're extraordinary. I can't discuss it over the phone. You need to see this."

He felt the familiar surge of anticipation, yet it was tempered by something new—a sense of belonging to a greater unfolding. "Of course I can. I'll head out within the hour," he assured her, then turned back to Massimo, regret in his eyes. "I'm afraid I have to leave town again, Massimo. Something's come up. I've enjoyed our conversation very much."

The barefoot monk nodded, his smile gentle, encouraging. "Go, my friend. And remember, what you're searching for in Francesco might be more than just a physical trace of the past. The greater discovery may lie within you."

As Anthony made the short walk to his hotel, Massimo's words echoed in his mind. He had always possessed keen instincts, and he felt confident in his inner sense of direction. The intensity of his dual quest—one for his family's legacy, the other for a deeper truth—remained with him, but it felt different now. The cobblestones beneath his feet seemed to pulse with their own hidden rhythm as though the very city was joining in the cosmic dance Massimo had described.

The road ahead held no certainties, but Anthony felt ready to embrace the unknown, sensing that both the relics and the spirit of Saint Francis held the keys to unlocking what awaited. As he departed the hill town of Assisi, the morning sun caught the façade of the Basilica and for a moment it seemed to shimmer with its own inner light—a reminder that sometimes the most profound truths are found not in the answers we seek but in the questions we dare to ask.

CHAPTER 25

The Laurentian Library, Florence
1:40 PM

Standing outside the visitors' gate of the Laurentian Library in San Lorenzo Square, Anthony felt a twinge of nervous anticipation. The unfinished façade of San Lorenzo, with its raw stonework laid in distinctive horizontal bands, rose before him like a massive pale sentry in the crisp February air. The austere beauty of its rough-hewn exterior contrasted sharply with the elegant Renaissance buildings flanking the piazza, where locals hurried past delivery trucks and empty café tables, their breath visible in the winter morning light.

As he waited, the hum of the city around him faded when he heard a voice call his name. Turning, he spotted Vera Valentino waving at him while loading a large hard-shell carrying case into the backseat of a navy-blue Land Rover. The insignia on the vehicle was impossible to miss—*Esercito*, the Italian word for army.

Vera gestured for him to approach as the driver, a tall man with the bearing of a soldier, stepped out. His posture was precise, and the Beretta 92 holstered on his hip caught Anthony's attention immediately.

"Signore Brunelli," the man greeted in a deep, formal tone, extending his hand. "I am Angelo Stillittano, a friend of Dr.

Valentino's. It's a pleasure, indeed, to meet you," he said in heavy, accented English.

"The pleasure is mine," Anthony replied, gripping the man's hand firmly. He turned to Vera, who was already settling into the backseat. "Where are we headed, Vera?"

"To the Art Commission Lab," she replied, her voice calm but tinged with urgency. "It's nearby."

With that, Angelo closed the passenger door, securing Anthony inside before heading to the driver's seat. The vehicle moved smoothly through Florence's cobblestone streets, the iconic cityscape blurring past. The short ride was a mix of silence and quiet tension, with Vera occasionally glancing at the hard-shell case beside her as if it carried the scale of an age beyond measure.

Arriving at the Art Commission Lab, Angelo escorted them inside, his military precision evident in every movement. In the lobby, he handed the equipment case over to Vera, who thanked him warmly. "I owe you one, Ange!" she called after him as he gave her a wide smile and a casual salute before departing.

Vera retrieved a keycard from her purse and used it to unlock the main entry, leading them down a stark, white hallway. The sharp sound of her heels clicking against the marble echoed as Anthony followed close behind. At the end of the corridor, she unlocked a set of large double doors and stepped into the laboratory, flipping a *Do Not Disturb* sign onto the handle behind them.

Anthony paused as he entered, taking in the room. The high-tech facility was a stark contrast to the ancient artifacts they carried. Stainless-steel tables gleamed under bright LED lights, and state-of-the-art equipment lined the walls. It was a modern sanctuary for unraveling the mysteries of the past.

Vera motioned to the central table and set the hard-shell case down carefully. Anthony joined her, watching as she pulled her hair into a high ponytail and slipped on a pair of white cotton gloves. Her movements were deliberate and precise as she opened the case, removed his Kevlar backpack, and began arranging its contents on the table. The familiar sight of the scrolls, parchments, and limestone cylinders filled him with a mixture of pride and apprehension.

"Anthony," Vera began, her tone serious, "I'll start by saying this. Everything you have here—the scrolls, the accompanying letters, the inks, the leather pouch, even the limestone cylinders—are authentic. The materials, the scripts, and the craftsmanship all date back to the period of Saint Francis. And this parchment here," she held up the weathered document he had always felt was significant, "was undoubtedly intended for you. But there's a problem."

His stomach tightened as Vera sighed, her gloved hands lifting one of the limestone cylinders.

"This cylinder, the one given to you by Benedict, has a wax seal that tested *negative*. While the cylinder itself and its contents are from Saint Francis's time, my analysis shows the seal was broken and reapplied within the last decade. It's the only item in this collection that shows signs of recent tampering."

Anthony's jaw tightened, the revelation striking a nerve. "I've suspected there may have been tampering all along," he admitted, his voice laced with frustration. "While the other two cylinders contained second parchments, this one did not."

Vera nodded. "This cylinder was opened and resealed at least once. The test results leave no doubt." She pointed to the scroll resting inside. "Look here." She indicated a faint indentation. "There's a very distinct impression where another parchment clearly rested."

Anthony's heart sank. "Who could have taken it?" He ran a hand through his hair, his mind racing. "I do find it hard to believe Benedict had anything to do with this. If someone tampered with it, it wasn't him."

"I'm not accusing anyone," Vera assured him, her tone steady.

His eyes widened. "Who could it have been?"

"There's no way to know," she said, shaking her head. "But whoever removed it likely had access to the cylinder before it reached you."

His mind swirled with possibilities, none of them comforting.

"But there's some good news," Vera continued, handing him a translated inventory list. "The third cylinder, the one your family guarded, contains the most crucial information. It includes an inventory of everything Francis prepared and even references the missing letter."

He scanned the list.

Cylinder I – Vatican Custodian

First Scroll: *Looming Danger (Pericula Ventura)*

Cylinder II – Minister General Custodian

Second Scroll: *Instructions for Allegory and Altrix Reference*

Cylinder III – Familia of Antonio Brunelli Custodian

Third Scroll: *Francis's Letter to* Designated *Heir, Antonio Brunelli's Account*

Vera took a deep breath, her voice dropping slightly. "Anthony, as incredible as these artifacts are, they're mere guideposts. This entire collection is designed to guide you toward something far greater. Saint Francis didn't just leave behind these documents, he left a legacy, something he called the *Sacred Order.* That's what this is all pointing to."

Anthony felt the significance of her words like a physical force. "Did Saint Francis describe what's in this *Sacred Order?*" he asked, his voice tinged with urgency.

"He didn't," Vera replied, her tone measured yet serious. "Apparently, that's something he intended only you to discover."

He absorbed her words in silence, the enormity of his role finally crystallizing. His thoughts drifted to his father—the endless conversations they'd had about Saint Francis, the stories that had once seemed like myths but now emerged as pieces of an intricate design. Those late-night discussions in their small den on Riverview Avenue in upstate New York took on new meaning, each memory illuminating another facet of what lay before him.

She gestured to a parchment containing densely written Latin text in a fine, precise hand. "This," she said, "is something I've only partially translated. It's a first-person account of a meeting between Brother Leo—Saint Francis's confessor—and Pope Honorius. It details their discussions about approving Francis's plan shortly before his death. This document was found inside the leather pouch."

Anthony leaned forward as she handed him the parchment. The delicate material felt almost symbolic, as though it carried the burden of the secrets it held. He scanned the text, taking in the depth of the words before carefully placing it back on the table.

"And then there's this," Vera continued, lifting another parchment. "It's an instruction letter meant for the successive ministers general of the Franciscan Order. I haven't fully analyzed it, but there's a directive regarding an allegory embedded

within it, something that might be crucial for you to understand."

"An allegory?" he asked, intrigued.

Vera smiled faintly. "Yes. A hidden—"

"Message or meaning within a work of art," Anthony
nodded, completing her sentence when his knowledge of symbolism and art history kicked in. "Something layered, meant to
be uncovered over time," he murmured.

"Exactly," Vera said, her eyes glinting with appreciation for
his quick understanding. "Your expertise as an artist might be
the key to deciphering it. That's a talent I wish I had."

Anthony studied the parchment more closely, his mind
racing before stepping away from the table. "Vera," he said after
a moment, his voice eager, "I can't tell you how grateful I am
for everything you've done. I would never have gotten this far
without you. You're not just a brilliant analyst, you're a gift."

Vera blushed slightly but maintained her composure.
"Thank you, *mio caro*," she said warmly. "Now, let's keep
the momentum going." Turning back to the table, she picked
up another parchment. "This missing document from the first
cylinder—*Pericula Ventura*—concerns me," she admitted. "Its
title translates to *Looming Danger*, and it might contain information we'll need. But for now, let's focus on *this*."

She handed him a carefully prepared English translation of
a letter thought to be written on behalf of Saint Francis himself.
"This is the letter meant for you, Anthony."

He took the translated document and settled into a nearby
leather chair. She stood behind him, her presence a comforting
anchor. As his eyes fell upon the ancient words now rendered
in English, his hands trembled. This was the moment—a direct
connection across centuries to Saint Francis himself. He read
the words aloud, his voice thick with emotion.

Speak forth thy name, and I shall hearken unto it. Art thou in true spirit born of mine most beloved and faithful companion, Antonio Brunelli? If such be true, then the miracle for which I have beseeched the Lord hath come to pass. Mine eyes behold great tribulations that shall visit the world hence, and I pray thou hast not witnessed such sorrows. My faith in thy bloodline remains unshaken, and I trust that this Divine charge shall not burden thy path but rather that thou shalt embrace the blessed purpose it shall bring unto all God's creation. Perchance thou dost already perceive the profundity of mine endeavor, the particulars of which I dare not commit to parchment lest they fall upon the eyes of others. If mystery yet shrouds these matters, look thou to the tales already told of my works, for in them lies truth. Sacer Ordo shall be revealed when thou findest what I have secreted within the marble vessel.

Anthony's hand moved to his chest, fingers finding the wooden tau cross beneath his shirt. Reading the letter again, his chest tightened with emotion. The mention of disasters in the future resonated with uncomfortable clarity—had Francis somehow foreseen the challenges of their modern world?

"Marble vessel?" he questioned. "Would that be the limestone cylinders we've found?"

"No, there's something more, something bigger," she retorted. "That's what he has called *Sacer Ordo*, or Sacred Order."

Suddenly, Anthony's expression shifted, his eyes lighting up as though a spark had ignited. "Vera," he said, his voice eager, "the word *Altrix* from the second scroll's allegory instructions…could it mean *enrichment*?"

She nodded, intrigued. "Enrichment is one of its meanings, yes. Why do you ask?"

Anthony sprang to his feet, locking eyes with Vera. "Because something clicked. When I was looking at Giotto's frescoes in the Basilica, I had this feeling, this…this inexplicable sense that the stories they depicted held more than just religious significance. And now, this letter from Saint Francis, it confirms that intuition."

Vera's curiosity deepened. "What exactly do you mean?"

"I'm not entirely sure yet," he admitted, grabbing his coat, "but I'd like to get back to Assisi. There's something I have to verify—something important. If I'm right about the connection between the *Altrix* reference and what Francis mentioned about a *sacred order*, I'll be able to decipher the message from all three scrolls."

Vera smiled knowingly. "That works for me. I'll email you the completed translation of the Brother Leo account as soon as I'm done."

"You're a lifesaver, Vera," Anthony said, patting his pocket for his keys. He gave her a grateful nod as he headed for the door.

T

The consequence of their shared quest pressed heavily on Vera, but another thought gnawed at the edge of her mind—she still hadn't contacted Alessandro, and time was slipping away.

CHAPTER 26

The Basilica of Saint Francis, Assisi
5:25 PM

After racing back to Assisi, Anthony left his rental car in the parking lot of Hotel Giotto and made his way to the Basilica. The evening air carried a chill along with the faint aroma of wood burning in distant hearths. The sight of the Basilica standing tall against the fading light stirred something within him—both urgency and respect.

Once inside, he paused to let his eyes adjust in the dimly lit interior. He began studying the frescoes again, this time with the focused intent to uncover any allegories Giotto may have embedded. Moving methodically, he traced each scene with his eyes, absorbing their intricate details.

Slowly, it dawned on him that every fresco was more than a mere depiction of Francis's life. Each was a visual sermon layered with religious symbolism and allegorical references to Christian virtues—faith, humility, poverty, and charity. Together, they formed not just a narrative of Francis's journey but a spiritual guide pointing to the essence of his teachings. Yet, despite their profound beauty and meaning, nothing stood out to Anthony as a clear answer to his quest. He exhaled slowly, before stepping outside into the crisp evening. He wandered the medieval streets surrounding the Basilica, allowing his thoughts to roam freely. The letter from Saint Francis echoed in his mind, urging him to uncover what was hidden.

Returning to the portico, he spotted Massimo sitting serenely on his usual bench. Barefoot and composed, the monk's presence radiated calm. "Antonio! *Buonasera*," he called out warmly. "I had a feeling you might come back today."

"Massimo?" Anthony paused mid-step. "*Buonasera*... What made you think that?"

"Oh, you know..." Massimo gestured vaguely at the evening air. "After you left here this morning, I thought to myself, *That young man is searching for something. And where better to search than here?*" His eyes crinkled with gentle humor.

Anthony dropped onto the bench beside him with a weary sigh. "You're right about the searching part. I've been in Florence all day, chasing leads, trying to make sense of everything. Actually"—he turned to face Massimo—"I could really use your insight on something."

The monk shifted to face him, his expression open and interested. "Tell me what's on your mind, my friend."

"I've been trying to emulate the spirit of St. Francis...not just his actions but his essence. How did he see the world? How did he become so deeply connected to life itself? I've read about him, walked these streets, even stared at Giotto's frescoes for hours, but I feel like I'm still missing something. How do I find his spirit?"

Massimo smiled knowingly. "Antonio, the spirit of San Francesco isn't something you find *out there*. It's something you awaken *within* yourself. His connection to life, to God, wasn't about intellectual understanding. It was about living in harmony with creation, with a heart full of love and humility. Perhaps you're trying too hard to see what can only be felt."

Anthony nodded, absorbing the hermit's words. "I think you're right. Where do I start?"

Massimo leaned forward, his expression thoughtful. "There are two sacred places I would suggest you visit, the Porziuncola and San Damiano. Have you been?"

Anthony shook his head.

"Then you must go. These places hold the essence of Francis's transformation. Go early, before the crowds, and let yourself be still. You may find answers in their silence." The monk reached into his satchel, scribbled the names of the two churches on a scrap of paper, and handed it to Anthony.

"Thank you," Anthony murmured, though his mind was already shifting. "There's something else I'm searching for. Do you know where Francis confronted his father? The actual place where he let go of everything?"

Massimo's eyes lit up with recognition. "Ah, yes! The renunciation of his patrimony, such a pivotal moment in his life." Rising to his feet, he gestured for Anthony to follow.

They crossed the lower plaza, ascending the Basilica's exterior staircase. Massimo took an abrupt left turn, walked toward the Basilica's entrance, and halted in front of the main double doors.

"Here," the monk whispered, his tone reverent.

Anthony's brow furrowed. "Here? I thought it happened in the town square."

"If you ask the scholars, most will tell you the confrontation occurred in the main square, but the legend claims otherwise. It may have started in the town square, but it ended here. After being humiliated and disowned by his father, and confronted by the bishop in the town center, Francesco ran from the square. The crowd, captivated by the unfolding drama, followed him like a procession. It's believed that Francesco deliberately led them to this spot. And here, in a bold and deeply symbolic act, he stripped himself of all his garments, casting aside not only his material possessions but the very identity tied to his father's wealth and expectations. It was a public spectacle, yes, but for Francesco, it was a moment of liberation, an outward expression of his inward transformation."

"And why did Francis do this? Why would he give up everything his father provided him?" Anthony asked.

Massimo gazed at the Basilica's façade for a moment. "You see, Antonio, Francesco wasn't just rejecting wealth. He was choosing something far more precious. His father, Pietro, was a wealthy cloth merchant who wanted Francesco to follow in his footsteps, to pursue profit and prestige. But Francesco had experienced something profound during his imprisonment in Perugia and his long illness afterward. He began to see how the pursuit of wealth had hardened people's hearts, including his own father's."

He leaned forward, his voice softening. "The final break came when Francesco took expensive cloth from his father's shop and sold it to rebuild the church of San Damiano. His father was furious about the stolen goods but also that Francesco was rejecting everything he believed made a man worthy—status, wealth, reputation. But Francesco…he had discovered that true worth lay in something else entirely, that it begins with one's relationship with God. Not a superficial relationship but a true, deep, and personal relationship, one that takes work and sacrifice to build. And in that moment of stripping naked, he wasn't just rejecting his inheritance—he was declaring that he would be clothed only in God's grace, that he would be a son only to his heavenly Father. It was a complete surrender of his old identity to embrace a new one."

"I see that now. It's making more sense," Anthony replied in a somber tone. "I've read a lot of this, but the way you explain it really helps me see how it was for Francis in those days."

"What his father saw as madness, Francesco understood as perfect freedom. And you know what's remarkable? Years later, many of the same wealthy young men who had once mocked him became his most devoted followers. They too discovered that in giving up everything, they gained something far greater."

Upon hearing those words, Anthony looked down at his friend's bare feet, feeling his sacrifice.

Massimo's eyes sparkled. "And back to the renunciation. You know, I've reenacted this moment several times over the years," he added with a smirk. "It's an incredibly humbling experience, standing exposed beneath the open sky, vulnerable in every sense. Of course, the authorities don't quite see it the same way. I've been arrested twice for it." He chuckled, though his admiration for the act remained evident. "But for Francesco, this wasn't about self-glorification. It was an act of surrender, of freeing himself from every worldly tie so that he could find complete reverence. For him, this place wasn't just symbolic— it was sacred."

As Massimo spoke, Anthony found himself imagining the scene vividly. Francis, with a growing throng of townsfolk trailing behind him, arriving at this very site. Stripped of his fine garments, standing bare before the crowd, vulnerable yet resolute, a man shedding not just his clothing but the unyielding grip of an entire life lived in privilege.

Massimo's expression grew solemn. "Years later, Francesco made it known to his brothers that he wished to be laid to rest here at the Hill of Hell. I mentioned that to you before. This place had borne witness to so much death, a site of mass executions and unthinkable suffering.

"By choosing this place for his resting place, Francesco honored those persecuted souls, transforming a place of despair into one of hope and renewal. He saw this ground as fertile soil for a new beginning. After Francesco's passing, Brother Leo and the other Franciscan brothers knew that this very site would become the entrance to something extraordinary—a great church that would bear his name. It would be a place where all who entered could feel enriched, inspired, and uplifted by the steps Francesco took to embrace the Divine within himself." The monk gestured toward the structure. "When the Basilica was completed, Francesco's remains were transported here. And just as he'd envisioned, the Hill of Hell became the Hill of Paradise."

As the hermit's words faded into the quiet of the evening, Anthony's gaze dropped to the stone slab where they stood. Intricate Latin carvings adorned its surface, their ancient etchings glinting faintly in the fading light. But one word made him freeze mid-breath.

ALTRIX

His heart hammered against his ribs as recognition blazed through him. "It can't be," he murmured, fighting to keep his voice steady.

Massimo looked at Anthony with wonder. "What is it?"

"Oh, nothing," Anthony said quickly, careful to mask the tremor of excitement in his voice.

His thoughts raced as he pieced together the significance of the word beneath him. He clenched his fist in triumph, as if solving a riddle that had eluded him for years.

"Massimo," he said, his voice taut with carefully controlled urgency, "how soon after Francis's death was the Basilica constructed?"

"Almost immediately," Massimo responded. "He passed in 1226, and within two years, he was canonized. The Basilica's construction began the very next day, overseen by Brother Leo himself. Virtually everything you see here has remained unchanged since then."

Anthony exhaled sharply, a smile breaking across his face. "That's exactly what I was hoping to hear."

T

Walking back to Hotel Giotto, Anthony's mind drifted to his father. The wind cut through his coat, but the cold wasn't what made him shiver. He stepped into an alcove along the medieval street and pulled out his phone to call Rick, who had just been liaising with the police.

"They found your dad's wallet," Rick said, his voice tight, "in a dumpster behind that abandoned garage. Everything was still inside—credit cards, driver's license, even an old family photo." He paused, letting the implication sink in. "The leather was weather-damaged, like it had been there for days."

Anthony's silence spoke volumes. His father would never willingly part with his wallet.

"Look, I know you're overwhelmed," Rick continued. "But we can't give up hope. Captain Rossi has his best people on this. They're working around the clock."

"Rick, we need to know what happened to him," Anthony pled, watching his breath form clouds in the cold air. "My mother's beside herself. She deserves to know what happened to him. We all do. Even if…even if it's not what we want to hear."

CHAPTER **27**

The soft glow of a desk lamp bathed Vera's office in a warm light. Outside, dusk pressed against the windows, deepening the stillness within. Her fingers moved steadily across the keyboard, finalizing the email to Anthony. Attached was the completed translation of Brother Leo's document, the fullness of its revelations heavy in her thoughts.

The words on the screen seemed to pulse with significance, drawing her further into the tangle of mysteries she was unraveling. Beside her, a bowl of pasta carbonara ordered hours earlier, sat untouched. She noticed it only when the faint aroma of pancetta and pecorino Romano cheese broke through her concentration. With a distracted sigh, she pushed it aside and leaned back in her chair, her gaze falling on the shelves of books lining the walls.

As she reached for the Latin text of the allegory, her phone's chime pierced the quiet. She fumbled through her purse, pulling it out just as the screen lit with a familiar name—Father Alessandro.

"Vera, I'm glad you finally picked up. Why haven't you returned my calls?"

Caught off guard, she hesitated, searching for the right words. "Well, Father, I've been immersed in this assignment.

It's been far more complicated than I initially imagined and taking twice as long."

A pause followed. When Alessandro spoke again, his annoyance was unmistakable. "Vera, this is the fourth time I've called you."

She closed her eyes briefly, exhaling through her nose. "You're right. There's no excuse for not calling back. I had planned to reach out later this evening."

"I need to know what's happening," he pressed. "I assume Brunelli has recovered all the documents by now?"

Vera straightened in her chair, choosing her words carefully. "Father, I don't think this is a conversation we should have over the phone."

Alessandro's sigh carried through the line. "Then we need to meet. I'm growing increasingly anxious about this. I'll also need to review copies of all the original documents."

"Of course," she responded. "But I'm still working on the translations. As you know, Father, these things take time. You understand better than anyone how precise this work has to be."

The line fell silent, tension stretching through the pause. Finally, Alessandro's voice returned, cooler but insistent. "Listen, tomorrow, I have business to attend to near Pompeii. I'll call you once I'm finished, and we'll arrange a time and place to meet. I don't care if the translations are incomplete. I need an update."

From his end of the line, Vera caught the faint toll of church bells, their somber tones amplifying the unease coiling through her.

"Very well," she replied softly. "I'll wait for your call."

The call ended, and its unsettling echo lingered in the quiet of her office. She stared at the phone, her fingers curling around it as though holding it tighter could ground her racing thoughts. Alessandro's insistence felt more than urgent—it felt calculated, as if he were steering the unfolding events toward a purpose she couldn't yet discern. She exhaled sharply, forcing herself to focus on the glowing Latin and ancient Italian text before her, but her resolve wavered.

What is Alessandro's true motive? she thought.

The question haunted her, its relentless pressure growing with every passing second. She grabbed her notebook and began jotting down the threads she needed to unravel. One thing was clear—she had to uncover Alessandro's intentions before it was too late.

CHAPTER **28**

Hotel Giotto, Assisi
6:25 PM

Back in his hotel room, Anthony powered up his laptop and immediately noticed Vera's email in his inbox. The subject line read, *Brother Leo's Account – Full Translation.* His hand trembled slightly as he clicked to open the message and its attachment.

Vera's note accompanied the document:

Hi Anthony—

I will be ready to share more specific details about the contents of the documents with you tomorrow. Plan to arrive at my office at the Laurentian any time after noon. Attached is the first-person account written by Brother Leo that I told you about. It vividly describes his meeting with Pope Honorius just before Francis's death. The details are extraordinary and filled with possible clues, so read carefully. As you'll see, Honorius was residing at the Archbasilica of St. John Lateran in Rome at the time. (Saint Peter's, as we know it, wasn't yet constructed.)

Settling into the desk chair, Anthony opened the file. The words drew him in immediately.

Translation of Brother Leo's Account:

After three days' journey from Assisi, I came unto the Archbasilica of Saint John Lateran in Rome. The morning light streamed across San Giovanni Square as I approached the grand entrance, where the scent of dew mingled with holy incense wafting from the nearby chapels. Marking my Franciscan habit and tonsure, many folk greeted me warmly, calling me "Brother." Their gentle words strengthened my resolve before the mighty wooden doors. Within, Pietro Capocci, the cardinal nephew of Pope Honorius, greeted me with a familiar smile that eased my weary spirit.

"Brother Leo, thou art welcome! His Holiness awaits thee with great eagerness. Pray, follow me."

We traversed the maze of corridors leading to the Apostolic Palace. Guards in polished armor stood like stone wardens in the dimly lit halls, stepping aside in silence as we passed. At last, we entered the chamber where Pope Honorius awaited—the same chamber where Brother Francis and I had stood years past, seeking approval for our Holy Order. The memory filled me with both pride and sorrow, knowing Francis's health now failed.

The vast chamber lay in shadow, with flickering candlelight dancing across the marble walls. Honorius sat elevated upon a cushioned throne, his weathered face bearing the significance of his office beneath the papal crown. His deep-set eyes, still sharp despite his advanced years, softened upon beholding me.

"Brother Leo," said he warmly, "it is an honor to see thee again. Didst thou journey all the way from Assisi on foot?"

"Indeed, Your Holiness," I answered, bowing. "And I am deeply grateful for thine audience."

"How fares my dear friend, Brother Francis?" he asked, leaning forward with visible concern.

I lowered mine eyes. "He is not well. Sister Death lingers near, and his time on this earth grows short."

Honorius's face darkened, the candlelight deepening the creases of worry. "Then why art thou here, Leo? Should thou not be at his side?"

"It was Francis who sent me," I explained. "He entrusted me with a message for thee alone."

The pope dismissed the other clergy with a wave of his hand, leaving us in solemn privacy.

Anthony felt himself being pulled deeper into the narrative, each word connecting him more acutely to the historical magnitude of his task.

When Honorius beckoned, I drew nearer and took my seat beside him. From my satchel, I brought forth two letters. The first, addressed to His Holiness, was Francis's final written testament. Honorius read a portion of it aloud, his voice steady yet touched with emotion:

"Thy Most Holy Father, Pope Honorius III, I believe my final earthly days draw near. Accept this as my written

testament. Thou art, Most Holy Father, my sole hope in fulfilling the command I received from the Most High."

The second letter, His Holiness read in silence. As Honorius's eyes moved across the parchment, his countenance shifted like shadows in firelight. Wonder bloomed into reverence before settling into profound sorrow. Tears glistened in his eyes as he folded the letter and returned it unto me.

"Extraordinary," he murmured. "Francis is truly a disciple of Christ. But his vision… Leo, it is both a gift and a burden. There are forces rising within the Church—dark forces—that seek to destroy men like Francis and any who share his truths."

Honorius spoke of the Inquisition, his voice heavy with condemnation of its cruelty and grief over its perversion of Christ's teachings. "These are the same forces that crucified our Lord," he said gravely. "They feel threatened by the truth, for the truth dismantles their power."

He questioned me further about the Sacred Order Francis had entrusted unto us, but I revealed only what Francis permitted: the roles of the custodians and the eventual revelation to a chosen heir. Honorius nodded, his face etched with solemn understanding.

Before our meeting ended, I showed unto him the marble vessel and three limestone cylinders, explaining their purpose.

He smiled faintly and placed his weathered hand upon my shoulder. "Leo," said he, "ensure that those who guard these holy relics understand their sacred duty. The future of our faith may depend upon it."

Anthony exhaled deeply, his chest tight with emotion. The *Sacred Order* was no longer an abstract concept but tangible, sanctified, and undeniably bound to his family's legacy.

The sharp ring of the hotel phone shattered his contemplation. Still caught in the importance of what he had just read, he stared at it for three rings before finally lifting the receiver.

"Hello?"

"Anthony, it's Lara," the familiar voice said. "You have a visitor here. She's on her way up to your room."

"A visitor? Who is it? Vera?"

"No," Lara said, her voice taut with caution. "She didn't give her name, but she made it sound like you were expecting her. And…well, I have to say, her appearance is a bit off-putting."

"What do you mean?" Anthony asked, unease creeping into his voice.

"She's wearing a mink coat, red high heels, and I doubt much else," Lara replied, her tone dripping with sarcasm. "You'll see what I mean. If you need anything"—she paused deliberately—"the front desk number is by the phone."

Anthony set the phone down slowly, a chill spreading across his skin. The revelations from Brother Leo's account still whirled in his mind, but now they tangled with an uneasy anticipation. Whoever was climbing the stairs to his room had arrived at a pivotal moment—and he doubted it was a coincidence.

CHAPTER **29**

San Pietro in Vincoli, Rome
6:45 PM

Richard stood at the threshold of San Pietro in Vincoli—Saint Peter in Chains—gazing at the ancient façade as twilight set on the Eternal City.

The Basilica's cream-colored walls rose from the summit of Oppian Hill, a quarter mile north of the Colosseum, where ages of pilgrims had climbed the steep steps to reach its portico. The church's distinctive colonnade of five rounded arches stretched across the entrance, their weathered capitals supporting the upper story where rectangular windows glowed softly against the night sky. En route, Richard had passed the Torre dei Borgia two blocks away, an original medieval bell tower whose dark silhouette was now barely visible in the darkness. Only the streetlamps illuminated its weathered terracotta surface, a fitting shroud for the notorious family whose name it bore. Below the Basilica, the ruins of the Forum stretched westward into darkness.

The instructions given to him by the cowled monk echoed in his mind, urging him forward. With a deep breath that tasted of incense and age-old stone, Richard pushed open the heavy wooden doors and stepped inside.

The Basilica's interior commanded a somber grandeur, its double row of ancient Roman columns marching down the nave like pale sentinels. Even at this late hour, the white walls and barrel-vaulted ceiling seemed to capture and magnify what little light remained, while overhead, the magnificent, frescoed ceiling depicted scenes of glory in rich golds and vermilions. Despite the church's name and history, the space felt unexpectedly airy and luminous, with its high clerestory windows and polished marble floor reflecting the last remnants of daylight.

At the heart of the sanctuary, encased beneath the main altar, lay the relic that gave the Basilica its name—the chains that once bound Saint Peter during his imprisonment in Jerusalem. The black iron links seemed to contrast sharply with the church's bright interior, as if to emphasize the darkness of persecution against the triumph of faith. Struck by how this bright, classical space housed such dark memories, Richard brushed his fingers over the cool glass of the reliquary.

The chains bore silent witness to Peter's journey from prisoner to martyr. Divine intervention had freed him from these chains in Jerusalem, but Rome would ultimately claim his life. During Nero's reign, as the emperor desperately sought scapegoats for the great fire that had devastated the city's urban core, the Christians became his target. Among them, Peter. The apostle faced death by crucifixion. After enduring brutal torture at the hands of the Romans, he made his final act of humility, requesting to be crucified upside down, deeming himself unworthy to die in the same manner as his Savior. Iron spikes were driven through his wrists and ankles, fastening him to the wooden cross.

Peter's remains were interred near Nero's Circus, on a modest hill that would later become known as Vatican Hill. In 1942, Vatican archaeologists unearthed Peter's tomb beneath the original floor of Saint Peter's Basilica. His bones lay alongside fragments of regal garments in shades of purple and gold. Etched into the ancient stone were raw inscriptions in Greek that confirmed the site's sacred significance: *Petros Eni.* (Peter is Here.)

A distant creak of ancient wood pulled Richard back to the present. He continued as instructed, his footsteps whispering against worn marble as he walked the perimeter of the Basilica. Every shadow-filled corner revealed only emptiness. The monk's instructions were precise, and Richard dared not deviate. Finally, he entered the side chapel dedicated to St. Sebastian, where the air hung thick with the sweet musk of aging wood.

Stepping over the red velvet cordon blocking entry to the stone altar, Richard lowered himself to the ground and leaned back against the cool wall, using a nearby oak side table for cover. The wood's polished surface reflected candlelight in warm ripples. He sat motionless in the darkness as the sacristan made his final rounds, extinguishing each candle with efficiency. His footsteps echoed sharply against the marble floor, the sound reverberating through the Basilica's vast interior. Then came the heavy groan of the main doors, followed by the unmistakable sound of an iron lock sliding into place with bone-deep finality. In the sudden stillness, Richard found himself truly alone and surrounded by centuries of martyrs and their silent witness.

Reaching into his pocket, he retrieved the sheet of instructions and shone the light from his phone over the text. The monk's handwriting was meticulous, almost mechanical, its precision a reflection of the significance of what was to come.

Remain still for 30 minutes after the church closes. Then, walk down the right-side aisle, parallel to the main altar. At the front of the church, you will see an archway. Enter the archway and open the door directly to your left. It will lead you to the basement.

When the distant clangor of church bells marked that the allotted time had passed, Richard rose and followed the directions. Each step echoed ominously as he made his way down the aisle. The archway loomed ahead, its heavy stone frame radiating an almost imperceptible chill that seemed to reach for him with ghostly fingers. He found the door to the left, its iron handle cold and unyielding, but it creaked open under his grip.

The air grew heavier as he descended the narrow staircase into the basement, his phone's flashlight casting long, wavering beams across the stone walls. The musty scent of damp stone and ancient decay permeated the space, assaulting his senses. The basement was vast, its high ceilings and scattered debris— a mix of broken pews and forgotten statues—lending it the appearance of an abandoned crypt.

Walk straight across the entire length of the room. There will be an opening on the right. Enter that room and you will see a large fresco on the opposite wall. In the center, you will see a door within the fresco. There's an actual keyhole in the painted door.

The fresco was breathtaking even in the dim light. A vibrant tableau of divine and infernal imagery, it depicted saints in heavenly glory above, while below, twisted forms writhed in a hellish landscape. At the center of the fresco, the painted door almost seemed to glow, its details rendered with uncanny realism. Gilt highlights caught his light, creating the illusion of movement in the painted figures that surrounded it.

He located the first keyhole hidden within the painted door and inserted the key with his left hand. Then, stretching his right arm outward, he found the second keyhole embedded in the fresco's intricate border. Both keys slid into place with a soft click that seemed to reverberate through his bones.

Turn both keys simultaneously: the left clockwise, the right counterclockwise.

As he complied, the stone around him shuddered. A deep rumble vibrated through the walls like the awakening of some ancient beast. The grinding sound of stone against stone filled the chamber as centuries of dust rained down from above. Slowly, inexorably, the painted door into darkness shifted inward, revealing a narrow staircase spiraling deeper into the earth.

A blast of cold air hit him as he descended, the chill penetrating his coat and settling into the surface of his skin like winter frost. The scent of mildew and ancient parchment grew stronger, as did the faint metallic tang of damp stone and something else, something older and more primal. The stairs seemed to stretch endlessly, coiling downward like a serpent, each step taking him farther from the world he knew.

The beam of his light found the chamber floor at last but failed to make sense of what lay before him. Like a mouth opened wide, the space yawned beyond his light's reach, consuming every ray in its bottomless throat. The air hung dense and oppressive, each inhalation an effort against the unyielding grip of accumulated evil that seemed to permeate the very stone.

He located a dim overhead light, which flickered briefly before it turned on. Columns carved from the living rock stood tall, their surfaces etched with symbols that seemed to shift and change when viewed directly. Wooden shelves lined the walls, sagging under the sheer mass of countless scrolls and tomes, their pages yellowed with age and secrets. The very air seemed to pulse with forbidden knowledge.

And at the center of it all, bathed in a shaft of sickly light that had no visible source, stood a stone pedestal. Upon it lay a single object shrouded in velvet the color of dried blood. The fabric rippled slightly in air that should have been still, as if whatever lay beneath still lived and breathed.

Richard stood within the Bunker of Sin.

Chapter **30**

A series of rapid knocks echoed against the quiet stillness of Anthony's hotel room. Though Lara had called to warn him about an unexpected visitor, the sound still made him flinch. Curious, he moved toward the door and squinted through the peephole to find a striking woman with bold cherry-red lipstick standing on the other side. Her expression was unreadable, her crystal-blue eyes sharp and unflinching beneath perfectly arched brows.

She knocked again, her manicured hand resting on her hip with calculated patience as though she had all the time in the world.

Anthony hesitated, his muscles tensing instinctively. "Who's there?" he asked through the closed door.

"I have an important request to deliver, Mr. Brunelli," the woman responded. "It's urgent."

Curiosity warred with unease as he unlocked the door, cracking it open just enough to meet her gaze. His focus was immediately drawn to her polished appearance—bare legs that led to red high heels, a luxurious black fur coat draped to her knees, and a confident stance that demanded attention. The scent of expensive perfume—ginger with hints of jasmine—wafted through the gap.

"Who are you, and what's this about?" he asked, his hand still gripping the doorframe, knuckles white with tension.

The woman's smile was deliberate, almost disarming. "My name is Katarina," she said smoothly, her accent laced with Eastern European undertones. The way she pronounced her name—*Ka-ta-ree-na*—carried a musical quality that seemed practiced for effect.

Anthony's unease deepened, but her mention of an urgent request had piqued his interest. "And how do you know my name?"

Katarina's smile grew as she tilted her head slightly. "I've been in correspondence with Mr. Meisel," she said, her tone effortlessly seductive. "He informed me of your whereabouts. May I come in?"

At the mention of his art dealer's name, Anthony's apprehension gave way to reluctant curiosity. Against his better judgment, he stepped aside and allowed her into the room.

Katarina moved with grace, her fur coat sweeping the air as she entered. The suite's warm lighting caught the diamonds at her ears as she set a large designer handbag on the coffee table before lowering herself onto the edge of the antique couch. Her presence seemed to fill the room, her crystal-blue eyes flickering with unspoken intent as she took in Anthony's open laptop and notepad.

"You've been in touch with Louis and he sent you to me?" Anthony asked, skepticism evident in his voice. He remained near the closed door, one hand absently touching the solid brass handle.

"Indeed," she replied, crossing her long legs. "Although I must admit, I had to convince him. He wasn't eager to share your location, but he eventually relented."

Anthony moved to stand in front of the desk, his hands clasped behind his back. The protective stance wasn't lost on

Katarina, whose smile flickered briefly. Anthony knew Louis wouldn't have given up his whereabouts without good reason. He'd always been fiercely protective of Anthony since taking a chance on representing his work in the early 1990s. Their relationship transcended business, forged through years of trust and shared ambition. The only explanation Anthony could imagine was that Louis saw this as another opportunity to change his mind about accepting that commission.

"Can I offer you something to drink?" he asked, keeping his tone even while studying her reflection in the room's gilt-framed mirror.

"I'll pass," Katarina replied, her lips curling into a small smile. "I'll get straight to the point. I work for Bishop Giorgio Montefusco, a man with impeccable taste and a discerning eye for fine art. He oversees the largest private collection of religious artwork in Bavaria. Recently, he became quite taken with your photorealistic style, especially your Vatican commission."

Anthony raised a brow, leaning slightly against the edge of the desk. The wood creaked beneath him.

"The bishop would like to commission your work," she continued, her voice smooth. "But to our dismay, Mr. Meisel informed us you declined our initial offer."

Anthony frowned, his fingers drumming against the desk's worn surface. "The timing isn't ideal," he said, glancing meaningfully at his computer screen. "Right now, I'm in the middle of a significant project."

Katarina uncrossed her legs, standing fluidly and moving closer. The floorboards whispered beneath her heels as her tone remained composed, though a hint of insistence crept into her words. "That's precisely why I'm here, Mr. Brunelli. The bishop is willing to increase his offer to one million US dollars."

Despite his best efforts, Anthony couldn't mask his surprise. "A million?" he echoed, his hand stilling on the desk.

Katarina nodded, her expression confident. "For a master-piece depicting his palace in Bavaria, to be unveiled at the Art Monaco exhibition in April. It would be a crowning achieve-ment, Mr. Brunelli."

Anthony let out a slow breath, pacing slightly as he consid-ered her words. The offer was tempting—more than tempting—but something in her eagerness set off warning bells. "That's an incredibly generous offer," he admitted, "but I'm afraid it doesn't change my current commitments."

Katarina's eyes flashed with determination as she removed her fur coat, revealing a sleek black cocktail dress. She draped the coat over the arm of a nearby chair before returning to the couch, the leather cushions sighing beneath her. "I see," she said, a note of challenge in her tone. "Perhaps I will take a drink after all."

Anthony hesitated, his eyes narrowing slightly. The mini-bar stood in the corner, its crystal decanters catching the warm light. Offering her a drink now felt like surrendering ground in a game he hadn't agreed to play. Still, his manners wouldn't let him refuse outright. Suppressing a sigh, he moved toward the bar, each step deliberate.

"Red wine or Napoleon brandy?" he asked, his voice clipped.

"What label do you have?" she asked, her eyes following his movements.

He lifted a bottle, examining it in the light. "Brunello di Montalcino."

"Brunello is wonderful," she purred. "What's the year?"

"2010."

Katarina's smile widened. "Ah, an exceptional crop. I'll take the wine."

As Anthony uncorked the bottle, the *pop* echoing in the room's tension, Katarina leaned back on the couch, her gaze fixed on him. The space seemed to shrink around her presence, the air charged with unspoken intention. He poured the ruby liquid into a crystal glass, the stream catching the light like liquid garnets. As he handed it to her, his eyes inadvertently caught the shimmer of her dress as she shifted, her figure every bit as striking as her tone suggested. He frowned but said nothing, choosing instead to focus on maintaining professional distance.

"So, Mr. Brunelli," Katarina said, taking a small sip of the wine, her lipstick leaving a perfect crescent on the rim. "What current project is more important than the bishop's offer?"

"I'm afraid that's confidential." His voice carried a firmness that hadn't been there before.

Katarina's painted lips curved into a smile, but there was no warmth in it. She placed the glass down with a deliberate *clink* against the marble side table. "Surely there must be something I can do to make you reconsider." Without waiting for his response, she reached up to her hair, removing several bobby pins. Thick blonde curls tumbled down her shoulders, catching the dim light as she ran her fingers through them and spread them apart with theatrical grace.

"Katarina, I appreciate the offer," Anthony said, his voice definite as he took another step back, "but I—"

"Before you decide," she interrupted, her honeyed words masking steel beneath, "there's more. In addition to the million dollars, we've arranged for a paid board seat at a prestigious Italian fashion house. A position most would envy."

Anthony stood abruptly, his patience fraying. The chair scraped against the floor with a harsh sound. "I'm flattered, truly, but I'm not sure why you're so determined. I'm not the only photorealist out there. There are others, equally talented, who I'd be happy to recommend."

Katarina rose to her feet. "Shhh," she murmured, placing a finger over his lips. The scent of ginger grew stronger. "Take this offer, love, and you'll never have to worry again."

He stepped back, unsettled by her proximity. "I'm sorry, Katarina. You're very persuasive, but my answer is no. The timing simply isn't right."

Her expression darkened slightly, though she maintained her composure. Slowly, she sat back down on the couch, crossing her legs meticulously. She picked up the wine glass again, taking another slow sip as her crystal-blue eyes stayed locked on his.

A clock somewhere in the room ticked away the heavy seconds.

When she set the glass down, she stood and approached him once more, her steps slow and deliberate. Her eyes glimmered, not with seduction but with something sharper, more calculating. "You're a difficult man to persuade, Anthony," she said softly, letting his first name linger in the air between them.

"You're actually not the first to tell me that," he replied with a forced laugh, though unease crept into his voice.

He held her coat out to her, but she ignored it, draping it over the chair herself.

Katarina leaned closer, her perfume heavy in the air.

Anthony stepped back instinctively, his knees hitting the loveseat, leaving him no room to retreat.

She trailed a fingertip down his sleeve, her voice dropping to a hum. "You're an artist. Surely you appreciate beauty in all its forms. I've seen your work. It's breathtaking…so meticulous, so passionate. Just say yes, Anthony, and you'll never have to worry again."

Anthony's heart raced against his ribs, but his instincts screamed that this wasn't seduction—it was control cloaked in temptation. His hands trembled slightly as he gently but firmly pushed her away. "Katarina," he said, his voice shaking slightly but resolute, "this isn't going to work. Please, stop."

For a moment, she froze in the disbelief flashing in her eyes. Then her expression hardened, the mask of charm cracking to reveal cold fury beneath. The veneer of allure fell away completely, leaving only calculation and anger. "You're making a mistake," she said, her voice icy as a Bavarian winter. "You could have had everything."

"I'm sorry, but this isn't who I am. Now, if you'll excuse me, I have work to do." He gestured toward the door, his pragmatism asserting itself.

Katarina held his gaze for a long moment before slipping her coat back on, her movements sharp with suppressed anger. As she turned to leave, she paused at the door and glanced back over her shoulder. The warm hotel lighting caught her profile, turning it masklike and severe. "American arrogance is so… *unattractive*," she said, her tone venomous. "Remember this moment, Mr. Brunelli. You'll regret it."

The door clicked shut with quiet finality, leaving Anthony alone in an oppressive silence. He exhaled heavily, his hands trembling as he ran them through his hair. The half-read email from Vera seemed to watch him from the screen as he crossed to the window, looking down at the plaza below. He had done the right thing, but a nagging feeling told him that this encounter was just the beginning.

T

In the dim interior of a black Mercedes sedan, Katarina sat rigid in the passenger seat, her anger as profound as the darkness beyond the tinted windows. Enzo Nobili glanced at her from the driver's seat with a smirk that betrayed his amusement of her barely contained fury. The dashboard clock cast a pale green glow across their features.

"He rejected you?" Enzo asked, his tone laced with mock surprise. His fingers drummed against the leather steering wheel.

Katarina's jaw tightened, a muscle twitching beneath her perfect makeup. "I tried everything. The money, the board seat…myself. And still, nothing."

Enzo let out a low, dark chuckle. "Well, well. The great Katarina Rocca turned down by an American painter? That's a first."

"*Statte zitto!*" she snapped, her voice like a whip in the confined space. "You don't understand. This was supposed to be easy."

Enzo smirked, his grip tightening on the steering wheel until his knuckles showed white. "Relax, Katarina. He'll regret it soon enough. Next time, we won't bother playing nice."

Katarina's lips lifted into a cold smile, her reflection ghost-like in the window. "You're right. Our superiors will make sure of it."

Enzo nodded, his grin turning predatory in the dashboard's glow. "Good. Because he has no idea what's coming."

The Mercedes melded into the shadows of the medieval streets, its black paint reflecting the glow of centuries-old lanterns. In the distance, the Basilica of Saint Francis rose against the starlit sky, a reminder that in Assisi, even saints had enemies. And tonight, Anthony Brunelli had made unforgiving ones.

CHAPTER 31

San Pietro in Vincoli, Rome
8:25 PM

Richard's attention turned to the walls of the sub-terranean chamber—or rather, what covered them. Towering shelves lined every surface, bowing under countless volumes. Manuscripts and scrolls filled each nook, spines split, their pages yellowed by time. This was no ordinary hidden library—it was a hidden archive, a repository of the Church's darkest truths.

He approached the nearest shelf with hesitancy. The leather binding felt warm beneath his fingers, as if the secrets within still burned. He selected a volume, its mass settling into his palms like a confession seeking absolution. The pages spoke of scandal after scandal, each meticulously documented. Noble families purchasing salvation, gold exchanged for absolution, dissenting voices silenced under the banner of divine authority. With each revelation, unease coiled tighter in Richard's throat.

One tome detailed the Inquisition's reign of terror, its pages seeming to echo with recorded screams. Another exposed the Church's maze of political intrigue—sacred alliances forged and shattered, leaving trails of innocent blood. Among them, a scientific manuscript bore Copernicus's signature, its heliocentric theory preserved in defiant ink. Beside it lay Christopher Columbus's personal diary, its entries revealing the savage truth of his New World conquests. These weren't just documents—they were history's buried bones. The crushing magnitude of history pressed down on him with each turning page.

Richard turned back to the center of the room and the stone pedestal shrouded in velvet cloth. Lifting the cloth, he revealed a bound, crimson-dyed leather manifesto. Its title stood stark against the cover: *Ramorosso*.

The name struck him like a physical blow. *Ramorosso*—the whispered enigma. A clandestine group spoken of in hushed tones, whose existence the Church still denied. They were history's shadow puppeteers, architects of chaos and power. Richard's fingers trembled as he opened the volume, cautious of its brittle pages.

Within lay an intricate web of confessions, acts of brutality cloaked in justification. The pages chronicled assassinations, conspiracies, and the strategic manipulation of faith to cement control. It wasn't just a record but a blueprint, a guide to wielding sin as a weapon for domination.

As he skipped through to the manifesto's end, he discovered a tucked parchment. Its frayed edges and faded ink bore the title that made his heart stop, Filius Brunelli. His breath quickened as he studied the delicate sheet. Though written in ancient Italian dialect, the message was clear. The Brunelli bloodline carried a purpose that someone was attempting to hide. Richard carefully returned the parchment to the manifesto before sliding it into his satchel, its crimson cover vanishing into darkness.

As dawn approached, he noticed a faint outline beneath a dust-covered stone near the base of the stairs. With careful pressure, the slab shifted, revealing a hidden trapdoor.

Richard peered into darkness, his flashlight cutting through stale air rising from below. The chamber beneath was smaller, more confined. Knowing time pressed against him, he secured the trapdoor and began his ascent.

Emerging into the main sanctuary, he found the space bathed in pale morning light. Michelangelo's masterwork dominated the central alcove—Moses seated between two classical columns, flanked by standing figures in their own shell-topped niches. Following the monk's instructions, Richard slipped behind the massive marble throne, into the shadowed recess where the statue met the wall. The cramped space barely accommodated him, cold stone pressing against his back.

Through the narrow gap between Moses's draped arm and the niche wall, Richard watched dawn's light filter through stained glass. He clutched his satchel tight against his chest, conscious of its explosive contents. The statue's presence loomed above him, Moses's stern profile and flowing beard carved with such lifelike intensity that Richard could almost feel the patriarch's judgment weighing upon him.

He remained motionless in his marble hiding place, the sculptured folds of Moses's robe concealing him from view. Above, the figure's piercing gaze seemed to hold both warning and protection, a silent custodian guarding yet another of the Church's mounting secrets.

CHAPTER **32**

Hotel Giotto, Assisi
6:05 AM

Lara glanced up from her computer screen as Anthony approached the front desk. "You're up rather early," she remarked, her tone light despite the worried look on her face.

Anthony attempted a smile and held up a folded sheet of paper. "I'm going to grab some breakfast downstairs, then I've got a long day ahead of me. There are two churches Massimo suggested I visit today, the Porziuncola and San Damiano. After that, I'll be heading back to Florence to handle things with Vera."

Lara nodded, studying his face. "Anthony, wait…before you go… Is everything all right? You seem like something is bothering you."

Anthony paused, shifting his stance. He was aware of the dark circles under his eyes and that his movements were stiff with more than just fatigue. His reflection in the mirror that morning portrayed a changed man. What he should tell her though… On one hand, he wanted to share more with Lara. On the other, he didn't want to drag her into his drama. Yet it was hard for him to keep things inside. "You ever get the feeling something's not quite right but can't put your finger on why?"

"Sure, I do…quite often actually. Prime example, like with that woman last night?" Lara ventured, seizing the opening. "I didn't see her leave."

Anthony stiffened before meeting her eyes, masking his discomfort with a hollow chuckle. "Her? She's not who you think she is."

"And who exactly *was* she?"

He raked his fingers through his hair, exhaling. "She claimed to represent an art collector—a bishop, if you can believe it. Said he wanted to commission me for a major piece."

"A bishop?" Lara's voice dripped with skepticism. "That's…unexpected."

"Tell me about it," he muttered, now leaning against the counter. His posture eased slightly. "The whole thing felt wrong from the start. They wanted a painting for some event in Monaco, but something about it wasn't right."

"Are you considering it? Sounds like your kind of opportunity."

"The money was tempting, very tempting. But they need it in eight weeks, and with everything here and in Florence… It's impossible." The strain of juggling too many responsibilities was evident in his voice.

Lara's expression softened. "Sounds like the right decision. You've got a lot on your plate."

Something in her understanding expression brought him momentary peace. "Yeah, you're right," he whispered. "I guess I do."

Morning sunlight streamed through the lobby's tall windows. The silence between them felt comfortable yet charged with things unsaid.

Anthony pushed away from the counter, managing a genuine, if tired, smile. "Thanks, Lara. I mean it."

"Anytime," she replied steadily.

T

Something was different about him this morning. His normally composed demeanor carried an unfamiliar edge. Lara had wanted to reach out to him while they spoke, to offer more than just reassurance, but held back and then watched him disappear down the corridor. His confident stride couldn't hide the strain he carried—a tension that seemed to mount with each passing day. Beneath his practiced composure, she glimpsed something fragile, something human. *If only he'd let me in.*

CHAPTER 33

Santa Maria degli Angeli, Assisi
7:00 AM

Dawn's first light struggled against winter darkness as Anthony approached Santa Maria degli Angeli. The Basilica emerged into view from the lower, flat expanse of the hill town, its massive dome a silhouette against the pearl-gray sky. A bitter wind carried him toward the structure, drawn not just by its architectural beauty but by something deeper, magnetic.

Saint Mary of the Angels stood as a monument to humility and grace. Frost traced delicate patterns across its grand exterior, the towering columns and intricate carvings stark against the pale morning. As Anthony stepped inside, escaping the cold, profound silence gripped him. The air hung still as if time itself had paused in veneration. Despite its vastness, the space offered sanctuary, the walls bearing generations of whispered prayers.

At the heart of the Basilica stood the Porziuncola. This tiny chapel sat beneath the soaring arches like a pearl nestled within its shell. Its simplicity struck him, almost fragile against the surrounding splendor. Massimo had told him of its history, how in 1211 the abbot of Saint Benedict of Monte Subasio had given Francis this chapel, making it the motherhouse of his religious order and the birthplace of the Franciscan movement.

Above and around this humble chapel, the Basilica stood as a testament to faith transformed into magnificence. Built between 1569 and 1578, the vast edifice rose over the Porziuncola, its three naves and circle of chapels extending along the aisles like protective arms around a precious relic. The Porziuncola rested directly beneath the soaring cupola, its medieval stonework and painted façade a striking contrast to the Basilica's white walls and ornate Renaissance detailing. A geometric pattern of terracotta and marble radiated across the floor, drawing the eye to the chapel's entrance where gilded religious scenes crowned the arch, depicting Christ, Mary, and the angels above kneeling Franciscan monks.

Anthony picked up a brochure from an offering table, scanning the text about the Pardon of Assisi. The promise was simple yet profound—anyone who prayed within these walls with a penitent heart would receive full absolution. The concept resonated deeply with him, the burdens of his own life weighing upon his conscience.

His footsteps echoed softly on the polished marble as he approached the Porziuncola. The dim winter light filtered through small sconces, casting shadows across ancient stones. The walls seemed alive, holding the prayers of countless pilgrims before him.

Anthony sat in the first pew, hands clasped against the lingering chill. His eyes fixed on the unadorned altar, a testament to Saint Francis's humility. The brochure's words blurred as his mind wandered, consumed by the events that had brought him here.

He sank into the stillness, feeling the presence of something greater, as though Saint Francis himself sat beside him. Memories surfaced—choices made, ambitions that led astray, regrets that weighed on his soul. For years, he had hidden from these thoughts. But here, in the chapel's sanctity, there was no hiding.

His confession came without pretense, thoughts turning to those he had hurt, trust broken, moments of weakness that scarred his conscience. As he prayed, a lightness replaced the heaviness he had carried for so long. The prayers of countless others seemed to mingle with his own, weaving a tapestry of redemption.

When Anthony opened his eyes, something had shifted within him. The Porziuncola had been the beginning of Saint Francis's journey, and now it marked the beginning of his own.

Outside, his breath misted in the February air as he drove toward San Damiano. The narrow roads wound through the winter-bare countryside. Dormant cypress trees lined the path, their dark forms stark against the brightening sky. The hills of Assisi unfolded before him, silvered by frost in the strengthening light. In the distance, Saint Mary of the Angels stood sentinel. San Damiano beckoned—the place where Saint Francis had heard the divine call to rebuild the church. Its weathered stone walls nestled among winter-stripped trees, modest against the austere landscape. Anthony parked and ascended the worn path, the valley below a masterpiece of frost-touched fields and misty horizons.

The church's simplicity contrasted sharply with Saint Mary of the Angels. No elaborate façades or towering spires adorned it, just quiet humility echoing Francis's teachings. Inside, the scent of aged wood and stone filled the air, warmer than the biting cold outside. Unpolished walls bore the texture of an eternity illuminated by winter light filtering through narrow windows.

In the first pew, Anthony's gaze found the crucifix above the altar, a replica of the one that had spoken to Saint Francis. The figure's expression held both agony and grace, mirroring the sacrifice of a devoted life. His thoughts settled into a chaotic blend of past choices and present obligations converging in this sacred space.

The shadows deepened as he stared at the crucifix. His breathing slowed, mind quieting as peace enveloped him. Francis's teachings flooded his heart—good and evil, humility and pride, obedience and rebellion, poverty and wealth. The saint's spirit seemed to speak directly to him, burning with intensity. In the silence, he felt weightless, his spirit soaring beyond the church walls like the dreams of his childhood. Clarity washed over him. The worries that had clung dissolved, replaced by purpose. His task wasn't merely an obligation but a calling that demanded complete devotion.

When he finally stood, the church seemed brighter, winter sunlight now streaming through the windows. The crucifix held his gaze one last time as he offered silent thanks. He had shed his past's incumbrance, stepped into a new version of himself— one guided by faith and resolve.

The February air bit at his lungs as he emerged. Florence awaited, his path uncertain yet clear. For the first time in years, Anthony walked with peace and determination, his collar turned against the cold and his spirit aligned with the divine purpose that had brought him here.

T

Richard called Captain Rossi for his daily update on Ronald Brunelli's disappearance. More than three weeks had passed, and the family's demands for answers grew more desperate by the day.

"Richard, yesterday afternoon we processed all evidence from the garage and dumpster. The blood patterns found suggest severe trauma, but…" He paused, choosing words carefully. "The amount wasn't necessarily fatal. We're still examining security footage from every business within a five-block radius from his abduction point to his last known location."

Richard gripped his phone tighter, that familiar mix of hope and dread rising in his chest. "What about his wallet? Any prints besides his?"

"Only partials," Rossi replied, frustration edging his voice. "But I've assigned my best team to this case. We won't stop until we have answers."

CHAPTER 34

The Laurentian Library, Florence
12:45 PM

"*Identificazione?*" The security guard's voice cut through the crisp February air.

Without a word, Anthony retrieved his sleek, gold card key for entry. He pulled his wool coat tighter as he gazed up at the Laurentian Library's imposing façade. The structure had been commissioned by the Medici family in 1568 and stood as both sanctuary and fortress, housing treasures like Plato's *Dialogues*, Dante's *Divine Comedy*, and *Codex Amiatinus*, one of the oldest complete manuscripts of the Latin Vulgate Bible.

The guard studied the card, shaking his head. "*Mi dispiace, signore.* That pass is for Church properties. We are state-operated."

Anthony's face reddened, then he handed him his photo ID. The guard checked a list, nodding. "Ah yes, Dr. Valentino has authorized your entry." He unlocked the gate with a deep groan. "*Benvenuto alla Biblioteca Laurenziana.*"

The courtyard revealed itself beyond the gate. Arched colonnades encircled the space, their repeated curves casting rhythmic shadows across the stone walkway. At the center, an orange tree—its dark glossy leaves and bright fruit defying the season—rose above meticulously maintained boxwood hedges arranged in geometric shapes. The winter sun, tracking low in the afternoon sky, cast a pale golden light across the Renaissance façade.

Ascending the exterior staircase, his every step resonated with the weight of his mission. The air was filled with a quiet calm, a reminder of the historical significance of the ground he trod. Anthony entered the administrative offices where an assistant with dark curly hair, thick glasses, and a perpetually skeptical expression awaited him.

"Dr. Valentino's been expecting you. Follow me, please," she said briskly, turning on her heel without waiting for a response.

She led him through the corridors of the library, past towering shelves stacked with ancient volumes. Dust motes floated lazily in the streams of light, the air thick with the scent of old paper and history. They passed several small reading rooms where scholars sat hunched over manuscripts, their whispers blending into the ambient silence of the age-old office suite. A brass plaque marked their destination—Dr. Vera Valentino.

The assistant unlocked the door and ushered him into the room. "She'll join you momentarily."

The office spoke of scholarly prestige. Leather-bound volumes lined heavy wooden shelves, while an antique globe with ornate brass meridian rings occupied one corner, gleaming in the lamplight. Anthony's parchments commanded attention from the center of an oak conference table, each document preserved beneath protective glass. The air felt heavy with their significance.

As he looked around, the walls chronicled Vera's success with university diplomas, plaques of achievement, photographs with Pope John Paul II and Pope Benedict XVI, and an Italian magazine cover proclaiming her "The Renaissance Scholar."

His attention quickly returned to the table. The ancient parchments beckoned, their message waiting to be revealed.

His eyes drifted to Vera's chair, where her open bag revealed a glimpse of protruding documents looking eerily similar to his. Before he could look closer, the door swung open.

Vera swept in, unwinding a cashmere scarf. The wind had painted her cheeks pink beneath her winter cap, and she clutched several massive art folios against her wool blazer.

"Anthony!" She deposited the books with a thud. "Perfect timing. I ran home to grab these. I'll fill you in about why in a moment."

He straightened. "It's good to see you, Vera." His eyes moved from the documents to meet hers. "Thank you for this."

"Of course," she said, hanging her coat. Her smile faded. "I've made two more discoveries—one exciting, one troubling."

"Okay…" Anthony leaned forward. "I'm all ears."

"This letter," she began, her voice lowering, "was dictated by Saint Francis himself to Brother Leo. It's been passed down to a line of succession he called the Time Watchers. They will be handpicked by the reigning minister general and must support the decision of the pope to enact the unveiling of what's been hidden."

He held his breath. The name alone sent chills through him.

Vera continued. "In the letter, Francis warns of a time when 'evil in men's hearts will reside in the pinnacles of the Church.' He speaks of an age overtaken by nepotism, wealth, and power, a time when the richest families will be at war with the law and with each other. And this struggle"—she paused—"will give rise to great art. But not just any art…art used as a tool to indoctrinate and manipulate the masses as the most ruthless families vie for control of the sacred papal throne."

The words hung in the air like ancient scripture. Anthony's mind raced. *Art as manipulation?* he thought. He intimately knew of art's influence throughout history, but this suggested something far more sinister and calculated.

Vera continued in a whisper. "The letter also speaks of a great artist, someone pure of heart, who would be chosen to 'veil the instruction.' This artist would create a divine allegory and hide it within the shadows of the Church's power, guided by the Franciscan Brotherhood to preserve the truth while standing as a silent angel of God."

Anthony paced the room. "This is unbelievable," he said. "It feels like…a prophecy. He must be referring to the Renaissance, right?"

"Precisely," she replied without hesitation. "Saint Francis foresaw the dangers of wealth and power colliding with art at some point in time. He instructed his brotherhood to find a trustworthy artist, bury the clues, and not reveal them until the right time."

He nodded slowly, processing everything. "And the allegory?"

Vera nodded. "Yes, there's a description of the symbols that needed to be hidden. Unfortunately, the actual diagram or map no longer exists. Brother Leo ordered it destroyed after the instructions were carried out. So, this chosen artist, presumably from the Renaissance, would have been instructed to hide a map within a great work of art to fit the clues." She pulled out her notepad and read, "Behold the Stairway to Heaven; Behold the Temple of Solomon; Behold the Coat of Arms; For thy resting place sits under the Right Hand of God."

Anthony repeated the words under his breath, writing them in his notebook. "Okay, got it. But what does it mean?"

"That's what we need to figure out. I've brought these reference books on Renaissance art because I believe the allegory is hidden within one of the frescoes. We just need to find it. The problem is there are literally thousands."

Vera handed Anthony a thick volume on Donatello, opening a book on Raphael herself. They flipped through the pages, scanning for symbols matching the description.

"Behold the Stairway to Heaven…that could represent some kind of spiritual journey," he mused.

Vera glanced up, a thoughtful smile playing on her lips. "Yes, representing the ladder of life. Or perhaps it speaks to humanity's constant struggle with time. Our rush to ascend higher, only to look back and wonder if we missed something along the way."

Anthony nodded, his smile softening. "And when we finally get to the top, we realize the journey was more important than the destination."

"Exactly," she said, her voice tinged with quiet reflection. "It could be about that very struggle, the pursuit of happiness, the relentless climb. And by the time we reach the pinnacle, it's already too late to savor the climb itself."

Their quiet discussion gave way to a deeper focus. Anthony's thoughts drifted to the other clues. *Behold the Temple of Solomon; Behold the Coat of Arms; For thy resting place sits under the Right Hand of God.*

As they searched, Vera glanced at him. "Tell me. How did everything go in Assisi?"

He leaned back in his chair. "Well," he smiled. "I also have some exciting news. Remember I asked you if *Altrix* could mean enrichment?"

Vera nodded.

"I've been meditating on that, and I believe it's tied to a deeper context in Saint Francis's life."

"Go on," she urged, her eyes alight with anticipation.

"When Francis was young," he began, "he lived the life of a nobleman's son but found it hollow. He rejected his father's ambitions and refused to join his father's clothing business. His father was so furious that he imprisoned Francis in the basement of their home. While his father was away on business in France, his mother released him and he fled. He never returned home."

Her eyes widened as she listened.

"When he came back," he continued, "he was so enraged that he dragged Francis to the bishop to demand restitution. That's when Francis publicly renounced his father's wealth, stripped off his clothes and declared himself no longer his father's son. He gave everything away, not just material possessions but also the ambitions and expectations imposed on him. That moment, for Francis, was one of profound enrichment—not material, but spiritual. He always referred to that as his moment of enrichment, the beginning of his true journey."

He leaned forward. "So, if we interpret Francis's message from the cylinders as *Incipe*, meaning 'begin,' *In Puncto*, meaning 'at the point of,' and *Altrix*—"

"Enrichment!" Vera's eyes lit with understanding. "Good heavens, Anthony, that's brilliant! *Begin at the point of enrichment…* That's it!"

"And I'm quite certain I know the exact point in Assisi Francis was referring to."

Vera leaned forward. "How do you know that?"

"With the help of Massimo, from Assisi. He's like a walking encyclopedia, always one step ahead of me. When I asked about Francis's renouncement, he led me directly to the site." Anthony took out his cellphone and showed her a picture he took of the slab of stone from the entrance of the Basilica. "And get this." He grinned, his eyes sparkling with mischief. "It's located at the entrance of the Basilica of Saint Francis. The entrance to the church is the point of enrichment, or one might also say nourishment!"

"Of course," she answered. "Nourishment of the soul."

The room filled with renewed urgency. The pieces were falling into place, and they both felt closer than ever to the truth Saint Francis had hidden for centuries.

Vera began, "Now, as I mentioned earlier, there's something else I've translated that's bothering me. I keep finding odd references to the Virgin Mary. Something's going on, but I don't have all the pieces together quite yet. There's a reference to it in the letter that was in your family's scroll. There's a reference to it in the letter that sat inside the cylinder from the minister general. And what I'm coming up with is that there may be empirical evidence that Pontius Pilate possessed documents challenging the virgin birth narrative. The implications would shake the very foundations of..." She paused, shaking her head. "But I need more proof. These fragments only hint at something larger, but—"

While completing her thought, a text notification interrupted.

"Excuse me," Vera hesitated, walking away to check her phone. Her brow creased as she read. After responding to the message, she returned with an apologetic expression. "Anthony, I'm sorry, but I have an urgent matter to attend to. I'll be gone for a couple of hours, maybe more."

He glanced at the wall clock and shrugged. "Okay if I stay here to continue?"

"Of course, until the office closes at five. I'll let the staff know."

"Vera, before you go, what's the name of that restaurant you like?"

"Tito's."

"If you're back in time, meet me there."

"I'll certainly try, but go on without me. If I can't make it, I'll call you and we can meet back at my place." She adjusted her scarf as she moved toward the door. "Oh, and be sure to take your backpack and all the documents with you."

"What's that dish you love at Tito's?"

"Pasta Bolognese. It's to die for," she said with a grin, disappearing through the door.

Left alone, Anthony turned his attention back to the Renaissance books. The cryptic phrases swirled in his mind. *Stairway to Heaven, Coat of Arms, Temple of Solomon, Right Hand of God.* Each carried profound meaning, but their true significance remained elusive.

With renewed purpose, he leaned over the table and slowly flipped through the pages. The answers were there. Ancient truths concealed for generations lay ready to reveal what Saint Francis had insisted be hidden. He could feel it.

CHAPTER 3 5

Piazza Dante Alighieri, Assisi
3:15 PM

Richard stepped off the train at Piazza Dante Alighieri, the rhythmic clatter of wheels fading into the winter afternoon. The three-hour journey had allowed him the rest he so desperately needed. A chill wind swept across the platform, carrying the crisp scent of wood smoke from distant chimneys. Only a few travelers hurried past, wrapped in heavy coats and scarves.

He approached one of the waiting taxis and, after sliding into the back seat, quietly informed the driver where he needed to go. As they wound through the streets, the Umbrian countryside stretched stark and beautiful, winter-bare hills dotted with stone villas and dark cypress trees, then the Basilica of Saint Francis rose into view against a steel-gray sky. Still, his attention remained fixed on his task, his thoughts consumed by the legal-sized envelope he carried and by its intended recipient.

The taxi came to a stop outside the Hotel Giotto. It was exactly how Anthony had described it. The rolling countryside offered a panoramic view of Umbria's timeless beauty. Inside, the lobby exuded a quiet elegance. The patterned rug stretched across the polished marble floor, leading him deeper into its refined charm.

Behind the front desk, the clerk finished a phone call and then smiled at him as he approached with the large envelope tucked under his arm. "Good afternoon, sir. I'm Lara. How may I assist?" she asked, her voice warm and inviting, her posture radiating professionalism.

"I'm dropping this off for one of your guests, Anthony Brunelli," Richard said, placing the envelope on the check-in counter. Tony's full name, written in bold, precise lettering, stood out on the front. "He's expecting it."

Lara studied the envelope briefly, her eyes narrowing. "Of course. Any message?"

"Just say it's from Richard. He'll understand." He offered a brief, closed-mouth smile, the kind that hinted at something unspoken. He tapped the envelope with his fingertips, a slight unease threading through his tone.

"Are you his friend Richard from his hometown?" she asked.

"I am. How did you know that?"

"He's told me about you."

"Oh?"

"Well, that you and his father were traveling to Rome for his art reception, that's all."

Richard looked at Lara as if she knew too much information.

She continued. "We spent a lot of time talking when he was here for a couple of months working on his painting."

"I see. Well, it's nice to meet you. Please make sure he receives it. It's important," he added, his gaze further conveying the depth of his words.

Her welcoming smile faltered, if only for a moment. "I'll personally deliver it to his room," she assured, holding the envelope with care.

With a brisk nod, Richard turned and strode away, his shoulders rigid beneath his winter coat.

T

Lara had handled countless deliveries for the hotel's wealthy and influential guests over the years, but this time felt different. Something in Richard's deliberate manner—his tone, his unwavering gaze—stirred an unease she couldn't quite name.

Moments later, she ascended to Anthony's suite. Using her master key, she opened the door to a room of immaculate order, the bed crisply made, polished surfaces reflecting the afternoon light. Only a single detail broke the harmony—a large white towel draped over the bathroom door. The subtle scent of sandalwood hovered in the air, a quiet imprint of its occupant.

Her eyes drifted toward the window overlooking Assisi's rolling hills. Shafts of sunlight spilled into the space, lending it a serene warmth. Carefully, she placed the envelope on the desk, angling it so it would be the first thing he noticed upon his return. Yet as she turned to leave, a prickling doubt surfaced. Richard's urgency had been unmistakable, and now the density of the envelope itself seemed somehow heavier, as though it carried secrets too vital to simply set aside.

Reaching for her phone, Lara dialed Anthony's number.

It rang twice before his familiar voice came through the line. "Hello?"

"*Ciao*, Tony, it's Lara," she began. "A Mr. Richard Pescatore dropped by and left a large envelope for you."

"Hi, Lara. Yes, he sent me a message earlier about it. If you can leave it in my room, that would be best," he said.

"You read my mind. I just placed it on the desk in your room," she replied, hesitating slightly before continuing. "But I just remembered, my father has been begging me to visit his property in Florence. So, if it's urgent, I could bring the envelope to you. It would give me an excuse to get out of town for the rest of the day."

"Are you sure? That's quite a detour," he said, though there was a hint of interest in his voice.

"It's absolutely no trouble," she assured him.

A brief pause followed before Anthony spoke again, his voice warm. "Thank you, Lara. How about I repay the favor? Dinner, perhaps?"

Lara smiled. "Now that would be lovely. I'll leave shortly. It's less than a two-hour drive. Do you have a place in mind?"

"A place called Tito's. I'll text you the address. Let's meet around 5:30?"

Before ending the call, Lara agreed, her voice carrying a quiet thrill she couldn't quite hide. Her thoughts swirled with anticipation, not just for the evening ahead but for the mysteries surrounding Anthony and the envelope she now carried.

With a final glance around his room, Lara carefully clutched the envelope to her chest and closed the door behind her. The hallway seemed to hum with a quiet energy, as though the air itself held secrets waiting to unfold.

As she walked toward the elevator, a subtle tension stirred within her. She was already visualizing what she'd wear to dinner—something effortlessly stylish but not overstated, something that would catch his eye without revealing how much thought she'd put into it.

CHAPTER 36

Thirty miles south of Florence, Vera guided her car off the autostrada at Montepulciano and into the crowded parking lot beneath the towering Auto Grill. The massive structure stretched over the A1/E35 freeway, a concrete colossus linking northbound and southbound lanes. Faceless and ordinary to most, it was perfect for anonymous meetings—transient and easily forgotten. Yet, as she stepped out of her car, a prickle of uncase danced at the base of her neck. Father Alessandro's message had been brief and cryptic, and her instincts warned this would be no casual encounter.

She clutched her leather business bag, the scope of the centuries-old documents inside grounding her. She climbed two flights of stairs to the main dining area. Inside, the Auto Grill was a shifting tapestry of travelers and commuters, voices blending into a soft roar, forks clinking against plates, the aromas of coffee and grilled meats thick in the air. As her gaze swept across the space, searching, she spotted him.

"Vera, over here!"

The man beckoning her bore little resemblance to the Father Alessandro she knew. Gone was the meticulous priest who had hired her years ago for her first assignment. In his place sat a rumpled figure, his white T-shirt blotched with sweat, black dungarees ill-fitting and slack. His face was flushed, forehead shining, as though he'd just sprinted up the stairs. The dignified composure he once carried had vanished, leaving only an uneasy tension.

"Father," Vera said quietly, approaching the table. She inclined her head, maintaining a veneer of respect. "I came as soon as you called. Were you waiting long?" She kept her voice measured, concealing her distaste for his disheveled appearance.

"No, just sat down," he wheezed, gesturing for her to take the seat across from him with a clammy, trembling hand. "Sit, sit."

She hesitated only a fraction before sitting, then rested her bag on her lap, her posture straight and composed.

He glanced around as if suspicious of every passerby. "You're alone?" His voice was low, urgent.

"Yes," she assured him. "As you requested. I've followed your instruction with the Brunelli assignment. No complications so far."

He stiffened before meeting her eyes, masking his discomfort with a hollow chuckle. "Good, we are in delicate territory, Vera. Very delicate."

She sat in the chair opposite him, exhaling. "You've made that clear. I know the Church trusted me to assist Brunelli, to help him authenticate the parchments. I'm doing what you requested."

Alessandro's eyes flicked to her bag. "And yet Brunelli's progress troubles us," he said. "There are…rumors, Vera. Whispers of a Marian myth buried in those texts. If these revelations defy Church doctrine, we must contain them."

Vera's heart beat faster, though she kept her voice calm. She'd gleaned fragments from the documents about the Virgin Mary. Such a secret, if revealed, might challenge long-held interpretations of faith. "Father Alessandro, if these documents truly threaten the Church, then why were they given to Brunelli at all? Pope Benedict must have known their significance."

Alessandro's lip curled, a flicker of anger passing over his features. "Benedict's final acts are not for you to question. The hierarchy—those who truly uphold the Church's stability—know what must be done. Benedict was…idealistic. He believed knowledge could strengthen faith. But we who remain must guard the faithful from dangerous uncertainties."

Vera inclined her head, careful not to show too much defiance yet. "I understand the need for caution," she said gently. "But I must also understand what I'm protecting. Brunelli has not finished piecing things together, and he'll continue to need my assistance. I've only been able to translate fragments to this point. To act blindly—"

"You do not need the whole picture." He leaned forward, sweat beading on his brow. "What Brunelli possesses could alter core assumptions about—" Alessandro caught himself. "Look, if certain knowledge spreads, it could disrupt the faithful, undermine the very foundation we've protected for centuries."

Her fingers tightened on the bag. She pictured Anthony and the tireless hours they had both devoted to examining those fragile parchments late into the night. He had been entrusted by Pope Benedict himself. This was no accident. Any such revelation could illuminate the Church's history rather than destroy it, though she still couldn't fully discern Father Alessandro's motives.

She replied, "Father, Pope Benedict specifically chose Brunelli for this task. He must have believed that this truth, whatever it is, deserves to emerge."

Alessandro's face hardened. "Don't be naive. Benedict's departure changed the landscape. Now the Church's stability rests with those who understand the peril of certain truths. I hired you to keep Brunelli's work in line, to ensure he did not wander too far. I need those documents in my hand—*now*, Vera. Show them to me."

A tremor of resolve passed through her. She had maintained a professional distance, had obeyed Alessandro's directives without fully knowing his endgame. But now his intentions were falling into place. He wanted to stifle what Saint Francis had set in motion, smother what Benedict had hoped would come to light.

"I can't do that, Father," she said, her voice quiet but firm. "These documents were meant for Brunelli. He is trying to complete a task entrusted to his family line for eight centuries. To silence that now would be to deny history and faith a chance to evolve."

His eyes flashed, incredulous. "You report to me, Vera. I command your loyalty. If you refuse, you risk everything. The Church can make your life…difficult."

Vera inhaled slowly, forcing herself to remain calm despite the fire burning in her chest. "I've followed your instructions without question," she said. "But now I see this for what it is, an attempt at suppression, a desperate bid to strangle a truth too unsettling for you to accept. I won't be a part of it. If you insist on silencing Brunelli, then I must walk away."

Alessandro's voice dropped to a hiss. "Do you think you can stand against the Church's will? Hand over those documents or you will find no allies, no refuge. You'll be cut off, and Brunelli's efforts will be in vain." His gaze sharpened as he spoke.

She could almost feel the devastating pull of his silent threat. He had helped place her at the Laurentian Library, opening doors otherwise sealed by Vatican bureaucracy. A word from him could close them again just as easily. But as her heart hammered in her chest, she realized she would not be indebted to fear. No title, no professional standing, was worth sacrificing the truth entrusted to Anthony. If Alessandro thought the leverage he once had would keep her in line, he was mistaken. She refused to trade integrity for security.

She rose from her chair, holding the bag close to her side. Though her heart pounded, her voice emerged firm and unwavering. "You may have helped me secure my position at the library, Father, but don't mistake that for lasting control. The Laurentian Library answers to the Italian State, not the Church. And I will not be your puppet. If these documents indeed carry a long-lost key to our spiritual heritage, then Brunelli and I will see they are understood and never buried."

He stood as well, his fists clenched and rage transforming his face. "You are putting Brunelli in danger! If this secret gets out, there will be consequences beyond your control."

Vera's eyes never wavered. "If anything happens to Brunelli, you'll answer for it. I have my own resources, Father. And I'm no stranger to Vatican politics."

Alessandro's fury boiled over. "You'll regret this, Vera," he snarled. "You have no idea what forces you're challenging."

She turned away, determined steps carrying her toward the exit. "Perhaps not. But I know what's right," she said softly, not bothering to look back. The clamor of the Auto Grill seemed distant now, the world narrowing to the sound of her heels clicking on the floor. "You won't stop us."

Behind her, Alessandro's voice erupted in a roar that drew startled glances from nearby diners. "Damn you!" he bellowed, slamming his fists on the table, sending utensils and coffee cups rattling.

Vera never flinched. She descended the stairs with her heart ablaze and her mind clear. She would help Anthony Brunelli complete his task, no matter the cost. Today, she had chosen truth over fear. In doing so, she understood a battle had begun, one she intended they would win.

CHAPTER 37

Antica Trattoria da Tito, Florence
5:45 PM

Navigating the narrow aisles of Trattoria da Tito, Lara felt the presence of countless eyes following her through cozy, bustling space. The century-old eatery was alive with the sounds of clinking glasses, the hum of conversation, and bursts of laughter that echoed off walls graffitied with colorful signatures of past patrons. The aromas of garlic and simmering sauces hung in the air, pulling her momentarily out of her thoughts. However, this wasn't just dinner—it was a gamble.

Her chestnut hair flowed freely over her shoulders, the loose waves a deliberate departure from the tight ponytail she wore at the hotel. She'd traded her practical blazer and slacks for a fitted navy midi dress that accentuated her figure, paired with a bold crimson lipstick. It was risky—she knew she was overdressed for the trattoria's rustic vibe—but tonight, she wasn't a hotel clerk. Tonight, she was just Lara.

When Anthony finally spotted her, his reaction was worth the gamble. He froze for half a second, his eyes widening before he rose from his chair. The flicker of surprise on his face was unmistakable.

"Lara," he said, his voice warm yet tinged with disbelief. "You look…amazing."

She felt her cheeks flush, a shy smile tugging at her lips. "*Grazie*, Tony."

Then came the sting she hadn't anticipated. "Are you meeting someone for a date?"

Lara faltered, her confidence wavering under the casual remark. "No, no," she managed, recovering quickly. "I have some business to take care of after this. My father has interests in a hotel near the Arno." Her father had a financial interest in a Florence hotel, but having business there was a lie, an excuse to spend some alone time with Anthony. Handing him the neatly wrapped package from Assisi, she redirected the conversation. "Here's what you've been waiting for."

Anthony's expression softened as he took the package. "You have no idea how much I appreciate this." He tucked it carefully beneath his chair, resting it alongside his rugged backpack that never left his side. "Please, Lara, sit." He softly gestured with an open hand.

As she settled in, a waiter arrived with a basket of warm bread, a dish of golden olive oil, and a bottle of deep red Cabernet. Another waiter followed, placing a charcuterie board between them with thick slices of prosciutto, black-peppered salami, and wedges of Parmigiano-Reggiano.

"Thank you," Anthony said.

The waiter poured them both a glass of wine, the ruby liquid catching the soft glow of the trattoria's lighting.

Lara nibbled at a piece of Parmigiano, eager to break the silence. "So, I'm still perplexed about what happened with that woman last night. She seemed so out of place."

Anthony's features darkened. He swirled his wine glass, staring as if searching for answers. "Like I mentioned this morning, she made me a rather…aggressive proposition about a large commission. It was the kind of proposal where refusal wasn't an option." His tone dropped. "I refused anyway."

"How did she respond?"

"She was angry. Very angry." He hesitated, then added, "Her demeanor…it wasn't just about money or art. It felt like something more."

Lara smirked. "She didn't exactly strike me as the religious type. Honestly, she looked more like she should be walking the streets of Bologna."

Anthony chuckled, the tension lifting momentarily.

When the waiter returned, Lara picked up the menu. "What do you recommend?"

He grinned. "Do you trust me to choose?"

She raised an eyebrow but nodded.

"Two of the house special," he said confidently.

"Pasta Bolognese? An excellent choice," the waiter confirmed.

Anthony leaned in. "Actually, make it three, but box the third. We might have—"

"Ah, planning for the apocalypse or just a little carb-loading?" the waiter interrupted with a grin, cutting him off.

Lara laughed, and Anthony couldn't help but smirk.

Before he could clarify, the waiter clapped his hands. "Three it is!" With a theatrical spin, he vanished into the chaos of the dining room.

Anthony glanced at her, something heavy in his gaze even as he smiled at her still gently laughing.

"So," she began, tilting her head slightly, "your art—photorealism. You've mentioned the term, but I don't think I fully understand it. What makes the technique so different?"

He leaned back in his chair, his hands cradling his wine glass. "Photorealism isn't just about replicating a photograph," he explained. "It's about capturing something deeper. The emotion of a moment, bringing a scene to life. A photograph is an anchor, but the painting…the painting becomes the story."

Lara studied him for a moment, intrigued. "And you've found these stories all over the world. Vietnam, Prague, Monaco…" A small smile played on her lips. "Even here in Florence."

"Yes, but I don't decide," he said, a faint smile touching his lips. "Once the collector tells me what they're generally looking for, the scenes find me. I'll be walking through a market in Hanoi or standing on the top floor of a hotel in Monaco, and suddenly something clicks. A shadow, a reflection, the way the light falls. It's like the universe whispering, 'This is the one.' "

"That's simply incredible," she said. "It must be amazing to see the world through that kind of lens."

"It is," he admitted. "And I'm blessed to be able to do this work."

"You never did anything else?" she asked.

His smile was faint, almost wistful. "Art has always been my world, the only work I've ever known. When I was fresh out of college, Louis Meisel took a chance on me. He's a well-known art dealer in New York, and it was a gamble, trusting a young artist with nothing but a portfolio and a dream. But it worked. Louis and his wife, Susan, they've been like family to me. Second parents, really."

Lara's gaze softened. "That's rare, to find people who believe in you like that."

Anthony nodded. "Louis gave me a career, but there's been someone else who's been just as important. Richard Pescatore. He's been by my side through it all, championing my work, handling the travel and logistics, things I can't even begin to think about."

"Richard, who I met this morning?" Lara asked, recalling the man with the kind, steady eyes and an air of quiet confidence. His thin mustache and neatly combed hair gave him an old-world charm, as if he'd stepped out of a bygone era. The designer glasses perched on his nose added a modern edge, contrasting with his otherwise classic demeanor. "He seemed… dedicated."

"He is," Anthony said. "Richard has a knack for making the impossible seem effortless. I wouldn't be sitting here without him, or Louis. They've both taught me that art isn't only about talent. It's about trust, risk, and having people who see what you're capable of before you do."

The warm, rich aroma of the pasta Bolognese lingered between them as Lara set her fork down, curiosity dancing in her eyes. "You are fortunate to have them by your side."

Anthony nodded. "But I have to say, Italy is different though. It feels like home. Every cobblestone, every shadow feels familiar. I've painted Rome, Florence…just blocks from here, in the leather market, and now Assisi. There's something about this country. It seeps into your soul."

She leaned in slightly. "And how did you like painting in Assisi? I know you usually work in your studio, but Assisi must have been…different."

He smiled, the memory lighting his face. "Different is an understatement. Assisi has this timeless quality to it. I love your town. Every corner of it feels like it's holding its breath, waiting for someone to notice its secrets. Painting there was inspiring and maddening."

"Maddening?" Lara asked, a smile tugging at her lips.

He chuckled, taking a sip of wine. "Absolutely. I'm used to working alone in my studio. No distractions, no interruptions. At the hotel—and don't get me wrong, I loved it—but there was always something pulling my attention. The view from the parlor you let me set up in, the other guests stopping by to chat, even the way the light shifted throughout the day—it was impossible to ignore. And then there was your father…"

He smirked. "He had a lot of opinions about my choice of supplies."

Lara let out a laugh, covering her face with her hands. "He's actually an amateur painter. He has his own studio at the house."

"Yes, he told me…many times." Anthony smiled.

"Please don't tell me he interrogated you about your brushes."

"Not just the brushes. The canvas, the easel, even the way I set up my paints," he said with a laugh. "He's quite something."

"He's impossible," she replied, though her tone was fond. "He treats every guest like they're his personal project, but I guess it worked out. Your painting turned out beautifully. I still can't believe you finished it in just two months."

"No, you're right, this one was special," Anthony admitted. "The Vatican's timeline didn't leave much room for error. I practically lived in that parlor."

"You did live in that parlor. I think half the staff thought you were a permanent resident."

"It certainly felt like it. But honestly, it was worth it. Assisi is one of those rare places where the past feels alive, like it's woven into the air. Capturing that on canvas was…well, it was one of the most rewarding experiences of my career."

"I remember watching you work sometimes, just for a moment when I passed by. It was mesmerizing, the way you brought everything to life. You could almost feel the Basilica breathing in your painting."

Anthony raised an eyebrow. "You were watching me?"

"Hardly," Lara shot back, her cheeks warming. "I was usually delivering you a fresh espresso, if you must know."

"Well, I'm glad you broke your father's No Mingling rule long enough to notice. I certainly know how strict he is about keeping you separated from guests."

She glanced down at her wine glass. "He has his reasons. He's always believed the hotel comes first, and that means keeping things professional. No personal connections, no exceptions."

"And yet," he said with a grin, gesturing to their table, "here we are. I guess Florence is neutral territory?"

"It's far enough from Assisi to keep us off his radar," Lara admitted, her tone playful but tinged with rebellion. "Besides, you're not just any guest. You were practically part of the furniture by the time you finished that painting."

Anthony laughed, shaking his head. "I'll take that as a compliment."

"You should. I think everyone will be sad to see you go. Even my father."

"Maybe you're right," he quipped. "And I appreciated his hospitality. The Giotto isn't just a hotel, it's a part of Assisi's history, and your family keeps that alive."

"That's kind of you to say. My father would be thrilled to hear it, though he'd never admit it. He takes everything so seriously. I sometimes wonder what he'd think of me sitting here now, breaking all his rules."

Anthony leaned forward, his gaze steady. "He'd be proud. You're not just breaking rules, you're living. And that's something I've learned is worth any risk."

She held his gaze, her cheeks warming again. For a moment, the noise of the trattoria faded as if it were just the two of them. She leaned forward slightly, her chin resting on her hand. "And now I have the privilege of having dinner with one of the most sought-after photorealists in the world. So, tell me, Mr. Artist, don't you feel wonderful to be able to do what you do?"

"Yes, it is wonderful. But also…isolated. Every painting, every commission is its own world, and once it's done, you leave it behind. That's the price of creating—you're always moving, always searching."

For a moment, neither spoke. The clamor of the trattoria swirled around them, but their table seemed suspended in quiet understanding.

Just as Anthony started to say something, a voice rang out.

"Anthony! There you are!"

Lara's stomach dropped. A beautiful, poised woman approached their table, her tailored suit radiating authority. She exuded a cool confidence that turned heads as she passed.

Anthony stood, a flicker of surprise crossing his face. "Vera," he said, his voice caught between warmth and awkwardness. "This is Lara. You've met her at the hotel in Assisi."

Vera's lips curved into a polite smile, but her eyes betrayed a more urgent matter. "Yes, of course. Lovely to see you again."

The air grew heavy. Lara felt suddenly out of place, her earlier confidence evaporating.

"Everything okay?" Anthony asked, his brow furrowing as he turned to Vera.

Vera leaned in, lowering her voice. "We need to talk. Didn't you get my message?"

He grimaced, reaching for his phone. As he scrolled through his notifications, Lara rose abruptly, her coat already in hand.

"I should go," she said, forcing a smile. "I don't want to intrude."

"Stay," Anthony urged.

"Yes, do stay," Vera added, though her tone felt more like an obligation than an invitation.

Lara shook her head. "Thank you, but I really must be going."

Anthony hesitated for a moment before turning to Vera. "Watch my backpack and the envelope, please," he said, gesturing toward his seat, then he followed Lara out the door.

The cool evening air brushed against them as they stepped outside.

At her car, Anthony hesitated, searching for the right words. "I'm sorry," he said finally. "This isn't how I wanted tonight to go. And it's not what it looks like. I meant to tell you earlier that Vera might be joining, but…I kept getting distracted."

Lara smiled faintly, though it didn't reach her eyes. She stepped closer, wrapping him in a tight hug. "I had fun," she whispered. "Now, go to your work."

T

Her words hung in the air, laden with a bittersweet finality. Anthony searched her expression, but she only smiled—a gentle curve of her lips—before stepping into her car and driving away.

He sighed, sinking into his chair again. He waved at the waiter for the check. "You're probably wondering why Lara was here."

Vera waved dismissively, her interest elsewhere. "What's in the envelope?"

"I haven't opened it yet," he admitted. "I thought we'd do it together."

Her playful demeanor evaporated, her expression sharpening. "Good call and right now, we need to leave."

"What happened?"

Vera took in a deep breath through her nose. "I met with Father Alessandro," she said, her voice dropping. "He's not himself. He demanded the documents, threatened me when I refused."

"Threatened you how?"

"He said I'd never work with the Church again. But it was more than that. He implied we're in real danger."

The muscles in Anthony's jaw tightened as the implications of Vera's words settled over him. "You think Alessandro is part of something bigger?"

Vera nodded, her lips pressing into a thin, grim line. "Yes. This isn't just about protecting the Church's reputation. There's something darker at play here, something he's hiding."

He exhaled slowly, his mind racing to connect the tangled threads of the past few weeks—his father's disappearance, the cryptic messages, the secret documents, the veiled threats from Katarina, and now Alessandro. The pieces were scattered, but they all seemed to lead back to the same sinister web.

"Vera, there's something else you should know," he said, his voice steady but laced with tension. "It happened last night."

"What is *it*?"

Anthony shifted the package in his hands, his grip tightening, his voice darkening. He recounted his encounter with Katarina. "The offer wasn't a request, it was an ultimatum. Turning her down wasn't an option. When I refused, she made it clear she wasn't happy. Her tone changed, and the things she implied…" He shook his head. "It felt less like a business proposal and more like a warning."

Vera's eyes narrowed. "Sounds like there's a connection to Alessandro?"

"It wouldn't surprise me," he admitted, his voice low. "Katarina had the same disregard for boundaries, the same ruthless determination. Either they're cut from the same cloth, or they're working for the same people."

Vera nodded slowly, her expression grim. "We're dealing with people who don't make idle threats. If Katarina and Alessandro are connected, then we're up against a network far more dangerous than we've realized."

Anthony exhaled, his breath heavy with the depth of the moment. "I know. And the more we uncover, the more convinced I am—they'll stop at nothing to get what they want."

The waiter returned with the check, and they made their way out of the restaurant.

As they stepped into the quiet Florentine streets, the wind picked up, sharp and biting, carrying with it the unmistakable chill of uncertainty. The distant sound of church bells echoed faintly through the narrow alleyways. As they walked, Vera's apartment building came into view—a centuries-old structure with weathered stone walls, its history etched into every crack and crevice.

Anthony's grip tightened on the large envelope tucked under his arm. It wasn't just a bundle of papers—it was a key, a cipher that could unlock the truth they were desperate to find. Yet with every step, the abundance of it grew heavier as though the mystery itself was resisting discovery.

Once they reached her apartment, Vera unlocked the heavy wooden door and stepped inside, motioning for Anthony to follow. The loft was a striking blend of old and new. Exposed wooden beams crisscrossed the high ceiling, their age darkened by time, while sleek, modern fixtures adorned the open kitchen. Soft lighting reflected off polished concrete floors, and minimalist furnishings created a sense of understated elegance.

But it was the room's atmosphere that struck him most, a quiet intensity as though the walls themselves held secrets. A single floor-to-ceiling bookshelf occupied one wall, filled with a mix of antique tomes, modern texts, and what appeared to be meticulously organized files. The scent of aged parchment mingled with the faint aroma of espresso, a blend that was comforting.

"We need to open that envelope," Vera said, her voice steady as she gestured toward a long oak table in the center of the room. The table, illuminated by a single overhead light, seemed almost like an altar, waiting for the secrets within the envelope to be revealed.

Anthony nodded, stepping inside as the door clicked shut behind them. The sound echoed faintly in the loft, a reminder of how isolated they now were. He placed the envelope on the table, its surface catching the fractured light from the lamp. The shadows stretching across the walls seemed alive, bending and twisting as though they too anticipated what was to come.

This was no longer about art or faith. The game had shifted. It was a chessboard, and Anthony had just realized how dangerously outnumbered he was. Every move would count, and the stakes had never been higher.

CHAPTER 38

San Pietro in Vincoli, Rome
8:10 PM

While Anthony was north of Assisi in Florence, Richard headed south to Rome. His heartbeat steadied as he once again stood before the hidden passage in the depths of San Pietro in Vincoli. In each hand, he gripped one of the ancient skeleton keys, their weight cold and heavy with the secrets they protected. Taking a deep breath, he inserted the keys into the concealed locks embedded within the fresco—a masterful artwork hiding an entrance no one was ever meant to discover.

He turned the left key clockwise and the right counterclockwise until the faint metallic click echoed through the silence. The mechanism released, and the fresco slid open to reveal the door into darkness—the Bunker of Sin. The stagnant air rushed out to greet him, thick with the smell of centuries-old decay and the oppressive force of untold stories.

Carefully, Richard descended the narrow staircase, each step reverberating faintly in the claustrophobic space. The deeper he went, the darker and more suffocating the atmosphere became, as if the bunker itself were alive, resentful of his intrusion. Reaching the bottom, he placed his foot on the cold, dusty floor and fumbled for the trapdoor. With a grunt, he lifted it open, then descended the iron ladder into the chamber below.

He again switched on the dim overhead light. The room, no larger than a modest pantry, was lined floor to ceiling with cabinets and shelves, each meticulously labeled with dates ranging from the eighth to the fifteenth century. Richard's eyes widened as his gaze roamed over the labels. These were older records than those he had previously uncovered above. If the upper archives had been damning, these were certain to be catastrophic.

Since the fifteenth century, San Pietro in Vincoli had served as the spiritual stronghold of the della Rovere family, a legacy rooted in the ambitions of Francesco della Rovere. Once a devout Franciscan, Francesco rose through the Church's ranks with unwavering pride in his Franciscan heritage. He held the titles of Cardinal Protector and Minister General of the Franciscan Order, later becoming Cardinal Priest of San Pietro in Vincoli. Ultimately, he ascended to the papacy, adopting the name Sixtus IV. However, Richard could now see that beneath the pious façade, Sixtus IV was nothing more than a kleptocrat, his reign steeped in deception and self-interest.

It was almost inconceivable that such an enormous collection of evidence still existed. It was a testament to the arrogance of the della Rovere family, who had chosen to preserve their sins rather than erase them. While Sixtus IV's accomplishments as pope were undeniably significant, such as constructing the Sistine Chapel and establishing the Vatican Secret Archives, his legacy was equally marred by infamy. He was the architect of the Spanish Inquisition and the mastermind behind the Pazzi Conspiracy, a failed plot to assassinate two Medici brothers who ruled Florence.

The deeper Richard delved into the archives, the more Sixtus IV's influence became inescapable. His shadow loomed large over nearly every document, a testament to his relentless drive for power. Sixtus's strategy of consolidating control was evident in his elevation of family members, particularly his nephews, to Cardinal positions, many of whom were deeply tied to the Franciscan Order. Among them was Giuliano della Rovere, who would ascend to the papacy as Julius II. His legacy, marked by ambition and controversy, was immortalized in his tomb, crowned by Michelangelo's iconic statue of Moses towering in the Basilica above where Richard now stood.

What disturbed Richard most was the realization that many of the Church's most influential figures, those entrusted with safeguarding and guiding its spiritual mission, had been shaped under the Franciscan Order's tutelage. These men, draped in the symbolic authority of the Franciscan Coat of Arms, had wielded their religious devotion as both a shield and a weapon, concealing their darker, self-serving ambitions behind a veneer of piety.

It was more than mere historical corruption. It was a deeply entrenched legacy of darkness, a shadow organization whose reach spanned centuries.

Through the night hours, Richard pored over the documents, selecting the most damning pieces to take with him. His briefcase grew heavy with parchment, each page a weapon that could dismantle the illusions of power. When he finally closed the last volume, his nerves were raw, his mind reeling from the suffocating reality of the truths he now carried.

Richard sealed the briefcase and climbed the ladder, the case growing heavier with each rung. As he emerged into the church basement, the cool air carried notes of stale incense, a momentary reprieve from the bunker's suffocating history.

A sound—barely perceptible—made him still.

From the shadows stepped four figures: one in a Franciscan habit and hood, and three in tailored black, their faces hidden behind white Venetian masks. The porcelain caught what little light existed, their fixed smiles at odds with Richard's mounting dread.

Without warning, he was struck with an iron bar. Pain flared across his shoulder as he crashed to the floor, the briefcase sliding away from his grasp—underground truths spilling toward waiting hands.

He struggled to rise, but a second blow collapsed his ribs, emptying his lungs. He gasped as gloved hands twisted his arms behind him, zip ties biting into his wrists. A blindfold descended, returning him to darkness.

Richard began to yell, but a swift strike silenced him.

They bound his ankles, transforming him from threat to package. He understood with terrible clarity that the della Rovere guardians had anticipated him. His intrusion was expected, and his discoveries would never see the light of day.

As they hauled him over worn marble, his fading awareness caught fragments of their hushed conversation—Italian words, crisp and formal. These weren't common thugs but educated men, caretakers of della Rovere secrets who had likely neutralized threats like him before. The cold stone against his face was the last clarity before darkness took him.

CHAPTER 39

Vera's Apartment, Florence
7:15 PM

The glass table gleamed under the bright overhead light, its surface reflecting the stark white glow that illuminated every corner of Vera's loft. The envelope lay in the center like an artifact waiting to be dissected, its edges sharp against the pristine glass. Anthony moved with purpose, his focus unshakable as he reached for it. The light cast sharp angles across his determined features. Vera stood nearby, her arms loosely crossed. The modern lines of the apartment around them contrasted with the presence of the secrets they were about to unveil.

"Whenever you're ready," she said, her voice brimming with expectation.

"Let's get started," Anthony replied.

He removed the flex band wrapped around the large envelope and began carefully removing its contents. The first item was an old, untitled leather-bound book, its pages filled with tightly packed Italian text. He handed it to Vera, trusting her expertise to decipher its secrets. But it was the second item—a sealed envelope addressed to him personally—that made his pulse quicken. The neat handwriting spelled out Anthony Brunelli: Personal.

His hands trembled slightly as he opened the envelope, revealing a letter written in Ricks's familiar script. The room seemed to fade around him as he read the urgent words.

Tony,

In the event something happens to me, the documentation I provided will answer all your questions concerning the money I received and the group of extremely dangerous individuals plotting against you. My time in Rome has been spent uncovering a dark conspiracy that reaches the highest levels within the Church. I was led to a secret place containing the most incriminating information I believe has ever been collected. It's here I uncovered documentation about a group called the Ramorosso, a secret society that has operated since the Renaissance.

On the last page of the book, you'll find a letter enclosed. It appears to be addressed to the patriarch of your family. I haven't had time to translate it, but it's obviously something important. You should have it translated as soon as possible. Finally, Tony, be careful. Do not, under ANY circumstances, reveal to anyone that you have possession of this book! You are most likely being followed. I pray you can fulfill your obligation.

Anthony's breath hitched as he absorbed the enormity of Rick's warning. The urgency in his words, the peril they implied, sent a chill down his spine. Just as he finished reading, Vera's voice broke through his thoughts.

"Anthony, you have to see this," she exclaimed, her glove-protected finger tapping the page of the bound book in front of her.

Still clutching the letter, Anthony looked up, his focus reluctantly shifting. "What is it?"

Vera's eyes gleamed with a mix of excitement and dread. "This is no ordinary book. It is the secret manifesto of the Ramorosso..."

"The Ramorosso?" he repeated, his brow furrowing. "Richard mentioned them in his letter."

Vera nodded. "Most scholars had believed the group to be a myth. They're one of the oldest underground Catholic factions, dating back to the Renaissance. This manifesto"—she pointed to the date on the cover—"is from 1517, a year of immense flux for the Catholic Church."

Anthony leaned forward. "What exactly do you mean?"

"Two pivotal events occurred," Vera replied. "First, it marked the split within the Franciscan Order after decades of tension. The Order divided into two sects—the Conventuals, who practiced a less rigid interpretation of Franciscan principles, and the Observants, who adhered strictly to the original ideals. Second, it was the year the Protestant Reformation began, a seismic shift in Christianity sparked by Martin Luther and later John Calvin. Luther's *Ninety-Five Theses* challenged the Church's authority, particularly its practice of indulgences. It created a ripple effect that reshaped Catholicism for decades. At the time, Pope Leo X, formerly Giovanni di Lorenzo de' Medici, was at the helm of the Church. Unsurprisingly, Luther's actions didn't sit well with the Medici." She gestured toward the manuscript. "Let me read into this some more."

Anthony had barely taken another breath when Vera's sharp whisper cut through the air. "Oh Dio!" She began to read aloud.

In this grave hour, the Holy Mother Church confronts an unprecedented peril not witnessed in the course of fifteen centuries. By decree of the Holy See, strict obedience to the sacred laws is hereby demanded, including the prohibition of possessing the Holy Scriptures in any tongue other than the sacred Latin, and only by those duly ordained. Many illicit translations, including those in the vulgar tongue of Italian, are spreading heretical teachings among the faithful. Any who are discovered with such forbidden texts shall be brought before the Holy Tribunal of the Roman Inquisition to receive due penance. Likewise, any who openly espouse the seditious doctrines contained within the Theses of the monk Martin Luther shall face trial under the authority of the Governor Inquisitor of the Holy Church. Moreover, should there be evidence of communion or collusion between the heretical sect of the Spirituali and those aligning with the Protestant heretics, punishments shall range from excommunication to, in extreme cases, the penalty of death. Such heresies strike at the very heart of the Church's divine doctrine and threaten the sacred authority of the Holy Father and the Apostolic See.

Vera's adrenaline surged as she locked eyes with Anthony, her voice taut. "Listen to this!"

Our principal adversaries include Lady Vittoria Colonna, Cardinal Ercole Gonzaga, and the scholar Reginald Pole. Furthermore, there is a renowned artist, whose name shall remain unrecorded until such time as his association with this circle of dissenters is undeniably proven. Should his guilt be established, we shall seize all his personal sketches, letters, and manuscripts. If deemed necessary, documents shall be crafted to expose his errors and strip him of his heretical inclinations. For many years, he has veiled his subversive thoughts within his works, cunningly disguising them from the righteous judgment of the Church.

"Who's the artist?" Anthony asked, leaning forward.

Vera bit her lip, her brow furrowed in thought. "That, I'm not sure of yet."

"Any clues?"

"I'll need to read further," Vera replied, flipping through the pages. "But I'm familiar with the three individuals mentioned. Vittoria Colonna was a poet of immense talent and influence, hailing from a prominent Roman family. She was well-educated, privileged, and deeply connected with artists, intellectuals, and reform-minded clergy. Ercole Gonzaga and Reginald Pole were powerful cardinals. Together, they formed the Spirituali, a secret fellowship that sought to reform the Church from within. They believed in *sola fide*—faith in Christ alone—as the path to salvation, rather than through the institutional Church, indulgences, or good deeds. They argued such acts should flow naturally from faith, not as a prerequisite for redemption."

She paused, her voice taking on a sharper edge. "Their philosophy was closely aligned with Franciscan teachings, which made them a threat to the more conservative factions in Rome. Their staunchest opponent was Cardinal Giovanni Pietro Carafa, a fierce critic who became the driving force behind the Church's most reactionary elements. He convinced Pope Paul

III to reinstate the Roman Inquisition, targeting reformers like the Spirituali."

Anthony absorbed her words, the toll of the Church's tumultuous history consuming him. "And this artist, if they're not named, they must have been someone significant."

"Exactly. The fact they've gone to such lengths to obscure his identity suggests he posed a real threat to their control. Let me dig deeper. I'm certain the answer is in here somewhere."

"I wouldn't be surprised if Carafa had direct ties to the Ramorosso," Anthony said, absently stroking his stubble.

"Most likely," Vera agreed. "He knew there were plenty of cardinals determined to maintain the status quo, which led to an all-out assault on both the Protestants and the Spirituali. They systematically began eliminating anyone who opposed them. Decades of tension culminated in a dramatic standoff at the 1555 conclave between Cardinal Pole and Carafa. Pole was the favorite to become pope, but he fell just one ballot short of ascending to the papal throne. Instead, Carafa was elected and took the name Paul IV. His confirmation was the death knell for the Spirituali. With him in power, the wealthiest families consolidated control, ensuring their grip on influence. Even the Laurentian Library and the entire San Lorenzo complex were built out of this, all to glorify the Medici."

She paused, testing her own memory. "And Pope Leo X, who I mentioned earlier, was also a Medici. He granted indulgences in exchange for gold donations to rebuild St. Peter's Basilica. It was the ultimate exploitation of faith for profit. Before him, Julius II of the della Rovere family—The Fearsome Pope—was infamous for his arrogance. He had the original St. Peter's Basilica torn down simply because he refused to reside in the same structure that had once housed the Borgias, one of his family's most bitter rivals. Then came Pope Clement VII, another Medici, who carried on their legacy of corruption."

"Unbelievable," Anthony muttered, running a hand over his face. "No wonder this group has remained so dangerous for so long."

Just then, he recalled Rick's mention of another letter hidden within the *Ramorosso Manifesto*. "Vera, may I see that book for a moment?"

She handed it to him. He flipped to the last page, his fingers carefully tracing the fragile parchment until he found it—a letter written in elegant ancient Italian script, the ink faded yet remarkably intact. He passed it back to Vera with care.

"What's this?" she asked, her curiosity immediately piqued as she examined the delicate writing.

"Richard said there was a letter for me hidden in the manifesto. This must be it."

Vera's eyes widened as realization dawned. "Anthony, this isn't just any letter…this is the missing letter from the first cylinder! Remember? I told you there was a letter listed in the inventory that was never found. This is it!"

His expression mirrored her astonishment. "What? The missing letter from the limestone cylinder Benedict gave me? I didn't think we ever stood a chance of finding it."

"Me neither," she said, her voice laced with urgency. "But here it is, perfectly intact and preserved."

Anthony shook his head in disbelief. "Things sure are starting to fall into place, but it feels like we still have a ways to go. Richard uncovered some things in Rome he wasn't supposed to. Things that were never meant to resurface."

Vera turned her attention to the letter, her finger hovering over the ancient Italian text as she began to skim it. "I'll need time to translate it fully tomorrow at the lab, but from what I can see, this appears to be part of a two-part correspondence. Now it's starting to make sense. I told you the letter found in the third scroll seemed incomplete, like the first part had been torn away. This letter appears to be the missing piece."

She set the letter aside, her eyes sharp with determination. Returning to the *Ramorosso* manuscript, her gaze landed on another passage and she murmured, "This is interesting. There's a reference here to the Ramorosso keeping close tabs on Luke Wadding and his writings. They suggest he knows more than he's letting on."

"Who was Luke Wadding, and why would they care about him?"

"He was a Franciscan friar and historian from the mid-1600s who wrote extensively on Franciscan history. His entire collection is preserved in the Laurentian Library." Vera rose and slipped on her black velvet coat. "It's a long shot, but I'm heading over there to see if I can find anything relevant in his work."

Anthony glanced at his wristwatch. "Now? I'll come with you."

Her expression softened, a sympathetic smile gracing her lips. "Finish going through the envelope from Richard and get some rest. You've been through enough for one day. Besides," she added with a hint of regret, "guests aren't allowed in the Laurentian after hours. There's a spare bedroom down the hall, second door on the left. Make yourself comfortable."

Reluctantly, he replied, "Alright, but let me know if you find anything."

"I will. I'll call if anything urgent comes up," Vera promised, grabbing her bag and keys.

As the door clicked shut behind her, Anthony leaned back on the couch and slipped off his shoes. He pulled out the legal documents from the envelope, intending to review them. But exhaustion quickly weighed on him, and within moments, the pages slipped from his hands as he drifted into a deep, dreamless sleep.

CHAPTER 40

The Laurentian Library, Florence
8:30 PM

Vera balanced herself on the top rung of a wooden, rolling platform ladder inside La Cripta de Biblioteca Medicea Laurenziana, also known as the Laurentian Library central vault. The air was thick with the vastness of centuries, faintly perfumed by aged paper and ink. Around her, towering shelves housed some of the most valuable manuscripts in history, including Luke Wadding's entire first-edition collection. The sacred repository held over 11,000 ancient texts, though only about 1,500 were sequestered within the central vault.

Her fingers danced lightly across the spines of Wadding's works, twelve volumes of *Duns Scotus* and eight of *Annales Minorum*. At first glance, nothing appeared unusual. The books were pristine, their leather covers well-preserved. But then her eyes caught something odd at the far end of the top shelf—a duplication. Two copies of a large volume titled *Presbeia* were positioned side by side.

Vera's brow creased. Duplicate volumes in such a curated collection were exceedingly rare. Her curiosity ignited, she descended the ladder, slid it a few feet to the left, and climbed back up to examine the books more closely.

The first copy was flawless, its pages thick and smooth to the touch. She thumbed through it quickly, finding nothing out of the ordinary. But the second copy was different. It was noticeably heavier, as if concealing more than just its contents.

Her pulse quickened. When she tilted the book, she felt an odd movement within. It had been vaulted. The latter two-thirds of the book's pages were glued together, its core hollowed out—a centuries-old technique used to hide valuable or incriminating items. She peeled back the final page and found a smaller book tucked inside. Its black leather cover was worn with age, and the title, *Commentarius*, was inscribed in delicate, slanted script. Her heart raced as she read the first page. A note, handwritten in Wadding's neat script, greeted her.

The knowledge contained within this volume hath been imparted unto me in utmost secrecy by Miguel Angel Catalani, Minister General of the Franciscan Order, upon the solemn condition that it be safeguarded within the Biblioteca Laurentian and not laid open to any eyes ere the year of Our Lord 1750.

Vera's breath hitched. This was a treasure, a hidden narrative preserved through the ages. Cradling *Commentarius* under her arm, she replaced the hollowed-out book and descended the ladder. She moved swiftly toward the main reading room, the ancient space eerily quiet other than her footsteps echoing against the marble floors.

Seated at a long wooden table, she opened the *Commentarius*. The entries alternated between Latin and English, with occasional scribbled notes in the margins. As she read deeper into the journal, the room seemed to hold its breath, the air charged with the magnitude of what she was uncovering. One of the overhead lights flickered for a moment, giving her pause.

Then, a sharp crash broke the stillness.

Vera froze, her ears straining to catch any further sounds. The crash echoed through the halls like shattering glass, but no voices or footsteps followed. Clenching her fists, she rose and cautiously approached the library entrance. Everything appeared undisturbed, yet the uneasy sensation of being watched lingered.

Brushing off her apprehension, Vera returned to her table and refocused on the *Commentarius*. An hour passed unnoticed as she sifted through its pages. Then, near the journal's end, she found an entry that made her blood run cold.

Wadding had written about the Spirituali, the reformist movement tied to the Franciscans and documented secret instructions from Miguel Angel Catalani.

I was entreated to commit to parchment a most peculiar secret. Though its full meaning escaped my understanding, I was commanded to render account of the shrouded labors of a certain artist whose name I am bound not to reveal. This work, it was imparted unto me, doth signify the occasion to commence afresh, to uncover that which may already dwell within our very souls.

Vera's pulse quickened as she drew parallels between Wadding's revelations in *Commentarius* and the details unearthed in the *Ramorosso Manifesto*. The threads connecting the two were undeniable, too compelling to dismiss. The weight of her discovery pressed heavily on her, stirring an impulse to take the *Commentarius* with her for deeper study. But she knew the Laurentian Library's immutable rule—no book, regardless of its significance, could leave its sacred confines.

Determined not to risk the loss of this invaluable evidence, she moved to the photocopier, duplicating the key pages. Upon completion, she carefully replaced the decoy book, *Presbeia*, and its concealed treasure, *Commentarius*, within the locked display case at the center of the library's rotunda.

Gathering her belongings, Vera departed. By the time she reached her apartment, her mind still reeled but exhaustion was settling in. She unlocked the door and entered quietly.

Anthony was sprawled on the couch, fast asleep, the package from Pescatore resting protectively on his chest. Gently, she lifted the package and placed it on the coffee table. Then she draped a blanket over him.

For a moment, she stood there watching him. Tomorrow would bring answers—perhaps even more danger—but for now, rest was their only sanctuary. She turned and retreated to her bedroom, the echoes of Wadding's words still lingering in her mind.

CHAPTER 41

The Laurentian Library, Florence
7:20 AM

Arriving early the next morning, Vera unlocked the heavy wooden doors of the Laurentian Library's vestibule, the ancient mechanism creaking as it swung open. The grandeur of this vertical foyer always struck her. Its magnificent tripartite structure and the central flight of elliptically-shaped stairs rose like an invitation to ascend into history itself. Today, though, something was different. She froze when her gaze settled on the reading room door. It was slightly ajar, a thin sliver of dim light escaping from beneath it.

Her pulse quickened and her instincts went on alert. Before entering, her gaze darted downward, catching sight of a small wooden tau cross attached to a thin, brown leather cord lying just in front of the door. She bent to pick it up, her fingers brushing its worn surface. The cross felt unsettling in her hand. She was no stranger to symbols and their meanings, so she hesitated for a long moment. Should she leave it? But, against her usual cautious judgment, she slipped it into her purse, her mind whirling with questions.

When she stepped into the grand rotunda, the sight before her took her breath away. Soft morning light filtered through the hexagonal coffers in the domed ceiling, making the scene all the more shocking. Small shards of glass lay scattered across the terracotta floor, glinting like dangerous jewels. At the center of the room, a display case lay broken, the scattered fragments forming a ring of evidence around it.

Luke Wadding's personal journal, *Commentarius*, was gone.

Panic bloomed inside her, spreading through her chest like wildfire. She rushed back down the vestibule stairs. In the main office, she fumbled with the phone, fingers trembling as she dialed 1-1-2, Italy's universal emergency line. Within minutes, members of the carabinieri and polizia arrived at the main gate, their faces grim with understanding after her brief explanation. Their next words, however, brought a fresh wave of anxiety:

Tutela Patrimonio Archeologico (TPA)—a special unit of the Finance Guard specializing in the recovery of stolen art— was on its way. This was bigger than she had imagined.

Soon, the square outside the Laurentian Library buzzed with life. Several dozen bystanders gathered along with employees from the San Lorenzo Church, the library, and nearby museums, all craning their necks for a better view. The carabinieri cordoned off the entrance with red-and-white crime scene tape, keeping the curious at bay. As the crowd grew, additional officers arrived to ensure a roughly twenty-by-twenty-meter perimeter for Captain Daniello Rossi's helicopter to land.

An A109 helicopter descended smoothly into the square, its rotor blades stirring up a gust of wind that scattered loose papers and forced street merchants to hurriedly dismantle their stalls. The moment the helicopter touched down, Captain Rossi disembarked, his face set with determination as he strode toward Vera. Behind him, his team followed, carrying cameras, backpacks, and fingerprinting kits.

"When I heard it happened at the Laurentian, you were my first thought," Rossi said, offering a reassuring smile despite the gravity of the situation.

"It's been a while, Daniello," she replied, feeling an unexpected wave of comfort as he pulled her into a brief, friendly hug. Although her body relaxed slightly at his familiar touch, the urgency of the situation remained at the forefront of her mind.

He patted her back. "Too long, Vera."

As they approached the grand rotunda, Rossi's sharp gaze swept over the scene. He bent as he ducked under the crime scene tape, then scanned the area for any signs of forced entry. "Is there any other way in or out of the library?" he asked, his voice steady but laced with curiosity.

"There's a fire escape at the rear of the building," she answered. "And an emergency escape route through a tunnel."

Rossi's attention snapped back to her, intrigued. "A tunnel?"

Vera nodded, her tone matter-of-fact despite the growing anxiety. "It's a small passage leading from the library to San Lorenzo. That's how I usually exit, it's a closer walk to my apartment."

He jotted something down in his notepad before they began to ascend the outdoor stairwell to the second level of the complex. Below them, the noise of the crowd faded into the background as they approached the grand rotunda where the crime had taken place.

Nearing the top, Rossi paused, shifting on his feet as though carefully considering his next words. "Before we go inside, I have to ask you, Vera… Why haven't you called me? I thought we had something special."

Vera halted, feeling a rush of conflicting emotions. Daniello had always been a complicated chapter in her life, one she'd never quite closed. She turned to face him, her voice soft but firm. "I could ask you the same, Daniello. But right now, we have bigger issues." Without waiting for his response, she strode forward, her shoes tapping sharply on the stone floor as she entered the rotunda.

Rossi followed close behind, until he froze at the sight of the crime scene.

The shattered glass gleamed in the light like fragmented truth scattered across the floor in a chaotic array. His team immediately set to work, securing the scene, collecting evidence, dusting for prints, and snapping photographs of the damaged display case.

"Was anything else taken besides this journal?" Rossi asked, his voice low as he surveyed the area with a sharp, methodical gaze.

"No," Vera replied, her voice equally quiet. "Just the journal. The other artifacts are still in their places."

He stood in silent contemplation for a moment as he processed the scene. Finally, he turned to her. "Can you think of any reason why someone would want this particular journal?"

She had known this moment would come, but saying it out loud made it all the more real. Leaning in, she lowered her voice. "I'm working on an extremely confidential case directed by the Vatican. I believe this journal is closely tied to it."

Rossi's eyes darkened with concern. "Is your case connected to an American artist, Anthony Brunelli, perhaps?"

Her breath caught. Her hand flew to her mouth as she gasped. "How do you know?"

"I've met him," Rossi replied, his voice now a whisper. "His father's been missing from Rome."

The news hit Vera like a punch to the gut. "I'm aware. Anthony confided in me…he's been extremely worried. Do you have any leads?"

"Not yet," he murmured. His pen clicked as he tapped the shattered glass, carefully probing through the fragments for any additional clues. Then he turned back to her. "Other than the open door, did you notice anything else out of the ordinary this morning?"

Vera racked her brain, mentally retracing her steps. Then it hit her. "Oh Dio!" she gasped, raising a hand to her head. "I almost forgot. I found a tau cross at the top of the stairs."

Rossi's eyes sharpened with immediate interest. "Show me."

Vera led him to the reading room entrance. She pointed to the spot where she had found the cross and then reached into her purse, carefully showing it to him.

His expression grew serious as he snapped on a pair of latex gloves. "May I?" he asked.

Vera nodded, allowing him to take the cross from her.

He crouched down, balancing on the balls of his feet as he inspected it closely. Once calm, his face now bore a deep frown as he slowly raised his gaze to meet hers. "This is important, Vera. Can you tell me exactly how it was positioned when you found it?"

She closed her eyes, trying to visualize the moment. When she opened them, he had already placed the tau cross on the floor in the exact position she remembered.

"That's it," she said, her voice shaky. "That's exactly how it was."

A grim look settled over Rossi's face, his jaw clenching in a way that made Vera's stomach tighten. "Vera, this wasn't just dropped. Someone left this intentionally, as a sign."

A chill crawled up her spine. "What do you mean?"

Rossi's eyes flicked upward as if searching for the right words. "It's a scare tactic. The inverted cross—or in this case, the inverted tau—is used by certain underground circles, the equivalent of the mafia's black hand. It's called the *fallen cross position*, a symbol of a severe threat."

Her pulse raced and her knees felt weak as the words sank in. She stared at the inverted tau cross, the symbol now taking on a sinister load. "A severe threat...for whom?" she asked.

"Most likely for you. Or perhaps Anthony Brunelli. Or both of you. This is their way of telling you that whoever took this journal is not playing games. They're sending a message—back off or face the consequences."

Vera instinctively reached down to the floor and touched the tau cross trying to sense the malice it carried. Her mind swirled with fear and confusion, the situation escalating with every passing second. She swallowed hard, trying to regain her composure. "Who could be behind this?"

Rossi sighed deeply, folding his arms as he mulled over the possibilities. "Given the nature of what's been stolen and your connection to Brunelli, I'd say you've drawn the attention of people with deep, dark interests. We're not just talking about art theft or ordinary criminals here. This is something bigger, more dangerous."

Vera's hands trembled, and she quickly hid them in her pockets while attempting to calm herself. "Could it be the Ramorosso?" she asked cautiously, testing the waters.

His eyes sharpened. "The Ramorosso? You know of them and think they're involved?"

She nodded slowly. "Daniello, of course I do. Anthony and I recently uncovered information that points directly to this secretive group."

Rossi probed, "What exactly do you know about them?

"They've been around since the Renaissance," Vera responded, "and I believe they're still active, protecting something or trying to uncover something important that Francis of Assisi left behind. The stolen journal might hold the key."

Rossi's expression darkened further. "If the Ramorosso is involved, then we're dealing with a group that won't hesitate to eliminate anyone who stands in their way. They've been hiding in the shadows for centuries, and they'll go to any lengths to protect their secrets."

Vera bit her lip, thinking about the ramifications of the stolen journal and the threat now hanging over both her and Anthony. "But why now? Why are they surfacing at this moment?"

He shook his head, clearly troubled. "That's what we need to find out. Whatever they're after, it's something they don't want the world to know. They'll stop at nothing to ensure it stays buried, just like they've done for centuries."

The intensity of the situation pressed down on Vera. She couldn't shake the image of the inverted tau cross, its meaning now clear and terrifying. She knew she couldn't back down, not now. The stakes had just risen to life-and-death proportions.

She took a deep breath, trying to steady her nerves. "What should I do?"

Rossi met her gaze with a hardened expression, the seriousness mirrored in his eyes. "You need to stay vigilant. Don't go anywhere alone. Make sure Brunelli is aware of the threat. We're going to get to the bottom of this, but until then, I need you to be extremely careful."

Vera nodded, feeling the enormity of the danger ahead. Despite that she and Anthony were in grave peril, she couldn't abandon their quest. Too much was at stake—more than just the journal, more than just the Ramorosso. Something far bigger than both of them was at play.

As Rossi turned back toward his team, Vera stood frozen, her thoughts consumed by the growing storm around her. The Laurentian Library had become a battlefield, and she was standing in the eye of it. With the *Commentarius* missing, the road ahead had become perilous.

"Daniello," Vera called out suddenly, her voice shaky. "What severe threat are they trying to communicate?"

Rossi turned, his eyes dark with a grimness that sent chills down her spine. He stood slowly, gripping the tau cross in his gloved hand, his gaze never leaving hers. "Vera," he said, "it's a death threat."

CHAPTER **4 2**

Vera's Apartment, Florence
8:40 AM

Anthony's eyes snapped open, his pulse still keeping pace with a fading dream's unease. For a moment, he couldn't recall where he was, but the warm hush of Vera's apartment—spartan yet reassuring—brought him back to his present reality. Early morning light slipped through half-drawn curtains, illuminating the few precious items laid out around him, the large envelope from Rick, the delicate sleeves holding ancient parchments, and the limestone cylinders entrusted to him by powers beyond his understanding. The faint aroma of espresso drifted in from the kitchenette, beckoning him toward focus and resolve.

He swung his legs over the edge of the couch, clearing the lingering haze of sleep. Now, as he stood in Vera's apartment, these mysteries pressed against him like an iron mantle he could not remove. Just weeks ago, he was simply an artist unveiling his commissioned painting at the Vatican Art Gallery. Then came that private meeting with Pope Benedict XVI, an audience he'd never imagined in his wildest dreams, where the pontiff entrusted him with an 800-year-old limestone cylinder and urged him to welcome the aid of Vera, to seek out Minister General Marco Tasca and uncover a truth hidden for centuries that was cemented by his bloodline. His father's disappearance, coupled with the cryptic instructions to pursue a third cylinder buried in a relative's grave, only tightened this web of intrigue. This was no ordinary errand. This was destiny bending toward him.

Anthony was not a historian like Vera, yet here he stood tethered to relics as old as the faith itself. The parchments he carried, the secrets locked in stone, and the Vatican's quiet but urgent directives had pulled him into a realm far beyond the comforts of the art world.

Yet it was Massimo who guided him to uncover the true essence of Saint Francis. He'd urged Anthony to open his heart at the holy places of the Porziuncola and San Damiano. This action had stirred his soul. Saint Francis's legacy wrapped him like a gentle but insistent embrace. Inside those hallowed spaces, something ancient had stirred in his heart. He could no longer deny he'd changed. The old Anthony Brunelli had sought perfection on canvas, acclaim in hushed galleries. The new Anthony Brunelli carried a spiritual charge, an invisible current of purpose older than Rome's cobblestones and as potent as the faith that had built empires—and toppled them. He felt a connection to the saint who had relinquished all worldly trappings to follow a calling more urgent than comfort. Now, attempting to walk in Francis's footsteps, Anthony sensed he too was being called to relinquish his old self and embrace the unknown.

Barefoot, he moved into the kitchenette where a hot moka pot of espresso awaited him on the stovetop, steam curling upward like a beckoning spirit. Beside it lay a folded note bound with a red ribbon.

Anthony,

I've gone to the Laurentian. Make yourself at home. Take a shower, gather your belongings, including the envelope, parchments, and the Kevlar backpack, and *meet me there when you're ready. The library is just a ten-minute walk away.*

See you soon.

—V.

He allowed himself a small, tight smile at her directness. Sipping the espresso, its bitterness sharpening his senses, he felt his mind focusing like a lens adjusting to perfect clarity. This was no casual morning stroll. Every action now felt loaded with significance.

In the shower's stream, the fatigue and fear that clung to him washed away. As the water poured over him, his thoughts returned again and again to the crucifix at San Damiano. Before that icon, Francis had found his calling, and now Anthony felt he was absorbing a hint of that same divine whisper. The saint had begun a revolution of the spirit with nothing but faith and courage. He did not presume to equate himself with Francis, yet he could not deny a sense of alignment, as if he'd stepped onto a path the saint had traced centuries before.

Dressed and composed, Anthony fitted the parchments back into their protective sleeves. He took the envelope from Rick, double-checked the limestone cylinders, and placed them gently in his backpack. Securing the zipper felt like sealing a promise that he would follow these clues wherever they led, no matter the cost.

Exiting Vera's apartment, he paused on the landing and inhaled the crisp Florentine air. Down below, shopkeepers rolled up their shutters and early patrons drifted through the streets. The Laurentian Library stood only minutes away, yet those mere minutes felt like an epoch—an interval within which he would cross an invisible threshold. Stepping onto the cobblestones, his every footfall resonated like a heartbeat, each echoing the legacy of a man who had dared to renounce wealth and comfort for truth and love.

A street vendor offered pastries, but Anthony shook his head, his mind elsewhere. Francis had wandered fields and forests. Anthony now wandered a landscape of manuscripts, cryptic codes, and Vatican secrets. Yet the essence of pilgrimage remained the same, to move forward guided by faith rather than certainty. At the Porziuncola, he had felt something gentle and encompassing, a warmth that signaled he was not alone. At San Damiano, the silence itself had seemed to listen as if awaiting his consent to undertake this journey.

He imagined Francis walking beside him, not as a distant historical figure but as a guiding presence, a humble friar beckoning him beyond the safe limits of his old life. The limestone cylinders nestled in his backpack felt heavier with every step. They were no longer inert relics, had become keys, responsibilities, and instruments of change. With each stride, Anthony felt himself shedding layers of doubt and fear. He was an artist whose canvas had expanded from the surface of linen to the breadth of history itself. He was painting now in strokes of faith, using centuries as his palette and courage as his brush. He felt the transformation weaving its subtle tapestry within him. He understood that the path before him was carved not just by intellectual curiosity or familial duty but by something deeper and more luminous. He had stepped into the aura of Saint Francis's legacy, and it had changed him forever.

With a steadying breath, Anthony was mentally prepared for whatever came next. He would press forward. He would trust that he had been called, as Francis was called, to confront whatever lay hidden in these centuries-old secrets. In this moment, he was both witness and participant, pilgrim and guide, answering a summons that transcended art and ambition. In this moment, he belonged to something greater than himself.

As he neared the Laurentian Library, the city's colors grew more vivid, each hue a reminder that beauty and danger often commingled. His father's fate, the Vatican's urgent trust, the centuries-old puzzle—these realities pressed in. Still, he moved forward. Just as Francis had stepped into an uncertain world armed only with conviction and humility, Anthony Brunelli stepped now into the heart of a mystery that demanded transformation from within.

The moment he turned the corner, he caught sight of flashing blue lights. As he stood at the edge of San Lorenzo Square, he scanned the crowd. Any of these people could be watching him, working against him. His heart pounded at the sounds of raised voices and the hum of police radios. Instantly, he imagined Vera inside—frightened or hurt—and panic settled over him like a heavy cloak.

CHAPTER 43

The Laurentian Library, Florence
8:50 AM

Captain Daniello Rossi knelt at the top of the library's vestibule steps, the inverted tau cross resting in his gloved palm. Its small, wooden form—twisted upside down, slashed by time—seemed to radiate malice. Several of his agents gathered nearby, their camera flashes snapping through the hush like distant lightning.

Vera hovered behind them, her heart thudding as she watched Rossi handle the artifact as though it were a loaded weapon.

"Inverted tau," Rossi said quietly to his team, shaking his head. His voice carried the measure of old scars, cases that still haunted him. "It's not arbitrary." He looked up, meeting the eyes of his team and then Vera's. "I haven't seen this since that mess outside Siena a decade ago. Whoever placed this knew precisely what it meant."

He produced a blue evidence tag from his jacket and placed it carefully beside the cross. After one of his agents photographed the scene, Rossi slipped the relic into a sealed bag with slow and deliberate movements. When at last he turned to Vera, worry etched hard lines into the corners of his eyes.

She swallowed, forcing her voice to remain steady even as dread coiled in her stomach.

"Your report says the stolen book was by Luke Waddling?" Rossi asked, squinting at his notepad. His pen hung just above the page as though each word he captured would carry substance in the case to come.

"Luke *Wadding*," Vera corrected. "He was a Franciscan friar, a renowned historian from the seventeenth century."

Rossi nodded, pen scratching a quick note. "Why steal it? There are plenty of rarities in this library. What makes this one worth leaving a threat behind?"

Vera took a breath, scanning the hallway as if the ghosts of the past might step forward to explain themselves. "It's not just any volume. Wadding's personal journal recorded pivotal Church events during the Renaissance—events that could still shake the foundations of certain institutions today. It's been locked away for over three centuries, unnoticed and untouched in the Medici holdings. Until last night." Her voice dropped to a near whisper, as though admitting a dangerous secret. "It was hidden inside another book, a volume of *Presbeia*. The *Presbeia* is still here, but the chamber within it is empty. The journal's gone."

Rossi's brow furrowed. "Book-vaulted," he repeated quietly, as if tasting a bitter truth. "Someone knew exactly where to look."

"Exactly," said Vera. "They knew precisely what they were after and how to get it. It should never have been handled by anyone without clearance, and now it's vanished just hours after I examined it."

His dark eyes narrowed. "Then they were watching you. Were you here alone last night?"

She bit her lip, replaying the events of the previous evening in her mind. "Yes, I was alone. But, Daniello, you know better than anyone, that's not unusual for me. I often work late, sometimes very late, finishing research." Her expression clouded with doubt. "Now that I think about it…" She grimaced. "I may have heard glass breaking before I secured the journal in the display case. I dismissed it as noise from the street below. I never imagined…"

A tense silence fell.

Rossi's jaw tightened. "This wasn't an amateur job," he said. "Whoever did this was prepared, and I doubt it was their first break-in. They timed their entry perfectly, most likely while they were watching you. They waited until you vacated, then moved in with surgical precision."

Vera's phone buzzed, shattering the quiet. She glanced down, finding multiple missed calls and a text from Anthony.

What's happening? I'm outside in the square.

She could almost feel his panic through the screen. Her heart skipped a beat, knowing he must be worried out of his mind.

T

Anthony wove through a tightly packed crowd that had gathered in the wake of the break-in. He surveyed the scene of police tape cutting across the cobblestones, flashing blue-and-white lights illuminating the old stones, nearly a dozen official vehicles parked haphazardly, and a helicopter resting ominously in the center of the square.

Fear seized him, unleashing a torrent of worst-case scenarios. Vera's safety overshadowed every other concern as he pushed forward, squeezing between onlookers until he reached the police line.

An officer stepped forward, firmly blocking Anthony's path. "*Mi scusi, signore,*" the officer said firmly, raising a hand. "This area is restricted."

"But I know someone inside!" Anthony's voice cracked, raw and urgent. He craned his neck, searching beyond the cordon for any glimpse of Vera. His pulse hammered. This morning he had stepped out of her apartment a changed man, determined to forge ahead. Now he feared something had derailed that journey before it truly began.

His eyes locked on the Laurentian Library courtyard where he spotted Vera walking toward him beside a man who appeared to be a detective. The lawman's badge glinted in the sunlight, but Anthony's focus sharpened as recognition hit him. This was the same detective who had appeared at the Residenza di Ripetta in Rome on the day his father vanished, the one giving Rick daily updates.

Adding to his unease, the two stopped walking momentarily, and Anthony noticed the way Rossi's hand lingered lightly on Vera's arm as they spoke in hushed tones, their heads inclined close together. For a fleeting moment, unease coiled in Anthony's gut. The sight of Rossi's hand resting on Vera's arm, coupled with their apparent ease with one another, stirred an unspoken tension within him. It wasn't just the familiarity between them but the connection to the case that gnawed at him.

Then Vera turned, her eyes locking onto Anthony's. The urgency in her gaze cut through his thoughts like a blade. She broke away from Rossi and strode toward the exit with purposeful resolve.

"Anthony, follow me," she called, ducking under the police tape. "We have no time to waste."

Anthony quickly fell into step beside her as they wove through the crowded square. The tension in Vera's face was unmistakable. Her jaw was set tight, her pace swift and determined. He wanted to ask a dozen questions, but her resolve silenced him. Whatever had happened, it was clear there was no time for idle chatter.

CHAPTER 44

Autostrade, Florence
9:50 AM

They emerged from the tight confines of Borgo la Noce, a narrow Florence side street flanked by weathered apartments. Vera unlocked the doors to her Alfa Romeo Giulia with a soft, echoing beep. The cobblestones beneath their feet radiated the quiet charm of early morning Florence, but her mind remained far from serene. She motioned for Anthony to hand over his Kevlar backpack, then placed it carefully into the trunk alongside her own business bag and several large art volumes before closing the trunk with a decisive snap.

Sliding into the driver's seat, she tucked the photocopies of Wadding's journal entries above the sun visor. She adjusted her mirrors as Anthony settled into the passenger side. He pulled down the sun visor, squinting against the brilliant morning light that bathed the ancient city in a golden hue.

The Giulia maneuvered expertly through winding Florentine streets, its engine's hum echoing softly off the stone façades. They were heading south, aiming to reach the autostrada, but first they'd have to navigate the city's intricate grid of old roads and obstacles. As they neared an intersection, their eyes met—wide and anxious—and Anthony let out an exaggerated, forced breath, trying to release the tension trapped inside the car. The silence between them stretched, charged with unspoken questions.

Abruptly, Vera slowed the car as they approached a railroad crossing. A lumbering freight train rolled past, each ironclad car dragging the next in a seemingly endless procession. The rhythmic clatter against the tracks combined with the metallic clang of the crossing bell intensified the tension that had been simmering between them since leaving the Laurentian Library.

As they waited for the train to crawl by, Anthony said with an apparent measured restraint, "Vera, the detective at the library—Rossi—he's the same man who appeared at the Residenza di Ripetta in Rome the day my father vanished. He's overseeing the case, providing my friend Richard and our family constant updates." His voice trembled. "I recognized him immediately. You two seemed…close. Is there something going on that I should know about?"

Vera's shoulders stiffened at the question. She had hoped to explain things gently, but given everything that had happened, his concerns were understandable. "Anthony, I'm so sorry," she said softly, sincerity threading through her voice. "Daniello told me he knew you because of your father's case. I didn't mean to keep it from you. In all the chaos, I forgot to mention it. I see how it must look, but please believe me…you have my word, you're not being deceived."

She exhaled deeply, still watching the freight train as it inched past. The metallic din amplified the tension in the confined space of the car. "There's more," she continued. "Daniello and I had a relationship in the past. It got complicated, and we ended things." She glanced at him from the corner of her eye. "I should have told you sooner."

The final cars of the train rumbled past and the crossing arm began to lift. Vera pressed the accelerator lightly, and moments later, they merged onto the bustling autostrada, the city's ancient architecture giving way to open road and the hum of modern traffic.

T

Anthony's thoughts churned. He recalled how Vera had insisted he stay behind last night, how she'd left early this morning without warning, and now Rossi—connected to his father's disappearance—had appeared unexpectedly in Florence. Still, when he looked at her face, he found quiet sincerity rather than cunning.

"Vera, you don't owe me an explanation about your past relationships," he said. "I just need to know you're not shutting me out and I'm not being kept in the dark."

She leaned forward slightly. "Anthony, no…nothing like that. I'm sorry if it ever felt that way. We're in this together, and I'm not going anywhere, or doing anything without your knowing."

He nodded, the tension in his chest loosening fractionally. "So, what exactly happened back at the library? What was all the commotion?"

Vera provided Anthony an entire rundown of the events that had transpired the previous night and that morning. "Thankfully, I made photocopies of the key pages from Wadding's journal," she said as the Giulia sped down the freeway.

"What exactly did you find in the journal?" he asked, directing the conversation to the heart of their predicament.

Vera shot him a quick, urgent glance. "Wadding's entries mention an artist entrusted with safeguarding the location of a Sacred Order. He actually names the order and explains how its existence was encoded in the artist's work. He also notes that the artist had strong ties to the Franciscans, which explains the immense trust placed in him." Reaching up, she retrieved the photocopies from the sun visor.

Anthony studied the pages carefully.

"Wadding never names the artist outright, but he refers to him as *Il Divino*."

His eyes widened as realization dawned. "Wait...*Il Divino*—you mean The Divine One? That's famously associated with Michelangelo. Even I know that."

"Correct," Vera confirmed, a flicker of satisfaction crossing her face. "This could be our biggest breakthrough yet. But as you know, Michelangelo's body of work is vast, and pinpointing what we need won't be simple."

He leaned back in his seat, his mind racing. "So, I take it we're heading to the Vatican?"

"Indeed, we are," she replied, a faint smile breaking through the tension. She paused, then murmured, as if piecing together a puzzle, "And now...I'm recalling his strong tie to the Franciscans. Hmmm..."

Anthony thumbed through the photocopies, his attention snagging on a cryptic passage Vera had translated in the margin the night before. "What do you make of this? 'Its length, twice its height, threescore its width'?"

Vera's grip on the steering wheel tightened as she glanced briefly toward the page. "This dimensional reference is likely a map or an architectural detail. If my hunch is correct, Michelangelo's frescoes might hold the answer. I spent years immersed in his work at the Vatican, collaborating with a team dedicated to restoring and decoding his frescoes. As a matter of fact, my thesis on the Sistine Chapel ceiling had been groundbreaking at the time. In addition to my knowledge of Michelangelo, we're going to need to rely on your artist's eye."

If anyone was prepared to help him tackle this mystery, it was Vera. Combined with his natural ability to look at the frescoes beyond the foreground—understanding what was deliberately painted in the background—this would be immensely important for uncovering the mystery.

Breaking the silence, Anthony turned to Vera. "A moment ago, you mentioned Michelangelo's ties to the Franciscans. What did you mean?"

Vera's eyes stayed fixed on the horizon, her voice taking on the tone of a lecturer. "Upon his death, Michelangelo's body was immediately taken to Santi Apostoli, where it was placed in a stone coffin and later secretly removed."

"The Church of the Twelve Holy Apostles?" he asked. "That's where the minister general lives."

"Exactly," she confirmed. "What makes this even more interesting is that Michelangelo was a Third Order Franciscan. He took their vows and maintained close ties with the Franciscan Friars at Santi Apostoli. While working at the Vatican, he attended daily Mass there. When news of his death broke, Pope Pius IV ordered that Michelangelo's body be brought to St. Peter's to lie in state before being placed in a permanent tomb at the Vatican. But in the early hours of the morning, Michelangelo's nephew, Leonardo, secretly removed his uncle's body from the stone coffin, hid it in a carriage filled with hay, and fled to Florence. A few weeks later, Michelangelo was buried in Santa Croce, another renowned church under Franciscan protection. That's where he rests to this day," she finished, sighing. "Many believe his nephew was simply honoring his uncle's wishes, all quietly supported by the Franciscans."

Anthony pressed his lips together in thought, the puzzle pieces slowly aligning. "So, he was deeply religious but didn't align with the papacy?"

"That's correct," Vera said, her tone laced with admiration. "While he was well-paid for his work, they essentially treated him like a slave. He never had time to rest. He went from one commission to the next without any pause, which led to much resentment."

Anthony nodded, the connection solidifying in his mind. "So, even in death, Michelangelo stood against the papacy."

She smiled faintly. "And here's where it gets even more intriguing. Remember when I was reading from the *Ramorosso Manifesto* and it mentioned the name Vittoria Colonna? She was Michelangelo's closest confidant and a prominent member of that group, the Spirituali. Given their shared ideals, it's highly likely Michelangelo was closely connected to them."

He leaned forward, his curiosity ignited. "Vittoria Colonna…she was listed in the manifesto as one of the Spirituali's founders."

"Yes," Vera said, her excitement evident. "And let me give you some history. The Colonna family restored Santi Apostoli in the fifteenth century after it had fallen into neglect, and the Franciscans have been indebted to them ever since. Michelangelo's connection to Vittoria and her ties to the Franciscans link him directly to this mystery."

Anthony exhaled deeply, the wholeness of the revelation settling in. "It's almost too logical to ignore. You're right, Michelangelo *has* to be connected to the Spirituali, and he must be the unnamed artist Wadding wrote of."

Vera's smile widened, her confidence evident. "I'd bet my career on it." She glanced at him. "Historians have debated his ties to the Spirituali for centuries. While there's no definitive evidence, rare sketches by Michelangelo were discovered in Vittoria Colonna's personal library after her sudden and unexplained death, which many believe hints at their intimate connection. But before Michelangelo died, he burned nearly all of his personal papers, writings, and drawings. If there had been any proof of his involvement with the Spirituali, it was likely reduced to ash."

"Why would he do that?"

"To protect everyone connected to the Spirituali, including the Franciscans he associated with," she explained. "Had there been any evidence linking Michelangelo or his inner circle to the group, the Church would have seen it as a direct challenge to papal authority, equating it with the Protestant Reformation. The Spirituali weren't looking to fracture the Church like Luther or Calvin. They wanted peaceful reform, a restoration of spiritual integrity within the institution. Michelangelo and Vittoria Colonna shared that vision."

As the Giulia continued down the autostrada, Anthony turned his gaze from the passing landscape to the photocopies in his lap. For the first time, he was viewing Michelangelo not just as a towering figure in art history but as a human being who had lived under the pressures of the Church and chosen to align himself—at least spiritually—with ideals reminiscent of Saint Francis. It was as though the artist, in some quiet corner of his soul, had embraced the Franciscan calling without ever donning the habit, finding solace in a worldview that placed humility and service above wealth and status.

He cleared his throat. "Vera, I'm starting to see something here. It's not just about Michelangelo or the Spirituali. It's about why Michelangelo would align himself—at least conceptually—with Franciscan ideals. He worked in the heart of the Vatican, surrounded by all this grandeur and power, yet he gravitated toward something simpler, something that valued every living thing, every brushstroke, as part of a divine connectedness."

Vera glanced at him, intrigued. "You mean you're understanding why someone like Michelangelo, forced to create under such constraints, would long for a more authentic spiritual life—something Saint Francis represented?"

Anthony nodded. "Right. Francis chose poverty and humility, not to belittle himself but to understand his relationship with the entire world and with God. Michelangelo might not have renounced all material goods, but his close ties to the Franciscans and Vittoria Colonna's circle suggest he wanted to break free from the chains of expectation. He wanted to paint truth, not just commissions. He embraced their vision because it acknowledged that everything, from a blade of grass to the largest cathedral, was connected through the Divine."

Vera's voice softened, her scholarly tone giving way to something more contemplative. "That's the essence of the Franciscan lifestyle, seeing creation as an interconnected whole, alive with God's presence. It's not about the title or the robe. It's about the heart."

His eyes drifted toward the horizon as he imagined Saint Francis roaming the Umbrian hills, speaking to birds, comforting lepers, and embracing all of creation as kin. Quietly, he said, "The time I've spent with Massimo…he never called himself a Franciscan, but he lived it, welcoming strangers, seeing God's reflection in every face. He guided me more than I realized, lending me books, encouraging me to visit the Portiuncula and San Damiano, and challenging me to look deeper within myself. People say he's the purest modern embodiment of Francis's spirit. I can't help but agree."

A gentle silence settled in the car until Vera broke it. "So, you're realizing this path is more than a label. It's about experiencing the world differently, about humility and love, about seeing no separation between oneself, God, and the world He created."

Anthony sighed, but this time it was not a sigh of frustration or uncertainty. It was a breath of understanding. "The Spirituali, Michelangelo, Francis, Massimo—they all point toward the same truth, that faith isn't trapped in buildings or dogma. It's alive and breathing in the way we choose to live, in how we honor the beauty and worth of every person, every creature, every moment."

Vera smiled. "Yes, Anthony, I see it too. It's a relationship with creation itself rather than mere adherence to religious decorum. And if Michelangelo encoded that understanding into his work, then this mystery we're unraveling isn't just about art or hidden clues. It's about a legacy of spiritual insight that survived centuries of turmoil."

Anthony looked back down at the photocopies, seeing them through new eyes. "Then let's find these clues," he said. "And let's do it with this new understanding, remembering that what we're ultimately searching for is more than an artifact. It's a reminder that no matter how dark the corridors of history might seem, there's always a guiding light, a hidden wisdom woven into the fabric of creation itself."

The rolling countryside gave way to the urban sprawl of Rome, the Eternal City's iconic skyline rising on the horizon. Anthony couldn't help but feel a surge of energy as they approached the Vatican, a sense that they were on the cusp of a monumental discovery.

✝

Vera sped through the Tunnel Vaticana, the towering walls of Vatican City looming closer with each passing second. Her eyes darted toward the side streets around the Vatican, searching for a parking spot. Finally, she pulled into a space on Via di Porta Angelica, just under two blocks from Italy's sacred heart.

She grabbed her business bag as Anthony pulled out his Canon 5D camera, then tightened the straps of his Kevlar backpack across his shoulders. They set off at a brisk pace, weaving through the bustling streets as they moved toward St. Peter's Square.

"Once we're inside, we'll start in the Pauline Chapel," Vera said decisively as he adjusted his backpack. "I have a theory about one of the frescoes there."

Anthony raised an eyebrow as they approached a discreet Vatican entrance. "A theory?"

"You'll see," she replied.

He produced his gold card key for instant access through security. As they walked through the vast halls of the Apostolic Palace, the cool marble beneath their feet amplified the sound of their steps. The grandeur of the Vatican surrounded them, the ornate ceilings, towering statues, and intricate tapestries whispering centuries of intrigue.

Vera spoke softly to Anthony along the way. "The Pauline Chapel is another testament to the tension between power and artistry. Pope Paul III commissioned it in 1538, dedicated to the Feast of the Conversion of St. Paul. It was meant to be both a sacred space for worship and a demonstration of the papacy's absolute authority."

Anthony tilted his head. "And Michelangelo was their ultimate instrument?"

"Yes, sir," Vera said, her pace quickening. "By this point, Michelangelo was already hailed as The Divine One. There was no greater artist alive. Paul III knew this and decided Michelangelo was the only one worthy of decorating his chapel. Never mind that the artist was exhausted and anxious to finish his commitment to Julius II's tomb. What the pope demanded took precedence. These frescoes would reflect not only the stories of the saints but also Michelangelo's inner struggles. St. Peter crucified upside down represents ultimate humility, while St. Paul's dramatic fall captures a moment of blinding truth. Michelangelo poured his own conflict into these works."

When they entered the Pauline Chapel, they were met by a hush that magnified the frescoes' power. Michelangelo's works dominated the walls, their muted colors illuminated by soft light filtering through high windows. *The Conversion of Saul* and *The Crucifixion of St. Peter* faced each other in a silent, eternal dialogue. The magnificence of these images was almost breathtaking in the chapel's intimate space.

Vera stepped forward, her gaze immediately drawn to *The Conversion of Saul*. In the fresco, Saul lay sprawled on the ground, just thrown from his horse by a searing bolt of divine light. He shielded his eyes with his left arm, temporarily blinded. Above him, Christ appeared amid a cluster of muscular, twisting figures reminiscent of the Sistine Chapel's monumental forms. She murmured to herself, "For thy resting place sits under the Right Hand of God."

Anthony moved beside her, studying the painting with equal intensity. "So, you think something is hidden here?" he asked quietly.

Around Saul, chaos reigned. One figure raised a shield against the unbearable glare. Another gripped the reins of the panicked horse. A third covered his ears as if to shut out the thunderous vision. The composition teemed with desperate reactions to this supernatural event.

"I do," she said, her voice gaining an edge of excitement. "Michelangelo wasn't merely illustrating scripture. He was weaving layers of symbolism. Even under immense papal pressure, he found ways to embed messages in his art. Consider the varied poses, the shift in perspective, how Christ's outstretched arm points toward Damascus. Look at the tension in every stance, the interplay of light and shadow. There's more here than meets the eye."

Her eyes lingered on Paul's newly altered face—astonished, caught between worlds. The soldiers' weapons angled awkwardly, their bodies poised in disbelief. Every element seemed laden with meaning, each gesture a potential clue.

"The Right Hand of God," Vera repeated softly, following the beam of divine radiance. Yet something felt incomplete. Paul's conversion marked a profound shift, not a serene conclusion. The clue they sought suggested finality, a place of rest, and this scene was all upheaval and beginning.

"We're missing something," she muttered almost to herself.

Anthony took a few steps to view the fresco from another angle. "Maybe it's not about rest," he offered quietly. "What if it points to a path yet to come?"

She pressed her lips together and stepped back, taking in the entire composition once more. "Paul's fall is a catalyst," she said. "It's the start of his mission, not its end. This isn't the resting place we're searching for."

Her eyes drifted to *The Crucifixion of St. Peter* on the opposite wall. The brutal image of Peter's inverted crucifixion was equally striking, but it too seemed at odds with the idea of a peaceful resting place. Chaos and pain didn't align with the clue's suggestion of a final, restful haven.

As Vera studied this fresco, she noted how the crowd clustered around Peter's cross seemed caught in a moment of frantic urgency. Unlike Saul's sudden, blinding revelation, here the tension was drawn out, deliberate, each figure grimacing, straining, or recoiling at the unsettling spectacle. Peter's upside-down position symbolized profound meekness but also underscored the fresco's atmosphere of violent upheaval. Instead of serenity, Michelangelo had depicted a scene of raw human struggle, a testament to faith forged through unimaginable suffering rather than tranquil repose.

After several minutes of silent examination, she sighed. "I thought this was it," she admitted quietly. "It fits so closely, but it doesn't feel right. Neither of these frescoes represents the final rest we're seeking."

Anthony moved beside her, sensing her frustration. "Then it's time to move on."

Vera nodded reluctantly, her gaze lingering on *The Conversion of Saul* as if it might suddenly divulge its secrets. Yet deep down, she knew this wasn't the place. That nearness without resolution gnawed at her.

Saying nothing more, they left the chapel, their footsteps echoing softly through the corridors as they ventured deeper into the Apostolic Palace. Vera's mind churned with new possibilities, her resolve crystallizing with each step.

"It's time," she said. "We must pass through the most inconspicuous door of majesty's past."

Anthony glanced at her, curiosity brightening his eyes, but his footfalls did not hesitate. The path ahead was uncertain, and yet one truth remained clear—the answers they sought were still hidden within these hallowed walls, waiting to be revealed.

CHAPTER 45

The Sistine Chapel, Vatican City
2:15 PM

Enzo and Katarina worked meticulously alongside Alessandro, their eyes scanning the pages of Wadding's journal with an urgency that crackled in the air. Inside the Sistine Chapel, Salvatore Aquilani—a renowned papal art historian and restoration expert—awaited them. They pored over the cryptic passages, convinced that Michelangelo's work held the key. The stakes were impossibly high, the secrets they sought buried beneath centuries of history and hidden within the frescoes towering above them. Their task was clear, their time fleeting.

The group made their way toward the Sistine Chapel, their footsteps echoing ominously through the intricate corridors of Vatican City. Contrary to popular belief, the Sistine Chapel had not always served as the traditional setting for electing popes. In its early history, only twelve popes had been chosen within its sacred walls. The first was Cardinal Rodrigo Borgia, who took the name Pope Alexander VI in 1492. His tenure remained infamous, marked by scandal, corruption, and the controversial sale of Cardinal positions to fund his extravagant lifestyle. It wasn't until Pope Julius II, a fierce opponent of the Borgia family, introduced stricter reforms in 1503 that the process of papal elections began shifting toward greater integrity. By

1513, under Pope Leo X, the Sistine Chapel fell out of favor. For over three centuries, it ceased to host the conclave. Only in 1878 did the tradition resume, and since then, the Sistine Chapel had been synonymous with the sacred act of electing the Vicar of Christ.

Its history weighed heavily on Enzo as he stepped into the chapel. Vatican City was already abuzz with preparations for the upcoming papal conclave. Electricians worked tirelessly at wiring concealed lighting, carpenters adjusted raised flooring, and Vatican security meticulously swept every inch of the premises. The urgency of the conclave heightened the risk of discovery for anyone navigating these shadows. Alessandro, ever the taskmaster, urged the group forward.

Jean Lucca, one of Alessandro's loyal operatives, had already confirmed that Vera and Brunelli were close by, piecing together clues in the Pauline Chapel.

Alessandro's jaw tightened. Competition for the secrets they sought was not ideal. They were now locked in a race. Whoever uncovered the hidden clues first would secure the advantage and forge ahead, leaving the other party fumbling. There was no second place in this quest—only the first to succeed could claim the prize.

Aquilani offered a curt nod as they entered, his gaze flickering nervously toward the frescoed ceiling overhead. He looked as if he knew that precious time was slipping away and each second brought more pressure to find what they sought before Vera and Brunelli succeeded.

"Call me the moment you find what we're looking for," Alessandro growled to Enzo, his grip on the man's arm firm enough to bruise. "We don't have the luxury of patience. People far more powerful than you or me are growing restless."

Enzo nodded, a sharp tension gripping him under the devastating pull of Alessandro's warning. As Alessandro strode away,

Enzo exchanged a tense glance with Katarina. Her expression was dark, her mind still circling her unresolved encounter with Brunelli. A vindictive spark lit her eyes. She wasn't here solely for the mission. She intended to settle a score.

The Sistine Chapel's frescoes stretched high above them, Michelangelo's work commanding reverence even from those too preoccupied to truly admire it. The vaulted ceiling and altar walls, adorned with scenes from the Bible, radiated both divine inspiration and elusive meaning. For centuries, these artworks had been studied, admired, and debated, but now they formed a puzzle the team needed to solve—a path leading to truths buried deep in time. The group dispersed, carefully examining every detail, searching for concealed allegories or hidden symbols that might unlock the secrets they so desperately sought.

Before long, Jean Lucca alerted Enzo that Vera and Brunelli were on their way to the Sistine Chapel. Reacting swiftly, Enzo and his companions slipped into the choir gallery, concealing themselves behind a heavy red velvet curtain that hung like a shroud of secrecy.

T

Most of the contractors had vacated the Sistine Chapel, leaving only a few electricians and carpenters to finalize their tasks. Vera and Anthony slipped inside during this opportune lull, just after a newly constructed raised floor had been installed to create a uniform surface throughout the chapel. Scaffolding, some towering over twenty feet high, was still scattered around the room, while workers methodically sealed the windows to ensure absolute isolation. Before the conclave began, the chapel would be swept with cutting-edge equipment designed to detect any hidden surveillance devices or bugs, ensuring the world outside remained completely unaware of the proceedings within.

Anthony, who had visited the Sistine Chapel a decade earlier, now felt a profound connection he couldn't quite explain. Standing in this hallowed space, surrounded by Michelangelo's breathtaking frescoes—Old Testament scenes on the ceiling and New Testament narratives on the altar wall—he was overwhelmed by a sense of awe. It was as though the divine stories had come alive, resonating more deeply than ever before.

Vera adjusted her powerful binoculars, focusing intently on the ceiling. Methodically, she passed over the six central panels, each laden with intricate detail, including the iconic image of God. Every subtle brushstroke seemed to whisper secrets, urging her to uncover their meaning.

Meanwhile, Anthony unzipped his camera case and pulled out his Canon 5D. He climbed onto one of the scaffolds, ascending to the uppermost tier, and shrugged off his backpack. Lying flat on his back, he positioned himself directly beneath the frescoes, carefully aiming his lens at the vast expanse above. With each shot, the camera's shutter echoed through the chamber, a sharp, pulsing sound that underscored the sheer immensity of the space. The reverberation felt like a heartbeat, a subtle reminder of the infinite nature of the heavens depicted overhead.

His gaze locked onto Michelangelo's *The Creation of Adam*, the iconic moment where God's outstretched right hand reaches toward the first man.

Could this be the clue? he wondered. *The right hand of God? Or does it connect somehow to Vera's earlier explanation about the human brain?*

During their journey to Rome, Vera had shared an intriguing theory with him, something that had lingered in her mind for years. She recounted how, two decades ago, an American doctor had published a groundbreaking hypothesis about *The Creation of Adam*. The crimson shape encircling God and the unborn souls, long interpreted as a womb symbolizing creation, bore a striking resemblance to a cross section of the human brain. This doctor proposed that Michelangelo, renowned for his deep understanding of human anatomy, had encoded a profound message—the Divine connection resides not in external rituals but within the very essence of the human mind.

For centuries, the crimson form had been revered as a representation of life's origin, yet this new interpretation revealed another layer of meaning, a subtle, revolutionary idea that humanity's bond with the Divine begins within. As Anthony reflected on this, he recognized how Michelangelo's blend of art and intellect could serve as a commentary on the Spirituali's ideals.

Gradually, patterns emerged and repeated before his artist's eye, forming an intricate tapestry. Vera had explained how the Spirituali—a secret fellowship of devout reformers—believed salvation came not through the Church's institutional structures, indulgences, or deeds but through *sola fide*, faith in Christ alone. Their vision of reform aligned with the conviction that spirituality was an intimate, personal experience, unmediated by earthly authorities. Now Anthony saw the connection between the Spirituali and the Franciscan movement, both pointing toward the same underlying truth of an internal, unencumbered relationship with the Divine. He had felt it stirring within him since his visits to the two churches Massimo urged him to explore—experiences that had reshaped his understanding of faith and further solidified this new, deeply personal perspective.

His thoughts drifted back to the cryptic verse that had guided their journey, its essence and meaning settling upon him.

Behold the Stairway to Heaven;
Behold the Temple of Solomon;
Behold the Coat of Arms;
For thy resting place sits under the Right Hand of God.

This verse, once distant and abstract, now seemed closer to yielding its secrets. In the context of Vera's theory and the Spirituali's defiance of ecclesiastical hierarchy, it began to take shape. Michelangelo's frescoes were not merely grand expressions of faith—they were messages encoded to endure centuries of scrutiny and silence, waiting for the right moment and the right eyes to reveal their truth.

T

A faint rustle in the gloom caught Vera's attention. She froze, senses taut as if the air itself had stilled. Something felt off, a subtle wrongness that pricked at the edges of her awareness. Carefully shifting her footing, she scanned the dim recesses near the choir gallery, eyes narrowing as they adjusted to the half-light.

That's when she saw it—*Commentarius*, Wadding's stolen journal. It lay on a small table as if casually abandoned, yet its placement was too deliberate, too conspicuous to be mere oversight. Her pulse hammered in her ears.

Why here, of all places? she thought.

Moving slowly, she crouched lower, her gaze drifting beneath the gallery's *cantoria*. The faint outline of a curtain swayed almost imperceptibly. Behind it, the vague silhouettes of several figures hovered in tense stillness lurked, waiting. A quiet, relentless presence seemed to emanate from that corner as though the shadows themselves had grown watchful.

She fought the urge to back away. Every instinct screamed caution, yet her curiosity flared. Maintaining a mask of calm, Vera slipped the journal into her bag, then rose and walked slowly toward the scaffolding. Each step felt deliberate, her posture relaxed despite the tension coiling inside her. Reaching the base of the metal structure where Anthony lay above, she tapped lightly on one of its supports, careful not to draw un-wanted attention.

"Anthony," she murmured, leaning in just enough for her words to carry to him and no one else. "Don't look now, but there are people behind the curtain near the choir gallery. And...I've got the journal."

T

Anthony's eyes widened at her words, though he remained outwardly composed. He stretched, rolling his shoulders as if easing stiff muscles, then slowly lowered his head beyond the scaffold's edge to survey the space below. His body language was casual, calculated—a mask for the tension gripping them both.

As Vera resumed studying the frescoes, he refocused on *The Last Judgment*. Despite the looming threat, he found him-self drawn deeper into Michelangelo's masterpiece. From his elevated vantage point, he examined the intricate details with a near-meditative intensity, each element beckoning him into the work's staggering complexity.

He allowed his gaze to sweep across the colossal fresco dominating the altar wall. Michelangelo's depiction of the second coming of Christ and the final judgment of souls un-furled like a grand celestial drama, meticulously crafted to evoke awe and introspection. For Anthony, it was not just a painting. It was a puzzle layered with symbolism and human emotion, a testament to Michelangelo's genius.

His eyes settled first on the central figure of Christ rendered in divine majesty. Christ's right hand was raised in judgment, his left lowered in mercy. Around him, saints and angels circled like a cosmic entourage. Anthony noted the muscular intensity in Christ's form, a stark departure from the serene depictions common in Renaissance art. Here, Michelangelo presented

Christ as a powerful, almost unsettling arbiter of humanity's fate, commanding both respect and fear.

His attention drifted upward to the assembly of saints. He identified Saint Peter clutching the keys to Heaven, his expression mingling solemnity and hope. Nearby, Saint Bartholomew held his own flayed skin, traditionally associated with his martyrdom. Anthony lingered on the haunting detail of the empty skin—Michelangelo's self-portrait, pensive and somber. The artist seemed to wrestle with his own fears of salvation and damnation, a struggle Anthony found profoundly relatable.

At the fresco's upper portion, bathed in divine light, the redeemed souls ascended toward Heaven. Anthony traced their upward journey, marveling at their dynamic poses—their outstretched arms, their relief and joy. Even here, Michelangelo suggested struggle, souls clinging to one another as if their ascent were hard-won, not guaranteed.

Shifting his focus downward, Anthony studied the chaotic scenes of Hell. The contrast between Heaven's radiance above and the shadowy depths below was striking. Anatomical precision and fluid movement gave form to the damned, each figure contorted in anguish, separated eternally from God. Anthony's gaze fell upon Charon, the infernal ferryman, driving the damned with his oar, and Minos, the underworld's judge, twisted grotesquely, his serpent-entwined body adding a mythical dimension to the horror.

Anthony lingered on the subtleties embedded within this infernal tableau. Some faces were resigned, others defiant, and a few almost pleading. Michelangelo had imbued each damned soul with its own humanity, a reminder that these were not mere symbols but representations of individuals, each carrying their own story.

Between Heaven and Hell, he explored the realm of purgatory. The figures here existed in a liminal space, caught between despair and hope. He found himself drawn to the tug-of-war between angels and demons over a single, struggling soul. The angels' quiet resolve contrasted sharply with the demons' grotesque ferocity, their talons digging into vulnerable flesh.

Anthony marveled at how Michelangelo had seamlessly woven these realms into a single, cohesive vision. The interplay of light and shadow was more than aesthetic. It was symbolic, guiding the viewer's emotions and focus. The divine light emanating from Christ illuminated the saints and ascending souls, while the shadows deepened below, shrouding the damned in oppressive darkness.

As Anthony studied the fresco, he felt a profound bond with Michelangelo's work. It seemed the artist had embedded his own fears, hopes, and questions into its fabric. This was not merely a depiction of the final judgment but a meditation on the human condition, a reflection on the eternal struggle between light and darkness.

Lingering on the space between St. Bartholomew and the underworld, Anthony's mind returned to the cryptic verse.

Behold the Stairway to Heaven;
Behold the Temple of Solomon;
Behold the Coat of Arms;
For thy resting place sits under the Right Hand of God.

The words repeated like a mantra, drawing him deeper into the fresco's mysteries.

In that moment, Anthony made a calculated decision to approach the clues in reverse order. *For thy resting place sits under the Right Hand of God.* This was the most obvious clue, and he was locked in. *Behold our Coat of Arms.* He squinted, searching intently beneath the Right Hand of God for whatever might serve as the coat of arms.

Then he saw it—subtle, almost impossible to discern without a trained eye. Hidden within the chaos between Christ and the underworld lay the infamous coat of arms. The intricate design was unmistakable, larger than life. Michelangelo had carefully integrated it into the tumultuous scene, weaving the symbol into the fresco's narrative with masterful precision. It was a clue for those who understood how the foreground and background intertwined, how certain shapes could be both revealed and obscured by the very complexity of the composition.

Its outlines, faint and elusive, emerged from the swirl of figures suspended between salvation and damnation. From Anthony's inverted vantage point on the scaffold, the code stood out clearly, its intricate form like a beacon amidst divine turmoil. Had he viewed it from a conventional angle, he might have missed it entirely. Only his artist's eye, attuned to Michelangelo's language of allegory and balance, allowed him to perceive the sign.

Anthony marveled at the artist's genius. The coat of arms had been placed with deliberate care, hidden in plain sight beneath the Right Hand of God, nestled within the fresco's chaotic tapestry of Heaven, Hell, and Purgatory. Michelangelo's subtlety demanded not just keen observation but an understanding of the deeper meanings layered in every brushstroke.

Heart pounding, he began snapping photos, his camera's shutter clicks echoing through the Sistine Chapel like a rhythmic heartbeat. Still lying flat on his back, he carefully adjusted the angle for the sharpest, clearest image. He zoomed in, capturing every nuance of the coat of arms, revealing Michelangelo's brilliance in its hidden placement.

Satisfied with his photographs, Anthony forced himself to look away, returning his gaze to the ceiling and feigning interest in the familiar panel depicting God and Adam. He took a few extra shots of the iconic fresco as if merely recording a masterpiece, all to mask his true purpose. Slowly, he strapped his backpack over his shoulders, climbed down from the scaffold, and approached Vera with deliberate calm.

He locked eyes with her, trying to communicate silently. Then, leaning close, he twitched his eyebrows. "I found it," he whispered, his voice barely audible in the chapel's hush.

Her eyes widened, searching his face for confirmation. "Are you certain?" she asked, her voice trembling with excitement and disbelief.

Anthony leaned in closer, his breath steady now as he whispered into her ear, "Yes, absolutely. We need to go, before they realize."

Vera nodded, and they waited a moment longer, feigning casual interest in the frescoes overhead. She snapped a few photographs of her own. Beside her, Anthony stood poised, every sense attuned to their surroundings.

At last, their chance came. The final lingering workers had moved to another part of the chapel, and the shadows behind the choir gallery curtain remained still. Vera and Anthony slipped across the open space, their footsteps muted by the newly installed flooring.

As they exited, the significance of their discovery pressed in like never before. They had entered the Sistine Chapel in search of answers and emerged bearing a revelation. Together, they stepped into the cool Vatican night, armed with newfound knowledge and the resolve to see Anthony's commitment through no matter what obstacles stood in their way.

T

Attempting to decipher Anthony Brunelli's revelation after his departure was proving maddeningly difficult. High above the polished marble floor of the Sistine Chapel, Enzo, Katarina, and Salvatore Aquilani climbed onto the central scaffold, their gazes fixed on the frescoed ceiling. Brunelli's earlier presence lingered like a phantom, hovering at the edges of their thoughts. They shifted from angle to angle, struggling to replicate his line of sight. Frustration etched lines into their faces.

"Salvatore, you're the expert. We're counting on you," Katarina snapped, her impatience evident. "What did they find?"

Salvatore felt the profound heft of their expectations crushing inward on him. He was supposed to be the key—the one who could unlock the mystery. Lying on his back in the same spot Brunelli had occupied, he raised his binoculars toward *The Creation of Adam*, trying to see what he had seen just moments before. At first, the fresco's colors and intricate lines dissolved into a blur of shapes and shadows. Then, as though struck by lightning, he jolted upright.

"I've got it!" he exclaimed, excitement charging his voice. "It's about man's relationship with God—Michelangelo's greatest masterpiece!"

Enzo and Katarina turned, curiosity halting their complaints.

Salvatore's voice trembled with fervor as he pointed toward *The Creation of Adam*, his hand shaking slightly. "What Michelangelo captured here—what he immortalized—is the essence of humanity's connection to the Divine," he said, eyes gleaming. "Adam represents all of humankind. His body is the temple we must preserve so our eternal soul can ascend. Look at how God extends His hand. It's not just a gesture. It's an *invitation.* An invitation to unite the physical body with the divine spirit!"

Enzo and Katarina exchanged puzzled looks. They wanted something concrete, a tangible clue, not a theological lecture.

Despite their dismay, Salvatore pressed on, tapping his temple for emphasis. "Michelangelo was a master of human anatomy," he continued. "He's showing us that our relationship with God occurs right here—in the mind!" He grinned, certain he had made a breakthrough.

Enzo's patience snapped. "We don't care about the brain, Salvatore! What did Brunelli see? Where are the clues?"

Salvatore's enthusiasm faltered. He was lost in his own revelation. "I-I'm still working on that," he stammered. "But I'm close. I can feel it." His voice wavered, trying to convince himself he was on the right path.

T

Enzo grabbed Katarina's arm and pulled her aside. "This guy is useless. We're wasting time. I'm calling Alessandro."

Katarina's eyes narrowed, her lips pressing into a thin, furious line. "Brunelli's slipped through my fingers twice," she hissed, glaring at Aquilani, who remained absorbed in Michelangelo's imagery. "I won't let it happen again."

Without another word, Enzo and Katarina climbed down from the scaffold, leaving Aquilani behind still muttering about symbolism and salvation. They slipped out of the chapel, their footsteps echoing in the hallowed darkness.

Outside, at the edge of Vatican City, they spotted Jean Lucca crossing a busy street.

"You just missed them," he said. "I trailed them. They left in Vera's car, headed that way." He pointed down the dimly lit road.

Katarina cursed under her breath, bending forward as if physically struck by the realization. Again, they were too late. She cursed, fists clenched. "This ends now."

Enzo nodded, tension coiling through him like a drawn bowstring. There would be no more errors. They would find Brunelli and Vera—and this time, there would be no escape.

Il Gianicolo, Rome
4:05 PM

Vera's Alfa Romeo Giulia hugged the tight corners of Viale Vaticano, tires screeching as she steered into the ancient streets. Anthony, his mind racing as quickly as the car, suggested finding a secluded spot where he could show her precisely what he'd discovered. She headed westward toward Il Gianicolo, a serene hilltop park offering a quiet view of Rome.

"Where's the Michelangelo book?" he asked.

"In the trunk," Vera replied, eyes fixed on the road. "Just a minute. We're almost there."

Within moments, they reached the base of Il Gianicolo. Known for its monument to Garibaldi and the eighty-four busts of Italy's national heroes, the park also offered sweeping views of Rome's bell towers and historic churches. Tonight, however, the beauty of the panorama was secondary.

Vera parked swiftly, retrieved the book from the trunk, and slipped back behind the wheel. "Okay," she said, handing it over. "Show me what you saw."

Anthony wasted no time, opening the volume to a full-page of *The Last Judgment*. The print paled in comparison to the fresco itself, but it would suffice for his purpose. "Look here, directly beneath the Right Hand of God," he said as he pointed to a specific section of the image. "See anything familiar?"

She squinted, studying the intricate details closely. "No," she said at last, shaking her head. "I see Mary, San Lorenzo, the clouds…everything I've seen a hundred times before. Anthony, I've never noticed anything unusual."

He turned the book upside down, mimicking his vantage point from the scaffold. "What about now?"

Though skeptical, she studied the image again. Then she gasped, her hand flying to her mouth. "Oh my God," she whispered, breath catching. "The tau cross…the Franciscan coat of arms…it's right there."

Amid the painted sky, hidden in plain sight under the Right Hand of God, was the unmistakable shape of a tau cross. It blended so subtly into *The Last Judgment* that it felt almost like an optical illusion.

"It's profound, isn't it?"

"Incredible," she murmured, still staring. "How did I never see this before? A massive tau cross, hidden in the sky… Michelangelo was a genius." She lowered the book to her lap and tapped another area. "Look, beneath Mary's foot," she said, indicating a strong male figure. "That's San Lorenzo. The Basilica of San Lorenzo, where the Laurentian Library is housed, was the parish church of the Medici family.

"Michelangelo himself designed the Laurentian Library and worked there extensively, even hiding in a secret chamber beneath the Medici Chapels during turbulent times in Florence. San Lorenzo was martyred in the third century, burned alive on a gridiron. Here, Michelangelo uses his image as another allegory. Anthony, the gridiron is our Stairway to Heaven."

He nodded, a smile spreading across his face. "You're right! It symbolizes a path to salvation. It all fits."

Vera traced the image thoughtfully with her index finger, marveling at Michelangelo's subtle brilliance. "San Lorenzo's martyrdom, the stairway to heaven, right under God's hand…

astonishing. And something just struck me—look at this woman behind San Lorenzo, her eyes peeking just above the gridiron."

Anthony leaned in, nodding in anticipation.

"That figure," she said quietly, "is widely believed to be Vittoria Colonna. Michelangelo placed her there with purpose, to meet her gaze in such a subtle yet deliberate way. By situating her behind San Lorenzo, Michelangelo seems to be linking Colonna's spiritual purity and reformist piety to the courage and sacrifice that San Lorenzo represents. In other words, he's visually endorsing the Spirituali's inward spirituality, aligning Colonna's moral and intellectual influence with a saintly model of devotion. But I think there's a dual meaning here. Michelangelo used Vittoria Colonna's figure as a hidden point of trust, revealing this is where the Stairway to Heaven can be found. Anthony, Michelangelo left this clue in *The Last Judgment* for you!"

He shook his head slowly, still staring at the fresco as if seeing it anew. "This is all so surreal," he said quietly, his voice tinged with amazement. "To think Michelangelo—under instructions from the minister general of his time—would hide these clues so intricately, all so they could one day be discovered by me." He ran a hand through his hair as if to steady himself. "It's astounding, Vera. Centuries of history unfolding right here, right now, through this painting. I've spent my life studying art, but I never dreamed art was studying me back."

Now, only Solomon's Temple remained—the last clue to solve. Anthony reached into the backseat and retrieved his sketchpad, eager to translate this revelation into lines and shapes. As he drew, Vera watched, captivated by his talent.

"What were those measurements Wadding mentioned?" he asked without looking up.

"Its length, twice its height, threescore its width," Vera recalled promptly.

The memory aligned perfectly with his emerging sketch. He worked quickly, drawing a three-dimensional form. "Vera, this is our last clue. This is Solomon's Temple," he said softly, voice influenced with realization. "These are our coordinates."

"Behold the Temple of Solomon," Vera repeated. "Anthony, that's the fourth and final clue. You've found the map… You've solved the puzzle!"

"No," he corrected gently, meeting her eyes. "*We* solved it."

T

A flush of pride and affection lit Vera's face. She lifted the book again, turning it upside down to marvel once more at the hidden tau cross, emotion welling inside her. "What makes this even more astonishing is that the Sistine Chapel was built with dimensions closely reflecting those of Solomon's Temple. Michelangelo not only provided the coordinates referencing Solomon's Temple but also placed the fresco itself within the Sistine Chapel, its…its modern-day architectural echo of that ancient holy site.

"Historically, scholars and historians have noted that the Sistine Chapel's proportions, about 40.9 meters in length by 13.4 meters in width, were deliberately chosen to echo the biblical dimensions of Solomon's Temple. Although not an exact match, the chapel's architects drew inspiration from the ancient temple's measurements, hoping to evoke its sanctity and significance. This architectural homage was well-known in certain scholarly circles, yet the subtle integration of Michelangelo's frescoes—both referencing and encoding the temple's symbolism—added another layer of meaning."

Setting the book aside, she leaned closer and pressed her lips to Anthony's cheek in a tender, meaningful gesture that left them both breathless.

He smiled, dazed. "What was that for?"

Her laughter was soft, warm. "Because you're not just talented, you're *brilliant*. I've studied that fresco for years and never thought to look at it upside down."

Before Anthony could respond, his phone rang and sliced through the quiet moment. He fumbled and answered on the third ring. "Hello?"

A cold, high-pitched voice crackled on the line. "If you want to see Richard Pescatore alive, return to the Sistine Chapel. You have thirty minutes."

The call ended before he could reply.

Eyes wide, she spoke in a hushed tone. "I heard. Who was that?"

Anthony's expression darkened. "I don't know, but they mean it. We can't ignore this."

Fastening her seatbelt, Vera's eyes flashed with urgency. "What do we do? Are we going back?"

He nodded grimly, attempting Rick's number again, only to be met with voicemail once more. He pressed his lips together, unease and frustration etched in every line of his face.

She stared straight ahead, her mind racing. "Wait," she said quietly. "I think I know where Richard might be."

"You do?" Anthony asked, his voice edged with tension. "Where?"

She pressed her lips together, her gaze fixed on the road. "It's a secluded location not far from the Vatican. But first, I'm calling Daniello."

CHAPTER 47

Though it had been nearly twelve hours since his capture, Richard had no clear sense of time. His world had shrunk to a dark, cramped space smelling of old wood. Blindfolded, hands and feet bound, his senses were dull but not extinguished. He could tell he was in a confined area, perhaps a booth or small room. The air felt stifling, and his limbs ached from their unnatural position. Occasionally, a faint breeze drifted through what he guessed was a screen nearby.

Then it struck him—a confessional.

Shifting uneasily, he strained to listen. He could hear muffled Italian voices seeping through the heavy wooden door, their accents unfamiliar and their tones sharp, aggressive. The danger pressed in on him, suffocating.

His throat burned with thirst. He called out for water, voice hoarse and cracking, but received only silence. In the distance, faint church bells tolled every fifteen minutes, mocking him by the count of the passing hours.

As the final chime signaled, footsteps broke the oppressive hush. Keys jingled, followed by the swift snap of a zip tie slicing off his ankles. He flexed his legs, relief flickering but not lasting. Before he could react, rough hands yanked him from his seat and dragged him onto a larger chair. The air felt different, more open now, but still his blindfold stayed firmly in place. A forceful shove planted him in the chair.

Then came a voice, low, familiar, dripping with malice.

"Richard, Richard…so we meet again. You've really outdone yourself this time."

Richard's breath caught. The voice was older, raspier, punctuated by strained wheezes, but he knew it. A figure from his past.

"And you were supposed to be the clever one," the voice sneered, each word laced with contempt. "The one trusted with such an important task…watching over that precious child. The one with a pure heart."

Richard's mind raced, pieces snapping into place. The bitterness, the scorn—he recognized this man.

The voice turned colder, slicing through the dim space like a knife. "Well, let me show you what your cleverness has earned you."

Rough hands grabbed him again, hauling him upright and dragging him toward a window. A sudden yank tore off his blindfold, and harsh light stabbed his eyes.

Blinking, he struggled to focus, stomach churning at the scene below.

Hanging upside down from an iron stake in the courtyard was the lifeless body of Friar Basilio Heiser, former Minister General. His corpse swayed in the night breeze, cassock torn and bloodied.

"The minister general should've chosen his allies more wisely," the voice taunted.

Richard turned to face the speaker and froze.

Standing just a few feet away was Father Alessandro delle Rovere, a once-devout man now rogue and corrupt. Malice radiated from his lined face, his eyes blazing with vindictive satisfaction. Time had etched bitterness into every crease, and his hatred burned as fiercely as ever. He had become apostate, renouncer of the very faith he had once vowed to serve. Alessandro stepped closer, wheezing softly. Without warning, he spat into Richard's face.

The vile mucus ran down Richard's cheek, a final insult. Though fury simmered within him, he forced himself to remain silent.

Two captors seized Richard's arms, binding his limbs even tighter.

Alessandro hovered above, voice low and venomous. "I have a few questions for you, Richard," he said, tone deceptively calm. "Where is Anthony keeping the cylinders?"

Richard held his tongue, defiance in every taut muscle.

Silence stretched, tense and suffocating.

Alessandro nodded to one of his men, who advanced and sliced open Richard's shirt with large scissors. Cool air brushed his bare back, raising gooseflesh.

"I'll ask again," Alessandro growled. "Where are the cylinders?"

Still, Richard refused to speak, jaw clenched in unyielding resolve.

Alessandro patience snapped. Another captor handed him a leather whip, its surface cracked and worn with years of use. Alessandro ran his fingers along it almost tenderly, then stepped back. With a sharp crack, the whip bit into Richard's back.

The pain flared instantly, but Richard bit down hard, refusing to cry out.

Again and again, the whip struck, each lash carving fresh agony into his flesh. He counted silently, focusing on the rhythm to endure the torment. Blood trickled down his back, and every nerve screamed, yet his resolve stood firm.

After more than ten lashes, Alessandro leaned in, breath hot and fetid. "This is your last chance. Tell me where the cylinders are, or Brunelli will be next."

Richard met Alessandro's gaze, unflinching. He would not betray his friend.

Alessandro's sharp nod signaled a new horror. A brute named Fargazo stepped forward hefting a polished wooden club. Without hesitation, he swung it down. The impact jolted through Richard, pain exploding in white-hot sparks. Darkness rushed in as he slumped to the floor, unconscious.

Suddenly, the door burst open.

"Polizia! Polizia!" a voice rang out, sharp and commanding.

Alessandro's men scattered as chaos erupted, boots thundering across the stone floor as they fled through an emergency exit. In their panicked haste, they left Pescatore behind—bloody, broken, and alone.

After an urgent call from Vera, Captain Daniello Rossi and the Italian authorities, along with the TPA arrived at the villa within minutes and moved swiftly to secure the scene. Inside, they found Pescatore barely clinging to life. His body, battered and torn, gave no response to their initial attempts at resuscitation. He was ghastly pale, deep lacerations running across his back and torso—evidence of brutal torture. Blood loss had driven him into hypovolemic shock—his pulse weak, his breathing shallow.

EMTs rushed in and worked frantically to stabilize him. They applied pressure to the wounds, wrapped makeshift bandages, and, after a tense twenty minutes, managed to place him on a gurney. Navigating the villa's steep, narrow stairs was treacherous, but time was precious. Every second counted as they hurried him to the nearest trauma center, his life hanging by the thinnest of threads.

Outside, one of Rossi's men urgently beckoned him to the rear courtyard. There, he faced a scene of horror: the lifeless body of Friar Basilio Heiser—what remained of it—hung grotesquely from an iron stake. Flesh burned beyond recognition, the minister general's identification lay neatly at his feet, along with his cap and overcoat, as if mocking the concept of identity itself. The murder's cruelty conjured disturbing echoes of mafia brutality, surpassing anything the Italian police had encountered in recent memory. Even Rossi's most seasoned officers struggled to mask their revulsion.

Rossi stepped away from the crime scene to call Vera.

T

The phone rang just as she guided the Alfa Romeo onto a quieter stretch of road. She tapped the speaker button. "Daniello, I'm here."

"Vera," Rossi said, his tone grim. "We found Richard Pescatore."

Vera and Anthony exchanged a quick, anxious glance. "Is he…?"

"He's alive," Rossi continued. "Barely. He's in critical condition. Severe blood loss, multiple lacerations. The EMTs are rushing him to a trauma center now, but his chances…" He paused. "It's bad, Vera. And don't even think about going to the hospital. I don't want you or Brunelli anywhere near there."

Anthony lowered his head, burying his face into his hands, far too upset to speak.

Vera swallowed hard, her knuckles whitening on the steering wheel. "My God. Daniello? Is there anything we can do?"

Rossi's tone hardened. "No. Not now. Whoever did this is still out there, and your presence could make things worse for both of you and for Richard. Let the doctors handle it. I need you focused and keeping your distance."

Vera took a shaky breath, resisting the urge to argue. "Alright, we'll stay away. Just…keep us posted, please."

"I will," Rossi promised, his voice softening a fraction. "But remember what I said, Vera. Be careful. And call me if you learn anything that might help."

"You have my word. We left Rome about thirty minutes ago, now heading to Assisi. It's been quite the day. I don't have time to explain it all now, but we found the Wadding journal. I'll fill you in about everything when we talk next."

"You found the journal and you're just telling me?" Rossi's voice sharpened again. "Vera, you can't leave me in the dark. I need to know what you and Brunelli are up to. The crime scene is still active, and whoever's behind this is extremely dangerous."

"Give me until tomorrow," Vera replied. "I'll have more answers then, I promise. Let's talk in the morning. And, Daniello…thank you." She ended the call.

T

Anthony sat in silence. His father still missing and now Rick's life was in peril. Yet he couldn't let fear cloud his judgment—not now. Too much depended on what they were piecing together, and time was running short.

Vera maneuvered through Rome's bustling streets while he flipped through the materials on his lap, trying to refocus. *The Last Judgment* stared back from the open pages of the large book, the answers they needed buried somewhere in Michelangelo's tangled symbolism.

Breaking the silence, Anthony said quietly, "It's hard to concentrate with all this happening. Where were we? I need the distraction."

"We were discussing the Temple of Solomon," Vera replied.

"We have the map. We just need to assemble it. We're close."

Anthony's thoughts drifted to Michelangelo's revelations, the centuries of politics and rivalries woven into these secrets. "Do you think Michelangelo knew exactly what he was doing?" he asked. "He must have understood the power struggles around him. The Medici, the della Rovere…he was caught in the middle."

Vera glanced at the sketches Anthony had made. "Michelangelo was brilliant. He knew how to navigate their schemes. The della Rovere were Franciscans, sure, but they weren't innocent. They exploited their positions. Michelangelo understood the stakes, and he knew how to hide his secrets."

Halfway to Assisi, Vera pulled off the autostrada into a quiet, dimly lit fuel station. After refueling, she retrieved the Kevlar backpack and her business bag, then tossed the keys to Anthony. "You drive," she said, settling into the passenger seat with her materials. "I need to review and translate the rest of the parchment Richard found. There might be something we've overlooked."

Anthony nodded, sliding behind the wheel. "Fine by me. Honestly, I almost forgot about that parchment."

T

Vera slipped on white cotton gloves and carefully extracted the parchment from the *Ramorosso Manifesto*. The handwriting was ancient but remarkably clear. It didn't take her long to confirm a hunch. Her breath quickened as she read. "Anthony, this is it. This is the missing piece."

Anthony glanced over, then refocused on the road. "The missing piece, meaning?"

"It's confirming what I thought all along," Vera said, eyes tracing every line of script. "The whole business with Pilate and his story about the beloved Virgin Mary. He confessed that he lied. And the Church knew that if his original documents were to get into the wrong hands, it could potentially shatter a belief based on an untruth. The parchment from the first cylinder made it seem that the false story of Mary might be true, meticulously crafted to fool anyone. But this parchment…it's the second part. The truth."

Anthony kept his eyes on the road, but she could tell he was hanging on every word.

Vera slipped on her reading glasses, her voice hushed as if someone might overhear even though they were in her car. "Alright," she began, swallowing hard. "It says here, 'Three years after Pontius Pilate ordered the crucifixion of Jesus Christ, he was removed from office by Emperor Tiberius. Summoned to Rome, Pilate carried a parchment he claimed disproved the virgin birth, that Mary had been violated by an unknown assailant and Joseph only posed as her husband to maintain her dignity en route to Bethlehem. Pilate hoped this so-called proof would secure his station, but by the time he reached Rome, Tiberius was dead and Caligula had taken the throne. When Pilate confessed he'd converted to Christianity—calling Jesus the King of the Jews—Caligula demanded he verify his claim that Jesus wasn't divinely conceived. Pilate couldn't. Infuriated, Caligula made things extremely difficult for Pilate. He fell into misfortune and likely took his own life under Caligula's reign.' "

Anthony stiffened, knuckles whitening on the steering wheel. "So Pilate's 'evidence' was just a desperate attempt to save himself. Unbelievable. And all these centuries, the Church was guarding it?"

Vera nodded. "The parchment says it was held as Church property under Roman rule until Emperor Constantine ended the persecution of Christians with the Edict of Milan in 313. That allowed confiscated Church possessions to be restored, Pilate's parchment among them." She flipped to another section, her eyes scanning lines of ancient script. "Over time, it reached the popes. In 1221, Pope Honorius III came to Assisi, asking that the parchment be buried and its location recorded.

This formed a trust between the Catholic Church and the newly founded Franciscan Order."

Anthony's brow furrowed. "So, Honorius tasked Francis with protecting this secret? That's an enormous responsibility. But why hide it?"

Vera exhaled slowly, her gaze drifting out the windshield. "Because even the rumor of this secret—let alone the truth of it—could shake the very foundation of Christianity. Honorius knew the Church's entire identity, its power and influence, rests on Christ's divine nature. If Pilate's false claim got into the wrong hands, it wouldn't just erode faith…it could become a weapon. By entrusting Francis and, in turn, your family, with this burden, Honorius ensured the secret remained buried, guarded by those with no personal ambition to exploit it. For centuries, it's been locked away, waiting for the right moment, and the right people, to decide what to do with it."

He inhaled sharply. "My family… So that's the reason we hold a piece of this puzzle. Francis entrusted it to us to ensure the truth—this terrible, destabilizing truth—would remain hidden until the right moment."

"That's why we must find the Sacred Order to see what else, if anything, might be hidden." She resumed reading, voice taut with tension, " 'If found, know that Francis's dying wish has come true.' "

Vera sighed. "The parchment also mentions Pope Honorius entrusting Francis of Assisi with this truth and the original Pilate Stone, where Pilate had first inscribed the false account. The pope must have known that only someone like Francis could safeguard such a dangerous truth. Something is not adding up because the Pilate Stone, a limestone block, was discovered in June 1961 by Italian archaeologist Maria Teresa Fortuna Canivet during an excavation campaign in the area of an ancient theater in Rome. I researched this excavation heavily. The theater was constructed by decree of Herod the Great around 15 BC. Today, this stone rests in a museum in Jerusalem. I've seen it for myself."

She performed a quick internet search on her phone. "The stone reads, *To the Divine Augusti Tiberieum…Pontius Pilate… prefect of Judea…has dedicated this.* The fact that the parchment mentions the Pilate Stone is not adding up, so for now, that piece remains a mystery." She gently refolded the parchment, her eyes flicking to Anthony's reflection in the rearview mirror. "What we do know is that Michelangelo, the Franciscans, even your ancestors—they all played a critical part in this. Pilate's lie became a deadly secret. And now we're holding the key to it all."

"So Pilate's false account, this vile accusation, was never about truth. It was about power, extortion, and survival. And now it's resurfacing, threatening everything."

Vera placed a protective hand over the parchment. "Yes. And the Ramorosso knew if they were to get their hands on the entire tale, the reigning pope becomes a puppet. They'll dictate Church policy, siphon wealth, steer the world's largest religious institution for their own gain. We can't ever let that happen."

They drove on in tense silence, the headlights carving a path through the darkness. The vastness of eight centuries of secrets pressed down on them both, as Vera's last words echoed in the hush of the night. "You have to finish what Francis started, Anthony. You're the last line of defense."

✝

Seventy nautical miles away, a Gulfstream 150 circled over Rome's airspace. The pilot's voice crackled through the cabin, announcing, "Your destination is Perugia-Sant'Egidio Airport, just outside Assisi. We'll have you on the ground in fifteen minutes."

Enzo and Katarina exchanged tense glances.

CHAPTER 49

Parked on Via San Francesco beside Piazza del Pace, Vera and Anthony pored over ancient documents and scrolls, their anticipation growing with each passing moment. The air felt charged, as though centuries of secrets pressed in around them. They were certain the final clues to the Sacred Order's whereabouts lay hidden within these parchments.

"While we're waiting for Lara and her cousins, I remember something Massimo told me," Anthony began quietly. "After Francis died and work began on the Basilica, Brother Leo had a falling out with the brotherhood. In a fit of rage, he hurled a marble box full of offertories over the Hill of Hell. The box shattered, and that was it. Brother Elias demanded Leo's expulsion from the Order. But Leo negotiated two conditions. First, the Basilica's entrance had to be placed exactly where he specified, with the word *Altrix* etched into the entry stone; and second, that the land east of the Basilica be preserved and named Piazza del Pace, never to be built upon."

Vera leaned over the center console, her eyes bright with understanding. "That explains why everything we need is still intact!" She reached for the first scroll, her fingers trembling. "Hand me the scroll."

Anthony retrieved the limestone cylinder from his backpack and passed it to her.

She carefully removed the cap and drew out an ancient scroll. Unfurling it, her gaze settled on Roman numerals in the top-right corner. "LX," she muttered, then compared these numerals to the others, XX and XXX. Her eyes widened. "These Roman numerals are coordinates! You've already sketched the gridiron out as Solomon's Temple, and these Roman numerals represent paces leading us to the Sacred Order."

Anthony studied his sketch, piecing it together. "Michelangelo deliberately omitted the height dimension in *The Last Judgment*. Otherwise, it would've been too obvious."

"You're right," Vera agreed. "The gridiron corresponds to Solomon's Temple, but we need the exact dimensions of the Temple as mentioned in the Bible."

Anthony tapped at his phone. "I've got it. The measurements are thirty, ninety, forty-five."

Vera's shoulders sagged. "Those numbers don't match the Roman numerals from the scrolls."

A heavy silence fell.

Soon, Vera straightened. "Anthony, search again, but this time add *Vulgate*."

"V-u-l-g-a-t-e?" he spelled out, eyebrow raised.

"Yes. Francis and Leo would've only had access to the Latin Vulgate version of the Bible, not the King James. The King James came much later."

He typed again. A new set of results popped up. "Here it is…twenty, sixty, thirty."

"That's it!" Vera's voice rose in triumph. The numbers matched perfectly with the parchments left inside the limestone cylinders, also matching the Roman numerals from *Kings 6:2*.

They exchanged a look of shared understanding—they'd cracked the code.

"We've solved the mystery of the Roman numerals," Anthony said. "We have everything we need."

"We're so close…"

"Vera, how would Leo have measured distance? Would it be paces or meters?"

"Well, one pace is roughly a meter," Vera replied. "But we still need direction."

T

Anthony's attention was momentarily drawn to the windshield where he spotted Lara walking toward them. He hopped out. "Any luck with that permit?"

Lara grinned mischievously, brandishing a slip of paper. "Today's your lucky day."

Behind her, Lara's four cousins waited in a large white caravan loaded with equipment. She handed Anthony an official certificate—PERMESSO—granting them permission to excavate at Piazza del Pace.

"You're unbelievable," Anthony said, giving Lara a high-five.

"What can I say? It helps when your uncle's the town clerk," she teased. "And my cousins came prepared. They brought every tool known to man."

Anthony laughed, relieved as he glanced at her cousins, eager and ready. Then he excused himself and returned to the car.

Inside, Vera had been busy. She explained, "I called a colleague in Germany, an expert on medieval directional symbols. He identified the markings next to the numerals. The first scroll's symbol is a Maltese cross indicating sixty paces due east. It aligns with a wind rose pointing toward Jerusalem."

Anthony's heart pounded as he reviewed his sketch.

"The second scroll's symbol," Vera continued, "calls for twenty paces northeast, and the third for thirty paces south."

Anthony mapped the directions on paper. The gridiron, the Roman numerals, and these symbols formed a grand map to the Sacred Order.

"I'm ready," he said, opening a compass app on his phone.

He started at the Basilica's entrance where *Altrix* was carved into stone. "Sixty steps east," he called, counting carefully as he walked each pace. "Now, twenty northeast. And finally, thirty south," he called out, halting in the square's center. "Here!"

Lara's cousins wasted no time erecting a small tent and getting straight to work. After digging several feet into the soil, they found nothing.

Doubt knotted Anthony's stomach. "What are we missing?" he asked.

Vera bit her bottom lip in deep thought.

"Was there another way they calculated distance in the Middle Ages?" Anthony asked.

Vera pressed a hand to her forehead. "Cubits!" she exclaimed.

"Cubits?" Anthony repeated.

"Yes," Vera said, excited again. "A cubit is roughly a foot and a half, the length from a man's elbow to his fingertips."

Anthony's hope rekindled. He recalculated the map using cubits before pacing off the distance again—sixty cubits east, then twenty cubits northeast, then thirty cubits south. This placed them closer to the Basilica, still within Piazza del Pace's grassy area.

"I've got it!" he shouted.

Vera hurried over, eyes shining. "Let's try again!"

Lara's cousins relocated the tent and began digging at the new location. Shovels scraped earth, each clang echoing through the still night. After a few minutes, Fabrizio's shovel struck something solid, the sound of metal against stone slicing the silence.

"Stop!" Fabrizio called.

Everyone crowded closer, craning their necks, hearts pounding.

Anthony knelt at the hole's edge, peering in. "Careful," he urged.

Gently, Fabrizio cleared away soil, revealing a stone slab etched with ancient markings. Time had worn its surface smooth, but one symbol stood out—the tau cross, unmistakable and profound.

"Oh my God…" Vera whispered. She looked up at Anthony, her eyes brimming with awe. "This is it."

Anthony knelt beside her, fingertips tracing the ancient stone. "We've found it," he said. "I don't believe it."

As they cleared more dirt, they realized this stone was more than a marker—it sealed an entrance.

"You've got to be kidding," Anthony muttered. "It looks like there's an underground chamber?"

Vera's voice shook. "Hidden all along, right here."

They paused, the depth of centuries bearing down. Then Anthony placed his hand on the slab. "Let's open it. We have to see what's in there."

Lara's cousins pried at the stone, centuries of dirt and silence resisting them. Finally, the slab lifted and they removed it completely. A gust of stale air rushed out, carrying the scent of ancient earth. Below, a dark void waited with stone steps descending into the earth.

Anthony took a flashlight from his pack, its beam slicing through the gloom. "I'll go first," he said.

Vera gripped his arm. "Go slow," she advised. "Be careful."

He nodded before stepping onto the first stair. The stone steps creaked but held firm. Vera followed close behind as they moved deeper underground. At the bottom, a small, ornate door awaited, its carvings and symbols mirroring the scrolls.

"This is it," Anthony murmured, awe and astonishment interwoven in his tone. Together, they pulled open the heavy door, its hinges groaning.

Inside the dim chamber, a small stone slab stood at the center. On it rested an ornately decorated chest—a marble reliquary. Anthony's breath caught, and he reached out, hand trembling. The moment his fingers touched the chest, he knew their journey had led them here.

The marble reliquary Saint Francis called the Sacred Order was now within his control.

T

Hidden amid the dense woodland north of the piazza, Enzo and Katarina arrived, crouched low, eyes locked on a large white tent illuminated by dim lights. The night air was still, and every scent, every whisper of movement felt amplified. They had the perfect vantage point.

Without a word, they prepared to strike. Moving with the fluid grace of seasoned operatives, they scaled a low wall using thin climbing ropes, their motions swift and silent. At the top, they dropped down and sprinted toward the tent. Their footsteps barely made a whisper on the frost-kissed grass, each step calculated, their training sharp as a scalpel.

Enzo slid a Pico Beretta from its holster, the familiar grip reassuring in his palm. Katarina flipped open the safety latch on her weapon, a V-42 Italian stiletto, the devil's brigade blade known for its needle-sharp precision. Approaching the tent's rear, they moved in tandem, their breaths shallow and controlled.

Enzo raised a hand beside his ear, signaling to Katarina with subtle finger motions. One, two, three. In a single fluid motion, they rounded the corner of the tent like living shadows. Enzo led with his Beretta, eyes sweeping the interior. Katarina followed, stiletto poised to strike.

After a tense heartbeat, both realized the tent was empty. Not a soul stirred inside. There was only a four-foot hole in the ground and a mound of freshly turned earth.

Katarina lowered her blade, frustration tightening her features. "Not again," she snarled under her breath.

Enzo took a step closer to the hole, lowering his weapon slightly. "They were here," he murmured, "but they're gone now."

A man stepped into the tent and asked, "Can we help you?" His imposing frame cast a deep shadow, his words firm and unwelcoming.

Caught off guard but quick-witted, Enzo forced a casual smile and put the gun in his right hand behind his back while holding up his phone in his left as if taking photos. "Oh, we're just curious tourists! What was dug up here? Part of a historical tour, perhaps?"

A second man appeared from behind the taller man, folded his arms and stepped forward, closing the distance. Enzo guessed by their resemblance that they were brothers.

The first man's voice remained stern. "This is a restricted area. You need to leave."

Even for Enzo, the brothers' presence was menacing.

T

Reading the situation, Katarina managed a bright, false smile. "So sorry," she said smoothly, tugging Enzo's arm. "We must've gotten separated from our group. We'll be on our way."

They exited the tent swiftly, retreating as fast as they'd arrived. Her anger simmered beneath her cool façade. Crossing the square, her footsteps crunched over frosted grass. By the time they reached the sidewalk, she'd had enough.

She halted, her hand drifting to her hair tie and pulling it free, letting pale strands fall loose.

"What are you doing?" Enzo asked.

She didn't answer. Instead, she rounded the parked car nearby—Vera's car—inspecting it with predatory calm. Satisfied no one was watching, she leaned against the trunk, her fingers curling around the handle of her stiletto. With one swift, practiced thrust, she plunged the blade into the rear tire. A soft hiss escaped as air rushed out, the tire deflating in seconds. Katarina straightened, pulling the blade free, a satisfied smirk tugging at her lips.

Turning to Enzo, her voice dripped with satisfaction, "Now they won't be going anywhere too quickly."

Together, they melted into the shadows, leaving the crippled car behind.

CHAPTER 50

Sacro Convento, Assisi
9:15 PM

In the moonlit courtyard, Anthony called Friar Martin. The friar answered after several rings, sleep evident in his fumbling with the phone. Despite being awakened, he agreed to meet them.

Anthony stood beside Vera, cradling the marble chest wrapped in her silk scarf. The night air held that peculiar Assisi stillness. His gaze swept the scene, settling on a familiar figure under the portico. There sat Massimo, barefoot as always, his presence as constant as the portico itself.

"Give me a moment," Anthony said gently to Vera, setting the reliquary carefully at their feet. As he approached Massimo, the hermit's calm eyes tracked his movement with quiet awareness.

"Antonio? Is that you?" Massimo's voice carried softly through the evening air.

"Yes, Massimo," Anthony replied. "I know it's late, but I've found something remarkable and I'd like you to join me."

"No, no, Antonio. Please, go on without me." Though curiosity flickered in the hermit's eyes, true to his nature, he seemed content to let fate run its course without his direct involvement.

"Massimo, I insist," Anthony urged, his voice firm. "Whether you realize it or not, you've played a tremendous part in making this possible. Please…come with me."

The monk studied him with eyes that seemed to peer through centuries. After a moment's contemplation, he rose silently, his weathered hands gripping his walking stick. His bare feet made no sound against the ancient stone as he followed Anthony back to where Vera waited.

Vera offered a polite smile, though Anthony could sense her uncertainty about this mysterious figure. He placed a reassuring hand on her shoulder, a silent promise that all was well. "Vera, I'd like you to meet Massimo."

Massimo dipped his head and extended his hand. "*Buonasera*," he said softly.

Vera shook his hand, a surprising warmth in her tone as she said, "It's a pleasure, Massimo. Anthony has spoken very highly of you."

Massimo's lips curved in a faint smile. "I fear he flatters me. I'm honored by your presence."

Their host arrived then, appearing like an angel sent from God. Friar Martin Breski, a tall, lean figure with kind eyes behind thin-rimmed glasses and short, graying hair, smiled warmly and unlocked the gate. Behind Anthony and Vera, Massimo lingered, giving Friar Martin a respectful nod. Although Massimo was not ordained, he was well-regarded by the friars of Assisi. Few lived as he did, preaching to pilgrims by day and sleeping on a bare wooden bench each night.

Anthony introduced Vera to Friar Martin. Massimo stepped back slightly, unwilling to intrude on the conversation.

Their greetings were cut short by the arrival of a royal blue Fiat rolling under the lower plaza's archway. Its headlights sliced through the darkness at a steady pace. Anthony knew at once who it was. The car halted, and out stepped Minister

General Tasca, whom he had phoned earlier that evening. Tasca had driven straight from Rome to witness these events.

"You made it quickly," Anthony said as the minister general locked his car.

Tasca, wearing a black top hat and a dark wool overcoat, inclined his head. "I wouldn't miss this for the world," he replied, gaze drifting to the reliquary at Anthony's feet. "It looks like you found what you were searching for."

"We have," Anthony responded, barely containing his excitement.

Tasca greeted each of them in turn. Although he hadn't formally met Vera before, he said he knew of her work and her years of devoted service to the Church. After their brief, courteous exchange, he turned to the barefoot hermit. "My friend, Massimo," he said, placing his hands gently on the hermit's shoulders. "It's wonderful to see you again."

The small group followed Friar Martin to the interior of Sacro Convento. Once inside the convent's dim corridors, Anthony set the chest on a nearby table to rest his arms. He turned to their host. "Friar Martin, can you take us somewhere secure to open this chest?"

"By all means, Anthony," Friar Martin said, nodding. "I know just the place. Follow me."

Anthony hefted the chest again, adjusting his backpack. Guided by Friar Martin, they headed through a hidden side door. Flickering sconces cast long shadows across the stone walls as they descended winding stairwells. Each step felt colder, heavier, taking them deeper into an underground channel beneath the Basilica. They emerged into a small chapel. Friar Martin walked to the far end and stepped behind the altar. He slipped an arm through the seam of a large beige curtain, revealing a hidden wooden door.

The air thickened with centuries of faith and mystery. The scent of old stone and wax mingled with something indefinable. They went down ten more steps into a small chamber displaying relics of Saint Francis—his tattered brown tunic, his leather moccasins, and a parchment bearing his distinctive tau cross. Vera lingered over these treasures while Anthony eyed the tau, aware they stood on sacred ground, as if Francis himself hovered in the silence.

Friar Martin led them to another nearly invisible wooden door. His hand hovered over the iron handle before he turned it, reverence in his gaze. "This way," he whispered, as if ensuring they were alone.

Beyond lay a small, secret chamber no bigger than 150 square feet. Its thick stone walls sealed off the world outside, dividing the space into three modest sections, a tiny chapel, a sparse living area, and a simple sleeping nook.

Inside, Vera spread her scarf across a small table at the chapel's center, and Anthony set the reliquary on it. His palms were damp as he retrieved a flat-head screwdriver from his backpack and began scraping away centuries of grime. Each scrape of metal on hard residue felt endless, tension coiling in the silence. Vera, Massimo, Friar Martin, and Tasca stood nearby. They had seen many artifacts before, but this overshadowed them all.

Anthony paused, noticing a painting of Joseph of Cupertino levitating as he gave a sermon—a reflection of how weightless and surreal the moment felt. Finally, the last of the grime flaked away, revealing the coffer's seam.

Anthony pried open the ancient lid. Inside lay an ornate golden reliquary no larger than a foot and a half by three-quarters of a foot, but radiant with centuries of history. The light from the sconces danced over its filigreed surface, revealing delicate arches, biblical scenes, and saintly figures etched with breathtaking intricacy. Each panel seemed alive with silent stories as though the artisans had poured their devotion into every curve and contour. He found himself enthralled by the reliquary's regal majesty, and for a fleeting moment, it felt as if they were peering through a window into the past. It looked like it had waited all this time—untouched, brimming with secrets on the cusp of revelation.

With a steady hand, Anthony lifted the reliquary's lid. Inside were two objects: a limestone cylinder identical to the ones that once held the other scrolls and a chipped block of carved limestone bearing a partially intact inscription.

Vera and Anthony slipped on white cotton gloves to protect the artifacts. He picked up the limestone cylinder, familiar in size and shape, its wax seal intact. He reached into his Kevlar backpack for the proper tools.

T

Vera gingerly lifted the block of limestone from the reliquary. The inscription read:

PRAEFECTVS·IVDAEAE·CONFITEOR

PRO·MEO·HONORE·SERVANDO

FALSAM·FABVLAM·NOMIN
I·MARIAE·COMPOSVI

HIC·LAPIS·TESTIS·SIT·MEAE·CVLPAE

ATQVE·INTEGRITATEM·NO
MINIS·EIVS·RESTITVAT

Vera translated the Latin text into modern English:

I, THE PREFECT OF JUDEA, CONFESS

IN UPHOLDING HONOR, I MADE
A FALSE TALE AGAINST THE

NAME OF MARY. LET THIS STONE
BEAR WITNESS TO MY GUILT
AND RESTORE THE INTEGRITY
OF HER NAME.

Vera stood, stunned. What she'd translated was a confession from Pontius Pilate entrusted to Saint Francis of Assisi. This stone would forever quell any rumors about the Blessed Virgin Mary. For five centuries, the Ramorosso had chased a lie they believed was truth purely to threaten, intimidate, or coerce with it.

She set the carved block back into the reliquary as Anthony carefully broke the wax seal on the cylinder. He used rubber-tipped tweezers to unroll the parchment within. It crackled softly as she helped him. Her eyes misted. This moment felt more real than any discovery she had ever witnessed. Two large parchments emerged, impeccably preserved. In a familiar Umbrian script, they carried Saint Francis's words from eight centuries prior.

As she began to translate, Massimo, Friar Martin, and Minister General Tasca stood motionless, awe washing over them in the cramped chamber as they absorbed each phrase from the saint's text—a revelation of timeless power.

" 'Unto you, beloved child of a distant dawn, who by Divine providence shall discover these words: Peace be upon you, and may the light of the Most High shine in your heart…' " she read.

For five minutes, Vera read Francis's words aloud.

Anthony's eyes filled with emotion as he stood by her shoulder, recounting the trials that had led them here. When she finished, he said, "Now it all becomes clear, why Francis endured what he did, why he safeguarded these truths, entrusting them to my family for centuries."

Tasca and Friar Martin listened reverently as though a holy presence hovered in the quiet. Massimo knelt, humbled.

Anthony spoke again. "It started with Francis's vision at San Damiano…but only nearly twenty years later did he fully grasp the command he'd received. Everything—his imprisonments, renouncing his father's wealth, his radical transformation, the circle of friends he gathered, Pope Innocent's acceptance, the miracles, his attempt to end the Crusades, his advocacy for women via the Poor Clares, the founding of the Third Order that eventually attracted such varied figures as Michelangelo, Joan of Arc, and Christopher Columbus—every step was necessary. He lived in poverty, comforted the hopeless, endured illness and hardship. In the end, short on time, he could only entrust his unfinished work to the future."

He paused, eyes on the parchment detailing the Sacred Order. "But no one from his generation could handle this burden, not with the Inquisition on the rise and the Church plagued by internal strife. Francis recognized only time could heal those wounds. Nepotism would flourish. Indulgences would persist. It wouldn't be the right time until watchers—like us—could confirm its unveiling in unity. Now I see why my father, and his father before him, labored so tirelessly to guard the saint's wish. It was our family's crown jewel, surviving centuries, the vital link in fulfilling Francis's ultimate desire."

He hesitated, focusing on the sheet that bore the Sacred Order. "That final gift Francis received, bearing the stigmata, lifted him above our comprehension, letting him enter a level of spirituality few ever achieve. Francis truly became a Mirror of Christ."

Taking a steady breath, he went on, "This Sacred Order is not just for me. It's for all of us, humanity's treasure forwarded by a simple man from Assisi, a man with a will stronger than any other who loved every living thing and accepted each gift freely, apart from the sacrifice demanded by genuine devotion. We need to understand why we exist, the simple truths for a decent, honest life. Francis paid that price, learning perfect love and living moment by moment as he wrote in the *Canticle of the Sun*, acknowledging that love defies all boundaries—no race, color, or religion. Even praising what we typically fear, Sister Death, which no one can escape." He gazed again at the artifacts.

Silence, thick and meaningful, settled over them for a time.

Finally, Minister General Tasca gently broke the hush. "Anthony…forgive me, but your task isn't finished," he said quietly. "Your journey doesn't end here."

Vera and Anthony exchanged glances.

"What do you mean?" he asked.

Tasca's manner grew gentle. "You're called to do something extraordinary. I arranged it earlier, hoping you'd discover what you have. As you know, the whole world waits for the conclave that begins tomorrow to elect a new pope. You've been asked to address the College of Cardinals and share this story. Vera, you too are invited."

Anthony glanced at Vera, who smiled brilliantly.

"Okay," he said. "And…when does it happen?"

Tasca checked his watch. "Tomorrow morning, nine sharp. Anthony, you're the last speaker before the Sistine Chapel's doors close to the outside world for the College of Cardinals to choose the next Vicar of Christ."

Anthony took only a moment to decide. "I'll do it under one condition," he said. "I'd like to have a large screen and a slide projector ready for when I speak."

CHAPTER 51

Anthony and Vera followed the minister general into a hidden passage concealed deep within the Sacro Convento. Constructed during the friary's late medieval expansion under the commission of Pope Gregory IX, this underground tunnel had once served as a discreet refuge. Popes in earlier centuries could slip away to Assisi, either fleeing Rome's relentless summer heat or escaping the threat of unrest. Now, centuries later, its old stones bore silent witness to another urgent departure.

Beneath the Sacro Convento's lower levels, behind a nondescript door, stretched a hidden passage. Winding beneath Assisi's main gates, it skirted the Basilica's lower plaza—an ancient artery of escape. As they advanced along the damp corridor, Anthony clutched the ornate reliquary tightly in his arms, its priceless contents secured within, while his backpack—heavy with precious documents and artifacts—was strapped firmly over his shoulders. Vera followed close, their footsteps muted on the damp stone floor.

The tunnel's path mirrored the western edge of the portico. The air felt cool and stale, carrying a faint scent of earth and distant history. When at last they emerged into the crisp night air, Anthony and Vera hurried one block to the Hotel Giotto.

There, his rental car awaited, its quiet motor and empty seats promising a swift getaway.

Earlier, Lara had warned them of two suspicious individuals spotted lurking near Vera's Alfa Romeo and that her tire had been deliberately punctured. Before they left, she and her cousins pledged to fill in the dig site and restore the ground exactly as it was, ensuring no trace remained of the night's secret excavation. Anthony promised her he would reach out as soon as the conclave ended, to share every detail of their discovery. Now, with his car ready and the reliquary secure in his grasp, they wasted no time. The chill nipped at their cheeks as they climbed in, hearts pounding with anticipation.

Anthony dashed down the winding autostrada, the engine's roar reverberating like a caged tiger unleashed. The road stretched ahead, a dark ribbon of opportunity beneath a starless sky. Pushing the limits, he shaved nearly thirty minutes off the usual two-and-a-half-hour drive to Rome, forging ahead as though each gust of wind carried whispered urgings from a distant past.

Inside the car's warm cocoon, he and Vera navigated a tangle of memory and meaning as they recounted their month-long journey—her long evenings in the lab, his enlightening talks with Massimo, and tender moments of understanding he'd shared with her over small cups of espresso. They spoke of the Sacred Order they had uncovered, marveling at how Saint Francis's legacy had guided them to truths both ancient and painfully relevant. Vera reminded him of the night they nearly lost hope when Alessandro threatened them both. He recalled the quiet dawn when he'd visited the Porziuncola and San Damiano and how it had impacted his every decision since.

They laughed over their early misinterpretations—Vera's initial skepticism that Anthony had met with Benedict XVI directly, and Anthony's hesitancy about trusting Vera with the artifacts—and how mutual respect had forged them into bountiful allies. Emotion welled up as they remembered the price others had paid along the way—Anthony's father, vanished without a trace; former Minister General Heiser, murdered; and Rick's delicate grip on life. Each tear was a silent tribute to those who suffered because they dared to seek the truth.

In this rolling confessional on wheels, Vera inquired about Anthony's father's fate. He admitted that with every mile, he grew more determined to discover whether his father yet lived or lay in some unknown captivity. She offered what comfort she could, suggesting new leads to pursue once they reached Rome—perhaps Vatican insiders they had not yet consulted, or a hushed meeting with Rossi's carabinieri contacts to glean any whispered intel.

They reflected on the Church's future and the conclave's imminent decision, marveling at how these ancient rituals would soon yield a new shepherd, possibly one who might knowingly, or unknowingly, carry forward the essence of the Sacred Order's revelations.

"I keep wondering," Vera said softly, turning to him, "what if after you spoke to the conclave, the next pope truly embraces the embodiment of Francis? It would be a welcomed change from the regal formalities."

Anthony kept his gaze on the dark highway ahead. "That's my goal. We've seen how deep the Church's divisions can run," he replied. "Still, that doesn't mean hope is lost. Maybe this new pope will be the one who understands the spiritual struggles of the common person and will listen to the message from Saint Francis that I'm going to deliver."

Vera nodded, optimism kindling in her eyes. "It would change everything if someone in that position of power took Saint Francis's message to heart, not just as folklore."

Anthony allowed himself a fragile hope that their month-long odyssey had not been in vain. "If anyone can open the door to that truth," he said, "it's someone who understands that the Sacred Order isn't just a relic of the past but a call to see the world with new eyes."

They let the possibility hang in the air between them, carrying them through the night with a quiet sense of hope. Perhaps, for once, history might pivot toward the conclave choosing a leader who embodies Saint Francis's compassion.

Vera scrolled through headlines on her phone. "They're saying Cardinal Scola of Milan is considered a front-runner." She glanced across the front seat at him. "He's intellectual, close to Communion and Liberation…definitely not Franciscan though."

Anthony tightened his grip on the steering wheel, the passing highway lights flickering across his face. "Scola's name keeps popping up," he said. "But let's see who else is in the running. There must be someone with a genuine Franciscan tie… someone who truly embodies Saint Francis's ethos."

Vera tapped her screen. "There's Cardinal Marc Ouellet of Canada, Cardinal Odilo Scherer of São Paulo, and Cardinal Peter Turkson from Ghana. None of them appear to have Franciscan backgrounds."

"What about Cardinal Timothy Dolan from New York?" he asked. "I love that guy."

Vera brightened. "He's been mentioned but is a long shot. Some say his frank, outgoing style rubs traditionalists the wrong way, and historically, no Cardinal from the US has ever been elected pope." She kept reading, then let out a gasp. "But listen to this. Cardinal Seán Patrick O'Malley is indeed a Capuchin Franciscan and is listed as a potential *papabile*. Although he's a possibility, I'm reading here that many don't see anyone from the States as a likely choice."

Anthony shook his head lightly. "That's not exactly the Franciscan way," he teased. "Still, I wouldn't count anyone out just yet. A Franciscan connection feels perfectly in step with everything we've uncovered. Saint Francis's message might be precisely what's needed to renew the Church. Maybe O'Malley *is* the one."

Vera looked back at her phone. "I hope so, but I wouldn't get your hopes too high. It's a long shot at best."

Anthony allowed himself a small smile. "Whoever they choose, we can't deny the Church is at a crossroads. If the next pope views the world as Saint Francis did, maybe this institution can still be put back on course."

Vera nodded, turning her attention to the screen. "Guess we'll find out soon enough. The white smoke and the bells will tell us everything, but first they are going to hear from one Anthony Brunelli," she teased gently. She lowered her phone, and for a moment the car's interior fell silent, the hum of the engine the only sound.

Both of them held onto a glimmer of hope that just maybe the Church's next shepherd would embody Saint Francis's living legacy. Once they reached Rome, their plan was to meet the priest arranged by Minister General Tasca for their hospitality, contact Rossi, and finalize Anthony's speech.

In that intense two-hour crucible of conversation and recollection, they knitted together resolve out of anguish and turned fear into purpose. By the time the lights of Rome shimmered on the horizon, they had laid bare their doubts and dreams, forging a unity no darkness could easily unravel. Anthony knew his job was far from complete, but in Vera's quiet determination he found strength, and in her unwavering gaze, he saw the reflection of a future worth fighting for.

Vera clung to the overhead handle, her eagerness apparent in the dim interior as the car thundered forward. Approaching their exit, they were forced to stop at a traffic light. The red light lingered, giving Anthony a moment to reach over and rest his hand atop Vera's. His fingers tightened slightly, seeking reassurance.

"Anthony," Vera began, "I need to confess something." She hesitated, eyes fixed on the road ahead. "As I told you… Daniello and I had a relationship. It ended due to a misunderstanding, but I think it's something I'll rekindle. I've been drawn to you, deeply, but I've always kept business separate from personal matters."

He met her eyes, his expression unreadable. After a beat, he spoke. "Vera, you owe me no explanation. I've been in this position before…in fact, more times than I'd like to admit." As the light turned green, he continued ahead. "Truth is, I have something to confess too…"

✝

Meanwhile, Enzo received a notification from his operatives. The tracker they had placed on Brunelli's phone pinged its approximate location, confirming their southbound route toward Rome.

Enzo, Katarina, and their reinforcements waited, prepared to intercept them at St. Anne's Gate. Officially, they were tasked with bolstering conclave security. Unofficially, they awaited Alessandro's orders.

✝

Anthony had been instructed to avoid the main Vatican entrance and instead use the museum's access point, a secluded route a quarter mile from the imposing perimeter walls. Vera, familiar with the layout, guided them carefully, hoping the alternative path would let them slip in unnoticed.

At precisely 12:35 a.m., they reached the museum entrance. A young priest awaited them, tension evident in his brisk gestures. Without a word, he slipped into the back seat of the rental car. Pressing his thumb to a sensor, he opened the gates and guided Anthony to the guest suites.

"You have a few hours to rest and prepare," he said, handing them keys to two adjacent rooms. "I'll be back to get you at 7:00 a.m."

Anthony and Vera exchanged weary glances before grabbing their belongings and retreating to their rooms.

"Do you want a hand with your speech?" Vera asked.

"I'm okay, thanks. It's something I need to do for myself. Get some sleep, and I'll see you bright and early," he said, smiling.

Morning came quickly, and the young priest returned right on time, knocking on both of their doors. Dressed in slacks, a dress shirt, and a sport coat, Anthony carried the Sacred Order reliquary in his arms, his Kevlar backpack tightly secured around his shoulders. The priest escorted them to a private room where a continental breakfast awaited. Anthony savored the aroma of the hot espresso, filling a small plate with parmigiana cheese, prosciutto, and bread. Vera had an espresso and a cup of fresh fruit. The priest then led them through the Vatican's halls. They moved silently toward St. Peter's Basilica, its grand interior sealed off to the public for the conclave.

"Any special requests inside the chamber?" the priest asked.

"Can you have this displayed on a table before I speak?" Anthony asked, glancing at the reliquary.

"With pleasure," the priest replied.

"Oh, and is there a projector screen available by chance?"

"For you, there will be," the priest replied. "In fact, Friar Tasca has already made arrangements. Please wait here until they call you," he instructed, then slipped away through a private access door.

St. Peter's vastness loomed around them, marble floors gleaming under faint morning light filtering through high windows. Anthony paced, the intensity of his impending speech weighing heavily upon him.

T

The Vatican's private passageways were reserved only for authorized clergy and staff, connecting St. Peter's Basilica to the Sistine Chapel within the Apostolic Palace complex. Used strictly for official Church purposes, these corridors guarantee the discreet movement of the pope, cardinals, and select personnel. The average visitor never encountered a direct interior path from one site to the other, so Brunelli's presence there for the conclave was an extraordinary exception.

Nevertheless, Alessandro devised a plan to exploit the confusion within these off-limits corridors. "Intercept and force Brunelli and Vera into the Scavi. Once we corner them in St. Peter's, we'll drive them down into the Necropolis. You know the rest," he instructed.

The Scavi—an underground area beneath St. Peter's usually associated with guided tours—lay within what was formally known as the Vatican Necropolis. Though people often used *Scavi* and *Necropolis* interchangeably, the *Necropolis* was the literal cemetery of tombs and relics, whereas the *Scavi* usually referred to the excavation work and visitor access that occurred in that same subterranean region. Discovered in the early 1940s under Pope Pius XII, the Vatican Necropolis was a subterranean maze of graves and tombs stretching back to the first centuries of Christianity. During a conclave, every Vatican tourist area— including the Scavi—closed entirely to ensure strict privacy for the Church's sacred proceedings. The tangle of the Necropolis would be deserted, free from watchful eyes, and Alessandro was counting on that emptiness to stage a stealthy ambush.

Though he would not be present, he devised a ruse under the guise of providing a "safe route" as a supposed escort for Brunelli for the upcoming papal election. Following his plan, Enzo and his operatives would inform Vera and Brunelli there was a change in plans and they were both requested by Minister General Tasca. That, coupled with the confusion of conclave preparations, would lull them into complacency. By the time the pair realized their true destination, centuries-old crypt walls would have blocked off all possible escape routes and no one else would be around to hear them call for help.

As Enzo's team closed in, Katarina's glare warned the others not to fail. The trap was set.

Disguised as Vatican staff, Enzo and his team guided Brunelli and Vera through secure checkpoints, steering them step by step toward the Necropolis entrance under the pretense of providing a shortcut. Dressed in his phony Franciscan habit, Enzo led the way, walking briskly ahead of the others.

T

Only after they had moved deep into the winding corridors did Vera realize their true destination. By then, the centuries-old crypt walls almost guaranteed they couldn't signal for help. They'd been deceived.

A group of eight stalwart men deftly overpowered them with a tightly orchestrated ambush. Neither Anthony nor Vera had time to react as they were lifted into a horizontal body lock. In a matter of seconds, they descended two stories below the papal altar, entering the Vatican Necropolis.

Anthony gasped as his Kevlar backpack was yanked from his shoulders. In a final, desperate move, he grabbed for the luggage tag, but the force of the pull shredded it from its fastening. The tattered tag fluttered to the ground as his attackers hauled the backpack away, taking his precious discoveries with it. He struggled against the iron grip holding him, but it was futile. Beside him, Vera's attempts to break free were equally unsuccessful against her captor's crushing strength.

Their assailants dragged them deeper into the Necropolis, pulling them into the bowels of ancient tombs where light barely reached. The faint glow of flashlights danced off crumbling stone, revealing fragments of Latin inscriptions and faded murals that whispered centuries of hidden history.

Vera's mind raced, her breath quick and shallow as they were hauled down narrow passageways. She needed a plan. She glanced at Anthony, being dragged a few feet ahead, his face pale but resolute.

As the group rounded a sharp corner, she seized her chance. Summoning every ounce of strength, she twisted her body and lunged upward, her hand finding an emergency electrical shut-off lever mounted high on the wall. With a sharp yank, she pulled it down.

The tomb plunged into total darkness.

"Damn it!" a voice echoed, sharp and frustrated.

The female among their assailants hissed in annoyance, fumbling for her flashlight.

In the chaos, Vera dropped to the ground, pressing herself flat against the cool stone. "Run forward!" she called out in deliberately broken English, hoping to mislead their captors. "Stay by the wall opposite your right!"

The sudden darkness disoriented the attackers, buying Vera and Anthony precious seconds. She scrambled to her feet, her hand brushing Anthony's arm. Gripping him tightly, she guided him through the labyrinth of ancient mausoleums. They moved swiftly but silently, weaving through a maze of faded inscriptions—S, T, U. Each turn felt like a gamble, the air growing colder and more oppressive. Finally, she spotted a narrow passage leading toward Mausoleum M.

They ducked into the corridor and pressed themselves against the wall. Vera pulled out her phone, shielding its faint glow with her hand, and sent a desperate text to Captain Rossi:

In danger, need help! Under St. Peter's in the Scavi. Hurry!

Her heart pounded as she watched the message struggle to send. For a moment, the signal flickered. Then, with a small chime, it showed as delivered.

Anthony and Vera remained crouched in the shadows of Mausoleum H, their breathing shallow. The faint sound of boots on stone reached their ears, growing louder by the second.

"I see them!" a voice shouted in Italian, echoing through the tomb. "They're just ahead!"

Vera and Anthony exchanged a desperate look. With no time to lose, they forged ahead. Their footsteps echoed in the tight space as they took a sharp left, then a right, narrowly evading their pursuers. Ducking into another corridor, they pressed into a hidden gap in the wall, cloaked in shadows.

Their pursuers stormed past, flashlight beams skimming the area but missing the hiding spot by mere inches. Vera held her breath, nails digging into Anthony's arm as she clutched him tightly.

T

In Saint Martha's House, cardinals gathered for breakfast. The air charged with expectation, today the conclave would begin—an event that would shape the Catholic Church's future by determining its next leader. Conversations were hushed, as though each whispered word might tip the balance of destiny. Outside, Vatican City stirred under a gray morning sky, while within these walls, hearts quickened with anticipation.

In a small private chamber off the main corridor, Cardinal Stefano Ferraro stood at a polished mahogany table. Pietro and Alessandro listened intently as he rehearsed his remarks for the day's proceedings. A single window let in a pale shaft of light, illuminating the tension etched in Ferraro's features.

"And as I conclude," Ferraro said, "I urge you to reflect on the Church's legacy. Yes, we have not been perfect and for that have faced criticism, but our decisions have strengthened our foundation. We have endured through strength of faith and perseverance."

Arms folded across his chest, Cardinal Pietro della Rovere frowned. "Stefano, be cautious. You can't highlight the Church's controversies. It will undermine your message." The somberness in his voice made the small room feel even tighter.

Ferraro glanced at the ornate clock near the door. Time was running out, each sweep of the second hand a reminder that he would soon stand before fellow cardinals to deliver this speech. Doubt gnawed at his confidence. He could feel his heartbeat pulsing in his throat, the enormity of the conclave looming larger than his own ambitions.

Alessandro cleared his throat, leaning forward. "What my uncle means is that if you dwell on our past struggles, you risk shifting attention away from the unity we're trying to build. The College of Cardinals needs reassurance, not more reasons to hesitate."

Ferraro exhaled slowly, setting his notes down on the table. "So, you're telling me to gloss over the darkest chapters in our recent history?"

Pietro shook his head. "Not ignore, just frame them carefully. Remind them of the Church's resilience and the path ahead. Give them hope, not scandal."

A tense silence lingered in the room. Through the single window, the faint toll of a distant bell signaled the passing of time and hinted at the monumental choice soon to unfold in the Sistine Chapel.

Steeling himself, Ferraro collected his notes. "You're right," he said, his voice softer now. "I must offer them something to believe in, not a mirror of old shadows. God willing, we'll choose a pontiff who will stand with us."

With that, the three men exchanged resolute glances, each aware of how high the stakes were. Outside, the low hum of conversation in Saint Martha's House continued like a subdued chorus heralding the dawn of a momentous day in Church history.

T

Boots pounded through the passageways as Enzo and Katarina regrouped. Their orders had been clear. Capture Brunelli and Vera, deliver them to Alessandro. But just as they closed in to corner their targets again, chaos erupted.

The Raggruppamento Operativo Speciale (ROS), which translates to Special Operations Group, stormed into the Necropolis, their movements swift and precise. The clash was immediate and brutal. Enzo's henchmen fought fiercely, but they were no match for the elite operatives.

In the struggle, one henchman seized Vera, pressing a knife to her throat. "Drop your weapons, or she dies!" he snarled.

Rossi hesitated for only a moment before firing a precise shot into the assassin's ankle. He collapsed with a howl, releasing Vera. Brunelli seized the opportunity, driving his elbow into another attacker's gut.

"Run!" Rossi shouted, covering them as they dashed toward the exit.

The Necropolis echoed with the sounds of grunts, shouts, and the sharp crack of fists on flesh. After a grueling fight, the ROS subdued the remaining henchmen, cuffing them firmly.

As Enzo and Katarina were dragged away, their eyes burned with defiance. But their reign of terror had ended.

CHAPTER 5 2

Vatican City, Italy
8:35 AM

Despite the tumult that had struck scarcely an hour ago, the new morning offered no reprieve from the intensity gripping Vatican City. Thunder rolled across Rome's early morning sky, echoing like a celestial drumbeat as rain lashed the cobblestone streets of Vatican City. The storm seemed to mirror the intensity of events unfolding within the walls of the Holy See.

Captain Daniello Rossi jogged through the downpour, water splashing up around his boots, until he reentered Saint Peter's Basilica where Vera and Anthony waited. Both were badly shaken from the incident inside the Vatican Necropolis.

Rossi was happy to return Brunelli's backpack and report that Enzo and Katarina, along with their cohorts, were all in ROS custody. He took off his sport coat and wrapped it around Vera's shoulders. She clenched the lapels together, crisscrossing her hands underneath the coat.

Anthony had ten minutes before he would be called into the waiting area, where he would remain until it was time to deliver his address. Neither Vera nor Rossi would be allowed inside due to the intense security and temporary ban on all visitors into and around the Sistine Chapel for the duration of the conclave.

Ⴕ

The private entrance door opened, and three priests appeared to escort Anthony inside. To his surprise, one of them was the Minister General Friar Marco Tasca.

Holding his backpack, Anthony turned toward Vera as she embraced him with a farewell kiss, one on each cheek, wishing him luck. Rossi winked, giving him a nod.

Anthony walked alongside the minister general, down a long hallway before slowly approaching the rear entrance door to the Sistine Chapel. Swiss Guards stood by in their signature stoic pose.

"Are you ready, Anthony?" Tasca asked gently as muffled applause drifted from inside the chapel.

"As ready as I'll ever be," he replied.

"Speak from your heart and don't hold back," Tasca advised.

With that, Anthony was ushered over the chapel's threshold and into a modest holding area behind a makeshift partition.

"You're next," a young priest murmured.

"Thank you," Anthony responded, letting a sacristan help him into a simple white linen alb tied with a matching cincture around his waist.

The next two minutes blurred, the hush of anticipation wrapping around him. Anthony had no written speech, only the convictions forged in the crucible of the past few weeks. He'd given lectures at art galleries and universities, but never had he imagined facing an audience such as this.

A nod from the priest signaled it was time.

Anthony advanced along the marble floor, silence falling like a drawn curtain. On either side of the aisle, rows of red-clad cardinals fixed their gazes upon him, many appearing puzzled. The priest handed Anthony a printed list of dignitaries and placed a glass of ice water on the top shelf of the podium. A small table stood to his right, holding the reliquary of the *Sacer Ordo*. Drawing a steady breath, he leaned into the microphone, took in the cardinal names, and began:

"Cardinal Bishop Naguib, Cardinal Priest Ouellet, Cardinal Deacon Montesari, and to all members of the College of Cardinals here today…good morning. My name is Anthony Brunelli. First, let me say how honored I am to stand before you in this sacred chapel, an experience I never imagined. I feel privileged to share a remarkable account, one that defies every expectation and might well sound like a modern miracle. You may note I'm the only layperson in this assembly, and I'm grateful you've granted me this voice behind closed doors. Please keep what I share in your confidence."

He took a sip of water to steady his nerves. "For the past twenty-two years, I've traveled worldwide as a professional artist. Life has been generous, though I admit I drifted from the Church some time ago. My mother, Carol, often reminds me of that, praying for my return. But recently, something happened—something that not only altered my spiritual outlook but also transformed me personally. So here I am, offering you a story that might be nothing short of miraculous, one I hope will resonate with you as you prepare to choose our next pope.

"A year ago, the Pontifical Council for Culture commissioned twelve artists from across the globe to produce specific works. I was blessed to be one of them. While showcasing my piece at the Vatican Art Gallery last month, I was then called upon to do something extraordinary…to complete a duty my family was called upon to fulfill—protecting the legend of *Sacer Ordo*, the Sacred Order. My bloodline was entrusted by the Franciscans of long ago, taking a vow passed down through generations and enduring the test of time. Today, I have been asked to share the details of this sacred oath with you, and I'm very proud to do so."

A low murmur rippled across the Cardinal ranks, anxious to hear more.

"The Sacred Order," Anthony continued, "is a genuine discovery akin to a hidden trove that was revealed piece by piece, connecting centuries-old artifacts and documents. Carefully assembled, these items led me to a hidden crypt dating back almost eight centuries in a small yet renowned commune not far from here that you all know as Assisi.

"I've had the opportunity to spend some quality time in Assisi over the past few months. One thing I've come to realize is that there's a spirit in Assisi with a magnetic pull, an attraction drawing in thousands of tourists each day and millions each year. It is a New Jerusalem, and aside from St. Peter's, it may be the only place on earth with a reputation spread so exponentially by word of mouth. But why? What is it about this small medieval town that the rest of the world lacks? The answer to this centuries-old mystery lies not in the stone and mortar of its walls but in the hearts and souls of its people and the countless generations before them. Ultimately, the essence of Assisi's appeal can be distilled into a single word—*love*. The mystery of Assisi, and the allure it holds, is its heartfelt love…love for one another, love for our Creator, and love for the priceless gifts of life that we too often take for granted. The spirit of Assisi is a force of nature too strong to describe unless one experiences it firsthand.

"However, it was in fact the example, leadership, and sacrifice of one man…a man who seemed to embrace life in a way considered fanatical for his time, a man who was not an ordained priest yet was able to start his own order for the ordained. This single humble man fully embraced the Holy Order he wrote—one that was blessed and approved by the pope. He was a man who loved his fellow human beings whether rich or poor, sick or well, Muslim, Christian, or Jew. And this man, this simple and humble man, rid himself of all he had, every possession and material comfort except for a single cloak, a pair of shoes, a tau cross, and his Holy Bible. He sacrificed his life for his passion for the Son of God…a God with whom he had a direct connection, who spoke directly to him first as a young man from the cross at San Damiano.

"He devoted his life to God and encouraged others like his beloved Clare, along with countless followers who also decided to take his solemn oath and live the same order he created and endured, embracing vows of poverty, chastity, and obedience… a life of prayer and a life of peace. This man, who lived but a brief life and died at the vibrant age of forty-four—what should have been his prime—received the ultimate miracle and gift from above. He bore the wounds of Christ after receiving the stigmata on a lowly mountaintop at La Verna, his place of solitude and incredibly intense prayer. Those wounds remained with him until his final years, though many doubted their authenticity until they saw the open marks with their own eyes.

"The man I'm speaking of—a man you all know of—was born Giovanni di Pietro di Bernardone, better known as Francis of Assisi, nicknamed Francesco, or the Frenchman, by his father. It's been said he was not a man of great intellect, but I'd debate that tale. After what I've experienced, I dare say he had greater insight and foresight that could rival anyone in his day. This man of peace, love, and humility connected with thousands through both his words and actions. Though not a scholar, he founded the Franciscan Order, which had tens of thousands of followers when he walked this earth. To put that in perspective, the popularity of Francis of Assisi might rival that of today's most prominent figures.

"But what is it about the legend of Francis of Assisi that makes him so special? How could one man still today command such reverence and draw millions to the place of his birth and death? Gentlemen, Saint Francis was indeed an extraordinary human being, not because he preached to the birds or cared for the sick but because he was *elevated* and possessed a superior state of mind beyond most comprehension. He was also a reformer who strove to improve the Catholic Church without a thought of overthrowing it, even embracing a position of *sola fide* before the Latin term gained popularity. Though his order was built on unwavering faith, he also advocated for good works.

"He lived like no other and loved like no other before or after his time, because for him, there was simply no other way. No one man since then has been so superior, and none before him with the exception of Christ himself. I'm not suggesting Francis of Assisi was the second coming, but he reached a level of consciousness so far beyond what we typically grasp. He attained the ultimate state of mind, one of pure enlightenment, an intensity of love so great that it remains unshaken to this day.

"Now back to the story of the modern-day treasure trove, the reason I am here before you today. For the past four weeks, I have been on a journey, or a mission of sorts…a mission to uncover some of the most significant historical documents, writings, and artifacts discovered in the modern era. Sometime before his death, Francis devised a plan and instructed that a protective crypt be buried, which—remarkably—was unearthed from the ground in Assisi only last night." Anthony gestured with his hand toward the reliquary propped on a table at his side.

The cardinals shifted and craned their necks to catch a glimpse.

"Many steps had to be followed, and generations of people who came long before me, as well as others still among us, fulfilled their promise so this moment could become reality. There were messages, parchments, and works of art absolutely crucial to the cause and many key individuals who selflessly contributed to this effort over the past eight hundred years. It seems implausible that such an event could even occur. There are countless names we don't know, and a handful we do, who made this moment in time possible. In fact, Michelangelo, a Third Order Franciscan, was among the most critical individuals who cooperated with the plan, providing the final clues to the puzzle found right here in this very sacred chapel, embedded in the famous fresco on the altar wall behind me." Anthony gestured with his right hand while glancing over his shoulder at *The Last Judgment.*

"Like Francis, it was the Franciscans and the succession of popes who provided the unswerving resolve to keep what we now know as the Sacred Order alive all this time. But it was also the cooperation of my ancestors, dating back to Francis's time, that is the main reason I'm here. After all, Saint Francis knew he could not complete God's will while faced with his own mortality and the fierce reality of such turbulent times. Peering into his figurative crystal ball, he knew there would be hundreds upon hundreds of turbulent years ahead. He knew the Church would rise, then fall, and rise again. He knew it would battle itself through nepotism and hypocrisy and there would be many more holy wars before the world could progress and mature. And he knew the evil of Satan would persist in every age, but he believed there would be an opening…a tiny window in time when change would be welcomed more than ever before, when a leader could rise above the darkness, above the hatred, and not succumb to daily pressures. Deep in his heart, he trusted that good overcomes evil and that someone would eventually emerge as the successor to Saint Peter, leading the effort to repair God's house, which many fear has again fallen into ruins.

"Most respected College of Cardinals, the time is indeed now. This is the time the leader of the Order of Friars Minor—the minority of lesser brothers, or in fact the radical underdog—the one who devoted his life in matrimony to Lady Poverty, the man who honored Sister Death as dearly as a newborn child, the fanatical *jongleur* who was canonized a saint—this is the moment he envisioned. The world is watching…only good can prevail. God has left the future state of His Church in your hands."

Anthony scanned the hundreds of eyes fixed upon him. "Now, what I'm about to reveal would not have happened without the competence and dedication of your own Dr. Vera Valentino, the Vatican's top art historian and restoration expert, a gem reflecting light where others find darkness and turning impossibility into opportunity. I'd like to publicly thank her, because if it wasn't for her, I would not be standing before you today."

Anthony took a step back and inhaled deeply as he reached for Vera's translated documents from the podium. He turned and gestured toward the reliquary beside him. "Within this vessel, Saint Francis preserved two remarkable relics. The first is a block of limestone bearing an inscription that will forever silence one of the most insidious attempts to undermine our faith—a sacred truth entrusted to him by Pope Honorius III in 1223, the same year he blessed the Franciscan Rule."

The cardinals stirred at the mention of the thirteenth-century pontiff, their attention sharpening.

"What I'm about to share with you demonstrates the profound foresight of Saint Francis. When Pope Honorius shared this relic with him, Francis understood its magnitude. He also knew, with divine insight, that revealing it during his time would have caused upheaval the broader Church wasn't prepared to weather. Instead of immediate disclosure, he chose to preserve it for a future moment—this moment—when both the Church and the world would be ready to embrace its truth."

He slipped on his white cotton gloves and lifted the ancient limestone, turning it carefully so the assembled Cardinals could see the Latin inscription carved into its surface. "This Latin inscription comes from none other than Pontius Pilate himself. Pilate faced a crisis of conscience that would ultimately lead to his downfall. As it's well documented, in the year 36 AD, Tiberius removed Pilate from his position as procurator of Judea following his violent suppression of a Samaritan uprising at Mount Gerizim. Summoned to Rome to answer for his actions, Pilate attempted to secure his position by fabricating a terrible lie about the Blessed Virgin Mary—one that has caused rumors, speculation, and doubt since the time of Jesus's death. He claimed he had proof she had been violated by an unknown assailant and that Joseph merely posed as her husband to preserve her dignity as they made their way to Bethlehem. However, the political landscape in Rome was rapidly changing. Shortly before Pilate's arrival, Tiberius died and Caligula ascended to the throne having no allegiance to Pilate."

Anthony's voice grew stronger as he continued. "When Pilate announced he'd converted to Christianity and proclaimed Jesus as the King of the Jews, Caligula demanded he prove his earlier claim about Christ's conception. Unable to do so, Pilate faced the emperor's wrath. According to the historian Eusebius, under Caligula's persecution, Pilate fell into such misfortune that he took his own life...but not before leaving this testimony."

He set down the ancient limestone and returned to the podium. "The words before you," he explained, "were etched in

Latin by Pilate's own hand, preserved for nearly two thousand years. Thanks to Dr. Valentino's translation, I can share with you its profound message in English." He cleared his throat before reading from Vera's documents:

I, the Prefect of Judea, confess: In upholding honor, I made a false tale against the name of Mary. Let this stone bear witness to my guilt and restore the integrity of her name.

Gasps echoed through the Sistine Chapel. Several cardinals crossed themselves, their faces reflecting both shock and reverence.

"Saint Francis understood that this truth needed to mature like wine in God's cellar," Anthony continued, his voice resonating with conviction. "He knew that its revelation would come at a divinely appointed time, when the Church would need it most—not just to silence ancient lies but to demonstrate God's perfect timing in unveiling sacred truths. For five hundred years, an underground faction of this body pursued what they believed was truth, wielding it as a weapon of threat and coercion. Today, that lie is finally laid to rest exactly when Saint Francis, in his wisdom, foresaw it would be most needed."

He carefully withdrew the second relic—a parchment containing Saint Francis's own words—and held it up for all to see. "And now, most respected Cardinals, please, look at your hands, envision the pain Francis endured as you cast your ballot today. I share with you the spiritual testament Saint Francis left for this very moment in time, entitled Sacer Ordo."

Anthony set the relic back down and once again read Vera's translated text.

Unto you, beloved child of a distant dawn, who by Divine providence shall discover these words: Peace be upon you and may the light of the Most High shine in your heart.

Know that the truth I would impart is both ancient and ever-new. The world about you, which seems so vast and apart, is not foreign to your deepest self. As Brother Sun warms the earth and Sister Moon gentles the night, so too does the Divine Spirit breathe equally through all things. It is in the rustle of leaves, in the chorus of birds, in the stillness of stones, and in the silent mystery of the stars.

In the hour of grace, when you awaken to who you truly are, when the veils of separation are lifted from your eyes, you shall behold that you and the rest of the world are not two, but one. This is the sacred knowing, the mystical experience I have longed to bequeath. In that blessed moment, the boundary between "I" and all that moves beyond you shall vanish like morning mist before the rising sun.

The very breath in your chest is breathed forth by the Eternal One who sings through the rivers, who dances in the branches, who kindles every star in the firmament. What you do and what the heavens do are not separate. All are movements of one and the same Divine Wholeness. The truest, deepest "you" is not being borne along by fate, but the entire cosmos awakened to life in the place you know as this moment in time.

You need not learn how to make your heart beat, nor how to set the sun aflame in its daily path. These marvels unfold as naturally as breathing, without toil or teaching. You hold a wondrous capacity to transform your very being, to bring forth and sustain all things, yet you do so without thoughtful strain. In truth, you are as the Eternal Weaver, spinning the living tapestry of existence, though you often remain unaware of your own skill.

All living beings, in every distant realm and hidden star, know themselves as "I," and yet they are not truly apart from one another. The Most High works through you as effortlessly as through all creation. Does it not astonish you that you are part of so wondrous a design, weaving life's pattern without ever having learned the skill? Yet so it is, and by this marvel you may come to see that what you call "the external world" is in truth your own body extended beyond measure. Do not feel isolated. You are a part of this marvelous creation as a wave is a part of the sea.

Consider too, the mystery of passing from this life. You behold death and tremble, believing it to be the cruel end of all. Yet this "darkness," as it may seem, is but the shadowed opposite that makes possible the miracle of new life and new beginnings. Without the quiet embrace of death, you could not awaken anew to the bright dawn of being. Each time the cycle turns, it is fresh and unforeseen so that you may discover life anew as if for the very first time.

Let it astonish and comfort you. As you become aware, recognize yourself in lilies and in stars, in sparrows and in silent stones. Your body, your mind, your soul extend into all creation, and all creation extends into you. When you stand in this knowledge, fear shall fade and your heart shall know the abiding peace that comes from unity with all that is and your direct connection to thy Lord.

When thy Holy Church lieth in ruins, know that true restoration dwelleth not within stone and mortar, beloved child, but within the sacred vessel of each mortal heart. Every soul that walketh upon God's earth is both sanctuary and cornerstone, each a living temple of the Divine Spirit. The mysteries of our interconnectedness with all creation lie beyond mortal understanding, and mankind must be guided gently toward this truth through countless seasons yet to come. Until that divine hour when souls are ready to embrace this sacred knowledge, thy Holy Church shall be as a shepherd, leading God's flock toward the light of greater understanding.

When the great awakening cometh forth, as certain as Brother Sun riseth in the heavens, thy foundation shall bear witness to the glorious flowering of thy Church in holy illumination. This restoration shall become as a living resurrection, born not of earthly hands but of Divine Love flowing through all of His creation. For when Love triumpheth, as it must, the countenance of the Eternal One shall be beheld in every creature, every blade of grass, every grain of earthly dust.

The greatest gift thou mayest bestow, unto thyself and unto all God's creatures, is this boundless Love that knoweth no division, that seeth in all things the presence of the Most High, and that discerneth in every heart the eternal flame of Divine unity.

Guard these words in your heart until the appointed time when the world hungers for this truth once more.

Then let them be revealed that all may remember what I leave to you now. In seeing yourself as one with Creation, you shall know the face of the Eternal in every being and discover that the whole of existence forever lives within you.

The cardinals looked at each other, whispering in disbelief, as though Saint Francis himself were speaking through Anthony.

"To conclude, the Sacred Order is a profound spiritual covenant embedded within a centuries-old tradition. It's a guiding principle—a timeless message entrusted to future generations for when the world would finally be prepared to embrace its truth. That time is now. At its core, the Sacred Order teaches that all of existence is interconnected and alive with the presence of the Divine, that the boundaries separating self from the world are illusions, and that true harmony and understanding arise from seeing oneself as both part of and at one with the entire universe. The Sacred Order is a spiritual blueprint intended to rekindle a deeper understanding of faith, unity, and eternal renewal. It calls upon humanity to remember that every heartbeat, every living being is woven into a single, sacred tapestry.

"Saint Francis, who safeguarded its message, intended it to serve as a guiding light, an invitation to recognize that love and interconnectedness transcend all barriers. By being revealed at this appointed time, the Sacred Order is meant to restore integrity, heal spiritual wounds, and inspire humanity to live with reverence, compassion, and authentic unity with all of creation.

"One of the things Saint Francis did best was live life as a drama. It was light and playful. But I must also remind us all, especially in this sacred assembly, that we cannot fulfill this vision while clinging to an *ego drama,* wherein each of us scripts our own story with ourselves at the center. Such self-centric ambition only leads to division and fear. Saint Francis's life shows us, instead, the power of a *theo drama*—God's greater narrative that enfolds us all. In the *theo drama,* we let go of self-serving control and place ourselves under the providence and guidance of the Divine. Only by setting aside personal agendas and trusting in God's higher purpose can we embody the Sacred Order's call to unity.

"I implore each of you to step beyond the boundaries of your own ambitions. Trust in God's greater narrative. Let the humility of Francis remind us that true leadership demands surrender—a willingness to serve, to open our hearts, and to seek God's plan rather than our own. Then, and only then, will this newly unveiled Sacred Order flourish among us, rekindling hope and anchoring our Church in a love that transcends all barriers."

Anthony gave a nod to the engineer controlling a projector.

The lights were dimmed and a large screen was erected, matching the width of the altar fresco, ascending nearly to the ceiling in front of *The Last Judgment.*

The artist continued. "Once again, we have reached a pivotal time in the Church's history, and as you look before you, you've been given a clean slate. It is a pure white screen…a blank page. The Church you lead and the church of your people, both need that same fresh start. I've come to realize and appreciate that every day here on earth can be a day of earthly paradise. If we live for today and use each precious moment to do good for all those we encounter, tomorrow will take care of itself.

"It is time to face evil head on with love, to empower leaders with that forgotten word guiding the righteous ahead. Humanity has looked forward to this day for thousands of years. It's a crucial time, a time to appoint a leader with unconventional rights, unconventional thoughts, and unconventional ties. A leader with the convictions of Christ and the courage of Francis to reform laws set forth by man…by you and your predecessors. And like Saint Peter who stands with you in spirit, holding the keys to the kingdom, we recall a man who faced death by way of an upside-down crucifixion, brutally nailed to a cross in total surrender. I deliver this message to you."

A crystal-clear image of *The Last Judgment* appeared on the screen, yet the image was inverted. Grumbles rose among the cardinals as many turned their heads and pointed, indicating the projection was incorrect. But then, a hush fell as others noticed something in the center of the screen, as though a ghost had appeared. There, in the middle of the digital fresco, before 115 cardinals, was the symbol of peace—the coat of arms adopted by the Franciscan deacon from Assisi, the patron saint of Italy. The tau cross was unmistakable, sending a message both loud and profound—Saint Francis was present.

"*Pax et Bonum,*" Anthony said in Latin. "Peace and be good. A simple message from a simple man who risked all in trying to restore the Church of his time, a Church turned upside down. Let us pray for the entire world that a great spirit of brotherhood might prevail. Like Saint Peter, you now hold the keys to a new judgment day…the future of this Church, and in many ways the future peace of the world, rests in your hands.

"Remember the words of Saint Francis. 'It is in giving that we receive.' Give your vote to the righteous one among you today. Be not afraid—go forth and steer this earthly institution right-side up. Stand tall and stand proud, elect a man you know in your heart has the courage, the stamina, the mindset, and most importantly, the willingness to see beyond any *ego drama*—any personal ambition or agenda—and trust in the greater story God is writing for His people. Recall how Francis recognized that true reform meant surrendering one's will to something far beyond human design. Let this new successor of Saint Peter carry forth dignity to the papacy and its people and restore a Church that can once again stand strong, guided not by self-interest but by faith alone in the God who authors every breath of its being."

CHAPTER 53

Vatican City
MARCH 13, 2013, 7:06 PM

Rainstorms had persisted for most of the day. Vera accompanied Anthony, who had just learned that Richard was under 24-hour observation in the ICU at the Rome-American Hospital.

Meanwhile, Massimo braved the cool, rainy conditions outside Saint Peter's Square. He knelt for hours, praying barefoot on the cobblestones amid thousands of pilgrims from around the world who anxiously awaited the election of the new pope. After a while, the barefoot monk attracted a small crowd and some among them even knelt beside him.

Following Anthony's address, the cardinals began with a *Pro eligendo Pontifice* Mass in St. Peter's Basilica, led by Cardinal Angelo Sodano. In the afternoon, 115 cardinal-electors proceeded solemnly into the Sistine Chapel, chanting the Litany of the Saints. They took their oath as prescribed by Church regulations, and once the doors were locked and Cardinal Grech gave the required meditation, they held the first ballot. Black smoke soon emerged from the chapel's chimney, signaling that no candidate had garnered the necessary two-thirds majority. Although early reports suggested Cardinals Scola, Ouellet, and Bergoglio led the tally, no one reached the threshold to become pope.

On the second day, the rain persisted and two more in-conclusive ballots released black smoke again that morning. Cardinal Scola's initial support waned, and votes increasingly coalesced around Cardinal Bergoglio by the afternoon.

Outside, the crowds expanded and so did the anticipation. The atmosphere was charged with expectation. Then, some-thing surreal occurred. A large seagull perched atop the Sistine Chapel's famous chimney and remained there for an unusually long time while the world watched and day slipped into night.

Now more than 100,000 strong, Saint Peter's Square exuded a tense tranquility until the seagull took flight. Miraculously, white smoke followed, billowing from the Sistine chimney while the great bells of St. Peter's rang in unison. A roar of cheers rose as pilgrims waved their national flags, as though a decisive match between good and evil were about to unfold on the global stage.

Inside the Sistine Chapel, the outcome had been that the Archbishop of Buenos Aires, Jorge Mario Bergoglio, would be elected Pope. He was overcome by humility.

Brazilian Cardinal Cláudio Hummes embraced him and whispered, "Don't forget the poor."

The new pope walked beneath *The Last Judgment* and en-tered the Room of Tears through a plain door on the left side of the altar. The small, unadorned room contained only a desk, a burgundy parlor loveseat, and a matching kneeler facing a window in an alcove.

There, he was taken to be vested in papal garments and, before signing his papal name into the conclave register, left alone to pray.

High above the Holy Door entrance of St. Peter's Basilica, behind a colossal crimson drapery, shadows stirred. The energy in the air intensified.

At 7:12 p.m., the drapes parted. Wearing a scarlet watered-silk biretta, Cardinal Jean-Louis Tauran, Cardinal Protodeacon, pronounced the two Latin words the world had been waiting to hear, "*Habemus Papam.*" We have a Pope. His voice echoed throughout the square, blending with the cheers as a new pope was announced.

The crimson drapery closed again, and at that moment, those present—and billions watching worldwide—were unified.

An hour later, the crimson draperies opened once again. A man with rounded glasses and a silver pectoral cross, flanked by senior cardinals and the master of ceremonies, stepped onto the central balcony of St. Peter's Basilica smiling faintly. Dressed in pure white, he raised his right hand to bless the crowds. The Holy See's marching band struck a triumphant note.

The new pope addressed the masses, not from a script but from his heart. "Brothers and sisters, *buonasera!*" he said.

The immense crowd in St. Peter's Square roared its welcome.

"You know it was the duty of the conclave to give Rome a bishop. It seems my brother cardinals have traveled to the ends of the earth to find one…but here we are. I thank you for your reception. The diocesan community of Rome now has its bishop. Thank you. And first of all, I would like to offer a prayer for our Bishop Emeritus, Benedict XVI. Let us pray together for him that the Lord may bless him and that Our Lady may keep him."

After reciting three traditional prayers—*Our Father, Hail Mary,* and *Glory Be*—the newly elected pontiff continued, "And now we begin this journey, Bishop and people. This journey of the Church of Rome, which presides in charity over all the churches—a journey of fraternity, of love, of trust among us. Let us always pray for one another. Let us pray for the whole world that a great spirit of fraternity may flourish."

The other cardinals listened intently, his words seeming to echo Anthony Brunelli's speech.

"It is my wish for you that this journey of the Church we begin today—and in which my Cardinal Vicar, here with me, will assist—will be fruitful in evangelizing this most beautiful city. And now I will give the blessing, but first…first I ask a favor of you. Before the bishop blesses his people, I ask you to pray to the Lord that he will bless me—the people's prayer for their bishop. Let us in silence make this prayer…your prayer over me."

St. Peter's Square fell still as the new pope bowed his head toward the people. "I will now give my blessing to you and to the whole world," he said.

T

"Brothers and sisters, I must leave you now. Thank you so much for your welcome. Pray for me, and I will be with you again soon. Tomorrow, I want to go and pray to the Madonna that she may protect all of Rome. *Buonanotte* and sleep well!"

Fittingly, this newly elected pope—the Bishop of Rome and Vicar of Christ—chose a name none of the previous 265 pontiffs had ever adopted, a bold break from tradition.

Instead, he chose the name Pope Francis after that humble poor man, the *light from Assisi*, the rising sun who eight centuries ago bestowed mystical legend and a hidden treasure called the Sacred Order, a final testament of his radical love, as his parting gift to all humankind.

EPILOGUE

One early spring morning some forty-four hundred miles west of Rome, in the small upstate New York town of Binghamton, Ronald Brunelli's funeral Mass was underway.

Anthony found himself in the first pew of Saint Patrick's Church, this time alongside his family and friends. Fittingly, the cantor led the opening hymn, "Prayer of St. Francis," and as he listened, he was reminded of all that had transpired over the past few months—and the void that now remained.

His friend and mentor, Richard Pescatore, sat behind him in the second pew. He had risked his life for Anthony and fortunately made a full and complete recovery.

Anthony knew that his true work was only just beginning. On the back of the Mass bulletin, the artist read the Bible verse he had requested be there, 1 Corinthians 13:3 attributed to the Apostle Paul. "If I give all I possess to the poor and give over my body to hardship that I may boast, but do not have love, I gain nothing." He then approached the pulpit to deliver the second reading. Though the words were familiar, they had taken on a whole new meaning.

The echo of Anthony's voice lulled the congregation into a peaceful hush as he read from 1 Corinthians 13, verses 4 through 13 (NIV).

Love is patient. Love is kind. It does not envy, it does not boast, it is not proud. It does not dishonor others, it is not self-seeking, it is not easily angered, it keeps no record of wrongs. Love does not delight in evil but rejoices with the truth. It always protects, always trusts, always hopes, always perseveres. Love never fails. But where there are prophecies, they will cease; where there are tongues, they will be stilled; where there is knowledge, it will pass away. For we know in part and we prophesy in part, but when completeness comes, what is in part disappears. When I was a child, I talked like a child, I thought like a child, I reasoned like a child. When I became a man, I put the ways of childhood behind me. For now, we see only a reflection, as in a mirror; then we shall see face-to-face. Now I know in part; then I shall know fully, even as I am fully known. And now these three remain: faith, hope and love. But the greatest of these is love.

When Anthony sat back down, he leaned forward in the pew, hands folded and forearms resting on his thighs as he reflected on his own life. Life itself would never be the same. Every aspect he once believed was reality had been an illusion of his own making. Now it was time to let go. He would no longer let his mind dictate his actions. Rather, he would yield control to his heart and soul, trusting that this was how it should be.

When our mind is in control, fear follows. When our soul leads, purity reigns. Allowing our mind to steer is where we've faltered. Letting our soul influence us is the path humanity must rediscover.

In that moment, he sensed his full conversion had taken place. His soul was firm in its resolve, and there would be no turning back.

T

The large envelope his father left for him remained mostly unopened except for the cover letter he and Rick had read once before. Retrieving it from his backpack, alongside the G. K. Chesterton book, Anthony opened it again, the words leaping forth with renewed clarity:

To my dearest Anthony,

The legacy of our family and its sacred duty now falls to you

His days were different now. His artistic creativity had taken on a whole new purpose and meaning. Physically, he'd changed as well, eating little—only enough to function—and selecting his nourishment more carefully. He was thin, yet lean and strong.

For the first time, love infused his brushstrokes, love resonated in his voice, love filled his eyes, and love permeated the air. He had reached a pinnacle of consciousness few ever experience.

Truly, love was in his soul.

Before long, Florence called his name for the second time in as many months. This time, there was no large commission awaiting him, no worldly duty to fulfill. Instead, he longed simply to capture Florence's view and spend time with the woman who had claimed a piece of his heart.

They'd agreed on a time and place, but he arrived early to capture the perfect shot. Sitting on the ground with his back to the Florentine cityscape, he stretched his arms behind him, tilted his head and neck as far back as possible, and then lowered his head to the ground, viewing the scene upside down for several minutes to take in its fresh, unusual perspective. Then his attention shifted to a single flower in a terracotta pot off to the side.

Everything began to make more sense.

From the red-brick patio below, the art historian called up to Anthony with excited enthusiasm, letting him know she had arrived. He smiled, then hurried down the stairs. They exchanged an Italian kiss—one on each cheek—followed by a warm hug. Over Vera's shoulder, Daniello Rossi appeared, first greeting Anthony, then clasping his left hand with Vera's right.

"I have something that belongs to you," Rossi said, reaching into his sport coat. He withdrew a weathered Snoopy luggage tag, its edges frayed but the cartoon beagle still cheerfully visible. "We found this in the Necropolis after the incident. I had it repaired and thought you might want it back."

Anthony took the tag, running his thumb over its worn surface. "Twenty-five years," he said softly. "I thought I'd lost it for good."

"Some lucky charms find their way back home," Vera said, squeezing his arm gently.

And so it was.

Moments later, Lara came running to Anthony, leaping into his arms with a lingering embrace.

Many more paintings would follow, but his life had changed irreversibly. Luxuries, extravagant meals, and worldly treasures had lost their former allure. He captured a small essence of what the poor man from Assisi left him with, an understanding that life itself is love and that it comes in many forms, like a parent's love for their child, a friend or sibling's love for one another, the unbounded devotion between two souls capable only through the Divine Architect.

There's no such thing as a coincidence or happenstance. Everything that was, was. Everything that has yet to happen, will. There is no past… There is no future… There is only the present moment in time.

All was well.

A sea of change had taken hold at Vatican City too, where Pope Francis declared his intention to live up to the name he freely chose. His words and deeds made this abundantly clear. He would be a pope of the people—*all* people. On Holy Thursday, he washed the feet of twelve young adults, including two women, in a juvenile detention center. He broke tradition by including women, a ceremony previously reserved for men. The Church found itself facing major reforms, perhaps the only kind of reforms that could mend its fractures.

After several months, the minister general secured a private audience with the pontiff. Humble and gracious, the pope listened intently. When the minister general pulled a large satchel from the floor and unveiled four limestone cylinders and a marble cask, objects that made up the Sacred Order, a gift from Anthony, the pope studied each piece attentively. He handed them back, instructing they be returned to Sacro Convento in Assisi, to the place from which they came and where they rightly belonged.

And it was at that moment that the world changed. The continuation of the command given to Francis some eight hundred years ago to repair the Church was now underway. And the secrets of the Sacred Order, once locked for so long inside the limestone cylinders and reliquary, would now forever be known.

Vatican City

February 14, 2025, 2:22 PM

Nearly twelve years to the day, Anthony Brunelli sat in the Papal Palace study, in the very chair where he had once met Pope Benedict XVI. The difference this time was that *he* had urgently requested the meeting with Pope Francis, citing matters concerning the Sacred Order. The subdued fragrance of beeswax candles and the silent dignity of the Papal private study settled over him, though comfort remained elusive. Pressed against his chest, the olive wood Tau cross felt like a reminder of unrealized hopes.

Reforms had come too slowly. The Church still clung to its archaic structures, its bureaucracy resisting true change. Anthony grew disheartened—not only with those closest to the pope but also with the glacial pace of transformation. The radical vision he had presented to the conclave in 2013—the very essence of Saint Francis's message—seemed to have been diluted by committees and compromises.

More troubling was a growing sense of a reemerging threat. He suspected the Ramorosso had reassembled, their shadowy influence once again seeping into the highest ranks of power. He recognized their tactics: critical information withheld from the Holy Father, progressive voices silenced, reform initiatives inexplicably stalled.

The Sacred Order's message was timeless, but realizing it required courage—the kind of courage Saint Francis had shown in his day. Gentle nudges would no longer suffice. The Church needed an upheaval on the scale of an earthquake.

A soft creak drew Anthony's gaze to the rear door, yet instead of Pope Francis, his assistant secretary appeared bearing a somber expression that telegraphed unwelcome news.

"Signore Brunelli," the secretary began, "I regret to inform you that your audience with His Holiness won't be possible today. He's currently on his way to Gemelli Hospital for precautionary treatment of advanced respiratory symptoms." He paused, adjusting his glasses.

Anthony stood, worry etched across his face. "I'm so sorry."

"Yes, thank you, we are all quite worried." The priest nodded as he looked up toward the high ceiling. "Signore, there's something else. Once it became known you were in the Apostolic Palace, I received a request from someone in town who expressed great interest in meeting with you."

"Oh? And who might that be?" Anthony asked, noting the half smile that crossed the secretary's face.

The priest inclined his head for Anthony to follow, then whispered, "Let's just say he's the most influential cardinal from your part of the world."

"*Not* Cardinal Dol—"

The priest raised a finger to his lips, silencing Anthony mid-word.

In that moment, Anthony felt the same rush of destiny he had experienced twelve years prior. A renewed glimmer of hope—and perhaps now, at last, real change—loomed on the horizon.

Though deeply concerned for the Holy Father's well-being, Anthony still sensed the timing was providential, as whispers of a papal resignation drifted through the Vatican's halls and the pope's health remained in question.

The next great renewal could arise not from Rome's time-worn traditions but from America's younger Church, where just maybe the Sacred Order's vision of radical transformation could finally break free from centuries of resistance. The prophecy of Saint Francis, after eight hundred long years, stood ready to fulfill its promise. And this time, Anthony knew no force on Earth could stop it.

FACTS BEHIND THE FICTION

While this novel is a work of fiction, several characters are inspired by or based on real individuals, adding a layer of authenticity to the narrative. Among them:

Anthony Brunelli is indeed a renowned photorealist artist whose work has been exhibited internationally. His family's ancestry traces back to Assisi.

Ronald and Carol Brunelli are in fact the parents of Anthony Brunelli.

Richard Pescatore attended the Franciscan seminary at Rye Beach, NH before discerning a different path in 1968, the same year Anthony Brunelli was born. He later became a friend and mentor to Anthony at the start of the artist's career in the late 1980s—a friendship that continues to this day.

Massimo Coppo is a well-known figure in Assisi who lives in intentional poverty, sleeping under the porticoes of the Basilica of Saint Francis. His powerful presence captured international attention when he prayed for the cardinals in St. Peter's Square before and during the 2013 conclave.

Louis K. Meisel is the pioneering founder of the photorealism movement and serves as Anthony Brunelli's art dealer in real life.

Friar Marco Tasca served as the 119th Minister General of the Order of Friars Minor Conventual from 2007-2019 and is currently serving as the Archbishop of Genoa, appointed by Pope Francis in 2020.

Friar Martin Breski, OFM Conventuals, served at the Basilica of Saint Francis in Assisi during the time period of this novel.

The novel's timeline intersects with actual historical events, including Pope Benedict XVI's historic resignation in February 2013 and the subsequent election of Pope Francis in March.

Many other characters in the novel are based on real individuals, though their roles in this story are purely fictional. This blending of fact and fiction serves to ground the narrative in reality while allowing the imagination to explore the mysteries of faith, art, and human connection.

For readers interested in learning more about the real people and places that inspired this novel, additional information and photographs can be found at the author's website: thesacredorder.com

www.ingramcontent.com/pod-product-compliance
Lightning Source LLC
Chambersburg PA
CBHW030740310726
48969CB00005B/1272